TEARS OF THE ALKONOST

YOUNG YAGA
and the
Thrice-Nine Kingdoms

TEARS OF THE
ALKONOST

Shea Michaels

Published by Nesting Doll Press

Opening up to the world within.

For my mother—who believed in my magic all along.

"Would that I might

From the world hide my poor self,

And in some place

Where no man ever comes,

Spend all my days in pray'r."

— *Princess Shikishi, Japan, late 12th Century*

PROLOGUE

Time is seldom faithful to memory.

Instead, we are told that history belongs to its victors. That the world was defined by the righteous men who stood atop the skulls of those they had conquered. The men who were heralded and praised for their deeds. And *feared*.

And what of those who opposed them? Long ago, their gospel was laid to rest, tucked down beside their bones in shallow, unmarked graves. The moldering consequence for having the courage to *tell the truth*.

Now, folklore and fairy tales may be all that remains for them.

Yet, their stories—of the vanquished and the inconvenient—have soured like milk within the mouths of men. Their lives putrefied by those who would suckle at the teat of the carrion sow; who turned away in fear from what they did not understand, only to be nourished instead by *lies*.

Now their words fall like curdled mash, spit out with contempt for those *who would dare*.

You've heard the tales, haven't you? The ones muttered under bated breath—shaped by fear and twisting with old superstition. The crone in the woods. The devourer of the lost. The monster who waits with a hunger that never fades.

But stories are not truth. They are merely what lives on when the truth has been buried.

For a moment, he stopped, wiping the sweat from his brow. With trembling hands, he stood in the darkness, chest heaving as a pale plume of steam surrounded his face. The young soldier was drowning now beneath the weight of the man he dragged. His arms burned and his lungs stung, parched by the smoke-filled air. His grip was slick with blood, making it hard to hold on to the other man. The young soldier's eyes filled with fear and desperation; he *wanted to run* from it all. Still, he lurched onwards, his own form sagging with the heft of the other, trudging beneath the bent bows of the twisting oaks overhead. He was moving away from the melee, drawn towards a faint amber glow in the distance.

Behind them, the forest pulsed with the fury of war. Dim torch lights, scattered across the undergrowth, moved like distant fireflies in the black. The dull thudding sound of bodies hitting the wet earth melded into a din with frenzied battle cries and the clang of metal. There was a smell of burning wood. And flesh. A man screamed—high and shrill—before suddenly falling silent.

The soldier did not look back.

The wounded man groaned. Pausing, the young soldier stooped over him, attempting to yank at the other's armor. As he fumbled with buckles and ties, his eyes darted around the wooded darkness on all sides. His heart was panicked now—there just wasn't time. The plates were too heavy—*too loud.* They needed to move. He scrambled down to the ground, straddling the man, tearing away at the armor. Then, rising to his feet, he dragged him deeper into the woods—away from the battle. *Away from the dead.*

He was guided still by the single light in the distance. A beacon, soft and steady. Perhaps a house.

Soon, the trees thinned into a small clearing that contained a dwelling. A cottage loomed above him in the darkness. Crooked and sprawling, it had been built onto the gnarled roots of ancient oaks.

And in the doorway, a figure.

She stood unmoving, cast in shadow. The young soldier, covered in dirt and sweat, squinted. Her form was dark—the light behind her framing the woman in a border of wild, unkempt hair. His breath ragged, the young soldier stumbled in exhaustion, dropping the legs of the man he had been dragging and falling to his knees in the mud.

Without warning, a brilliant, blazing light illuminated the space where he sat slumped. Though the soldier shielded his eyes, for one blinding moment, the night burned away. Then, just as quickly as it had appeared—the light flicked out.

The young soldier glanced towards the doorway to where the silhouette of the woman remained. Her face obscured, she stood motionless—watching him.

It was as though she had been waiting.

As though she had known he would come.

Chapter One

THE CAULDRON

Yaga's feet padded gently over the floorboards in the kitchen, their surfaces worn smooth by the passing of time. The room was dim, though not dark—illuminated by the soft yellow flames of several pillar candles and a few loose threads of sunlight streaming in through the windows. The air around her was filled with a pungent aroma of dried lavender and roses that mingled with the coiling wisps of woodsmoke emanating from the hearth. There, a heavy black cauldron hung down from an iron pot-crane, its sagging belly nearly resting on the glowing orange coals hissing and popping beneath. Within it, a liquid amalgam of oil, lye, and water bubbled away slowly—the sound forming a melody to the tempo of Yaga's footsteps.

Today, Yaga was dressed in a white linen *vyshivanka* blouse with delicate floral embroidery cascading along the sleeves and at the front. She had tucked it into a long, dark *zapaska* skirt, over which a simple gray apron had been tied snugly at her waist. Her chestnut-colored hair pulled back in a long braid, she paused briefly, blowing a few strands out from in front of her eyes. Then she began to hum, her feet carrying her to a nearby shelf where she collected a few jars of dried herbs.

In the cottage where Yaga Luchanova lived, this morning was like any other—full and heavy like a ripe piece of fruit with tasks and tendings.

A sleek tabby cat named Dobra stood beneath her, his body slinking between her feet. She stooped, scratching him gently behind the ears as he pressed his head into her leg affectionately. After a moment, she stood, making her way towards the worktable with the jars clinking together as she clutched them within her hands.

Yaga's cottage was a sort of treehouse, round and curiously assembled high upon the twisting roots of three ancient oaks. As a crisp autumn wind swept through the understory of the surrounding forest, it caused the wooden structure to sway slightly, the boards creaking and moaning in a way that, by now, formed a comforting din.

Inside, the cottage was divided into two levels—the lower being a living space with a high ceiling, and the other a loft, where her bedroom and inner sanctum were tucked behind heavy tapestries. The large open area of the first floor where Yaga stood presently had a kitchen and a hearth towards the back, along with a small washroom tucked behind the staircase. In the front near the door, a set of large cushions flanked a low table—a place to enjoy some tea and reading on quiet afternoons.

Nearby, at the room's center, an enormous wooden worktable housed several drawers filled with herbs, linens, and other staples. Today, Yaga had spread an assortment of items across its surface—a pair of shears, a small brick of wax, and some twine.

This place was Yaga's home, yes—though in the years since she had arrived in the forest, the cottage had transformed. It had become something of a place of study and healing—with all who entered stopping to marvel like curious children as they crossed over the threshold. The gaze of her visitors would invariably sweep over the scene before them—their wide eyes beaming up the circular walls where row upon row of shelves spanned towards the ceiling.

The shelving was stacked with heaps of books and miscellany—replete with glass jars and bottles of many sizes, each filled with herbs and other materials. From the highest reaches, green tendrils of potted plants dripped downward, while clusters of stone glistened out from every corner of the space—bright blues, shining black, and sparkling purples. From the rafters, bundled rosemary and sage hung, each a dried, fragrant bouquet swaying slowly with the movement in the kitchen below. And then, there were the eyeballs. Arranged as casually as a chipped cup or candle stubs, they littered nearly every available surface. Dishes and jars, set atop windowsills and tucked beside stacks of books—all overflowed with a curious assortment of colored glass eyes.

The only thing in the cottage more wonderous to behold was Yaga's collection of books—their countless spines stretching to the ceiling and encircling the cottage's interior in the shape of a crescent moon. At the end of the bookcase nearest the door, a sliding ladder stood at the ready, left in the spot where Yaga had last needed it. Sooner or later, it would be moved again, lifting her up to an out-of-reach place where important tomes lay waiting.

The cottage was ultimately a sanctuary—with Yaga making her life there in quiet comfort all through the year's turning. Other than the creaking ancient wood of the treehouse set against the soft, contented clucking of the chickens as they rustled through fallen leaves beyond the porch, the forest was mostly quiet today. In most ways, Yaga's world was peaceful—ever since she had left the house with her stepmother and stepsisters. It had been five long years since she had moved out of the estate, taking refuge under the forest canopy. Here, surrounded by dense forest and silence, Yaga felt free to do as she pleased—including practicing the crafts she had been taught by her mother.

Standing now before the cauldron hanging in the hearth, Yaga held a large wooden spoon with her bare hand, dipping it into the pot and stirring the mixture gently. Inside was a batch of soap she would take to the market in a few weeks' time, once properly cured.

She never wore gloves anymore when she worked with the lye—though, until it had been mixed into the oil and water, it could be dangerous. Still, Yaga felt no fear as she tended the pot; this task, despite everything that had happened, had always brought comfort to her. As she continued stirring, humming quietly to herself, a bittersweet feeling crept upward to the surface of her mind. She paused, pushing aside a memory—the faint image of her mother smiling and laughing vanishing with the steam flowing upward from the hearth.

With the mixture at the right consistency, Yaga used a pair of iron tongs to pull the heavy cauldron down from the pot-crane, straining beneath its weight as she moved it to a low, wooden round nearby on the floor. Scooping the liquid soap out with a ladle, she poured it smoothly into a rectangular mold, after which she sprinkled a few pinches of lavender and rose petals across the top.

She gazed at the delicate floral crumbles spread over the cream-colored, fragrant soap. Sighing, she moved to a nearby shelf, placing the mold beside several others to cure. Glancing across the room at the stacks of crates, each filled with soaps that had been carefully wrapped, she bit her lip pensively. One crate sat open, its lid ajar. *Just a few more bars,* she thought. Then, the following day, she would be ready to cart them off to the market at the village square.

Yaga's eyes swept over her kitchen once more as she wiped her hands across her apron. They settled on Dobra, now a soft orange ball curled up on a cushion near the fire. He looked remarkably like any other common cat—though Yaga knew better. He was a *Domovoi*—a House Spirit, and had been a loving, quiet companion over the years—especially since her mother's death so long ago. The creature—along with the impish House Spirit the *Kikimorra*—had followed her from the house in Valen out to the cottage, just after her father had passed away. Dobra's presence was comforting—though he was also a reminder of the past. As she eyed him, he yawned, stretching his neck slightly, before jumping to the floor and sauntering over to a patch of sunlight. Watching him settle down, Yaga smiled softly to herself.

Soon, she had once again moved to the worktable, where she would finish cutting strands of twine short enough to tie around the bars of soap. As her hands uncoiled the twine, running along its length, she had a flash of memory again—this time seeing a vision of her mother running her fingers through Yaga's hair.

Her mother, Vesna, had hummed liltingly as her fingers moved over Yaga's long chestnut locks with a wooden comb. Her mother's hands felt like anchors to that earlier time, tending and nurturing to Yaga all through her childhood. She could picture them now, recalling how her mother had carefully harvested herbs from the garden, or collected—with expert skill—mushrooms from the surrounding forests and countryside. Sunlight blanketed the figure of her mother in Yaga's mind as she imagined the two of them walking through a field in search of wild oats. *It helps soothe a worried mind*, Vesna had said to her. She had watched as her mother carefully plucked the tops from the milky plants, tossing them into a basket Yaga held.

Vesna was by trade an herbalist, and for most of Yaga's early life, she had been a healer—tending to the ailments of a never-ending stream of people from Valen, the nearby village where Yaga had been born. Self-trained and skillful, Vesna had been sought after by many in their small part of the Thrice-Nine. It was all Yaga had ever known—the broken and sick hobbling into a room attached to her family's estate. To Yaga, helping the vulnerable had seemed not just a type of work; it had been a way of life.

In many ways, Vesna's world had been a simple one. She had been raised in a modest farmhouse with her parents—hard-working farmers who had adopted her at an early age. Yet, this was a history that remained obscure to Yaga; the story of how Vesna had come to Stasa and Druven. As with most stories, this one had roots in something that had happened many years before—in a time and place far from Yaga and Valen.

Still, Yaga wondered about her mother's past—and about the grand-parents who looked so different from Vesna with their sandy blonde hair and blue eyes. They had died when Yaga was small—too young to recall even the sound of their voices. Yet, she could picture them in her mind, and remained curious about them still—a feeling that seemed to grow with every passing year. More than anything, however, Yaga had unanswered questions about the mysterious book, the grimoire. It had been found by Vesna in a drawer by Stasa's bedside when she was young. Now its leather-bound, yellowed pages rested just a few feet away on a shelf in Yaga's cottage.

Yaga stared blankly at the table before her, the vision of her own hands fuzzy and distant as she pictured her mother's fingers running over the pages of the grimoire late at night. Occasionally, as Yaga had peaked over her shoulder, Vesna had shown her daughter the drawings it contained—ethereal beings and strange beasts depicted within its pages. Yaga's eyes would sparkle as she stared in wonder at the creatures—half expecting them to come alive, leaping off the paper into the room around her.

Yaga's gaze came back into focus for a moment. Her eyes were fixed on her own hands as she played absently with the twine. Her face rumpled slightly as she recalled that even at a young age, she felt it odd that her grandmother Stasa would have kept such a curious book of ritual magic and beasts tucked away. Surely there was a story there—of how the book and Yaga's mother had made their way into her grandmother's life. After all, Yaga and her mother were *different* from most people. And yet, Stasa, like the grimoire, seemed to hold tight to the secrets of Yaga's world—and about her mother's past.

The book itself provided a record of things that had all but dis-appeared from the Thrice-Nine. Now, magic was more than uncom-mon—as was the meddling of the Old Gods in the affairs of humans.

Those with magic were scarcely encountered at all these days—even if small enclaves still existed scattered across the Kingdoms.

She shrugged as she recalled the peculiarity, continuing to run her fingers over the twine on the worktable as she uncoiled it. With a small knife and the flick of her wrist, she sliced a succession of pieces off, tossing them onto a pile.

Pausing, she glanced at the shelf where the grimoire sat. As she did, it seemed to shimmer—just slightly, as though it could feel her eyes upon it. A bit of enchantment that Yaga was used to. As with other things, the book seemed to respond this way on occasion—to wiggle or vibrate when Yaga was near. The grimoire was special beyond measure to her, having been a significant part of Yaga's life with her mother. Now, it was like an old friend, and Yaga had thumbed over every page more than once since she was a girl. For her, it was a strand of memory tethering her tightly to her mother.

Standing at her table, Yaga's thoughts drifted back to her mother's face. Vesna's eyes were a honeyed brown, tucked beneath dark lashes and lids that curved gently like the petals of a chamomile flower. She imagined her mother's porcelain skin dappled with a few freckles and framed by strands of straight, black hair. Often, Vesna had pulled it back into a neat bun, which Yaga had delighted in decorating in the summers—sticking small flowers and bits of lichen into the coiled rosette atop her mother's head.

When it was just the two of them, Yaga was happy. Across the seasons, they would spend every moment by one another's side. Even in cold winters, Vesna's love had warmed Yaga as she orbited her mother like the sun, basking in her mother's tenderness with quiet reverence.

Though, there were times when dark clouds loomed on the horizon, threatening to obscure the light radiating from Vesna's spirit. Yaga's father, Zoren, seemed to be one of those changes that rolled over the skyline of their life together. Often away sailing between ports on the Sable Sea, he was a reserved and impassive man—though not unkind. Yet, his exhaustion and ambivalence when he returned was a wound that Vesna had no remedy for—a malady for which the only cure was for him to stay away.

Vesna loved Zoren—and indeed, he loved her and Yaga more than anything in the world. Yet, he suffered in some way unseen—living as though there were a heavy door shut tightly over his heart. Yaga had the sense that if her father were to let her or her mother into his heart fully, he might burst open like a darkened sky—a torrential flood sweeping them all away. And so, he didn't let them in. Instead, he seldom remained long in Yaga's world—his travels as a merchant marine taking him back to the southernmost reaches of the Thrice-Nine Kingdoms.

When he left, she imagined he would travel on horseback for days—beyond the staggering mountains and dense forests of the Sclaveni dominions. For weeks he would traverse across vast highland plateaus, eventually making his way down into the open ranges of the lowland country that led toward the sea. *It is black, like velvet*, he would tell her of the waters he sailed upon.

Zoren rarely spoke when he returned home. When he did, Yaga's eyes would shine, captivated by her father and the fantastical world he had seen. Yaga hung on every word as he told her tales of the southern lands. Occasionally, too, Zoren would bring her a small gift from afar; a shell necklace, a sprig of fragrant herbs—even a carved wooden doll. She was mesmerized by him as though he were a character in a story, imagining his faraway travels.

Yet, his absences were long, and though Yaga loved her father deeply, his presence marked the inevitable return of heartbreak for her mother.

It was as though Vesna longed for someone else entirely—and that Yaga's father was an imposter. Someone who had taken the place of the man she had married years before. And so, despite Yaga's yearning for his return, Zoren remained an implacably distant man; when he was home, mostly, he felt like a stranger.

Her mother, however, had filled every gap within her beating heart, cradling Yaga in her girlhood like a tiny bird. Vesna had sought to nourish her daughter's mind with learning and love, and so it was. Yaga had been raised to care for living beings, to tend to them with herbal medicine. Throughout the seasons, she would move with her mother into the fields, valleys, and forests, learning to craft from the wild offerings of the earth. Together, she and her mother would make medicine, dye, and soap. Vesna wanted her daughter to be self-sufficient. She wanted Yaga to understand the world, and to develop her gifts. She wanted her daughter to know that no matter what, she was loved beyond measure.

Then, one day, when Yaga was seven, Vesna decided she was ready: Yaga was to be pushed out of the nest to take flight. This was the day that she first took her daughter's hand, guiding her through the misty realm beyond the liminal during *the quieting*.

Vesna and Yaga had sat together one afternoon on the colorful woven rug within the inner sanctum of their home. The moon had been full in the sky the night before—stretching the veil between worlds thin like gossamer. Dobra had watched curiously from a chair in the corner, his tail flicking back and forth as his eyes gleamed with anticipation.

To begin the ritual, Vesna lit several candles, placing them in a circle around a set of cushions. In a small dish, she burned a bundle of sweet-smelling dried incense, the wisps of smoke curling into their nostrils as they took their seats within the circle. They sat together, she and her mother, as the fragrant smoke of the incense wafted around the room like the specter of a pale snake, its body slinking around them in the silence before striking.

Perched beside Yaga, her mother swayed gently on her cushion. From her mouth, rote incantations began falling like music. It was a language that had been memorialized over the pages of the grimoire. As the words filled the air between them, Yaga began to drift subtly in her mind.

Soon, she felt her mother's voice guiding her—gently urging her to focus her awareness on her breath. Yaga's eyelids felt heavy—her attention squarely trained on the rise and fall of her chest as her breathing fell into a natural rhythm. Her consciousness shifted, slowly detaching from her—until suddenly Yaga found herself moving *beyond the bounds of her body.*

Her control over these journeys had been limited in those early years—though over time she would develop the ability to project her spirit outward, somehow jumping between various objects. Vessels like bowls, cups, pitchers—anything with a cylindrical or spherical shape seemed to hold her spirit for a time. In this way, she learned to move her consciousness around the room, and eventually the house. She even began to expand her consciousness past the bounds of the objects themselves—filling up the room beyond as though she were hovering at the ceiling. Yaga delighted in these moments of playfully exploring the house, feeling the strange coldness of each object as she passed through—sensing the vast emptiness of the liminal space.

These quietings, her mother had said, were a way for Yaga to feel the magic within her. This was the way Yaga had first accessed the world beyond the veil. Throughout, Vesna would remain beside her—a lighthouse to their world as Yaga's spirit slipped free of her body, anchored by the unseen thread of her own mortal coil. Each time Yaga returned to her body, her eyes would flutter open slowly—greeted by the watchful face of her mother.

The quieting was an elemental tool—one through which Vesna could teach her daughter about her gifts; blessings from the Old Gods to few humans now. Indeed, Yaga and her mother were rare in the Thrice-Nine Kingdoms—humans with magical abilities connecting them to a past now all but erased.

Yaga was a healer like her mother. A mystic.

A Witch.

Vesna had been her teacher and her friend—a champion for her daughter's life in every way imaginable. The two were linked by an invisible coil between mother and child—and by the blood that ran through the veins of all Witches. And so, Vesna—herself seemingly alone in the world—had forged a singular bond with her daughter Yaga. It was stronger than iron, cut into the marrow of their intertwined existence. Theirs was a life that was filled with boundless, real love.

And then, when Yaga was twelve, her world fractured.

The day of the accident had started like any other. Yaga and her mother were in the kitchen working on a batch of soap. It was a simple task, really. Still, soap-making required precision; lye could be dangerous if mishandled, burning flesh, or worse.

Yaga had been distracted that morning—a detail itself which was out of place. Working beside her mother, her mind had flicked back again and again to the memory of something strange—a presence she felt during a quieting the previous night. There had been something with her—a dark figure on the edge of her vision. She replayed the quieting in her mind: sitting alone in the inner sanctum, she had moved beyond the door and down the hallway, eventually landing in a silver cup next to the grimoire on her mother's bedside table. Her mother had been sleeping peacefully—her dark hair framing her face in the low amber light of a lamp. In that moment, Yaga had been overcome by the sensation that they were *not alone*. Whatever it was had felt vaguely familiar to her, a thought which puzzled her. In the air, there had been a kind of whisper—a faint rasping that moved through the room like a breeze. It had filled her with fear—her consciousness slamming back within her physical body in an instant. She had fallen asleep at once upon her cushion. Now, she felt uncertain; perhaps it had only been a dream.

It was at that moment in the kitchen the following day, with her mind focused elsewhere, that Yaga made a mistake. Absently, she had grabbed a bottle of oil, instead of a pitcher of water, pouring it into the cauldron hanging over the hearth. As the oil began to heat, she added the lye, which settled into a heap on the top of the oil—unable to sink down beneath the surface. Unaware of the mistake, she had continued on, her mind still turning over the unsettling intrusion of energy from the night before.

In the years since that day, the next moment had replayed in Yaga's mind without mercy. In the blink of an eye, the kitchen erupted into chaos. Yaga had poured water into the pot, her thoughts disconnected from the process she knew so well. As soon as it made contact with the mound of lye within, the mixture exploded upwards onto her hands. She screamed in pain as her mother rushed to her, submerging Yaga's small hands within a dish of cool water.

The pot continued to spit and spew, however, projecting lye and oil throughout the room. In a panic, Vesna attempted to rush the cauldron outside, grabbing it from the hearth with bare hands. But as she ran towards the front door there had been something at the threshold. It was the Kikimorra, the dark House Spirit who had plagued Yaga and her mother in small ways for years. She had briefly taken the shape of a step stool in the doorway. Yaga watched in disbelief as her mother tripped—tumbling outside with the cauldron and spilling it across the porch and everything else.

Vesna, too, had been covered head to toe.

The rest happened fast—a terrible nightmare unfolding in their waking life. Her mother fell to the porch, the hot oil clinging to her skin and clothes. A guttural scream pierced the air around the estate as Vesna—the caustic lye now sealed over her body—dragged herself down into the yard below.

Yaga ran to her mother, though she could not touch her. And the next moment—where she darted back into the house to fetch a pail of water—was forever etched over Yaga's heart. At the sink, she had listened to her mother's writhing howls echoing through the front door and up the hall. Time seemed to stand still as Yaga stared in desperation at the trickling water slowly descending from the tap.

Mama, I'm coming! Mama—I'm sorry! Mama! Yaga cried out over her shoulder, her eyes filled with tears. Yet, by the time the pot of cold water had been filled, it was far too late. Her mother, now horrifically maimed and soaked with the water to no avail, lay in a heap on the ground. With ragged breaths, Vesna slowly stilled, the whole of her body raw and burned. Yaga's final memory of her mother was Vesna's hands reaching out to her one last time—her flesh melted and hanging from her bones.

And then, the light left her eyes.

That was the day Yaga had killed her mother. She lived with this truth, wearing it over her chest like armor. She was dangerous.

Afterwards, there had been a flurry of hushed whispers in Valen between the villagers. They were told it was an accident, yet some, amongst themselves in private, wondered if there could be something *dark* about the girl. Still, despite the burden of guilt Yaga carried, most people felt only sympathy for her—even if the memory of the terrible event remained just the same.

For a time, Yaga had lived with Velimir and Mitza, a merchant couple who had known Vesna since she was a girl. Yaga spent her days lingering next to her mother's headstone, speaking to her aloud—asking for forgiveness. Only a somber melody of songbirds ever sounded in return.

Weeks after the burial, her father Zoren finally returned, though he offered no more comfort than before. Stricken with his own grief, he thought it best to move on, quickly remarrying in the months that followed. Soon, he had brought a widow and her two daughters into their home from afar. Afterwards, he returned to the sea where he remained, mostly absent from their lives entirely.

Yaga's new stepmother Branka was a disapproving woman with graying blonde hair and a terse smile that never managed to reach up to the corners of her hardened eyes. She had immediately disallowed the practice of herbalism and anything that carried so much of a whiff of the otherworldly. The House Spirits all but disappeared in Branka's presence, slinking off into the shadows and dark recesses between the floorboards of the estate. Even her two daughters, Nadia and Marfa, seemed to fear her scrutiny. They appeared more like pretty lamps and vases than living beings in their mother's cold presence.

But Yaga was determined to remain connected to her mother. At night, she would lie upon a mat in her bedroom in secret, practicing her quietings and projecting her consciousness out of her body. Her stepmother and stepsisters unsuspecting, she would study by candlelight, thumbing through the pages of the grimoire, practicing the incantations as she focused intently on the symbols and creatures depicted within it.

She had hoped that by continuing these parts of her old life, it would somehow bring her closer to her mother. It was all she had left to connect her to the world she had known before, for everything that had ever mattered—even her father—had become just a memory.

Then, when Yaga was seventeen, a town clerk received a message: Zoren had died at sea. The news was painful—though Yaga had suffered so much already she hadn't been able to cry. Her father was a hazy figure; an apparition she seldom saw. In his death, Zoren had left his estate to Branka. And so, with nothing left to keep her there, Yaga had retreated into the trees, with both House Spirits following her to the woodlands beyond Valen. She would make a home at the foot of three ancient oak trees there—away from her stepmother and stepsisters.

Over time, in the cottage she had built by hand, Yaga had resumed her soap making. She began selling it by the crate to Velimir and Mitza—their shelves emptying almost as fast as she could make it. And while it afforded her staples and sundries, the truth was—as with other things—it was an echo of the past with her mother. A world of memory she longed for.

Since her arrival in the forest, Yaga had sought to fill every moment of her time. When she wasn't making soap, she studied and practiced herbalism— helping those in need and spending countless hours searching through the woods and countryside. There, she would collect every possible medicinal plant, stone, or fungus she could—bartering in town for others still.

And bartering for *books*. As it was, in the course of five summers, Yaga had amassed exactly seven hundred and one books. She had books in languages she couldn't read and those filled with creatures from faraway corners of the Thrice-Nine. There were tomes about stones, medicine, history, and more. Still, her most treasured of all remained the grimoire.

Now, at twenty-two years old, Yaga's cupboards and shelves were a small window into the vastness of both the Thrice-Nine Kingdoms and the natural world itself. In addition to the staggering collection of books, Yaga had perhaps thousands of specimens for study and healing—all of them equally familiar to her, each tucked away in a bottle or a drawer, or suspended over lengths of twine to dry overhead.

Still, despite the abundance within her cabinets and the busyness of her days, what brought Yaga the most fulfillment were her quietings. Since retreating to the forest, she had developed the skill considerably—learning to project her consciousness far and wide, never knowing where she would end up.

Yaga was fascinated by what she had seen during those sittings as her spirit travelled to distant lands and buildings—visiting places and things she imagined to be far beyond the Sable Sea where her father had once sailed. From a dish or a vase in some unknown place, Yaga saw people who dressed and spoke in ways that were strange and exhilarating. And, while she couldn't control where her spirit would project to, she relished it just the same. These journeys were both a calling and a comfort to her; Yaga was somehow closer to her mother in those moments—and far from Valen.

Yet, despite this life that Yaga had filled to the brim, there would always be something missing. A specter remained, lurking in the corners of her own mind. A shadow of grief clung to her still—leaping out like the Kikimorra when she least expected.

Chapter Two

WARP AND WEFT

S etting the roll of twine down next to the stacked pieces she had cut, Yaga paused. The sun, higher now in the midday sky, warmed the cottage against the crisp of autumn beyond its walls. She chewed the inside of her cheek pensively, eyeing the remaining crate once again, its lid still ajar. She sighed softly; it was time for a short break.

With a final glance around the room, she turned, ascending the winding staircase towards the second floor. As she climbed, the treads of the stairs groaned gently beneath her feet. The handrail, made from twisting branches of oak, felt smooth beneath her hand as she ran it along its surface. She closed her eyes, her lips whispering silent words of gratitude for the trees as she ascended.

In truth, the oaks that held the cottage were more than just a home to her; they were a *sanctuary*. Ancient and sturdy, they loomed high over the small clearing below, their tops jutting beyond the canopy of the surrounding pine forest like lookouts. Below, anchoring into the duff, the trees' roots stood like sentries covered in bark.

At the top of the stairs, Yaga pulled back a large, heavy tapestry, revealing a doorway. The space beyond was simple and cozy, with a single window through which the light filtered down between the leaves outside. Centered within the room stood two wooden support beams, and beside them—two single beds, each neatly covered by a woven blanket.

Inside, Vasilisa sat near the window, her fingers moving over a loom.

"Vasa?" Yaga called softly.

Vasilisa tilted her head toward the sound slightly. Her face was small and pale, framed by a gauzy blue kerchief. The cloth was tied over her face and to the back—concealing the place where her eyes had once been. Beneath it, her long hair, dark as a raven's wing, fell in two thick braids beyond her shoulders and down her back. She smiled faintly, her hands gracefully pulling and pushing on the threads before her.

"I'm here," Vasilisa replied.

Yaga crossed the room, sitting down on the edge of one of the beds. Vasilisa remained seated, a tapestry continuing to form slowly before her as her small hands worked the warp. Quickly, she pulled at the dry birch sapling she used for the shed, passing the shuttle through. She repeated the process several times, building the weft as Yaga watched her quietly.

The weaving itself was filled with a miscellany of wooly tufts and strips of fabric—all dyed by Yaga the previous summer using plants from the nearby countryside. It was a bit like a kaleidoscope in its assemblage of colors, each strand skillfully threaded and tied to the next.

Vasilisa moved like a conductor as she worked, her hands pulling and twisting, never seeming to lose track of the tempo or the melody. The warp looked a bit like the pipes of an organ rising towards the ceiling—with Vasilisa its sightless player pressing every key in precision as her delicate hands glided over the keys.

Gazing at her friend, Yaga was taken with the juxtaposition before her: Vasilisa's expertise with weaving was matched only by what Yaga understood to be her profound *resilience*. Yaga knew that Vasilisa's life had been a difficult one, yet now, watching her pull each strand through the warp, Yaga felt only a deep sense of admiration. Her friend, once seemingly a broken bird dropped at the base of Yaga's tree, had remained whole;

undamaged despite the hardship that had befallen her. Yaga smiled softly as she watched her work a moment longer. Then, she stood, smoothing out the blanket upon her bed.

"I'm heading back down in a moment to finish up for the market tomorrow," Yaga said. She reached towards Vasilisa's arm, touching it gently. "Just wanted to check on you."

"I'm fine. Go finish your work," Vasilisa said. Unfurling a brilliant violet yarn, she sent it through the strands of the warp on the shuttle. Then, clutching a thick wooden comb, she tamped it down atop the previous layer made from strips of fabric that had been dyed a blazing orange using the roots of curly dock.

Yaga leaned forward, kissing Vasilisa on the top of head. Then she turned, making her way back out of the room and descending the staircase. As she moved, her thoughts drifted to the first time she had met Vasilisa. It was a day she would never forget. The girl—no, the *Vila*—had arrived with clipped wings. And, although some of her power had been plucked from her then, her spirit remained a force unlike any other.

When Yaga had first left Valen at seventeen, she had done so with a determination to create a life that was hers alone. With her father's passing, she no longer felt tethered to the estate where she had been raised by Vesna.

In the early days and at most times, it had just been her and the House Spirits, puttering about in silence within the cottage. She had spent months building the structure itself, adding to it as her small soap-making business grew. Each trip to the market afforded her new tools and materials. Month by month—room by room—her home expanded as she hauled lumber from the village out across the countryside and into the woods using a handcart. It was arduous work, but as the cottage formed around her, she had the sense her life was taking the shape it was meant to.

Over time, the dwelling she built became the centerpiece of her world, each passing year bringing a solitude that seemed to offer her a kind of mending. Yet, despite how much Yaga relished the gift of living the way she chose, there were times when the absence of connection stalked her relentlessly, creeping nearby in the quiet moments between thoughts. It was a feeling she pushed aside with haste; she didn't wish to think about her loneliness at all. It was an emotion that carried with it the weight of an anguish she hoped to leave in the past.

Yet, Yaga wasn't truly alone for those years. Instead, following her departure, the people of Valen had taken to visiting her at the cottage for medicine. She was, after all, the daughter of Vesna.

Over time, the villagers' trust in Yaga's skill as a healer began to grow, and with it, her reputation. People from all over their small part of the Thrice-Nine came, laying all manners of malady and complaint at her door. Bartering her skills as an herbalist, in time Yaga found that virtually every illness she encountered she could soothe, mend, or cure. Yaga, it seemed, was an herbalist now by trade.

Through the years, her compassion grew deeper for those who entered the cottage seeking her healing. She cherished her work, though not just because she wished to help those who could not help themselves. It was a way for Yaga to maintain a connection to her life before; herbalism was another thread connecting her to her mother. To the time when all who entered the small room attached to her family's estate had found healing in her mother's tenderness and care.

Then, three years to the day since Yaga had gone to live in the forest, Glúpyj arrived.

He had stumbled into her clearing like a hulking shadow. Immediately, the man surveyed Yaga's humble cottage, his eyes filling with greed. He knew who she was—everybody did. Though, he wasn't there for healing.

Instead, he had come to strike a bargain. Behind him, he dragged a small girl—thin and pale—her head bowed towards the ground. Over her eyes, a dirty cloth covering.

Yaga had never met the man before, though she sensed immediately as she spotted him enter the yard that he was a brute. She had heard whispers of such a cantankerous, vile individual made by the villagers at the market. It seemed he too had *a reputation*. He was known for his violent temper and an insatiable thirst for wealth—though by the looks of him, he had yet to find any.

That day, after marching through the undergrowth, Glúpyj had made his way across her yard hastily. Stopping at the base of the porch steps, he propped himself up on the handrail. Yaga appeared in the doorway, immediately letting out a small gasp upon seeing the girl up close.

"I've got something for you," he'd said, glancing at the girl before a small smile curled at the corners of his mouth. He grunted irreverently before wiping his brow.

Yaga could *feel* something seeping out of him—a contempt and malice dripping from his pores with the sweat. She eyed his stout, hairy hand with gnarled fingernails as he gruffly pulled the cloth away from the girl's face. Yaga's face twisted in horror as he revealed the girl had two empty eye sockets, red and raw beneath the rag.

"What happened to her eyes?" Yaga said, her fist taking the shape of a tight ball at her side.

"Oh, that. You know how these things can be. Took 'em to keep it from causing trouble," he said. "Anyways, it's useless to me—but I hear *you* like strange things." The man smiled up at her with teeth the color of rust.

Yaga's heart sank as she saw the girl's condition. She knew at once the girl was a Vila—something surprising on its own. She was part of a magical race of beings who had all but disappeared across the Thrice-Nine. A chill of disbelief ran down Yaga's spine. *How could someone be so cruel?*

Her eyes studied the captive girl for a moment. Despite the Vila's appearance of frailty—despite the filth covering her body and the rags she wore as clothes, she seemed to stand upright. There was defiance in her stance—though clearly, she was suffering.

"What do you want?" Yaga asked, her eyes narrowing. She widened her stance at the top of the stairs. From where she stood now, her shadow seemed to grow, looming out over the steps. It stretched across the place where Glúpyj stood, casting him in darkness.

Glúpyj shifted on his feet, gazing past Yaga towards the cottage's dim interior. He scratched absently at a red, angry patch on his neck, his grubby fingers working at the itch as he squinted past her.

"Well—what have you got?" he asked. His voice sounded like he wet rocks in his mouth; gravelly and overly soaked with saliva. There was impatience, too—it was clear the rash and the heat bothered him mercilessly. He rubbed the sleeve of his shirt against the sweat glistening on his forehead. His eyes flicked back to her.

"Got any coin in there?" He jerked his chin towards the doorway. "You must—you're known in every town in this part of the Thrice-Nine. Surely, you've stockpiled some bullion—what, with all the sick folk coming to see you."

Yaga's lips pressed into a thin line, her eyes meeting his in a way that made him uncomfortable.

"No," she said evenly. "I don't sell my healing. I trade for it."

Glúpyj scowled. Sweat darkened the fabric at his collar and beneath his ears. Tilting his head to the other side, he sighed loudly with annoyance. Yaga studied him. It was clear he was miserable in the heat. It was a hot summer day, and flies had begun to take an interest in his neck—or perhaps just in the man generally. They circled him now in slow, lazy arcs—his filthy hand swatting at them with an irritated grunt.

"Well, alright. A trade, then—what do you have?" He placed a foot on the bottom step, yanking the Vila with him as he moved.

Yaga turned her gaze back to the interior of the cottage, her eyes drifting over the familiar clutter. She considered the possibilities—the books and herbs, the bundles of dried flowers hanging from the rafters, the heavy cauldron resting in the hearth. Yet, she doubted he would find much appeal in most of it. Abruptly, her eyes settled on a crate of soap by the table, and an idea began to take shape.

"How about three crates of soap?" she asked.

Glúpyj exhaled sharply through his nose, rubbing at his face. He knew he needed to rid himself of the Vila. He felt the creature had become more trouble than he had anticipated, and that it would only be a matter of time before he'd have to kill it to keep it from running away—or worse. Still, he had hoped for something better.

"Make it four," Glúpyj grumbled, swatting at a fly that crawled over his cheek and down his face, its tiny legs wading through a sheen of oil. He scratched at the flesh of his neck, something purulent oozing from within. "And fix this damned rash," he bellowed, his feet clomping heavily up the steps.

As they ascended to the porch, Yaga watched the Vila intently. Like most Sclaveni, Yaga had heard the stories of the Vilé. They were ethereal beings who had once lived throughout the forests of the Northern Thrice-Nine. And though they appeared to be girls, they were forever young; this Vila looked no older than eleven years, yet surely she was older than either Yaga or the man whose hand gripped tightly around her thin arm now.

Yaga wondered how he had managed to catch her at all; despite their child-like appearance, the Vilé were known to be skilled archers. They could deftly command a set of enchanted, gold-dipped arrows—shooting with an unerring precision. And their eyes, well... they could kill a man with a glance. In any case, the Vila seemed to no longer have either.

Yaga's stomach churned with disgust as white-hot rage boiled up within her as she watched the man trudge up the steps. She would not let him take the girl away. The Vila wasn't human—but Glúpyj was the *real* monster. Yaga's breath hitched knowing he would not be inclined to listen to reason. So, she would bargain with him. But today's exchange would be more than a simple trade.

Yaga's eyes narrowed as he passed her, lurching forward into the cottage, the boards groaning loudly beneath his heavy footsteps. This man would pay for his malice—though, not by her doing. Before Glúpyj left her cottage, he would understand that his hatefulness and cruelty had *a price*. Yaga saw the truth in him as she did so many others; he was careless and filled with greed. Today, that would cost him.

"I'll make you a deal," Yaga said, her voice steady and unreadable as she closed the door behind them, moving to a stack of crates and resting her hand upon them. "I'll give you the soap you want—but you'll have to help me make it. It's just that I really can't part with it until I know I have more to replace it..."

Glúpyj scoffed at the prospect of having to put in any effort. Yet, he knew the soap was worth more than the creature he now felt burdened by. He flung the Vila's arm abruptly from his grip as though he were glad to be rid of her, wiping his hand over his pant leg.

"Two extra crates," he said, his tone rapacious.

"If you help," Yaga said, turning and moving towards the cauldron hanging in the hearth. Glúpyj sat down heavily upon a small stool which sighed loudly as though it might break. He folded his arms over his chest, his gaze sweeping over the cottage as though he hoped to see something more for the taking.

What Glúpyj didn't know was that Yaga might have easily taken the Vila from him then. She didn't *need* to bargain, or reason, with him at all—for perched above her home in the top of the oaks sat the massive Firebird, Zhar. A creature of magic and good fortune, she had been growing in the years since she had come to live with Yaga. Once no bigger than one of the hens clucking in the yard outside, Zhar had transformed.

And she was very, *very* big.

In the canopy, she roosted then, unseen—her once-white plumage now as black as the deepest night. Zhar had noticed Glúpyj while he stalked beyond the hedge of scrubby brush at the edge of the clearing. She had watched him curiously from above as he dragged the Vila towards the cottage. Just one feather from the bird; that was all it would take. One wish and he could be extinguished—or perhaps turned into a simple worm to be gobbled up by the chickens scratching beneath the trees. On the other hand, Zhar could have simply curled her taloned foot around his body, snapping every bone within his oafish form without any effort at all.

Yet, Yaga preferred to avoid overt acts of aggression. In truth, her life was built around mending those who could not help themselves; she was a friend to all creatures, great and small. But there was something different about the man that stood before her. Whatever had connected him to his humanity seemed to no longer exist. Whatever had replaced that which was once good within him sent a chill down Yaga's spine. The man was evil; his spirit was darkness itself.

And Yaga would make sure he did not leave *empty-handed.*

She worked quickly about her kitchen as she set up the soap-making station. Carefully, she explained the process, breaking it down to its simplest terms as she moved. While she spoke, she noticed from the corner of her eye the Kikimorra, having taken the form of a spider, climbing up a nearby wall. Yaga narrowed her eyes, shaking her head from side to side.

He will suffer today, she thought—*but he will do so all on his own.*

She shooed the spider away with a cloth, her spindly legs carrying her off into a dark crevice in the wall. Continuing on, Yaga took great pains to show the man how to handle the lye, the most dangerous part of the process. Soon, with every step accounted for, she looked him squarely in the eyes.

"If the lye touches you, use this cold water," she said, tapping a pail of fresh water with her finger.

Glúpyj nodded vaguely, his gaze now resting on a set of glittering crystals perched high on a shelf. He wasn't paying attention—a fact which Yaga had assumed would be the case. He was arrogant, mostly ignoring Yaga as though hearing her voice was an inconvenience.

As the water heated in the cauldron, Yaga handed him a pair of leather gloves and glass goggles, instructing him to wear both for his own safety. Finally, she carefully placed the lye and a wooden spoon for stirring on a small table.

With another log added to the embers below the cauldron, the temperature in the room began to climb. The man started working, sweat beading up on his brow. His goggles, too, fogged in the humidity. He tried wiping the sweat from his face, though he struggled; his oafish hands sweating inside the gloves which had become unruly and oppressive.

He glanced several times out of the corners of his eyes at the crates of soap Yaga had already made, grumbling loudly at having to help with another batch. More and more, as he worked, his frustration and contempt grew. He struggled to maintain what little composure he had; Glúpyj seemed increasingly like a vat of oil, roiling and ready to explode from the heat and pressure.

His impatience was palpable, enveloping him ever more as he stood before the cauldron, the steam puffing into plumes around his form. He really hadn't been listening to Yaga. He didn't break for rest, nor did he ask for help—instead standing squatly above the hearth in irritation. His mind twitched with resentment as perspiration dripped from every pore on his body. *I've better things to do*, he thought.

It wasn't long before his carelessness caught up with him.

As the man stirred the mixture over the open fire, he began clawing at his face with a gloved hand, attempting to move the goggles, now fogged over with the moisture of his own breath and sweat. Unable to grasp them, he yanked his gloves off with furious intensity. His voice filled with agitation, he barked and muttered, swatting at the glasses and knocking them off his face. They fell to the floor, cracking.

Yaga moved slowly in the periphery, watching him. Across the room, the Vila sat silently. Even without eyes, she seemed to be watching, too—sensing the mounting tension. In predacious silence, the two women waited.

And then, it happened.

Turning with a burst of frustration towards the cauldron, Glúpyj grabbed clumsily at the handle of the wooden spoon propped against the inner edge of the pot. His hands, now gloveless, knocked the spoon downward with a thwack. In an instant, the submerged portion of the spoon leapt upwards out of the cauldron, a bit of lye water splattering over the man's hands.

Outside, the chickens scratching about the forest floor paused as a roaring scream rang out through the air. Within the cottage, Glúpyj thrashed violently as the burning liquid ate away at the skin on his hands.

Yaga pointed calmly to the bucket of water—reminding him with a steady voice to dip his hands within it. But Glúpyj was frantic, and like a bear caught with their paw in a trap, he continued barreling into things and wailing with intensity. Too panicked to hear her, he grabbed a bottle of vinegar she had set on the worktable, drenching his hands furiously. Only, the vinegar reacted with the lye instead.

Zhar stirred in her roost slightly as a screeching cry pierced the sky and reverberated over the small planks of wood siding the cottage. It was followed by the sound of the man thundering out the front door and rolling down the steps, thudding onto the duff below and startling the nearby birds.

Yaga appeared at the threshold. She moved to the top of the stairs, dousing him with a pail of water while he raged in torment on the ground below. She dropped the bucket to the porch, where it rolled lazily beside her feet. She stared down at him, her face impassive.

"You—*you Witch!*" Glúpyj bellowed. He stood up clumsily, his chest heaving. He looked like a fat, wet muskrat that had just emerged from a foul, brackish pond.

"You did this to me *on purpose!*"

Yaga continued to watch him silently from the porch. She wouldn't bother to reason with him—what would be the point? He had done it all on his own—*in every sense*. It was he alone who had caused this. She had only set the stage for him to be punished for his avarice and greed.

Glúpyj's eyes filled with malice—yet as his gaze met with Yaga's, something unsettling arose between them. It crept over him like a spider suddenly clambering up the edge of a tabletop from beneath. In that moment, it wasn't anger he felt anymore. It was fear.

Like a terrified child, he broke into a run towards the forest, stumbling over roots and plants, before disappearing into the tree line.

For a few minutes, Yaga stood in the doorway to the cottage as she listened to the man crashing through the undergrowth, crying out into the empty understory. She sighed, heading back inside—though she didn't close the door. Instead, she turned her attention to the Vila, who seemed to be staring at her.

Yaga approached her slowly, wiping her hands over her apron.

"You can stay. Or leave—it's your choice," Yaga said. She moved closer to the Vila, whose face seemed expressionless.

"May I?" Yaga asked, gently touching the rag pulled over the Vila's face.

The Vila nodded, unflinching as Yaga lifted up the filthy cloth. Beneath it, two inflamed sockets—empty and vacant—stared back at her. Yaga bit the inside of her cheek, swallowing hard to hold back tears. She stood, moving towards the sink, leaving the Vila's face uncovered while she washed her hands.

"I'm Vasilisa," the Vila said, smiling faintly as she followed Yaga with her gaze.

Yaga moved next to the worktable, opening a drawer full of clean strips of linen. Then, pouring hot water from a kettle into a bowl, she added a bit of soap to create a lather. She returned to the spot where the Vila stood, bringing her hands slowly to the Vila's face with the warm, wet cloth.

"Pleased to meet you, Vasilisa. I'm Yaga," she said, dabbing the warm cloth across the Vila's skin tenderly. When she had finished, she took another strip of cloth and blotted the skin dry. Then, another, tying it gently over the open wounds and behind her head like a blindfold.

Yaga sat down on a cushion near the Vila. For a moment, there was silence, the room cast in an amber glow as the sun sank deeper in the afternoon sky. Only the sounds of coals crackling in the hearth filled the air of the cottage as the two sat together. Then, without warning, Yaga felt the small, doll-like hand of the Vila settling atop her own.

"I think I will stay here," Vasilisa said.

Yaga turned towards Vasilisa, a soft half-smile forming at her lips.

"Ok," Yaga said, placing her own hand atop the Vila's.

And so, she had. From that day forward, Vasilisa had lived in the treehouse with Yaga. They spent their days tending to various tasks—together and apart—living in what felt very much like harmony. The Vila had become like a sister to Yaga the past three years; there was a comfort and connection in their shared life in the forest. Together, with the Domovoi and the Kikimorra—and Zhar, who roosted above—they had become a strange, quiet household.

It was early afternoon now as Yaga stood at her kitchen table. Glancing towards the staircase, she smiled, her heart comforted by the thought of Vasilisa weaving in the loft above her.

After a moment, Yaga noticed Dobra from the corner of her eye; he was watching her from his cushion by the hearth. His black eyes gleamed in the low afternoon light, catching the flickering reflection of the glowing coals nearby. It was as though Dobra had something to say to her then—though he never had. Instead, he slipped off the cushion and sauntered over the floorboards towards her. Leaping onto the worktable, he stepped over the tools and strands of twine gingerly, purring as he brushed his orange fur against Yaga's arms. Yaga smiled, her hands scratching him behind the ears. He wasn't a cat at all—but it didn't matter. Yaga loved him just the same. He was family. *They* were a family.

Chapter Three

THE FIREBIRD'S MARK

It was midmorning the following day as Yaga stooped over the long worktable centered in the kitchen. Nearby, several rows of cream-colored, fragrant soap were wrapped in cloth and set into neat stacks. Around each bar, a strand of twine was tied in a simple bow at the center.

Before her was a single bar, above which Yaga held a thin candle she had lit from the coals beneath the hearth. In her other hand, she held a brick of green wax, drawing it near to the candle's flame. She watched patiently as the wax dripped down, forming a small green pool just beneath the bow. With her other hand, she quickly pressed a silver tool into the wax. Lifting it, she paused to admire the imprint left by the stamp. The batch of soaps was complete now—the delicate image of the Firebird adorning each one.

Placing the final bar of soap within the crate, she stood back, pausing to admire her work. The daylight had shifted, a gentle glow now falling over the cottage. The air inside felt warm and cozy now—a contrast to the crisp breeze of autumn carrying the leaves slowly to the forest floor beyond the walls. It would be followed, eventually, by the frost-laden winds flowing down from the mountains to the north. Then, all traces of the summer would be chased away. She glanced at her fur-lined jacket hanging on a hook since the spring. Sighing, she slipped it over her shoulders, then scooped up a few crates within her arms.

Outside, the chickens scuttled through the leaf litter as they wrestled grubs from the earth feverishly. Yaga glanced at them as she hoisted the crates into the wooden handcart set at the base of the porch. She considered the farmers in the nearby countryside. Like her mother's parents so many years ago, they would be toiling in the fields now—bringing their harvests into storage and to the market. And then, sooner than anyone was ready for, their world would be covered in snow and ice.

Yaga pulled her jacket snugly across her chest as she turned back to the cottage for the last of the remaining crates. Inside, Vasilisa stood by the door, her bandana resting atop her head. Reaching up to a nearby shelf, her small, porcelain-like hands felt about. Locating a jar, she dragged it off the edge. She rummaged through it for a moment before fishing out two glass eyes—one a soft green, the other a deep marine blue. Carefully, she slipped them into her empty eye sockets before setting the jar back upon the shelf.

"Ready?" Yaga asked.

Vasilisa nodded as she tied her braided hair back into a large, coiled bun. Then, pulling on a dark fur coat from a nearby hook, she made her way out the front door. The Vila was—though unable to see with eyes—quite capable of navigating the world around her. In the years since she had been mauled by the brute Glúpyj, she had developed a keen sense of the world. She *felt* the shape of things, perceiving an energy within them that formed a vibrating, living image within her mind.

After placing the final crate into the cart, Yaga picked up the handles. She turned, smiling at Vasilisa as they started to walk through the clearing towards the path through the forest. Yaga barely noticed the Vila's mismatched eyes anymore. Some days, they were the same color, and on others, not. But mostly, around the cottage, she preferred a colorful kerchief.

The eyes themselves had been a gift from Yaga, who, teaching herself to blow glass in the months following the Vila's arrival, had worked for more than a year to perfect them. Now, jars and dishes of glass eyes—evidence of her many attempts—were strewn about their home. They collected dust on shelves and poured out of dishes and drawers, their irises every color and shape imaginable. There were perhaps thousands of them—nowadays a curious decoration for those who entered the cottage. For Vasilisa, they were a comfort—a bit of normalcy when they went to the village. The townsfolk, it seemed, stared less at the strange "girl" when she didn't walk amongst them wearing a blindfold.

Before long, Yaga pulled the handcart over the forest floor, her feet accustomed to the gnarled roots and stones. She and Vasilisa chatted and laughed as they made their way through the woods, their boots crunching over the leaves that formed a shallow blanket on the ground.

Soon, the trees gave way to the open farmland cradling the small village of Valen, its rolling hills speckled with small homes and sheds. They passed by open fields and fenced areas with livestock, and farmers busily tending to their chores. The townspeople paused briefly to wave as Yaga and Vasilisa walked down the road towards the village; by now, they were as predictable a sight as the turning of the seasons itself.

The marketplace at the center of Valen bustled with the familiar clamor of life. There, merchants tended to displays of their goods: a potter's table with colorful bowls, a blacksmith banging out something in the back of his shed, a fabric seller surrounded by the reams of fine fabrics she had carted in that morning.

As Yaga and Vasilisa moved through the square, the sounds of mothers bargaining over prices floated through the air as children yelled and wove through the crowd, their little boots clopping over the cobblestones. Yaga maneuvered her handcart through the teeming streets with a smile over her face; she enjoyed the market and its energy—even if she didn't feel as though she truly belonged.

Continuing onward, Vasilisa's head turned slightly as they passed the fabric seller's booth. The Vila seemed to be focusing in on something, her blue and green glass eyes each turned just a touch off-center. She had sensed something then, just beyond the crowd.

Someone.

As Yaga and Vasilisa continued walking, a young boy stared back at the Vila. He grimaced slightly, his eyes widening in curiosity. The boy tugged abruptly at the tunic of a young man standing beside him. The man was well-dressed, tall, and handsome—features that rendered him somewhat out of place on the dusty cobblestone streets of the tiny village. Atop his broad shoulders, a mane of dark hair framed his face, falling just below a sculpted jaw that provided a shadowed contrast to his fair skin and blue eyes. The wool topcoat he wore opened at the front, revealing a cream-colored linen *kosovorotka* shirt beneath. It was open just slightly, the intricate red embroidery of the shirt cascading down the center of his broad chest.

The young boy beside him trailed Vasilisa with his gaze, tugging again at the man's sleeve.

"Alexey—look!" he whispered, pointing a finger towards Vasilisa. "Her eyes... they're... different..." he said, his face scrunching.

The man glanced down at the child before shifting his gaze in the same direction. Only, Yaga's and Vasilisa's backs were now turned as they disappeared into the crowd.

He met the child's eyes once more, though he said nothing. Instead, he turned back to the woman who was standing beside him, her fingers running over the edge of a ream of blue, shimmering fabric.

The woman was Tatiana, a stately woman in her mid-forties. Alexey, and the younger child, Misha, were her sons. Moving her delicate hands across the fabric before her, her gray eyes sparkled in the midday sun.

"This will do."

She smiled kindly, to which the fabric seller gave a polite nod, placing the ream of fabric over a long table within the stall of her shop. With a whisper and glance from Tatiana, a member of her household staff entered behind the fabric seller, a satchel of coin in hand.

Alexey's mother turned toward him, smoothing out the folds of her dress.

"The tailor assures me he can make a jacket expeditiously," she said. She paused, her eyes searching Alexey's intently. "Alexey, my darling—the gala... it will be a perfect opportunity for us to get to know our neighbors even better. And, well, you never know," she said, raising her brows slightly. "You might just find a nice girl there."

Alexey sighed inwardly, his eyes closing as they rolled in resistance. Though, he tried to hide his distaste.

"We'll see, Mother," he replied, his words carrying more than a hint of ambivalence. It was hard for him to hide—to pretend. Flatly, he had no desire whatsoever to go to the gala at the Casimir Estate—or to meet a girl there for that matter. Indeed, since their family had moved to Valen that past summer, Alexey had grown tired of the frequent social gatherings and house calls he had made with his family. Certainly, he had made a few acquaintances here or there—yet, just as before in his life prior to Valen, his focus was elsewhere.

Alexey's family, the Grishaevs, had come to live in Valen from Severyn. It was a town far at the northern edge of the Thrice-Nine Kingdoms. Severyn was the final outpost before the Ebon Tors—an impassable boundary of jagged, ice-laden mountains. They were mountains made of pure pitchstone; once trees in a massive, ancient forest, they had been toppled and scorched, their fibers replaced by towering minerals a shade of red so dark they nearly appeared black. The Ebon Tors were from a time distant in man's memory, and now, no human or animal dared enter. If they did, they seldom returned. Of those that survived the crossing into the Tors, stories came back with them. Tales of dark creatures—demons connected to the Old Gods themselves—making their homes on the shining, craggy slopes.

Yet, there were far more dire reasons why humans dared not venture into the Ebon Tors; to do so would mean being swallowed up into the depths of the *Mrak Navesin'*. The Nav, as they were known, were a labyrinth of fathomless crevasses, each yawning open like a hungry mouth into what seemed like an abyss of translucent, blue walls of ice. To enter, so it was said, meant death—for the underworld would pull you down with a burning hunger into the glacial, blue gloom. Only the men who had stopped their trek at the mouths of these deep trenches had lived to tell the tale of the Nav—to speak of the foreboding quiet and the hush that settles on the skin like frost. Some believe it to be where the world ends, beyond it laying only death and oblivion.

Back in Severyn, Dmitri Grishaev, Alexey's father, still operated a large commercial enterprise; a trading company. It was a lifeline of the Northern Thrice-Nine—a singular conduit of goods from the Sable Sea and across the northern lands of the Kingdoms, beyond the Sclaveni regions.

As the owner of The Volhynia-Severyn Trading Company, Dmitri had generally sought to strike a balance between being an astute businessman and a loving, present father. Though, he had somewhat struggled at the latter, and so recently decided to move his family south to Valen. They left the bleak, oppressive setting of Severyn to be closer to the southern port city of Volhynia—and to one another.

Volhynia was a bustling hub of trade and progress—a city situated along the Sable Sea, which itself was the primary point of access to the southern regions of the Thrice-Nine. Alexey's father had numerous enterprises in the port city, mostly in the wholesale procurement of goods and staples—items that would be sent by boat and horse-drawn cart to the far north.

Dmitri's travels had often taken him away from Tatiana and the children for prolonged periods of time. And, although Alexey had frequently accompanied him on his trips over the years, the family had felt the pressure of the distance; the absences had become a fracture. Moving to Valen had been seen as a resolution to this hardship; the Grishaevs would settle in this small village, halfway between the furthest edge of the Northern Thrice-Nine and the southerly border of the Sclaveni territories. It was close enough to Dmitri's business ventures in Volhynia, while still removed enough for them to raise Misha away from the chaos and bustle of a city. Their hope was to make a fresh start as a family. And Tatiana, herself looking to the future, hoped her children would eventually grow connections of their own.

Alexey, now twenty-six years old, had little interest in finding romance in Valen—at the gala or otherwise. It was true that in Severyn and Volhynia, there had been a stolen kiss here or there. A shared dance or two—perhaps a flirtation over a glass of mead. Yet, nothing ever grew from these trysts, for Alexey, it seemed, had been far more focused on other pursuits. He spent much of his time, instead, learning useful skills, looking after Misha, and walking the countryside with Kolya—the gray wolf he'd found as a cub in the forests near Severyn so many years before.

His mother was persistent, however. She saw that time was slipping away and feared her son would never settle down—never start a family of his own. With visions of large, celebratory dinners and the peels of children's laughter scattering through their estate, she felt resolved to sway her son.

Tatiana paused, drawing in a breath. She pressed lightly on the rosette of her dark hair, then smoothed a stray strand of gray against her head. A glint of determination flicked over her eyes.

Alexey's breath hitched as he squinted, his gaze turning towards the clear autumn sky as he heard his mother's voice float through the marketplace like a cloying breeze.

"Marriage is so important, my dear. My marriage to your father is the greatest thing I have done with my life—and I wouldn't trade it for anything in the world. It brought me the both of you, after all." She leaned slightly and kissed Misha on the top of his head, then placed one of her hands on Alexey's forearms.

"Mother, I know you mean well," Alexey replied softly, though his head shook slightly from side to side. He placed his large hand on Misha's shoulder, patting it softly. "It's just that I have other, more important responsibilities."

Before Tatiana could respond, Misha tugged on Alexey's sleeve, glancing up at him mischievously. "Are you bringing Kolya to the gala?"

Alexey chuckled, ruffling his brother's hair.

"No, Misha. I don't think wolves are allowed at *fancy galas*." Alexey stuck his pinky finger in the air, wiggling it side to side before pressing it to his lips. He raised his eyebrows, pretending to pick his own nose. At this, Misha let out a loud giggle, his feet shuffling as he spun around to dance over the cobblestones.

Alexey stopped abruptly, placing his hand gently on Misha's back. "Ok, ok, not too much, now," Alexey said. "You have to save that energy, remember?"

Misha paused, his small face sinking a bit. He knew too much excitement now would give him trouble for days to come. In truth, he had never known a life *without* pain and weakness. Since his birth six years prior, he had suffered to no end. And now, just as before, he would listen to his older brother—for it was Alexey's solemn charge to keep him safe.

Yaga and Vasilisa continued their walk through the village center, eventually reaching Velimir's mercantile. Yaga set her handcart down, unloading each of the crates. Vasilisa, positioning herself on a nearby bench, appeared both impassive and a bit otherworldly to passersby as she waited.

Entering the shop, Yaga placed each crate one by one upon the long counter in the back. Velimir took one of the soaps from the crate, his thumb gently running over the impressed image of the Firebird. Lifting the bar to his face, he inhaled the heavy floral scent.

"These are the best yet, darling," he told her, glancing towards Yaga as she entered with another crate. She smiled at him knowingly, setting the crate next to the others. Velimir always said the same thing, ever since she was a young girl.

He and his wife Mitza had adored Yaga, their words ever-encouraging and kind. After Branka came into her life, they carried a steady worry for the girl; she was lonely and grieving, trapped in a house without kindness and warmth. In their own way, the couple had sought to love her as if she were their own child, hoping it had been enough to help uplift her in spite of everything that had happened.

Still, Yaga's soaps *were* incredible. Velimir and Mitza sold them to merchants from neighboring regions, and the villagers alike—just as quickly as they arrived. And, as Mitza liked to say, the soaps seemed to do more than clean; it was as though each bar itself carried a bit of *enchantment*.

Soon, Yaga had finished unloading the crates, her face rosy from the exertion in the crisp autumn air. Velimir extended his hand, passing her a small sack of coins. Yaga lifted the sack as she moved towards the door, jingling the coins within.

"Say hello to Mitza for me," she said over her shoulder, pausing to scoop up a stack of empty crates near the door.

As Yaga stepped back into the streets, she turned towards Vasilisa. Without a word, Vasilisa stood, her feet gliding over the ground towards Yaga. Then, with Yaga pushing the handcart, the two walked in step back through the center of the village.

The sun beginning its slow descent, long shadows now loomed over the edges of the field as Yaga and Vasilisa slipped back into the tree line. Moving along, their cart thudded over the roots and stones scattered across the path. The forest was quiet now—the air brisk as the day turned towards dusk. Above them, the last plumes of blazing orange and yellow leaves still clung to the trees in vain; within a few weeks, they would join the others below.

Soon, they had come upon a small apple tree. Setting the handcart down, Yaga stretched beneath its branches, her hand reaching towards a cascade of bright red apples. Yaga plucked one, holding it up to her nose as she inhaled the sweet fragrance from its skin. She reached upward, plucking another and passing it to Vasilisa. The Vila cradled it within her small hands, turning it over between her fingers as she traced its smooth surface. Bringing it up upward, she too inhaled the apple's rosy sweetness—its scent unfolding like a thousand bouquets.

"So good," Yaga said, her mouth full of the sweet white flesh. She paused, offering her hand to Vasilisa. Without a word, the Vila grasped it, steadying herself as she climbed into the handcart. After, she sat patiently, her apple resting upon her lap.

Yaga plucked a few more pieces of fruit, gently dropping them into one of the empty crates. Soon, she was pushing the cart down the path once more, the woods darkening around them.

By the time they arrived at the cottage, the sky had deepened to a rich twilight. The chickens roosted now, their soft clucking sounds greeting the two women as they made their way through the clearing.

As Yaga stood helping Vasilisa down from the cart, she felt something around them shift. The air was calm—though, there was something nearly imperceptible moving in the air. A wrinkle in the energy.

"It's been like this for weeks now," Vasilisa said, her small boots clicking on the steps as she ascended the porch.

Yaga glanced around in the low light, not sure what she expected to see. She shrugged, gathering up the crates and climbing the steps. Yaga wasn't afraid, yet she felt as if *something were about to happen*. There was a difference—a sort of coldness beyond the crisp bite of autumn now settling over their region. And so, while Yaga had never locked the door to her cottage in all the time she had been there, closing it behind her, she turned the latch.

Safe in their beds, with only a few bands of pale light entering through the window over their darkened room, Yaga and Vasilisa rested. Outside, the forest stilled, with only an occasional rustle of leaves to break the silence.

But deeper in the woods, something else moved beneath the blanket of night. Heavy footsteps thudded over the dense earth of the forest floor, stirring up leaf litter and cracking errant deadfall with every step. Whatever it was, it moved with purpose, maneuvering through the undergrowth in the direction of Yaga's cottage.

Though cloaked in darkness, the beast occasionally passed through a patch of moonlight filtering down through the canopy, revealing its basic form. It was massive, with a human-like torso covered in grayish fur. Atop its head, an enormous rack of twisting antlers protruded, nearly snagging on the low-hanging branches it ducked beneath. It moved upright on its hind legs, its hooved feet sinking beneath the weight of its body down into the duff. Lurching through the undergrowth, it clutched at the nearby trees with strange, human-like hands.

High above, the oaks that held Yaga's cottage groaned as Zhar turned in her roost. She had heard the creature's movements below her, and now she shifted her weight, turning in its direction. As it crunched its way towards the cottage, Zhar's eyes opened, her fiery gaze flashing. Like twin suns blazing, the light from her eyes cut through the darkness, illuminating the forest beneath as though it were the day.

There, just at the edge of the clearing surrounding Yaga's cottage, was the creature. It was something grotesque—its appearance twisted and unnatural. As the bright light shone upon it, the beast let out a guttural screech. Turning back, it thrashed through the undergrowth, its massive body crashing through the brush loudly. Then, descending to all fours, it loped away in retreat, deeper into the woodland still.

As she watched it disappear into the black, the Firebird's eyes dimmed, returning the area below the oaks into shadow. Soon, the forest fell still once more, although a tension now lingered. Something had come there. It had been drawn there—but for what reason?

Yet, as alarming as its appearance had been to the other creatures of the forest, this deformed beast was not the only thing lurking near Valen. There were others still, drawn to their remote part of the Thrice-Nine like flies to honey. Or carrion.

And, as Yaga and Vasilisa slept peacefully in their beds, a chattering wind began to whip and howl outside, rasping over the hills and down the forest-lined valleys. Rattling the leaves from their branches, sending them swirling through the night air, it whispered of the darkness itself—and of the things to come.

The following day, the first rays of dawn filtered down through the dense forest. They created a soft ambience, glinting on the reeds and grasses that surrounded a modest pond nestled within a nearby meadow. A gentle mist hung low across the forest floor, flowing out in plumes across the surface of the water. The air, cool and still, was punctuated here and there with the stirrings of bird songs.

The pond, fed by a babbling brook that passed through the forest behind Yaga's cottage, was a watering hole and respite for woodland creatures. Along the water's edge, animals had begun gathering for a morning drink. A family of deer, their coats still darkened with dew, huddled together on an embankment. Chittering squirrels scurried and bickered as they whirled over the branches overhead, while slow-moving waterbirds waded near the shore.

Near a cluster of boulders half-submerged in the pond, a group of *Rusalkas* played, splashing water at one another with giddy laughter. Their grey skin shimmered in the dawn as though they were apparitions, the long, wet hair of the seductresses clinging to their bare breasts. As they splashed and played, their lilting voices carried into the understory—too far from any human men to be lured by. Nearby, tiny Fairies with wings of sparkling gossamer danced above the water, their reflections like giant dragonflies hunting over the pond.

One of the Fairies, her wings pink and delicate, flew away from the others to the far edge of the water. She was making her way towards a massive figure resting near the inlet of the brook. For a moment, she hovered next to the creature, taken with her own reflection in the glassy black orb of the creature's eye. Behind the surface, it appeared as though the Fairy could see the night sky itself hidden within.

Zhar blinked, though she remained undisturbed by the curious Fairy. Instead, the Firebird slowly bent forward to drink from the placid waters. As she moved, her black feathers gleamed, their iridescence shining. The Fairy flitted around her head for a second longer, then darted away back towards the others across the pond.

Just like the Rusalkas and the Fairies, Zhar—a Firebird—was an uncommon creature of magic. Indeed, the humans of their time rarely had a glimpse of such beings now, their numbers scarce and scattered through the Thrice-Nine Kingdoms. The Firebird was rarer still—the last, perhaps, to live at all. To the villagers who seldom saw her, she was more of a story; a bit of lore they told about the Witch girl living in the woods. A vestige of the time when the Old Gods roamed amongst them. To them, Zhar seemed strange, though harmless, nonetheless. So they didn't ask about the creature—nor did Yaga offer to tell them of how Zhar had come to live in their small part of the world.

As she finished drinking, the Firebird lifted her head. Her sharp eyes scanned the woods, her senses more alert since the intrusion the night before. A towering form the size of a small house, the Firebird was a vigilant guardian of the forest. In her heart, there was a dedication to protect others—matched only by the magic in her feathers. Above all, she and the *Witch girl* had an unbreakable bond—one that flared into existence the day she had entered Yaga's life.

It was nearly four years ago—before Vasilisa had arrived. In those days, the smell of freshly hewn pine resin still clung to Yaga's clothes as her pitch-stained hands worked daily, placing the last of the shingles on the outer wall of the cottage. By then, Yaga had grown accustomed to her solitude, even amongst the quiet ongoings of the House Spirits.

One summer morning, with her handcart filled with linen-wrapped soaps and bundled herbs for trade, Yaga had ventured into Valen to the village square. The market was alive that day—the voices of merchants calling out over the din as children scampered about.

Yaga, having just bartered for some flour and salt, was weaving her way back through the busy crowd. She had nearly made it out of the fray when one of the wheels of her cart became caught on the base of a barrel stacked high with apples. A horse clopped by her as she stooped to wrestle the wheel free, the sound of animals' hooves filling her ears.

After, as she wiped her hands on her apron, out of the corner of her eye, she caught sight of a small bird. Its eyes, black and shining, peered out from beneath the arm of a man who stood near the stall of the butcher. Yaga was about to pick up the handles of her cart to resume her walk—when something about the creature caused her to pause.

The voice of the man who held the bird cracked with frustration. He was attempting to trade the animal—for anything, so it seemed. He lamented sorely about having been turned away by the other vendors. None would trade him for the dirty, pale bird—not even for a few nails or a wedge of cheese.

Yaga listened, her eyes passing over the man. Beneath the grime of the fields and his tattered clothes, his face seemed worn and pocked, the skin around his neck raw and inflamed. His skin had a strange, scaly texture, corroded like bark stripped from a dying tree. Yaga had seen this condition before, watching her mother care for a few people in the past with the same malady. The disease was itchy and cumbersome—and off-putting to most who encountered it, as it deformed the appearance of those afflicted.

Yaga felt her stomach sink in pity for the man—and for the creature he held within his grasp. The bird squirmed faintly, the man tightening his arm around it.

"Go home and throw it in a pot," the butcher said, shaking his head.

Yaga frowned. The man holding the bird looked exhausted—like an animal who had begun to accept its suffering. She sighed slightly as her eyes passed over the bird once more. Pushing her cart to the side, she approached the man, who stared down at his feet, defeated.

"Hello there," Yaga said, glancing at the bird.

The man looked up, startled. His eyes flicked to the periphery, uncertain if the woman before him were addressing someone else.

"I overheard you," Yaga said. "You'd like to make a trade—for the bird?"

The man straightened, though he found it strange that young woman—beautiful as she was—might be talking to *him*.

"I am," he said, clearing his throat. He licked his thumb, quickly smoothing the plumage around the bird's face. "It just needs a little cleaning up, that's all."

"May I?" Yaga said, her hands gesturing towards the bird as she approached.

The man grimaced—though he loosened his grip, holding the bird at the front of his body.

With Yaga's hands gently cradling her face, the bird stared up at her, her black eyes blinking in the sunlight and sparkling like gemstones. *Surely this bird is not what she appears,* Yaga thought.

"It's not the prettiest but—it's—it's just not for me," the man said.

As Yaga stared at him pensively, the man's desperation began to well up within him. He had to rid himself of the bird—for good. The truth was the creature had been something of a bad omen since its arrival on his farm. The day it had hatched amongst his swans roosting near his pond, things had seemingly fallen into a state of disrepair. Nothing seemed to work anymore.

And now, he could barely get out of bed.

But he would not tell the woman that—no. He would trade this poor bird—what with its sharp, pointed beak and a tail that dragged over the ground only to be covered in dirt—for something better.

"You want it? I'd part with it for little, really—what have you got?" He forced a smile, his eyes passing over the items in Yaga's cart.

Yaga tilted her head, her face pensive as she continued examining the bird.

"Not for those—or for coin. But I could help with your skin. If you'd come to my cottage."

The man stiffened, his brow furrowing.

"You'd... what, heal it?"

"I can try," she said. "The rash. And your teeth, if you like."

The man's face fell with embarrassment, his gaze shifting back toward to his feet.

"Take her offer, Slepoy," a voice called out behind him.

It was the butcher, who abruptly slammed a large pork leg down upon a wooden block. The sound of a heavy cleaver chopping through bone rang through the air.

The man—Slepoy—hesitated for a moment. He looked down at the bird, then back to the woman standing before him. The offer seemed almost too fantastic to be true. And yet—he had no others.

"Well... alright then," Slepoy said.

"Pleased to meet you, Slepoy. I'm Yaga," she said, picking up the handles of her cart and maneuvering through the marketplace.

Together, they walked the cobblestones out of the village, following the road leading towards the forest. With Yaga pushing her cart, Slepoy trudged beside her, the bird nestled beneath his arm.

The bird was small, no bigger than a hen, and pale as a bone. Slepoy seemed ambivalent to her, however, holding the creature as though she were a sack of root vegetables. Still, he'd stopped to let the bird drink from a small pond beside a farm as they made their way towards the tree line. Yaga watched curiously as he held her near the water, the man's face grimacing as the bird lapped gratefully. Then, using a bit of his tattered sleeve, he dabbed the creature's mouth dry around the edges.

"There," he said, patting her gently on the back before standing up and shuffling onward.

Soon, the forest closed around them in shades of emerald and olive, the green leaves of midsummer contrasting with the curling white bark of the birches lining the path. They walked in silence for a time, the way to the cottage narrowing and bending between mossy roots and patches of fern.

Slepoy, as he ducked beneath branches and scuttled over the stones embedded in the path, found himself deep in thought. He was mulling over the possibilities—considering what could be if the woman made good on her end of the trade. As they neared the clearing that contained the cottage, his voice broke through the quiet.

"Yaga, I want the face of one of those noble merchants' sons. You know the kind—always having a way with the ladies and such." Sheepishly, he gave a crooked smile, though his lips barely parted, as though he hoped to conceal the rows of dingy, yellowed teeth.

Yaga nodded as she pushed her cart forward into the clearing, crossing through the yard with Slepoy trailing behind her. When she arrived at the base of the porch, she set the cart aside, hugging the salt and flour into her arms and taking a few steps up towards the threshold.

Behind her, Slepoy stood mesmerized, taking in the strange sight of the cottage.

"Come on, then," Yaga said, her foot pushing open the door and holding it. "We'll see what we can do."

As the man moved inside, Yaga observed him carefully. She felt pity for him and the bird in equal measure. *Perhaps they are both misunderstood,* she thought. Whatever the case, it was clear that he struggled to care for even himself, let alone this poor little bird he lugged at his side. Yaga would take the bird unquestioningly—and help the man with his condition as best she could.

As she closed the door behind them, she gently scooped the bird from his arms, cradling her with care as she whisked her away to a cushion near the hearth. The bird tucked her head down into her plumage, drifting off to sleep at once.

Slepoy's eyes widened as he glanced around the cottage, taken with the shelves brimming with glass jars and gemstones. Above them, bundles of dried plants hung from the ceiling, swaying gently in the breeze created by the closing door. Slepoy blinked; he could have sworn that the herbs had bent slightly toward Yaga as she moved.

Yaga turned then, gazing at Slepoy. Her eyes narrowed, examining him in a way that made him uncomfortable—like perhaps he'd made a mistake. But, just as quickly, Yaga began to hum, padding over to her kitchen where she filled a bowl with warm water.

"Have a seat over there," Yaga called to him over her shoulder.

Slepoy sat in a nearby chair, his back straight as he watched her working intently.

Soon, with fresh water warming in the cauldron, Yaga had placed a small bowl atop her worktable filled with clean cloths. She continued humming as she worked, her honeyed voice warming the air between them. He watched as she twirled, her feet carrying her towards a shelf near the hearth. There, she began searching through a cupboard, pulling out jars one at a time and examining them.

Hmm, hmmm, hmmm.

Yaga's humming wafted through the cottage like the scent of fresh pastries, a curious quality that made Slepoy feel a mixture of hunger and contentment. Suddenly, as he watched her move, he had the impression that a book had tipped forward from a stack above her on a shelf. He watched as it slipped down neatly into the front pocket of her apron. A puzzled expression formed over his face—yet, Yaga seemed unconcerned, instead continuing to rummage around her shelves and through a nearby drawer.

Finding what she had been searching for, she abruptly moved to the worktable, laying out an assortment of jars and vials. Pulling the heavy book from her apron pocket, she set it before her on the table with a thud. *Man's Maladies,* it read. She opened it, thumbing through the pages, her feet tapping out a soft rhythm beneath her. Shuffling and scratching sounds soon filled the air as she dragged a stand over the floor towards his chair. Then, back to the worktable she went, her lilting hum a pleasant melody over the percussion of footsteps.

Slepoy touched the top of his head. Yaga was... *strange.* The cottage, too, seemed unusual. Slowly, he realized that even *he* felt a bit off. Perhaps he was imagining things, he wondered. Still, he watched her curiously as she worked, mesmerized by the scene before him.

Soon, Yaga had fished out several walnut shells from a jar, placing them into the bowl of the mortar. Lying nearby, the pestle began to rock back and forth of its own accord. Suddenly, it rolled over the table, and—to Slepoy's astonishment, leapt up into the mortar. He rubbed his eyes as he watched the tool vibrate in the bowl. His eyes flicked to Yaga; surely she too was seeing it move unaided. Yet, Yaga seemed not to notice at all, instead continuing her preparations.

"*Rest, rest, my little bird,*

Softest wings, no need for words,
Sky is vast, the wind is true,
All the world sings just for you."

Yaga now sang as she breezed through the front door, her feet gliding down the steps and onto the ground below. Slepoy followed her, lingering at the threshold. Behind him, the rhythmic popping of embers in the hearth mingled with the steady grinding sounds of the pestle—an accompaniment to Yaga's song now drifting through the outdoors.

She worked quickly, pulling a birch log from a wood pile next to the cottage. Then, with a knife she unsheathed at her ankle, she shaved thin strips of the bark, her thumb steadying the blade. Soon, she was returning up the stairs, brushing past him at the doorway.

Yaga placed the birch into a metal bowl, ladling a bit of hot water over it and leaving it to stand on the counter. Then, wiping her hands on her apron, she turned to face Slepoy.

"Here, please," Yaga called to Slepoy, gesturing to the chair once more. As he sat, she stooped over him, continuing to hum as she cradled his jaw in her hands. Her brows knit together as she turned his head from side to side, examining his skin.

Behind her, the house seemed to buzz with movement and musicality. A clock ticking on the wall now formed a tempo. A metal spoon tipped and twisted into the air—twirling like a maple seedpod before settling with a clatter on the worktable. Glittering stones, too, seemed to lift themselves—jumping in time with the tapping of Yaga's foot on the wooden floorboards. Cabinet doors creaked open and shut ever so slightly. Dobra, too, had joined in; his coat shifting prismatically as he slunk across the floor.

To Slepoy, the scene was fascinating and otherworldly. He had heard things about a woman in the woods—Witch girl with magic in the forest near Valen. But—she was not a Witch in the way he had imagined one to be. In his mind, he had envisioned the dreaded Cave Witch Baba

Roga—or worse. Instead, Yaga was a delight to behold, and soon Slepoy slipped into a deep sense of ease.

His thoughts were interrupted by Yaga, who pinched the skin on his cheeks, forcing his lips apart. She grimaced; his teeth were badly stained. As her eyes moved over his complexion, her gaze sharpened. She leaned back, her arms folding in front of her body as she studied him intently. *This poor man*, she thought. He was suffering, and while she felt certain that the envy he had for others was a cause of misfortune on its own, she would try her best to help him. She glanced at the bird sleeping peacefully near the hearth.

In silence, Yaga walked to a small shelf near the sink. From a silver cup, she pulled a *brzytwa*—a cut-throat razor. With her other hand, she fetched a bowl of warm water and a bar of soap. Now, returning to the table, she tapped the blade of the razor against the bowl.

Ting, ting, ting.

"Your beard," she said, the clang of the bowl still ringing, "it's got to go."

A small gasp fell from Slepoy's mouth as Yaga made her way toward him. The idea of her holding a straight razor to his throat caused him to shift uncomfortably upon the seat. *Surely, she can be trusted*, he thought. And yet, Slepoy's heart began to beat a bit faster in his chest.

He swallowed hard as he felt the press of Yaga's fingers against his jaw. Tilting his head, she could see the pulse within his neck that thrummed beneath her touch, a quickened beat just below the skin. Slepoy clenched his fists in his lap, trying not to shift. As Yaga lifted the razor to his cheek, its polished edge glinted like a sliver of moonlight. Slepoy shuddered slightly, unnerved by the blade's appearance; sharp, thin, and final.

The room, once seemingly warm and uplifting, suddenly became eerily still. Yaga's feet had stopped moving, her voice no longer a pleasant melody filling the air between them. The fire in the hearth ceased to crackle, yet the light it cast stretched unnaturally—as if the shadows themselves were coming to watch. Abruptly, the room felt cold and oppressive to the man—a sudden darkness filling the space.

Unexpectedly, he heard a strange melody, sinuous and keening, wafting through the air like the smoke of incense. It was dissonant—haunting even, and it made the hair on the back of his neck stand on end. Nervously, he glanced at Yaga, quite sure that she heard it, too. Yet, she seemed unbothered—her expression steady and unchanged as she scraped at the bristle on his jaw.

Slepoy's gaze flicked to the edge of the room as something small skittered across the floor. There, he caught sight of a mouse darting near the leg of table. He released a relieved sigh—as though he had been holding his breath for too long. He watched the mouse scurry over the floorboards, its tiny claws clacking across the wood.

Then, abruptly—it stopped. A few feet away, the creature began to heave and convulse. To his horror, it began twisting and stretching into something gaunt and long-limbed, its bulging spine curling unnaturally. Slepoy gripped the chair as he watched, his eyes widening in disbelief. The creature's paws had grown, becoming a set of thin, clawed fingers that dragged across the floor.

A pair of large, dark, gleaming eyes flicked toward him. The monstrous creature tilted its head slightly as its mouth curled upward into a menacing smile. Inside, several rows of sharp, protruding teeth glinted in the low light of the cottage.

Slepoy jumped in his seat, nearly slicing his neck on the razor in Yaga's hand. Yaga stood back, her brow furrowing in disapproval. Then cupping his jaw in her hand, she held his face firmly.

"Hold still," she murmured, biting the inside of her cheek as she concentrated, steadying her grip. The blade ran over his skin once more.

Slepoy's heartbeat hammered—fast and loud. Yet, he stayed in his seat, too terrified to move. And so, the brzytwa rasped over his skin again and again as Yaga carved away rough bristle.

One slip. That was all it would take. Sweat beaded upon Slepoy's temples as the air in the room, heavy now with his own fear, pressed down on his chest like a large, black anvil. The shadows that loomed over them stretched again, and to his terror, something small chuckled from the rafters. The floorboards beneath him creaked, too, as if something demented had settled in, watching them. Watching him.

Slepoy's lungs tightened. Just as he felt the urge to run screaming from the cottage, never to return, Yaga leaned back, drawing the blade away from his flesh.

"There," she said, wiping the razor over her apron. "All done."

Abruptly, she moved towards the sink, humming once again as she walked.

Slepoy slumped in the chair, his chest heaving. As Yaga rinsed the blade, the room unexpectedly seemed to shift again. It felt lighter now, and as Slepoy relaxed into the chair he felt embarrassed by his own panic. *Surely, I must have imagined it*, he thought. Though, he was unable to shake the feeling that *he hadn't*. The thought lingered as he rubbed his fingers over his newly shaven skin.

Soon, Yaga returned, placing a clean cloth into hot water from the cauldron. She wrung it out into a bucket on the floor, then placed the hot, damp towel over his face. For a moment, the steam blurred his vision. He jolted slightly, swearing he had caught a glimpse of something darting just beyond the curtain of heat. Yet, by the time he peeled the cloth away enough to peek, all he saw was the soft glow of the embers in the hearth.

Above him, Yaga stared down quizzically. Slepoy smiled sheepishly, pulling the warm cloth back over his face—resigning himself to his fate once more.

The pleasant din of the cottage surrounding him, Slepoy soon felt Yaga's hands remove the hot towel. This time, she began scrubbing his face with a paste made of walnut hulls, removing the dirt and roughened skin. She took a second cloth, dipping it into the hot water, wiping away the excess grit. Slepoy sank deeper into his chair, his mind feeling distant and sleepy as the sound of her voice carried through the room.

"Hush now, hush, so light, so free,
Roots grow deep beneath the tree.
Streams will run, the leaves will sway,
All is well, you're here to stay."

As she finished, she draped another damp towel over his face, the scent of lavender wrapping around him. After several minutes, she removed it, revealing the tender, pink skin beneath. Then, bracing his head with one hand, Yaga carefully smoothed a thin layer of the birch water over his face. Slepoy shifted uncomfortably at the sting.

"It's fine," Yaga said. If he wanted his skin to heal, he would have to suffer—though only just a little. The bark's acids would treat his condition, and the discomfort was an unavoidable part of the process.

Soon, his skin had dried in the warm air of the cottage. Yaga slipped a small glass jar from her apron pocket; a blend of marshmallow root and sunflower oil. She continued humming as she gently patted the salve over his skin.

"You sure seem to know what you're doing, Yaga," Slepoy said, glancing up at her as she worked.

The corner of Yaga's mouth curved into a slight smile. She leaned back, her gaze catching his own. Slepoy marveled at her hazel eyes. Across her face, he noticed, the freckles looked like dark, inverted stars. He was enraptured by it all—her beauty, her skill, the magic of the house itself.

She smiled kindly, then narrowed her eyes, examining his skin one last time. Satisfied, she turned, moving across the room.

"Just one last thing," she said, her feet gliding back to the worktable. She continued humming as she mixed together a powder of ground stone and herbs within a bowl. Then, calling him to her sink, she showed him how to use the gritty paste to clean his teeth.

It was nearly nightfall as Slepoy stood in front of a mirror hanging from the wall. He grinned, turning his head from side to side, admiring his new appearance. Tracing his fingers over his face, he felt he was seeing it for the first time. His skin was smooth now—even handsome. A tear formed in the corner of his eye, though he quickly wiped it away.

"Take these with you," Yaga said, placing a small cloth pouch into his hand containing several vials of the remedies she had used to treat him.

Without a second glance at the bird, Slepoy hurried towards the door of Yaga's house. He paused briefly at the threshold, glancing around the room one last time—certain he could still hear a faint, melodic hum.

"Yaga," he said, his voice filled with sincerity.

Yaga turned towards him from the sink, their eyes meeting one final time from across the room. In that moment, it dawned on him that he had never experienced kindness like this—not from anyone. For his entire life, people had stared at him, judging him for his appearance. They had never wanted to know him for who he was on the inside. Over many years, a deep sadness and anger had taken root in his heart. Yet, today, Yaga had stirred something within him—though just what, he couldn't say.

"Thank you," he said, his eyes twinkling. Abruptly, he slipped out the door and down the porch, disappearing into the forest beyond the cottage.

Yaga sighed as she watched him scamper into the darkening woods. *Poor Slepoy*, she thought. He suffered in more ways than she could mend—and as she stood in the low light of her cottage, she wondered how he might fare in life if he continued to carry such envy and shame.

As she closed the door, Yaga turned, her eyes studying the empty space intently.

"You know, you really ought to be nice, Kiki," Yaga said, shaking her head. She knew that the Kikimorra had fed off the man's energy in some way—some broken part of Slepoy fueling her mischievous taunting.

But the other things—the jumping stones and grinding pestle? Yaga had yet to understand the force of her own nature. That she was a conduit—an amplifier of the energy that could connect with the anima of the world around her. One day, she would have to face the truth of the magic she called out to—in every root, every stone, and every beating heart.

Yaga glanced at the bird sleeping on the chair. Silently, she moved to her worktable where her grimoire lay. Thumbing over its pages for a moment, her breath hitched. Depicted before her was a small white bird, no bigger than a hen. Just a baby, she had a pointed beak and a long, unruly tail. And next to her, an adult—massive and covered with shining black plumage. A Firebird.

Zhar-Ptitsa.

In the stillness, Yaga gently scooped the bird off the cushion, holding her close to her chest as she moved. As she lifted her head slightly, the bird's eyes appeared like obsidian in the glow of the candlelight. Within them, Yaga saw something that looked like galaxies spinning in an ancient, quiet dance. The bird nuzzled closer, settling into her arms.

Yaga's heart swelled for the creature. She pulled her closer to her as she moved to the washroom in the back where she drew a small bath. The pale, disheveled bird was fragile and weak, and more than anything, misunderstood. From then on, Yaga would mother the creature until she could take care of herself. Gently, she placed the bird into the basin of warm water and began to sing, lathering soap into its plumage.

"Rest, rest, my golden spark,
Safe you are in light or dark.
Where you go, the earth will know,

Love will fill you as you grow."

That night, as she cradled the bird in her love, Yaga could not know their future. She could not begin to understand how important the bird would be to her own destiny. And now, years later, the Firebird had begun to sense something; an intrusion of energy moving into their peaceful world. There had been an unmistakable shift in the air the previous night.

Whatever was coming to Valen—had arrived.

As the morning sun lifted into the sky, Zhar spread her massive wings. With a single, powerful beat, ripples cascaded over the pond like small waves. The wind from her wings caused the reeds at the water's edge to sway as nearby leaves swirled in the sky like confetti. The Fairies and Rusalkas laughed and danced blithely in the wake of her departure as the Firebird soared toward her perch in the oaks above the cottage.

Inside, Yaga had already begun her day, humming as she tended to the morning chores. High above her, the Firebird now settled into the branches, her shining eyes scanning the forest one last time. Zhar was ready for what might come; she would protect her family at all hours and at all costs. For, unlike the waxen seal that bore her image, the Firebird could not be broken.

Chapter Four

THE WOMAN IN
THE WOODS

Pitchfork in hand, Alexey stood inside a stall at his family's stable. It was midmorning as he refreshed the hay in Kolya's quarters, and, working up a sweat from the exertion, he hung his long coat on a nearby hook. With a grunt, Alexey heaved a large flake of hay into an empty corner, breaking it apart on the floor with the forked end of the tool. He paused for a moment, wiping his brow. From the other end of the building, the soft whinnying of several mares echoed as they flirted with the neighboring stallions across the aisle. Here in Kolya's quarters, however, it was quiet and still—a small section of the building reserved entirely for the wolf.

Setting the pitchfork aside, Alexey walked from the open stall towards a long trough positioned below a faucet. Turning on the tap, he watched as the basin filled with a torrent of fresh water. Out of the corner of his eye, he noticed Kolya's penetrating gaze.

A gray wolf of considerable size, Kolya took up half of the empty stall across from the one in which Alexey worked. Neither Alexey, nor anyone else for that matter, had ever encountered an animal so large—save for a horse, as it were. Yet, despite his large stature, the wolf didn't appear unusual at all next to Alexey, himself a man towering above most others.

Alexey smiled faintly as he reached once more for the pitchfork, jabbing it deep into a bale of hay before twisting off another section. Still, he could feel Kolya's eyes upon him, and after a moment, he stopped, resting his arm on the tool's handle.

"Ok, what is it?" Alexey said. Kolya, as ever, remained silent as he continued staring at Alexey.

"I know—I know," Alexey said. "I promised I would bring you into the countryside again soon. Just not yet, ok?"

Kolya groaned, settling his large head onto his paws. He chuffed, sending a few bits of straw floating through the air. Turning, Alexey gazed out the window. As his eyes scanned the field beyond the estate, his thoughts went back to the first time he had encountered the wolf.

It had been nearly nine years since the day of the hunt in the woods near Severyn. There in the forested foothills of the Ebon Tors, a sudden storm had forced Alexey's hunting party to take cover. Kolya was smaller then, and seemingly lost and afraid. His silvery coat matted and damp, he had run beneath the tree under which Alexey and the other men sheltered. There, Alexey had gripped his hands over the wolf's wet fur tightly, steadying the cub as his body shook with every crack of lightning.

Alexey, only seventeen at the time, had pleaded to keep the poor creature when he returned home. His father, Dmitri, though deeply skeptical at first, had seen the love his son had for the animal, ultimately relenting. Wolves were, after all, venerated by the Karelian peoples, just as they were by the Sclaveni to the south. Still, the beasts were seldom kept by men, and Kolya's presence had hardly gone unnoticed; he had become nearly the size of a small horse since the day of his arrival into Alexey's life.

Despite Kolya's unusual stature, in the intervening years, he had become an important part of the Grishaev household. He and Alexey were inseparable now, both considering themselves to be the other's guardian.

In all ways, the wolf was a faithful companion to Alexey and Misha; a gentle giant with soulful, amber-colored eyes, completely dedicated to his family.

Alexey's thoughts were interrupted by the sounds of a stallion kicking at the sidewalls at the far end of the building. It seemed, he thought, that everyone was feeling a bit restless these days. Turning, he moved to the water trough once more, shutting off the tap.

Setting the pitchfork aside, Alexey slipped into the empty stall where Kolya lay. He stooped, scratching the wolf gingerly behind his ears. After a moment, Kolya rose to his feet, moving into the stall with fresh bedding. Padding around in a circle, he laid down with a slight groan.

"I'll be back soon, boy—I promise. I'll bring you a juicy piece of venison from the market, ok?" Kolya's eyes followed Alexey as he walked towards the door. "I'll take you with me soon."

Kolya set his head down silently as Alexey exited into the morning air. The wolf was free to come and go, though he knew better than to leave the estate unattended. Alexey was certain, given time, that the villagers would take a liking to Kolya. Though, he had learned over the years that the respect the Sclaveni held for wolves did not necessarily mean that they were not afraid of them. Especially one as large as Kolya.

They had seen him before; he would be hard to miss. Yet, his presence had initially been met with a wave of concern in those first few weeks after the Grishaev's arrival in Valen. Now, as the autumn leaves began their slow downward drift, the chatter had subsided to nothing more than a murmur. Still, Alexey thought it best for everyone to ease the townspeople into their familiarity—even if he wished to take the wolf with him everywhere he went.

Alexey glanced back at the stables one last time as he continued towards the house. Soon, however, his thoughts shifted to Misha. Today, the two brothers would head to the market together—an opportunity for some sunshine before the inevitable deep chill settled over the region.

In any case, Alexey knew his brother would benefit from the fresh air. Ascending the porch steps, he called through the screen door, summoning Misha to ready for their outing.

Walking along the road to the village, Misha sat perched on Alexey's broad shoulders. The young boy's gaze scanned the once-green fields where frost-killed tawny patches now spread like a creeping mist. He smiled, drawing in a full breath of the fresh air. Despite the dimming that came with the shifting seasons, the outside was alive. The breeze rolling over the hills carried with it the sweet, musky scents of the recent harvests. For Misha, it felt a sharp contrast to the stale air within his bedroom chamber, a place where he spent much of his time these days.

Before long, a carriage passed by the brothers, its outer walls ornate with painted trimmings. As the clopping of the horses hooves trundled up the road towards the village, Misha suddenly pinched his brother lightly on the arm.

"Alexey, when we go to the gala, do you think you'll meet a girl?" Misha's eyes sparkled in the midmorning sun as he imagined the feasts and dancing that would occur.

Alexey paused, craning his head slightly to see his brother's face, a smirk forming.

"A girl?" he said, his eyebrow arching. "Now why would I go and do that?" he said, continuing up the gravel road, his long coat swaying as he moved.

"Mother says..." Misha began.

"Now, brother," Alexey interrupted. "Mother says *many* things," Alexey said, smiling. "And what Mother says *today* is that she would like 'two bars of soap from the market,'" he said, imitating Tatiana's feminine lilt.

He smiled, hoping to leave the question behind. Yet, in the silence that followed, he could sense that Misha was worried; he knew that his young brother feared his absence, were he to meet someone and start a family of his own. Yet, despite his mother's frequent encouragement to marry and settle down, for Alexey, it was out of the question. He would not abandon his younger brother. Misha needed him more than anyone, and unless he was free of the sickness that had plagued him since birth, Alexey could not envision a future where they were parted. *Not ever.*

"I will *not* be meeting any girls at the gala, Mish," he said, hoping to reassure him. "Besides—it would take more than a pretty girl to steal me away from you. Only a *Witch* could do that!" Alexey teased, tousling Misha's hair as they broke into laughter. As they continued their walk toward the village, the topic changed, moving them away from the idea altogether.

Soon, the two brothers were making their way through the busy town square, admiring the booths, and taking in the morning's lively bustle. Weaving through the streets, they navigated towards a modest shop tucked between a spice merchant and a stand selling wooden trinkets. From high atop his brother's shoulders, Misha marveled at his view of things below; there were stalls and stands everywhere with people milling about. The sounds of laughter and conversation formed a pulsing hum that seemed to emanate outward from him and Alexey. As the wind rushed over his cheeks, Misha's heart felt full. From here, the world looked like it had been made for him—his vantage point no longer bound to his small, frail frame.

Alexey placed Misha on the stoop of the shop, then bent forward, ducking beneath the doorway. As they entered, a soft chime of bells jingled, announcing their arrival. Inside, the walls were lined with shelves displaying staples and various sundries. In the corner, neat stacks of soap were set—fragrant bars wrapped in cloth and tied with twine, each stamped with a green wax seal.

The shopkeeper, sitting on a chair behind the counter in the back, looked up from his book, waving politely. Immediately, Misha began to roam around, rummaging through bins of trinkets and stands stacked with curious items and various household goods.

Alexey moved towards the soaps, picking up a few bars and lifting them to his nose. The scent of roses and lavender was almost intoxicating, softening his brow with their earthy sweetness. He knew immediately that his mother—having come to covet the soaps—would be delighted by the batch. He smiled, walking to the back of the shop, where the shopkeeper, Velimir, sat. Pulling a bag of coins from the pocket of his overcoat, Alexey set the soaps upon the counter.

Velimir, who had been observing Misha moving about the store, had taken notice of the slight limp the child walked with. He had seen him before in town, and now, as Alexey rummaged in the sack of coin, the shopkeeper studied Misha intently. Then, in a quiet voice, he leaned forward.

"Your brother—he's unwell I see."

Alexey raised an eyebrow, his breath hitching slightly as a familiar twinge settled into his jaw. Over the years, many people—far too many to count—had commented on his brother's appearance. Most were simply curious, though, others offered to help—if only he or his parents would purchase some service or instrument. Alexey braced himself for an offer to buy something that would indubitably disappoint. It would be a waste of time, money, and hope—the latter of which Alexey had precious little of these days regarding a cure for his brother's ailments.

Gently, the shopkeeper placed the bars of soap into a paper sack as Alexey handed him several coins. "Have you taken him to see the woman in the woods?" the shopkeeper asked, though his expression betrayed he already knew the answer.

Alexey's eyes rolled slightly as he took the bag from Velimir's hands, turning on his boot without a word. Yet, just as he was about to call out to Misha to depart, the shopkeeper grabbed his forearm firmly.

"The soap you have—she makes it." Startled, Alexey looked down at the bag he held, the sweet fragrance still lingering in the air between them. His eyes flicked to the shopkeeper.

"*Take him,*" Velimir insisted, his grip tightening.

Velimir glanced at Misha across the room, nodding kindly at the child. Though Misha, playing with a wooden doll upon a shelf, barely took notice.

Once again, the man's eyes met Alexey's. Velimir narrowed his gaze. "She helps people with things... you've nothing to lose, my boy. Take him to her," he said, his grip suddenly releasing from Alexey's arm.

There was something unexpectedly certain in the man's insistence that Alexey found unsettling. Just like the soap in the bag, the mention of the woman living in the woods seemed to evoke something for Alexey—though what, he wasn't sure. He knew one thing with certainty, however: he was tired of fake cures and empty promises; he needed something real.

Misha needed something real.

Alexey glanced down at the soap once again, his expression pensive as Velimir placed the few coins in a box beneath the counter.

"Where did you say she lives?"

He had asked the question before fully considering it. Yet, as the words fell from his mouth—he knew, perhaps unreasonably—that he would go there. They would do so today. His back stiffened at the thought, for despite the small flicker of hope he now felt, he was more than a little wary. He had not a modicum of evidence to instill hope at this point. Still, with a winter to be spent indoors looming before his brother, he was more than a bit curious.

Could it be possible that someone would help Misha yet? He clutched the paper sack tighter in his hand as Velimir explained the route through town and towards the cottage.

With a final nod, Alexey took Misha's hand and headed for the door. Walking him out to the stoop, he stood on the cobblestones, hoisting his brother back upon his shoulders. Soon, the two were making their way through the market once more, stopping briefly at the butcher's to buy a few strips of cured venison. Then, as the sun climbed up higher into the midday sky, warming the air around them, Alexey and Misha turned down a narrow street winding away from the village. They were heading south, walking through rolling farmlands—a wall of forest growing in the distance.

Alexey's boots crunched over the brittle leaf litter scattered across the forest floor as he carried Misha on his back. The brothers chatted blithely as they moved, their voices echoing through the hollow understory. Here and there, Alexey crouched below a branch, his long coat dragging over the ground behind him.

It was early afternoon by the time the path narrowed, tapering beneath overgrown shrubs and low branches dappled in gold and shadow as the light filtered through the canopy. On foot now, Misha walked slowly beside his older brother, his tiny gait uneven and labored. His expression had twisted into a grimace, his small body hunching forward in an attempt to ease the pain growing within his knees and ankles.

Misha's face, though young, seemed to carry the weariness of someone much older. His skin was sallow and thin—a testament to the time he had spent in his bed. Alexey's heart clenched as he watched his brother struggle, his tiny boots disappearing as he waded through the leaf litter.

Alexey's brow furrowed. Within him, a hesitation swelled, his mind now tumbling over the many so-called healers who had come before. They had offered nothing more than false promises to his family. Yet, for a reason he couldn't begin to explain, something small in the shape of hope now grew alongside his trepidation. He would see what the woman living in the forest had to offer to Misha. He would go without expectation—though in truth, he wanted to believe in the possibility of a remedy. A *cure*.

Suddenly, Misha's voice broke through his thoughts.

"Look!" he chirped.

As they emerged from the tree line, a cottage came into view. Set upon three towering oak trees, it was a strange, unexpected sight. The house was completely unlike anything Alexey had ever seen, and as he hoisted his brother back upon his shoulders for the trek across the clearing, he marveled at its peculiar form.

Perched slightly above the ground, the cottage seemed to be built on the thick roots of the oaks that cradled it. In the yard below, chickens wandered, clucking and scratching at the duff, oblivious to the brothers' arrival. Drawing closer, Alexey could see a large iron cauldron in the yard, as well as bundled herbs swinging gently from the rafters of the porch. A small plume of smoke coiled out of a chimney, and as they approached, a gentle breeze passed over the cottage, carrying with it a pungent, familiar scent.

"Ok, Misha," Alexey murmured as they approached. "Let's see if anyone's home."

Soon, Alexey stood at the base of the steps leading up to the porch. Setting his brother down, they began their ascent—though just as they stepped up onto the first wooden tread, the door of the cottage creaked open gently.

There, standing at the threshold with the door ajar, an individual stood, half-cloaked in shadow. For a moment, there was silence, the figure seemingly observing them. Then, a woman emerged. Her chestnut hair shimmering in the midafternoon light, Yaga stood gazing down at the brothers.

Alexey blinked. Completely stunned by the woman's appearance, his mouth fell open in disbelief. Yaga's warm, freckled skin was wrapped in the soft linen of her embroidered blouse. Her hair fell in ropes, a few loose strands framing her cheekbones. And her eyes—each a slender willow-leaf holding a glistening, hazel dewdrop that sparkled as though it contained flecks of jade.

Alexey's heart dropped into his stomach as he watched her wipe her hands over her apron. Her full lips curved up into a gentle smile as she watched them curiously. She was unexpectedly beautiful, which Alexey found much more than a little surprising. He had not known who to expect, but it wasn't... *her*.

"You've come for your brother," she said. There was something about her tone that Alexey found unsettling; it was as though she had been *waiting for* them.

Alexey nodded, a lump now forming in his throat. His short interaction with the shopkeeper in town had not prepared him for the reality of the woman in the woods. As she loomed above him, she seemed self-assured and deliberate. Yet, here, tucked into this cottage in the oaks, there was something about her that appeared almost feral to him.

Suddenly, Alexey felt a small tug on his coat sleeve.

"Who is she?" Misha whispered.

Yaga's nose wrinkled, her gaze moving between the unexpected visitors.

"Uh, yes," Alexey began, his voice unsteady. Suddenly, for the first time in his life, he felt nervous. "My brother Misha. He needs... he's suffering," he stammered.

Yaga nodded gently, her eyes passing over Misha. Stepping aside, she motioned for them to come up the steps.

"Why don't you come inside and we'll have a look, shall we?" Yaga said.

The brothers glanced at one another, Misha's eyes searching his older brother's. Alexey took a breath, then nodded at him, steadying the child as he ascended the steps.

When he had reached the top, the woman knelt before Misha.

"Hello there, Misha," she said, extending her open hand towards him. Misha, clasping it weakly with his own, walked beside her stiffly as she led him indoors. Following them closely, Alexey stooped beneath the threshold, the door closing behind them with a soft thud.

"Have a seat right here, Misha," Yaga said, gesturing to a nearby chair.

"I—I can pay," Alexey offered, reaching for his sack of coins he kept in his breast pocket.

Yaga seemed to ignore him, however, kneeling before Misha.

"May I?" Yaga said, pointing to the boy's knees.

Misha nodded.

Yaga pulled the boy's legs forward gently, pressing her fingers lightly around his knees through the fabric of his pants. She could feel his joints beneath—swollen and stiff. Slowly, she rolled up the fabric from his ankle, revealing the lower part of his leg. His ankles, just as his knees, were knotted and red. Misha winced slightly beneath her touch. Yaga pulled her hands back, taking Misha's gaze into her own.

"You're a brave one—I can tell," she said.

Misha's eyes sparkled as they flicked to Alexey and back to Yaga.

After a moment, Yaga stood, her feet carrying her across the room. There, she began rummaging around a shelf, inspecting and sorting through jars and bottles with her back turned to the brothers.

In the silence, Alexey glanced around the space, taking in the strange collection of items. There were shelves spanning towards the ceiling, each stacked with glass vials, tinctures, and crystals. Potted plants dripped off the edge of cupboards while bundled herbs swayed gently overhead. In the air, the faint scent of woodsmoke melded with freshly baked bread lingering from the early morning, a fact that made his stomach groan faintly with hunger.

And then, at the same moment as his brother Misha, Alexey spotted the eyeballs.

They were strewn over the shelves and pooled into dishes and vessels on nearly every surface. From the windowsills, small prisms speckled over the floorboards as light filtered through the irises of the eyes stored there. They could see them in the corners and tucked behind chairs. Hundreds—no, *thousands* of glass eyeballs with irises in every imaginable color.

Misha's nose scrunched as he turned to Alexey, who himself was fishing one from a nearby jar. Alexey glanced back at Yaga, now humming at the center of the room as she busily sorted through several items on the worktable. Quietly, Alexey passed the eyeball to Misha, who marveled curiously as he poked at the dark green iris in his palm.

Tink, tink, tink.

The silence in the cottage was punctuated by the faint sound of Misha's fingernail rapping on the surface of the glass eye. Yaga turned, catching him in her gaze. Her lip curled slightly, a sly smile forming in the corner of her mouth. Without a word, she turned back to the worktable and continued humming, her focus on a book set open before her.

Misha glanced up at Alexey once more, who only shrugged. Yet, despite—or perhaps *because* of the oddity before them—Alexey now found the woman and the cottage itself unexpectedly endearing.

"Uh, I'm Alexey, by the way," Alexey said—his voice a little louder than he had intended.

The brothers watched in silence as Yaga moved abruptly from the worktable toward a massive bookcase across the room. Using her foot, she nudged a rolling ladder attached to the shelves, climbing up a few rungs where she retrieved a glittering blue stone. Soon, she had returned to the worktable, setting it next to the other items.

Pushing the open book to the side, she picked up a metal file and began to grind away at the blue stone. Misha and Alexey watched in silence, captivated by the shimmering powder that fell into the bowl below. Soon, she poured a bit of oil from a nearby bottle, folding it into the lustrous blue mineral within.

As she finished, she wiped her hands over her apron, glancing up at the two brothers.

"Yaga," she said, moving towards them.

"Pardon?" Alexey said, his expression puzzled.

"You can wait here," she said, touching Misha gently on the shoulder as she breezed by them both. To Alexey's surprise, the woman picked up a basket and headed out the door. He followed her, nearly bumping his head on the doorway as he tried to catch up.

Outside, her feet carried her down the steps and to the edge of the clearing on the backside of the cottage. She was walking swiftly now, her boots skimming through the leaves covering the familiar tangle of roots and stones that stretched over a narrow path leading into the forest.

"Wait!" he called to her. "Where are you going?" Alexey stumbled, falling behind her as his jacket caught on the scrubby brush. He could barely see her now as he walked deeper beyond the tree line, instead only hearing the soft hum of her voice echoing through the understory ahead.

Several steps behind her, Alexey soon emerged from the woods into a small meadow, his hand briskly wiping a spider's web from his face. Surrounding them, various grasses and plants seemed to have taken refuge here against the cold winds of autumn, their green leaves and stalks basking in the early afternoon sunshine.

The woman, now standing before a small stand of what appeared to be weeds, stooped, slipping a knife out from the sheath strapped to her ankle, as her other hand bundled a group of the plants together at their bases. With a swift slice, she had cut through their stalks, tossing their fleshy leaves into her basket as Alexey watched nearby.

Glancing over her shoulder at him, Yaga noticed a small twig with a bit of lichen protruding from his hair. She raised an eyebrow before shifting her attention back to the plants. Cutting another handful, she set them within the basket once more.

"These are nettles," she said, standing upright and turning to face him.

Now, just a few feet apart, Yaga could see the man before her more clearly. Though—it wasn't his height that caught her attention—nor was it his broad shoulders hugged too tightly by his overcoat. It was his hand, which sat perched at the hilt of the dagger at his waist.

Yaga observed him curiously, her eyes flicking down to the dagger. Alexey seemed puzzled—though, following her gaze, he widened his stance just slightly, clearing his throat. She stared at him for a moment longer, her brow furrowing slightly. Abruptly, she scooped up her basket, brushing past him back into the forest. He turned, trying to keep up with her once more.

"It's—it's for protection," he called out behind her.

"For whom—you, or me?" Yaga replied, her boots weaving through the forest nimbly as she made her way back towards the cottage.

"Wait—what? For you, of course," Alexey said. He stopped suddenly as a small branch entered his mouth. *Pfft, pfft.* He spit out the bits of leaf, then ducked below the branches overgrowing the trail as he tried once more to catch up to her.

"Interesting," Yaga said, her voice now distant as she walked briskly along the twisting, tree-line path.

Alexey pushed and thrashed his way through the shrubs and leaves as he followed behind. Suddenly, turning a bend, he saw her there, standing squarely before him. She stood silently, her face caught in a few strands of sunlight that fell through the canopy. Alexey swallowed hard, his heart now beating faster—though it wasn't from the walk.

"Yaga," she said, extending her hand to him.

Alexey raised an eyebrow, wiping a bit of bark from the front of his jacket.

"Meaning?" he said, straightening up as best as he could in the low-hanging understory.

The woman narrowed her eyes before turning, disappearing up the path once more.

"It's my name," she said, her voice now some distance away.

Alexey winced, a sense of embarrassment flushing his cheeks. *It's her name, you idiot.* He shook his head, grumbling to himself as he traipsed up the path.

After a few minutes, he had emerged from the trees into the clearing surrounding her cottage—just in time to see her leather boots clicking up the porch steps, her long skirt swaying as she moved. She stopped at the doorway, seemingly waiting for him—causing him to break into a jog to catch up.

Now, as he stood on the ground below the porch, she could sense his humiliation.

"Look, Yaga—I'm sorry," he said.

As she observed him, something unexpectedly warm stirred within her—if only briefly. Alexey was covered in tiny twigs and bits of moss, a sight which she found humorous given his stature. The man was handsome, yes—but there was something else about him that pulled at her, though what it was, she couldn't quite put her finger on. Looking into her eyes, he gave her a wide, bashful grin—to which Yaga only nodded slightly before slipping through the doorway, disappearing inside.

He grimaced, though quickly composed himself, turning his attention instead back to his brother as he entered. Misha, still seated in the chair, had gained a companion in their absence: upon his lap sat Dobra, his tail flicking as he purred and nuzzled into Misha's chest.

"I think he likes me," Misha said, his small hand placed lightly over the cat's shoulders.

"It seems like they *both* do," Yaga said as she knelt before him, slowly rolling up the legs of his pants once more. She had noticed a spider nearby, though she knew it to be the Kikimorra. She was perched on the ear of the chair—the carved upper corner just beside Misha's head. Yaga reached out gently, letting the creature crawl onto her finger, before moving her to an adjacent windowsill, where she crept amongst a trove of glass eyes staring out in all directions.

Returning, Yaga knelt before Misha, pulling a clump of leaves from her basket as she spoke.

"This will sting a bit," she said. "But only for a moment."

Misha's eyes widened as he glanced up at Alexey, though his older brother only gave a small, reassuring nod. Alexey was unsure of what would happen next, though he felt a sense of trust burgeoning in the time since their arrival.

The brothers watched as Yaga crushed up the leaves, rolling them gently between her fingers and Misha's knees until they dripped with green juice. She pressed the mash firmly over his knees, rubbing the wet material over the joint on all sides. On each of his ankles, she repeated the process.

At first, Misha winced, the sight of which made Alexey twinge with concern. However, to his surprise, he watched as a wave of relief washed over his younger brother's face.

"It tingles," Misha whispered, his face softening.

Yaga nodded as she fished out more of the leafy stalks from the basket, applying them to Misha's joints once more. Standing near the doorway, Alexey studied her as she worked, his curiosity growing. Surely it wasn't possible that this woman—in mere minutes—would be successful where so many, *many* others had failed. Yet, watching her silently as she tended to his brother with care and precision, he felt a small upwelling of hope.

Curious, Alexey bent forward, plucking a leaf from one of the stalks still laying within the basket. He rolled it around in his fingers—though quickly regretted it. Immediately, his skin became tingly and numb, soon filling with the sensation of a thousand tiny radiating prickles. He tossed the leaf back into the basket, shaking his hand vigorously while a strange numbness settled into his fingertips.

Soon, Yaga stood, her hands spreading green streaks over the front of her apron. Moving to the worktable, she fetched the bowl of the blue-tinged oil and a few strips of clean cloth. Returning, she knelt before Misha, and one by one, she dipped the strips into the oil. Straining off the excess back into the bowl with her fingers, she set to work wrapping Misha's knees and ankles with the fabric.

After a moment, Yaga rolled down the legs of Misha's pants. She stepped back, smiling at him kindly. The treatment was finished. Now, the three stood silently, with only the ticking of the clock and Dobra's purring punctuating the quiet of the cottage. Suddenly, Dobra stood on Misha's lap, stretching his striped, orange body out—before hopping to the floor and slinking away.

Misha glanced at Alexey, his face uncertain—as though to ask what would happen next.

"Misha, you should keep these bandages on as long as you can, ok?" Yaga said. She paused. "My name's Yaga, by the way," she whispered, as though just to him. She moved towards her worktable once more.

There, she poured the blue oil into a clear bottle, pushing a cork down into the opening at the top. She returned, handing Alexey two vials—one with the blue ointment, and another with a pungent-smelling brown liquid made from sweet onions soaked in honey.

"Rub this over his joints every morning and night," she said, instructing Alexey as she handed him the ointment.

"And this." Yaga turned to Misha, wrinkling her nose as she held up the brown liquid. "It's sweet, though strange. Sometimes it's the things that we don't want that can help us the most," she said.

Glancing back at Alexey, their eyes met briefly.

"One spoonful by mouth, each evening," she said. "And bring him back tomorrow for another treatment of the nettles." Yaga nudged at the basket of plants with her foot.

Alexey raised an eyebrow as he watched Yaga drift to the back of the cottage towards the sink. He realized then that he had been waiting—almost expecting that the woman would insist on payment. And yet, she hadn't. *Not once.*

Suddenly, Alexey's gaze flicked to Misha, who—to his great surprise—had darted past him towards a jar of glass eyeballs on the windowsill. He watched as his brother moved without the usual stiffness that was so familiar to him now. Slowly, he approached, stooping next to him at the window.

Together, they watched as Misha plucked an eyeball with a dark brown iris from the top of the jar, its glass sides clinking against the others lightly. Misha's face beamed with curiosity as he held it up to the light, a honeyed glow washing over the skin of his fingers. The brothers exchanged a glance. The cottage and Yaga were peculiar, indeed, for the eyeballs were an oddity unlike any they had seen before.

After a moment, Misha placed the glass orb back with the others. Then, looking past Alexey, his feet whisked his small body through the front door, out onto the porch. Alexey straightened abruptly. Casting his eyes towards Yaga briefly, he followed Misha outside, just in time to see him descend the steps unaided.

After a few minutes, Yaga, too, emerged from the cottage. There, she found Alexey standing at the base of the porch, watching as his brother stooped to gently pet a chicken, her soft clucking sounding in the yard. Running his frail hand over the bird's silky feathers, Misha smiled.

"His muscles," Yaga said. "They're weak."

The planks of wood creaked beneath her feet as she descended to the ground below.

"It will change—given time," she said, offering a kind smile.

Alexey, still mystified as he watched Misha moving about the yard, glanced down at his hand. His eyes flicked to Yaga as he wiggled his fingers, still tingling from the plant.

"The leaves—they sting," he said. "How…"

Yaga stared at her own hands, her shoulders shrinking just slightly.

"Just an old soap-making accident," she said. "Things just never felt the same after that."

"… in my hands," she added.

There was a pause between them, and in the silence, Yaga could sense Alexey's gaze upon her. She could tell he wanted to know more, though she didn't offer. Instead, she turned, her boots gently thudding as she walked back up the steps towards the door of the cottage.

"Wait," Alexey called after her, turning.

Standing above him now, their eyes met. For a single, fleeting moment, an energy, barely palpable, arose between them. Alexey cleared his throat.

"Thank you, Yaga—for today," he said.

Yaga's face softened as she studied the man standing before her. His shoulders were broad—his too-small coat open at the front, revealing just a bit of his chest. His blue eyes seemed to sparkle like topaz in the afternoon light—a peculiar contrast to the dark, midnight strands of his hair brushing just below his jawline. Something about him seemed a study in contrast to her; a brawny man charged with the tender care of a small child. She only nodded at him, however, before turning to wave at Misha. Then, she slipped into the cottage, the screen door thudding softly behind her.

Shifting his gaze toward the tree line, Alexey noticed the changing afternoon light. The sun would sink lower soon, disappearing beyond a distant mountain ridge and cloaking the woods in shadows.

"Come, Misha," he said, walking towards his brother with his hand extended.

Instead, however, Misha skipped ahead of him, laughing.

"Now, brother," Alexey said sternly, his brow furrowing. "Let's not get ahead of ourselves."

"You just don't want me to leave you in my dust!" Misha taunted—though he slowed his pace just the same, knowing Alexey was right. He had to be careful—always.

Soon, they had reached the edge of the clearing that contained Yaga's cottage. There, Alexey glanced back at the cottage one last time, before slipping beyond the trees. He hadn't seen her then, but as he looked back, Yaga, too, stood at the window half in darkness, watching the brothers depart. She had the strangest feeling that *she knew* Alexey from somewhere. As though she had met him before, yet she was quite certain she hadn't. Still, something about him felt familiar to her. She shrugged as they disappeared down the trail, returning to the kitchen to wash up.

As the brothers made their way back to the village, Alexey mulled over their encounter with the woman in the woods. He could admit to himself that he'd had an immediate attraction to her; she was beautiful. Yet, there was something more. He felt, inexplicably, an unusual sense of *safety* in her presence. It was a fact he found utterly strange; after all, Alexey was hardly in any danger himself. Yet, just the same, something about Yaga gave him comfort.

As they walked along, their feet kicked up bits of the leafy duff. All around them, Misha's chittering echoed through the understory. He rambled excitedly about eyeballs and orange cats, spiders, and chickens. Yet, Alexey was lost in thought as his mind considered the possibilities brought to their family and to his brother that day. Had Yaga truly helped Misha where others had failed? He wondered if she was the healer they had been searching for all along. Now, with his mind a tangled web of reflection and emotion, in his heart, a small ember of hope had ignited into a tiny plume of fire.

Still, he thought—*we will have to wait and see.*

As they emerged into the field that flanked the road winding back to Valen, Misha paused, reaching for his older brother faintly. He was tired now, and the long walk back seemed daunting. Alexey pulled his brother up onto his shoulders, feeling the boy's tiny chest slumping over his own head. As the two journeyed back toward the village, Alexey replayed his brother's burst of energy just before. He had never seen his brother walk as far without the dire consequence of days of exhaustion. Alexey winced, a pang of guilt flashing over his face. Misha had done too much.

Perhaps, he wondered, things were not as they had seemed after all; the woman in the woods hadn't really helped his brother as he'd hoped. The relief had been temporary. And then, a wave of fear crashed over Alexey as though coming to claim him back to the murky depths from which he had just surfaced for air.

Perhaps Misha wouldn't be cured after all.

Chapter Five

THE BOY IN THE CASTLE

With the low light of evening filtering through the windows of the cottage, Yaga stooped over the hearth, a small taper candle in her outstretched hand. Beneath the cauldron, she pressed the wick into a glowing ember, a bright yellow flame leaping up. Then, collecting a copper kettle with her other hand, she moved to the staircase, pausing to light a large lantern hanging nearby.

Making her way to the second floor, her bare feet pressed lightly over each step. Her shadow spanned upwards over the wall above her, looming over the lower level like a dark giantess. Steadying her steps, her forearm brushed lightly against the twisting handrail. Every familiar knot and groove beneath her skin felt like a smooth guide, while each groaning movement of the wood underfoot announced her ascent. It was as though they, too, could sense the day was nearing its end.

At the top, Yaga passed through the doorway framed with thick, woven tapestries, slipping into the room she shared with Vasilisa. There, seated before the loom, the Vila continued working despite the growing darkness. With the fading daylight now barely visible in their quarters,

Yaga set to lighting a few more pillar candles set on the small tables near their beds.

When she had finished, Yaga paused, admiring the growing tapestry as her friend's small hands pulled and pushed over the warp. It was an intricate masterpiece now—colorful like light bending out from a prism yet filled with dark strands of crimson and black. She had been working on it for weeks now, though, in recent days, the Vila seemed to be weaving at all hours. Vasilisa paused, fishing out a deep blue skein of woolen yarn from a basket beside her on the floor.

"Vasa," Yaga said softly.

Vasilisa tilted her head at the sound of Yaga's voice. The soft yellow kerchief covering her eyes contrasted starkly with the obsidian color of her hair. It reminded Yaga of a bumble bee, soft and gentle—though capable of stinging when threatened. Yaga smiled, her eyes passing back over the tapestry once more.

"I'm heading in now. I should be finished in time for bed," Yaga said.

Vasilisa nodded, her posture unchanging.

With that, Yaga turned, passing through another set of tapestries—this time entering a rounded room with a pitched, high ceiling. It was the inner sanctum—a space lit dimly by only the candle within her hand.

Windowless, the room had a small smoke hole cut into the high ceiling. The air within had an earthy thickness smelling of incense and burned resins. Yaga made her way to the center, plopping herself down onto a simple linen-covered cushion set atop a sheepskin rug. Pressing the candle down into a small holder, she stretched out her arms and legs, rolling each limb as she released the day's tension from her muscles.

She yawned, tilting her head upward, her gaze peering through the hole high above her head. For a time, she watched the oak leaves rustling in the gentle breeze coursing through the understory. This was her favorite time of day—a time to unwind and repair. A time just for her.

Outside, in the gloaming, the world was settling into darkness—a fact which brought Yaga a sense of peace and reprieve.

Closing her eyes, she listened to the faint clatter of leaves brushing over one another. Inhaling deeply, she focused her awareness; it was time for the quieting. Her consciousness would travel, though to where, she could never be sure. Now, as ever, the spirit world would pull her to a place that was beyond her control—and for reasons she couldn't comprehend.

She began by lighting several thin candles arranged in a semi-circle on the low table before her. Finishing, Yaga carefully collected a small, tightly wound bunch of herbs, lifting them up to a candle's flame. The smudge blazed brilliantly, though she quickly blew it out, a fragrant plume of smoke curling upward through the surrounding air.

Yaga closed her eyes, drawing her awareness to the natural ebb and flow of her own breath. The pungent smoke from the herbs filled her lungs, pulling her physical body down firmly on the cushion. She had the sense of being anchored now to the wood floor below—and beyond that, to the earth itself.

Opening her eyes softly, she focused on the flame of one of the candles, her chest rising and falling with each breath like a steady wave lapping against the banks of a placid pool. She gazed intently at the fiery wick for some time, its amber spire reflecting in the hazel green spheres of her eyes.

After a moment, she paused, retrieving a glass jar and a small clay cup from beneath the table. Setting them before her, she removed two small, white-stemmed mushrooms with gilded, button-shaped caps. These were the *Maryny Zoloti*—Mara's Gold. Named for Mara, the Goddess of dreams, death, and the space beyond the veil, they were a tool for transformation—and for transition out of the physical world.

Vesna had called them the *Golden Teachers*—and she had strictly kept them from Yaga when she was young. Now, Yaga was an experienced traveler; the mushrooms were a potent medicine for dissolving the illusion of confinement to a material form. They helped free Yaga, untethering her from her body and sending her consciousness out over great distances.

Placing a few of the dried caps into a mortar, she began grinding them with the pestle. With a spoon, she scooped some of the fine powder out and into the cup. From the kettle, she poured a bit of hot water over the shimmering, golden powder—giving it a final gentle mix with the spoon. Then she sat back, resting her hands gently in her lap, the steamy, warm vapor wafting up from the cup and encircling her face.

Her focus returned to the rise and fall of her breath now, her awareness slowly expanding outward from her body, taking in the rest of the room. The smell of burning herbs had merged with the muted, rhythmic hum of the forest at night beyond the cottage walls. Yaga's awareness pooled into a state of peaceful focus, where it remained for some time, her breathing steady—her senses fully attuned to the world around.

As she opened her eyes, her gaze fell upon the cup of tea. The concoction was brown, with a few specks of gold still floating at the top. Gently, she lifted it to her lips; the steam billowing past her cheeks. The taste of the brew was earthy and bitter—and as she swallowed her first sip, she felt a pulse—as though the energy of the Maryny Zoloti were unfurling within her.

After a few more sips, she set the cup down, laying back upon the soft sheepskin rug. As her body sank into its warmth, she gazed through the smoke hole once more. She could glimpse—though just barely—the stars glittering in the emerging night sky, obscured in patches by the canopy above the cottage. The branches of the ancient trees swayed gently overhead, the susurrations of their leaves pouring into the inner sanctum like rainfall.

Yaga let herself drift, the effects of the tea slowly unbridling her mind. Her thoughts wandered to the visitors who had just left—to the earnest concern for his young brother she had seen etched over Alexey's face. She sensed a stirring within her—an attraction between her and the man—yet she stopped herself. She could not allow her mind to entertain such impractical things. She would focus on Misha's needs alone; he was her patient, and that was all that should matter. *Besides,* she mused—she and Alexey were from *different worlds.*

Sighing softly, she let the thought pass. Closing her eyes again, rotating shapes and colors appeared before her. Most were familiar against the darkness blanketing her vision. However, the shapes began to change. Images entered her mind—familiar at first. She saw the Firebird—proud and soaring above a tiny patchwork of villages. Then, the grimoire—its pages fluttering by swiftly. A basket soon appeared, held by a woman whose face was framed by hair the color of coal. And then, a sword—one which she had never seen before, followed by a ring made of bone. Etched on its surface was a single, ancient sigil, though she could not place its meaning. And finally, an apple—gold in color—rotating against an ethereal, verdant background. All around it were rows of low, spreading trees—each heavy with a fruit unlike any she had ever seen—blushing and velvety, dripping with morning dew.

And then the vision was gone, replaced by an endless void. In that instant, Yaga was overcome with a chill—as though something ominous were about to unfold—though the feeling passed just as quickly. As she lay there, her mind pulsed. Images and visions were a part of this process, yes, though something had been different. This time, it felt like a message.

Whatever it meant, it seemed... important.

Soon, whirling shapes and colors returned—a familiar, kaleidoscopic tunnel forming before her. Then, the sensation of her spirit body peeling away from the heaviness of her flesh. The floor seemingly disappeared from beneath her, replaced with the vast emptiness of space, the tunnel of colors engulfing her. She let go, unafraid—she had done this before.

Abruptly, the creaking hum of the cottage within the trees faded as Yaga's consciousness barreled through the liminal, moving beyond the veil. She could feel herself condensing—shrinking smaller in size. Then, in an instant, she became aware of her surroundings, as though awakening from a dream. It took a moment for her to realize where she had projected to this time: a copper vase, polished but forgotten, set on a small table. She was in a corner somewhere—the joining of two long corridors spanning a distance in either direction.

Wherever she was, it was cold. The air around her held a dampness, filled with a musty odor which clung to every surface. This place felt impossibly *old,* with dark walls and floors made of stone, all covered in an unsettling slickness that glistened under the dim light of the few torches staggered down the hall. *This was a castle of some kind,* she thought. She felt certain, too, that she knew this place—that she had seen it before during another quieting. Yet, she had been somewhere else—a great room with massive ceilings and tattered banners. Now, as she peered down the shadowy hallway, she was overcome with a sensation that something sinister—*someone*—might be lurking within the same walls.

Suddenly, she heard footsteps, distant though growing nearer. They were accompanied by low voices—servants, perhaps—echoing from the black. Soon, the individuals had turned around a bend, their voices slowly fading.

In the hollow silence that remained, Yaga's curiosity grew. She wanted to know where she was—and why. Focusing her awareness, she reached out from the copper vase with her mind until her consciousness had slipped into a tall brass candlestick set upon a nearby stand flanking a doorway. From here, she could study the simple wooden door—noting an ominous, heavy iron lock that dominated its exterior. *Strange,* she thought. Moving again, she pooled her spirit body into the cylindrical mechanism of the lock itself, peering into the room beyond. Yet—her vision was obscured, with only the glass pane of a window on a far wall partially in view. She concentrated once more, separating her spirit body from the cold dark metal, passing into a delicate glass cup filled with water set upon a table within the room.

The moment she entered the cup, Yaga was overcome with a tremendous sense of *recognition.* Inside the room with her was an energy that she knew somehow. As she expanded her consciousness outward, she saw the bedroom chamber around her. Then she noticed him—a child sitting at a desk, his body slumped forward. He was facing a window—though, beyond the glass, there was only darkness.

Yaga watched his reflection on the windowpane. Illuminated by the amber glow of a candle, the child's face wore a mournful expression. He sighed heavily—a weariness etched over his young features. Yet, his eyes were a bright, honeyed brown—almost defiantly so. *He could be no older than ten,* she thought. And yet, the boy's complexion, draped in dark waves of hair, seemed unusually sallow and pale—as though he hadn't been outdoors in a very long time. She studied him hunched over the desk, apparently burdened by some invisible weight. As she watched, he stood slowly, pressing his hand against the windowpane and opening it outwards into the dark world beyond. For a moment, he stared vacantly. Still, Yaga could sense something beneath the surface; a profound longing.

Who was he? Her heart ached with something like recognition once again.

The boy seemed familiar.

The chamber around him was simple but well-kept. And yet—with a heavy bolt securing it shut from within the hallway, she knew that the door had been locked from the *outside.* A faint tremor of anger rose up within her.

This child was a prisoner.

As the boy stared into the distance, a shiver ran through Yaga's spirit body. She was overcome with a foreboding sense of danger. It wasn't the boy she had felt before in the hall. It was something deeper, something connected to him. Her thoughts swirled around the possibilities.

Unexpectedly, the boy turned. His gaze swept over the room searchingly, scrutinizing the air itself.

"Hello?"

Yaga froze as he spoke. *He couldn't be talking to me*, she thought. She had never once been noticed—at least not by any human. There had been a few times when some animal had sensed her, their curious eyes peering down into nothingness as they sniffed at the objects that she moved between. But a human child?

The boy stood, his feet carrying him slowly towards the glass cup holding Yaga's consciousness. He reached for it, his small hands clasping over the cool glass, lifting it upward from the table. As he looked into it, only his reflection waved in the water. His eyes shifted, darting over the room again, this time with more determination.

"Is somebody here?"

Yaga was stunned. Surely, this boy was more than he appeared. He had indeed sensed her presence. She felt something in him then; a faint pulse of magic she hadn't noticed before.

He looked around the room again, his brow rumpling. Peering back into the cup, he studied the water with a skeptical frown.

At that moment—bewildered by the circumstances—Yaga willed herself back, her consciousness snapping from the glass and returning back to her body on the sheepskin rug in the cottage.

As her eyes fluttered open, Yaga's gaze once again took in the night sky overhead. She could see the stars clearly now, more defined against the black velvety darkness beyond the canopy of leaves. Yet, she hardly registered them. Instead, her mind spinning, she was overcome with an unshakable feeling; she knew that boy. And, though she didn't know how or why, a certainty welled up from deep within her.

Somehow, they were connected.

Back in the castle, the boy paced his room restlessly. The presence of something—or someone—lingered on. He had sensed, against the dark, depressing backdrop of the space around him, an energy of warmth and light. Now, his room was still. Nonetheless, something remained; a trace of an intrusion. He crinkled his nose, squinting at the hearth across the room, half expecting something to reveal itself.

Sighing, he shrugged, his shoulders hunching deeper as he walked back to the window. Staring out at the vast, shadowed landscape beyond the walls of his chamber, a tear formed—though he quickly wiped it away.

Had he imagined it?

No, he thought. There was someone—somebody who was not supposed to be there. It was in that moment that a small seed of hope germinated within him: someone knew he was there.

Elsewhere, not far from the boy, a man stood before a grand fire within the castle. Above him, hanging motionless, were the tattered remnants of tapestries from a distant era. The man's appearance, too, seemed not unlike the castle within which he stood, as though he were from a time long since passed.

He was dressed in a long, black robe with mink cuffs and scrolling embroidery down the sleeves and front. His hair was white and straight, falling in thin, straw-like wisps over his shoulders. His face was worn—clearly the man was aging. Indeed, despite his shining black shoes, something about him seemed old and musty like the walls surrounding him.

Abruptly, the man's expression shifted. His sharp features slowly twisting, a cruel smile formed at his mouth—though his eyes remained hard as stone. With a sudden wave of his hand, the fire within the hearth blazed angrily—a nearby torch climbing higher up the wall.

The man reached behind him in the direction of a single scroll set upon a wooden desk. The scroll's seal—now broken in half—featured a majestic bird with upturned wings; a dove. It was centered within a circle, out from which expanded rays like the sun; a halo.

Without a glance, he flicked his wrist—instantly causing the scroll to burst into flames. For a time, he stood there, staring down into the hearth as the paper smoldered on the desk behind him. The waxen image of the bird melted before burning up into a pale plume of smoke. Soon, the scroll had disintegrated into a small pile of ash.

The man's faint smile was slowly replaced by a look of quiet rage. He turned abruptly towards a window, clasping his hands behind his back. A loud, heavy sigh—something of a growl—escaped from his mouth, reverberating through the room. Outside in the darkness, a cold wind howled over the exterior walls, whipping up the dense fog that now blanketed the surrounding land. The man stared pensively out into the pitch-black expanse of night. Slowly, he turned, walking back towards the fire, his mind burning like a seething ember. Within his veins, his blood simmered silently.

Far away, a hand unseen closed around what belonged to him like a phantom.

With impudence, someone would dare to trespass over his dominion.

Now, the fire crackling in the hearth hissed—rasping a warning into the chilly air.

Your power, Sorcerer, is not promised.

Chapter Six

A Silken Scarf

B ranka stood in a large upper bedroom of her estate, surrounded by household servants. It was midmorning now as the sun streamed in through a row of tall, curved windows, illuminating the room's dark, green walls. She had never liked the color, really—a remnant of when the estate had belonged to Zoren's first wife. Now, though the curtains and furniture had long since changed, something of the past still lingered. It seemed to her as though a bit of energy had been left behind by Yaga and her mother, Vesna—retained by the memory of the space. The feeling was one she tried her best to ignore, preferring ornaments and opulent décor to trick her senses. It mostly worked—though there were days that it didn't.

At present, her youngest daughter Marfa, now seventeen, sat on a small, cushioned chair in the corner, while Nadia, her eldest, stood within a large dressing area separated by two elegant, billowing curtains. Abruptly, Nadia emerged into the wider room, smoothing down the bodice of her dress.

Branka studied her daughter, noting to herself the pleasing contrast of Nadia's creamy white shoulders against the deep navy hue of the shimmering fabric.

"Nadia, darling, stand up straight," Branka said flatly. Her eyes narrowed as she continued her scrutiny of her daughter's appearance. Nearby, two servants—both expressionless—had positioned themselves next to a large, heavy mirror against the wall. In bated silence, they stared down at their shoes.

"We must leave a lasting impression tonight, dear daughter. Alexey is not like the rest of the boys in Valen. His family has connections that stretch to Volhynia and beyond, and—"

"He's *so* handsome!" Nadia gushed. Twirling in her dress, her yellow-blonde pin curls bounced and glinted like gold ornaments.

From her seat in the corner, Marfa rolled her eyes—though neither Nadia nor Branka took any notice. Instead, Marfa's older sister gave a haughty smile as she turned to face the mirror. Abruptly, the two servants lifted the mirror upright, struggling beneath its weight as Nadia admired herself. She seemed taken with her own reflection, sashaying and primping like a vain bird—oblivious to the sweat beading over the brow of one of the servants.

"I don't need to worry about the others, Mother."

A small, nearly imperceptible snort came from Marfa's direction.

Branka, ignoring the interruption, clasped her hands together, her bejeweled fingers sparkling as she continued examining her eldest daughter's appearance. Nadia, turning to the mirror a final time, practiced an exaggerated, ostentatious curtsy between the white-knuckled grip of the servants on either side.

"Indeed, my darling. Tonight will be splendid—and you do look absolutely perfect. But please—just remember your manners."

There was a slight tone of admonishment in Branka's words, yet Nadia seemed not to notice. Instead, her daughter gave a saccharine smile, followed by a shriek of self-satisfaction and excitement. Then, she hurried into the dressing area, flinging the curtain closed behind her. Another servant ducked into the space to help her undress. Though—Nadia was oblivious to the woman as she slipped the dress down past her corset, loosening each and every ribbon in the back. Instead, Branka's eldest daughter was lost in thought, her mind filled with visions of being married to a handsome, wealthy nobleman such as Alexey.

For Nadia, now twenty-five years old, the gala was the most important event of the year. She had been waiting all summer for the opportunity to dance with the eligible young bachelors—even more since the Grishaevs had moved to Valen. Now, with the event set for that very evening, she would use her time at the Casimir Estate to cement her goal of a marriage to Alexey.

In truth, since his family's arrival months before, Nadia's mother had been plotting. She hoped to secure a betrothal between her oldest daughter and the son of the wealthy newcomers. Almost daily, she had filled her daughter's head with ambition, so much so that Nadia had even erected a small altar to Lada, the Goddess of Love—even though the deity had been mostly forgotten in their time. And, despite her hollow aims, Nadia had implored the absent goddess incessantly to concretize her marriage to Alexey.

Beyond the curtains in the bedroom chamber, Marfa remained on the cushioned chair, having witnessed the entire scene with a sense of resignation. Her dress was a pale blue—simple yet attractive—though lacking the beaded adornments of Nadia's attire. Marfa tugged at the sleeves, looking down at her hands.

Branka's eyes shifted to her youngest daughter. In truth, Branka felt primarily a tepid ambivalence towards Marfa. She seemed dull next to Nadia—and her personality would win them no favors amongst the wider world. *Such a dour child*, Branka thought.

"Oh, Marfa, fix your posture. You look like you're about to wilt. And remember," she added with a sharp tone, "Borislav will be there. You really should make an effort."

Marfa's face paled as her stomach sank. The idea of being married off to the boorish, graying, middle-aged Borislav made her physically sick. Her mother—for reasons Marfa could not comprehend, had promised her youngest daughter's hand in marriage to the rotund, oafish town clerk. And despite the reality that he was decades older than Marfa, Branka had set this commitment into motion when her daughter was only twelve years old, promising that she would be wedded to the man after she had turned eighteen.

Marfa recoiled at the thought of being married to someone older than even her *own mother*. Yet, she had no voice in the matter, it seemed. Sensing her doom, Marfa merely nodded, dropping her gaze back to her lap. Inside, however, she was filled with a boiling resentment; an anger that grew with each mention of her impending fate.

Nadia, sensing her sister's discomfort from within the dressing room, smirked.

"Come now, Marfa, it's not as though you have any better prospects. Honestly, sister," she rebuked, her voice tinged with incredulity.

Marfa bit her lip. Nadia was the center of her mother's world, and she knew better than to express disdain for her sister's naked vanity and brazen insensitivity.

Branka cast her gaze outside, noting the sun had risen higher in the sky. Time was of the essence for the day's activities; she and her daughters had to prepare for the gala that evening.

"Enough dawdling, ladies," Branka said, her voice shrill and commanding. She snapped her fingers at the servants who had been carefully arranging jewelry and shoes on a small table.

"We have much to do, and the day is already slipping by," she said. With that, she exited the room, leaving behind a servant to help Marfa remove and hang her dress. Two more servants followed Branka down the hall and into the house beyond, off to the next set of tasks. The day's focus would be centered around making a good impression that evening.

She wanted each interaction with the Grishaevs to be nothing short of perfect.

Across town, a very different morning had unfolded in the estate where Alexey lived with his family. In the dining room, his mother, Tatiana, and his father, Dmitri, sat across from one another on the far end of a long table, sipping their tea and eating pastries. Dmitri, his lips smacking between bits, rambled on about their new business enterprise of shipping metal ore from the far Northern Thrice-Nine, down to the southern lands.

Tatiana, who held the *Village Herald* open in front of her, smiled flatly as her husband mused on about the endeavor. Suddenly, one of the household staff entered carrying an elegant blazer on a wooden hanger.

"Madam, the tailor has completed the jacket for Alexey's gala attire. Would you like to see it?"

Setting the paper aside, Tatiana studied the garment while Dmitri continued picking at a bit of pastry. Her eyes sparkled as they swept over the rich navy fabric with intricate yellow embroidery down the lapels and sleeves. The colors seemed exceptionally fitting to her eyes for Alexey's dark hair and fair skin.

"Oh, my—well it's absolutely wonderful, isn't it, Dmitri?" she said, tracing her fingers along the stitching. "You've all done quite an amazing job—and in such a short time. But please, do a final fitting to make sure of things." Her gaze shifted from the man to her husband, whose attention was now on a bit of sweet cheese curd that had fallen from the baked treat onto the plate.

"Dmitri, what do you think? Didn't they do splendidly?" Tatiana said.

"Oh, why—yes, look at that," he said, still chewing. "It's outstanding, I say," he added.

Tatiana raised an eyebrow as she watched her husband—a stout, amicable fellow—lift his plate to his lips, licking up some of the remaining honey. She blinked, pursing her lips, before returning her gaze to the member of the household staff.

"Just a final fitting, that's all," Tatiana said. "And thank you—really."

Like Branka, Tatiana had been preoccupied with finding a suitable marriage partner for her son. Still, their motivations for the gala were worlds apart. For Tatiana, her son's happiness was of the utmost importance, even if—with each passing year—a gnawing pang of worry grew within her. She feared she might never be blessed with the presence of grandchildren.

The man holding the jacket bowed, quickly exiting the room and making his way through the manor to Alexey's quarters. When he opened the door, however, he found the room empty. Having already made his bed, Alexey had left for the day, embarking on a journey back to Yaga's cottage with Misha.

Misha clung tightly to Alexey's back as they walked along the forested path. He was in pain again—though notably less than before. Holding onto his brother's shoulders tightly, he watched Alexey's boots kicking through the leaves below.

"Do you think Yaga will be able to help me again?" he asked, his voice hopeful.

Alexey glanced back towards him, smiling gently.

"I think so, brother. Either way, it sure is pretty out here, isn't it?" he said, hoping to quell his brother's fear by changing the topic.

Misha nodded, though as they continued along, Alexey sensed something more was on his mind.

"Mish," Alexey probed, "is there something else you'd like to say?"

There was a short pause, with only the sounds of Alexey's bootsteps trudging forward.

"Yaga is really nice, but... do... do you think she's pretty?" Misha asked.

Alexey paused, a nervous chuckle bursting out from him as a hint of warmth rose in his cheeks.

"Well—I suppose she is," he said. Clearing his throat, he continued. "But don't you worry for even a minute, Mish. Even if I *were* to meet someone special, that won't change a thing between us—not ever," he said.

Behind Alexey's head, Misha's face beamed. He knew his brother meant it—and what was more, Misha trusted him without question. It was true he worried about Alexey's absence were he to marry—a thing he often heard his mother pressing him to do. Yet, Misha felt warm in Yaga's presence. Safe, even. As they continued along, the thought of Yaga and her strange home brought a quiet smile to his small face.

Soon, they had arrived at the cottage, Alexey setting Misha on the ground before the steps leading up to the porch. Together, they made their way up the creaking wooden treads, gently knocking on the door.

After a moment, Yaga appeared, pushing the door open with her foot. In her arms were stacks of books; she was in the midst of reorganizing some shelves that morning. With messy long waves of hair hanging over her face, she pressed her lips together, blowing a few strands from in front of her eyes.

"Come on in," she said, smiling briefly.

As they entered, Yaga moved to the worktable, setting down the stack of books with a thud before wiping her dusty hands over the apron at her waist.

Immediately, Misha noticed the apron was covered with streaks of a deep reddish-brown color. To him, it looked familiar; like *dried blood*. His eyes grew wide as he glanced at his older brother.

Noticing his expression, Yaga's gaze shifted to her apron, then back to Misha and Alexey.

"Bloodroot," she said. "I'm preparing a dye bath for tomorrow, and I've just harvested the bloodroot." She pointed a red-stained finger across the room to a basket. Large leaves shaped like paper fans protruded out from the top while gnarled, crimson-colored roots poked through the basket's sides.

Misha and Alexey exchanged a glance before bursting into laughter. Yaga gave a sly smile as she made her way over to Misha.

"Shall we see how you're doing today?" she asked him, gesturing for him to sit on a nearby chair.

As Misha sat down, Alexey stooped, rolling up his brother's pant legs just past the knee.

Kneeling before him, Yaga gently unwrapped each of the bandages on his knees and ankles, placed there earlier that morning by Alexey. Gently, she clasped each of his joints between her hands, turning them carefully.

"We're off to a very good start," she told him, rising and walking towards a basket by the door already full of fresh nettles.

Grabbing a fistful of leaves, she set about preparing a poultice of the nettle by rolling it between her fingers. As before, she pressed the damp mash over Misha's knees and ankles. While still swollen, his joints showed small signs of healing. And, though he winced at first, he soon smiled as the stinging was replaced with the familiar sensation of tiny vibrations.

Nearby, Alexey watched over them, studying his brother closely.

After she finished applying the nettle, Yaga wrapped the bandages back over Misha's knees and ankles. Then, she moved to the sink, nodding at Alexey as if to say he should join her. As she washed her hands in the basin, he appeared beside her. She glanced at him briefly, before speaking in a soft, low voice beneath the hum of the faucet.

"He's doing better," she whispered. "But this will take some real time—to heal what has been for so long. He can come here as often as you are able."

Alexey watched as the green plant materials swirled down the drain, nodding his head.

"I know this is hard for you, too, Alexey," Yaga said, her eyes flicking towards him. "To have waited so long sounds..."

Alexey placed his hand gently on Yaga's elbow—a sensation passing through her like a jolt of electricity.

"Thank you. Really, Yaga. It means a lot," he told her, his expression sincere. Abruptly, he removed his hand, letting it drop to his side—embarrassed he had touched her so forwardly. *He barely knew her.*

Sensing a shift between them, Alexey gazed at her, his blue eyes catching like glass in the dim light within the cottage.

"Yaga, I..." Alexey started, though he was immediately interrupted by the sound of the screen door thudding shut, his younger brother's laughter reverberating from the porch.

Alexey sighed, smiling kindly as he followed after him. He glanced at Yaga one more time, though she had her back to him as she reached to hang a towel back on its hook. He bit the inside of his cheek, continuing after Misha. Stooping beneath the threshold, he exited to the porch.

Outside, Misha had skipped across the yard towards Vasilisa, who wore a rust-colored bandana tied behind her head. She was feeding the chickens from a pail on the ground beside her, and sensing Misha's approach, she paused.

"Can *I* feed them?" Misha asked, his voice inquisitive. Although they had not yet been introduced to one another, it seemed not to matter, for Vasilisa tilted her head slightly, her expression unchanging.

"Like this," she said softly, handing Misha a handful of grain. "They like when you scatter it about."

Misha's eyes rounded as Vasilisa scattered a handful of the feed across the ground with her delicate hand, prompting the chickens to dash towards each kernel, bounding over one another hastily.

Soon, with his hands full of grain, Misha walked back and forth across the small section of yard, leaving a fine trail of feed for the chickens to follow. As his laughter carried through the clearing, Yaga appeared at the doorway.

Alexey, who stood watching his brother from the edge of the porch, turned. As she made her way towards him, he noticed the slight jingle of the bracelets she wore today, matching with the beaded earrings dangling from her ears. Soon, she stood next to him in silence, her gaze passing over the yard to where Misha roamed with the chickens trailing his every step.

Alexey cleared his throat, uncertain of what to say.

"Do... you like living out here—in the woods?" he asked.

Yaga's fingers traced the wood of the porch rail absently.

"Well, I needed a place of my own—somewhere I could..." her voice trailed off. "I needed to be able to live my life."

Her words immediately struck something deep within Alexey. He nodded, pensive for a moment. Gazing out at the yard, he watched as his brother, seemingly more alive than he had been in years, carried another handful of feed from the pail. Misha's laughter continued, echoing into the understory beyond the yard.

"I...completely understand," Alexey said, his eyes flicking to the forest path leading to Valen. "Sometimes people expect things from you. Things you cannot give. Being alone..."

"It's just easier," Yaga said.

Their eyes met, and in an instant, something unspoken passed between them once more. As Alexey stared into the deep hazel pools of her eyes, Yaga was nearly overwhelmed by how *comforting* she found the man's presence to be; as though he had always been a part of her world.

And yet—*she barely knew him.*

Still, for Yaga, Alexey was something rather unexpected. Her focus over the years had been on building a life for herself—and eventually for Vasilisa and Zhar. But a connection with an outsider? She hadn't considered romance at all. The very idea seemed like a fantasy to her—something for characters in storybooks. Now, standing next to him, his scent and physical strength saturated the air around her. Within her, something stirred—deep and primal. His eyes were magnetic, seemingly pulling her towards him. Feeling the heat rise to her cheeks, she abruptly stepped back from the porch rail.

"I... I should go finish some things," she said, turning towards the door.

"Oh—of course," he said, stammering slightly. He winced, casting his gaze back towards Misha. "We—we should be going anyway," he said, his body straightening.

Yaga paused at the doorway, noticing the slight stoop in his shoulders as the man avoided bumping his head on the rafters.

"Back tomorrow for another treatment?" Alexey said, his eyes searching.

"Of course," Yaga replied, though she noticed a strange feeling arising within her. She wanted him to *stay.* She swallowed, collecting herself.

"I'll see you tomorrow, Misha," Yaga said, waving gingerly as she called out over the yard.

"Bye, Yaga!" Misha smiled at her as he spun in a circle, releasing the grain in a spiral pattern around his small body.

"Vasa, I'll be inside cleaning up," Yaga called out. Vasilisa nodded, though she didn't look up. Instead, she seemed preoccupied by her thoughts as she hung the now-empty pail upon a hook attached to a small shed.

Yaga turned, pulling open the screen door and stepping past the threshold.

"Thank you, Yaga—honestly," Alexey said. Yaga's gaze flicked towards him as she nodded politely. Then, she slipped beyond the doorway into the dim light within the cottage—leaving him alone on the porch.

In the yard below, Misha now stood next to Vasilisa, watching the chickens. The birds had moved on from the grain, now working feverishly at the dirt and scratching for insects in the leaf litter. Misha turned to face her, eyeing the cloth she wore over her face with curiosity. His expression shifted as he remembered seeing her at the market once before—with two different colored eyes.

"Are your eyes ok?" Misha asked her.

Vasilisa smiled. "That depends on what you mean by 'ok,'" she replied.

Misha paused as he considered it, his gaze passing over his own legs.

"Well, before we came here, my knees *always* hurt. But Yaga is fixing them! They feel ok now," he said, standing on his tippy toes as if to demonstrate his agility.

Vasilisa turned her head slightly at Misha's words, a faint smile forming at her lips.

"Well then, my eyes are 'ok,' too. *Yaga fixed them for me,*" she said, her voice a playful whisper.

Just then, Alexey appeared, having made his way down the porch steps and across the yard.

"It's time to go, Mish." Approaching, Alexey gave a quick nod, addressing Vasilisa. "Hello," he said.

"I'm Misha, by the way—and this is my brother Alexey," Misha blurted, sticking out his hand towards Vasilisa for a handshake. Vasilisa didn't take his hand, however—though not because she didn't sense it. Instead, she stood pensively, as though considering something else. Misha tugged at her sleeve, causing her to turn her head abruptly.

"Are you and Yaga going to the gala?" he asked her.

Vasilisa smiled wryly beneath her bandana.

"Gala? Yaga might prefer to be one of *those*," she said, pointing to a plump white grub being mercilessly devoured by a nearby chicken. Misha giggled at the comment, then paused, confusion spreading over his face.

"Hey!" he said. "How did you see that bug?" He glanced up at his brother, his expression puzzled. Alexey, just as perplexed, only shrugged.

Vasilisa turned her small frame towards the brothers slowly.

"You know, there are ways to see the world without the eyes," she said. "Things have an energy about them. Sometimes that tells you more than sight," she said.

Misha furrowed his brow as he considered it. "Ok," he said.

"I'm Vasilisa," she said, placing her hand firmly in the air in front of her as though he should take hold of it. "But you can call me Vasa."

Misha stared at her porcelain-like hand with surprise, clasping his fingers gently around it. It looked so *delicate* compared to his own—a fact he found more than a little peculiar.

Alexey nodded, smiling at Vasilisa. "Pleased to meet you," he said, bowing slightly.

Vasilisa nodded subtly, her expression impassive.

"Well—we should go," Alexey said, gesturing towards the path. Misha dropped his head with an exaggerated sigh. He quickly recovered, however, skipping off towards the tree line.

Alexey, unsure if Vasilisa could tell, gave a final nod and a wave. Turning, he broke into a fast walk to catch up with his brother.

"Walk or ride?" Alexey called out as he reached the edge of the clearing.

Misha giggled, darting down the path before him.

"Alright, slow down, Mish," he said, quickening his pace to keep up.

As the forest closed in around them, the sounds of insects and creaking branches formed a dull hum. After a few minutes of walking, Alexey scooped Misha up and onto his back. Continuing along the path, Misha seemed exceptionally quiet.

"Do you think Vasilisa is human?" Misha said, breaking the silence. His voice was edged with fascination.

Alexey thought for a moment. She certainly appeared human—only, she also didn't.

"Hmm," Alexey said, dipping to pass beneath a low-hanging branch. "I'm not sure."

After a brief pause, Alexey felt his brother unexpectedly tighten his grip, clawing into his arm.

"Take it easy, Misha," Alexey said.

"Do you hear that?" Misha whispered, his voice trembling.

Alexey stopped abruptly. At first, he heard only the distant movement of a high branch creaking rhythmically as it swayed in the breeze above. Straining to listen, he heard something else, however—like dissonant voices, soft and eerie. He gripped his brother's legs firmly at his sides.

"It's... probably just the wind," Alexey said.

They started down the path once more, Alexey's bootsteps crunching through the leaves—quicker now. Suddenly, the sounds grew louder—a rasping whisper echoing through the understory, whirling around them. But, just as quickly as it had started, it stopped again.

Alexey stood still. His heart pounded now—though he forced himself to remain calm. The sound had come from all around them, as though carried on the wind itself. But it wasn't wind—was it? Then—a cracking sound like a giant branch snapping nearby.

Instantly, the brothers gasped in unison when—out from behind a patch of ferns—stepped a small, delicate fawn. The creature stared at them, his dark eyes gleaming.

Alexey sighed loudly in relief—followed by a bit of laughter.

104

"Look, Mish. It's just a baby deer," he said with certainty. Though, there was a part of his mind that knew better. Something more than a small woodland creature had just rippled through the forest. For a moment, the fawn continued watching them both, his ears flicking. It, too, seemed to be listening. Abruptly, the creature stepped from the path, slipping into the undergrowth and out of sight.

Alexey patted Misha on the leg. Misha let out a shaky breath, resting his head upon Alexey's shoulder.

"Please—I want to go home now," Misha said, cradling his brother's neck tightly.

"It's ok, Misha. That was just a baby deer and nothing more," Alexey told him, hoping to comfort him. Yet, as they continued walking down the trail, Alexey couldn't shake the feeling they were being *watched*. From the corner of his eye he saw a movement—causing him to turn his head abruptly. Only—it was just a squirrel scampering up a tree, his dark eyes studying the brothers curiously.

As Alexey and Misha disappeared down the trail and out of sight, the squirrel paused, straining to listen. A low rumble swelled over the canopy—though it wasn't the wind. It was something else, moving like a blast of thick air, ripping over the branches in the trees. Soon, it passed by the creature, rattling the leaves and causing his fur to stand on end. A cacophony of strange whispers grew louder, sailing off in another direction through the understory. The squirrel stiffened, sniffing at the air as it passed. Shuddering, the animal scampered down into a hole within the trunk of the tree.

The strange torrent of energy whipped over the woodland like a malevolent wind, moaning as it pulsed angrily through the understory. It snaked its way between branches and beyond treetops, descending over the clearing surrounding Yaga's cottage.

Roosting high above, Zhar sensed the shift immediately, her eyes snapping open to reveal two burning, glowing orbs. As she raised her head, her feathers bristled. She stretched, her gaze scanning the surrounding forest, before settling back upon her perch. Her senses now alert, just like the squirrel, she had felt something strange—an intrusion, dark and sinister. Even if she could not know what was coming.

Far away, in the Sorcerer's castle, another kind of tension filled the air. Deep within the bowels of the oppressive fortress, the boy huddled at the man's feet. Slumped over the cold, damp floor, he sobbed quietly. His small hands were clenched now, still trembling from what he had done.

What he had been made to do.

"Ivan—again!" the Sorcerer commanded, his voice filled with impatience. His words echoed across the cavernous space. Leaning over the boy slowly, the Sorcerer grabbed his shoulders with long, bony fingers, dragging him up to his feet. He jerked the child's small frame around, compelling him to face the creature chained at the center of the room.

A horned beast, whimpering and wounded, quivered before them on the floor. The creature was as large as a bear—though built more like a mountain lion with its muscular frame. Sharp horns twisted, protruding from each side of its skull. And its fangs, sharp and menacing, glinted beneath the torchlight.

Yet, despite its ferocious appearance, the beast seemed helpless now.

Instead, it cowered before the boy, its red eyes filled with fear.

"Please, *no*! Please! I don't want to do this anymore! Koschei, please!" Ivan pleaded, his voice barely a murmur.

Sorcerer Koschei found the boy's anguished pleas infuriating.

"Use your power, boy! You *will* use it—you will!" His words were sharp, like daggers pressed deep into the child's spirit. The Sorcerer curled his long finger behind Ivan's head. From the tip, a flame grew—the fire licking at the back of the boy's neck and singeing his skin.

"Ow! *Oww!*" Ivan screamed, swatting behind him.

Koschei's eyes glared back down at him. Somehow, they appeared both empty and filled with contempt, their surfaces churning as though blackened blood roiled within.

"Do it—*now!*" Koschei bellowed. As his words filled the cavernous dungeon, the torch flames shot upwards along its high stone walls.

Inhaling slowly, Ivan closed his eyes, focusing his awareness on his breath. He felt its ebb and flow rocking him back and forth until he had sunk deeper into his own mind. Soon, against a backdrop of darkness, a red orb appeared in the distance within his vision. Though the beast still tugged on his chains in the room beyond, Ivan was surrounded by a fathomless quiet. Everything else had fallen away, leaving only the presence of the red object drawing nearer. As he watched it, the glowing mass moved closer until it hovered above him. Soon, it expanded further—enveloping him entirely. At that moment, he opened his eyes—a red hue cast over their spheres like embers within a fire.

Before him lay the beast, though now it stirred with restless anticipation, thrashing and yanking at its chains. With his eyes locked on the creature, Ivan's entire body began to shake. He reached towards it, his mouth opening as a primal scream filled the chamber. Then, a pulsing energy—red and coiling like a serpent—twisted out from his small hand. It spanned the gap between them, coiling over the beast's body.

This was a terrible power he had.

These were dark things he had never wanted to do.

The creature began to whimper and whine, brutally hurling its massive form against the chains in desperation. Ivan felt the beast's agony as the energy within him snaked around it, forcing its way down beneath the surface of the creature's body, burrowing deeper within.

Then—a surge of light.

An uncontrollable force of violence poured from the boy.

The creature screamed—a guttural, ear-piercing wail echoing through the dim corridors of the castle, causing the servants to stop in their tracks. With jerky movements, the beast's body contorted—as if being torn apart from within. Cracks and fissures formed over the surface of its body, a red-orange glow now pulsing beneath its flesh.

Ivan's eyes flashed back to honey-brown, his gaze quickly turning away. It was unbearable to watch—as though the creature's very essence was disintegrating. Beside him, Koschei's mouth curved upward into a sinister smirk. For a time, the beast writhed in agony behind the child, its tormented shadow twisting up the wall. And then, with a final tortured howl, the beast was no more. Nothing left but a wisp of smoke and a stain on the ground.

Ivan collapsed to the floor. His heart felt broken with shame and regret for what he had done. For what Koschei had *made him do*. He hunched forward, kneeling, as tears streamed over his face. Now, a heavy silence stretched across the chamber.

Suddenly, a sound broke through the quiet. A low, rumbling laugh—thick with satisfaction. The Sorcerer's voice echoed over the cavernous walls as he enveloped Ivan's crumpled body within his shadow. Soon, however, the laughter faded.

Koschei's thin lips twisted into a grotesque smile.

"You're growing stronger," he said, his voice filled with a thirst that made Ivan's stomach turn. He stooped over him, tilting Ivan's head upward with a bony finger beneath his chin. Ivan stared into the vast darkness beyond Koschei's face, unable to meet his gaze.

"You see? You have the power to destroy. And someday soon... soon, I will show you *what real power is.*"

Ivan's heart clenched. He hated this power—what it did. How it annihilated living beings. Even more, he hated that there was no escape—not from this castle, nor from the Sorcerer's twisted grasp. And above all, he hated who Koschei claimed to be.

He was Ivan's own grandfather.

How could someone so loveless and cold—so filled with hatred—be his kin? He had considered this nearly every day since coming to live with this demented monster.

Ivan's existence within the castle was different in every way imaginable from the life he had lived before. Before he had been taken. The surrounding forests were filled with hundreds of beasts, none as terrible as he knew their master—the Sorcerer—to be. And despite this power within him, Ivan refused to use it any more than he had already been forced to. Each time he destroyed one of the creatures, he felt something shrink—a small part of himself he feared he could not get back. And so, here he remained—unable to run away and leave this place forever.

More than anything, Ivan worried that one day he could become like Koschei himself—a demon no longer connected to humanity.

"Ah, well," the Sorcerer said. He sensed Ivan's misery—but it didn't matter. If anything, it seemed to fuel his desire to press the boy to harness his power. But still—the child's mind was *weak.* He took pity on the beasts, after all, and that just would not do.

Koschei sighed, gazing down at Ivan once more.

"It will be over soon enough, boy," he told him.

Without another word, he turned, his bootsteps echoing briskly over the stone floor. Ivan listened as the Sorcerer entered a narrow, winding stairwell—the clopping sounds of his movements fading into the distance.

The boy remained hunched upon the floor of the dungeon. Strange that he could feel safe down in this dark space that reeked of death. Now, cloaked in shadow, the chamber was still—almost peaceful—the only sounds a muffled dripping of water seeping between the stones within the wall.

Ivan welcomed the aloneness; it was a reprieve from his tormentor. Yet, despite the grim reality of his circumstances within the castle, Ivan also sensed something shifting in the balance. Something else was stirring. Someone had seen him—of that he was sure—and now, a single thread of hope had been woven through the tapestry of his own, lonely life. There in the brooding darkness, he saw them—thin strands of magic and destiny, lifting and weaving, shifting over the warp.

A stream of carriages lined the drive outside the Casimir Estate in Valen. It was early evening now, and the guests, dressed in exquisite attire, moved slowly up the gravel pathway leading to the arched entrance of the grand manor. Casimir, known for hosting extravagant dinners and soirees, held an autumn gala each year—a chance for the villagers and those from nearby towns to mingle and celebrate the turn of the seasons.

The estate was resplendent tonight, its marble floors gleaming beneath glittering chandeliers. Entering the foyer, the guests were greeted by overflowing vases, each intricately arranged with an array of flowers and decorative plumes of grass.

Inside, the party was already in full swing. Long tables flanking the edge of the dining room had been draped with embroidered cloths, their tops covered in spreads of exquisite foods—roasted meats, delicate pastries, cheeses, and fruits like apples and grapes from the recent harvests. Wine and cider, too, flowed freely, while the sound of laughter mixed with the music flowing from the ballroom. The lively, playful sounds of the *gusli* strings blended seamlessly with soft, ambient notes of *sopilka* flutes—adding to the festive atmosphere and beckoning young couples to dance. A time of celebration, the guests wore their finest clothes; women twirled about in elegant dresses, while the men's dark, shining leather shoes gave a pleasant, regal contrast to the brilliant white sheen of the marble floor.

In a corner of the dining hall, Alexey stood beside his parents as they mingled with the other guests. He was sharply dressed—his broad shoulders overlaid handsomely with his newly tailored blazer. His face, though unreadable, was cleanly shaven, too, and his hair had been combed into a sophisticated coif—more for his mother than anyone else. He nodded, smiling at the other guests—though he barely spoke a word. While the other attendees were curious to get to know him, there was a certain distance in his eyes.

As though he wished to be elsewhere.

His mother, on the other hand, appeared as regal and warm as ever this evening. Tatiana's dress was simple but well-made, a compliment to her salt and pepper hair pulled back neatly into a chignon. Dmitri stood beside her, happily sipping wine as he smiled, taking in the ambience.

Nearby, Misha sat at a table, a plate piled high with food before him. His face was content tonight, with no signs of the usual weary expression that accompanied his suffering. It seemed that his treatments were indeed bringing him relief; for the first time in years, he could savor the moment—a pheasant drumstick in one hand and a cup of cider in another.

In between social pleasantries with other guests, Tatiana leaned toward Alexey, placing her delicate hand atop his forearm. Her eyes were fixed on Misha now, watching him as he gulped from his cup.

"I just—I can't believe how happy he is," she said, giving Alexey's arm a gentle squeeze.

"I know," Alexey replied. "It's... *incredible.*"

"Just a miracle—truly." Tears formed in the corner of Tatiana's eyes—though she quickly wiped them away.

Alexey, seeing his mother's emotion, pulled her towards him, hugging her tightly. Finally—after all the years of suffering, Misha had begun to show signs of improvement. Tatiana patted her son gently, leaning back.

"Who is this skilled healer, Alexey? Misha says she lives in the forest beyond town?"

Just then, several guests stopped by, greeting Tatiana and Dmitri. Some of their first acquaintances in the town, they were excited to be caught up on the Grishaev's adjustment to life in Valen. Alexey, nodding politely, attempted to focus on the conversation that ensued. Though, he instead found his thoughts drifting.

To Yaga.

In his mind, he recalled fondly the way she had applied the nettle poultice to Misha's knees—the movements of her hands as she tended to his younger brother. The way her chestnut hair fell over her face when she leaned forward to harvest nettles the day prior.

Occasionally, as Tatiana and Dmitri continued socializing, his mother would observe Alexey with curiosity. She had noticed the distant look in his eyes, knowing full well he had something on his mind. And, while it concerned her seeing him like this, she knew he disliked social gatherings. Still, something about him seemed exceptionally despondent tonight.

As the hours slipped onward, darkness loomed over the Casimir Estate. Branka and her two daughters, having orchestrated themselves to be fashionably late, now sailed through the spacious dining hall toward Alexey and his family. Branka was radiant in a deep purple gown, the color bold against her pale skin. Behind her, Nadia walked gracefully, her navy-blue dress shimmering with each step. The fabric, intricately embroidered with a yellow-gold thread, hugged her petite waist snugly. Over each of her shoulders, a frilled sash draped, framing her face perfectly. Her blonde curls, too, had been pinned up in an elaborate style—each detail of her appearance attended to meticulously.

Beside her, Marfa seemed almost lost in her sister's shadow. Her pale blue gown appeared modest—even drab—in comparison to Nadia's. And, while Marfa's expression was pleasing, there was a faint flicker of discomfort in her eyes—or perhaps it was something else. As she walked, her gaze caught sight of Borislav across the room, causing her to shudder.

Noticing Branka, Borislav gave a small, eager wave. Though, Branka only nodded stiffly—turning her back towards him as she maneuvered towards the edge of the room, her daughters trailing behind her.

Marfa's thoughts churned in quiet discomfort as she watched her mother's heels peek out with each step from beneath the hem of her skirt. She knew, unlike the other guests present, that something calculated was at work this evening. Tonight was the first opportunity for her mother to build up her connection with Tatiana—the first necessary step in cementing an engagement for Nadia to Alexey. Every detail had been forethought—including the *very color* of Nadia's dress, for Branka had prompted her servants to stealthily gather this information from the fabric seller just days before.

This coincidence, though contrived, was more than just a minor detail. It was part of an elaborate scheme to engineer *success*. Marfa's mother was used to playing life as a game—and this would be no different. Still, the stakes felt rather high for Branka, as a marriage for Nadia and Alexey would secure her family's future for generations to come. He was more than an eligible bachelor; he was the heir to his family's business, The Volhynia-Severyn Trading Company.

Earlier that summer, after being introduced to Tatiana at the market and catching a glimpse of her strapping son, Alexey—Branka had sensed the woman's desperation to find her son a suitable bride. And, although Alexey was only twenty-six years old, Marfa's mother could practically *taste* the dread that Tatiana carried over the potential she might never have grandchildren. In the months since, she had been watching.

Waiting.

Now, as she and her daughters approached the Grishaevs in the dining room, Branka's face lit up with practiced warmth.

"Tatiana, dear, what a splendid evening this is," she said. "I know this is your first gala, but really—Casimir has outdone himself once again." Her voice carried an enthusiastic lilt and saccharine tone that Marfa found unnerving.

"Branka, was it?" Tatiana replied. She was kind, yet it was evident that their prior introduction had not left quite the impression that Branka had hoped for.

Branka gave a small laugh, quickly brushing the oversight aside. There would be enough time, she thought, to establish the rapport she needed tonight.

"Yes, that's right," Branka replied. She cast her eyes towards Alexey curiously. "And this must be your son, Alexey."

Branka then craned her head to see beyond Dmitri, her eyes settling on the nearby table where Misha sat eating.

"And your other son—why, isn't he a hungry one? He must be growing all the time. However do you keep up with two boys, Tatiana?" Branka placed her hand on Tatiana's forearm, smiling. It seemed that her words had the effect intended—for Tatiana gave a small, sincere chuckle.

"They certainly do keep me on my toes."

Just then, Nadia stepped out from behind her mother, her blonde hair shining beneath the chandeliers. She smiled politely, her full lips perfectly demure, while the tops of her breasts pressed up ever so slightly above the fabric of her dress. Despite this evocative subtlety, her posture was reserved—a contrast that was not accidental.

"Why, aren't you lovely?" Tatiana said, glancing at Alexey from the corner of her eyes.

"This is my daughter, Nadia," Branka said.

Nadia greeted the group with an elegant curtsy.

Tatiana looked to Dmitri, though his eyes were cast downwards at a plate of food held before him. He chewed busily, seemingly oblivious.

"Husband, have you met Branka's daughter, Nadia?"

Dmitri swallowed a hunk of bread hastily.

"Oh—yes. Pleased to meet you, dear," Dmitri said, small crumbs lingering in the corners of his mouth. As Nadia extended her hand, Dmitri clasped it, placing a small kiss on the back. He glanced at Tatiana, who gave a slight, approving nod.

Branka's eyes flicked between Alexey and his mother.

"I'm immensely proud of her, honestly. She's such a lovely, caring creature, my Nadia," Branka cooed.

Tatiana nodded and smiled, her eyes flicking to Dmitri once more—though to her dismay, he had resumed his focus on the buttered bread upon his plate.

Not wanting to let the moment go to waste, Branka enumerated on her daughter's finer points whilst Nadia projected a humility her younger sister knew to be false. In addition to Nadia's impeccable tastes for home decoration, she was, evidently, a talent at needlepoint, painting, and in the careful tending of orphaned kittens. The final detail was, of course, one Branka had concocted solely based on Alexey's fondness for the wolf he kept as a pet—though secretly, Branka thought the monstrous animal to be a brute. Still, Alexey and his mother, she had reasoned, could be swayed by the added knowledge that Nadia was tender and maternal.

Alexey, sensing the undercurrents of the conversation, remained silent, offering nothing more than a polite nod in response. Tatiana, keenly aware of her son's reserved demeanor, felt a slight sense of frustration building within her.

"Well, Nadia—you sound quite well-rounded," Tatiana said, her smile sincere and kind. Abruptly, Tatiana tilted her head to the side, her gaze cast just beyond Branka.

"And who do we have here?" she said, eyeing Marfa.

"Oh—of course. This is Marfa. She really is such a—" Branka paused as she searched for the words. "She's a very... *dependable* child. Always there when you need her." Branka took hold of Marfa's shoulders, her touch icy and loveless, as though her daughter were a prop.

Inside, Marfa recoiled.

"Hello," she said timidly, her smile faint.

Tatiana gave a pleasant nod.

"Well, it's lovely to meet you *both*," Tatiana said. Marfa nodded, bowing—then slipped into the shadow of her sister.

The conversation shifted then, with Branka and Tatiana walking together towards the tables of food as they chatted about the Grishaev's adjustment to life in Valen. Marfa, spotting a chair at the edge of the room, quickly shuffled away. Soon, she had flopped down upon it—intent to remain there until the gala's end.

Dmitri's eyes flicked to Alexey. Clearing his throat, he too departed—moving to the table where Misha sat and taking a seat next to him.

Seeing the opportunity, Nadia drifted closer to Alexey, who had himself begun to wander towards a large spread of food. Her eyes twinkled as she addressed him, her feet carrying her after him.

"Are you usually so... quiet?" she asked him. Alexey turned his gaze towards her briefly, then back down to the plate he had begun filling with bits of cheese and crisp wedges of apples.

"This kind of place doesn't exactly make me feel conversational," he replied. He gathered a few hunks of bread to finish off his plate.

Nadia seemed undeterred.

"Well, surely you might like to dance at least once before the night is over," she said, her voice hopeful.

Alexey gave a half-smile, though his disinterest was palpable.

"I've never been much of a dancer, Nadia."

"Oh, I'm sure you could manage if you tried," she said, her slender fingers suddenly curling around his bicep. Her voice was soft and coaxing, though it betrayed something deeper—an eagerness, perhaps.

"You just need the right partner," she added.

Before Alexey could respond, however, another voice interrupted. A tall, graceful young man had appeared beside them. He wore clothing that was glamorous—even exotic, moving with a lightness in his step.

"Excuse me darling, but may I borrow this fine gentleman for a moment?"

The man's voice was pleading as he took Alexey by his elbow, leading him briskly away from the table and towards a set of doors opening to a balcony. Munching on a bite of bread, Alexey nodded politely to Nadia as he walked away. Soon, the two men were outside beneath the night sky, overlooking the grounds of the estate.

"Admir, how are you?" Alexey asked, swallowing his food and wiping a crumb from his lip.

The two had met that summer at another dinner in town, forming a friendly acquaintanceship. Admir beamed, revealing a bright, perfect smile. His face was handsome and angular, set atop a red silken scarf that erupted like a plume of crimson blood from his violet-colored velvet suit. He cast his gaze over the sprawling gardens beyond the balcony, now cloaked in shadow. Grasping the stone railing, he craned his head back to look through the glass doors leading inside.

"Well," he began, his voice mischievous. "I've never had to rescue a puppy from drowning before. But now I know what it's like," he chided, glancing at Alexey.

Alexey smiled, letting out a small laugh as he placed a bit of cheese and apple in his mouth. His interaction with Nadia moments before had apparently been as awkward to endure as it was painful to watch. He sighed, relieved with appreciation that Admir had helped him escape for some fresh air and conversation.

"Ah, well. There will be more where that came from," Alexey said, shaking his head. He knew his mother would not stop worrying about him—or the prospect of grandchildren to smother with adoration.

Staring into the darkness, Alexey's thoughts drifted back to Yaga. Out beyond the manor, across the countryside, he imagined her in her cottage. He wondered what she could be doing at that very moment.

After a few minutes, sensing the distance in his friend, Admir pressed. "Somewhere you'd rather be?" he asked.

His thoughts interrupted, Alexey grimaced.

"Other than at a fancy gala with Tatiana Grishaev?" he replied, raising an eyebrow.

Admir chuckled.

"Really, though—you seem like something is on your mind, friend."

An audible whimper left Alexey's lips as he looked down at his plate of food, before scanning over the dark horizon line in the distance. A long silence followed.

"Have you ever been out to see the woman who lives in the forests south of town?" Alexey asked.

Admir tilted his head.

"Do you mean Yaga? Yes, I grew up with her. A friend," he said, hesitating. "Though—I don't see her much anymore. Why do you ask?"

Alexey felt silly as he digested the information, realizing that to him, something about Yaga seemed otherworldly—as though she were a riddle to be solved. He straightened, clearing his throat.

"I took Misha to see her. He's sick, you know..." Alexey fell silent for a moment, tension aching in his chest. "She—she's healing him." His voice cracked as he choked back his tears gruffly. "It's hard to believe, but she's *actually helping him*," he said.

Admir nodded, his brow knit together.

"I'm sorry—by the gods, I'm sorry. I should have suggested to you to go see her. I just—I didn't want to intrude, I thought..." Admir's face twisted with guilt.

"No—no that's not it," Alexey told him, shaking his head. "No one did—until the merchant in town. I suppose they were all just being polite. And really, I've been so disappointed before. My family—we've all been let down so many times... I... I don't think I would have listened anyways," he told him. "Honestly, Admir."

Admir sighed, relieved—though he felt a pang of regret just the same. He could have helped, and as he reflected on it now, Admir wondered if he had been too concerned by his own discomfort to speak up. He turned back to face the gardens beyond the balcony, the two staring out in silence.

After some time, Admir began to sense a lingering heaviness in the space between them. From the corners of his eyes, he studied Alexey. Something continued to weigh upon the man; his demeanor seemed practically forlorn.

Admir's gaze shifted back towards the beautiful statues of men and women now cast in shadow on the grounds below, studying them. Some of the figures were tangled in an embrace, their arms twisting over one another beneath carved cloth. It was then that he understood, and for a moment, he laughed inwardly.

The thing on Alexey's mind was obvious to him now: it was Yaga herself.

Admir smiled as his thoughts flashed to the girl he knew from so long ago. She had always been peculiar, different from most people in all the right ways. Now, she had grown into a shining gem amongst dull rocks and pebbles. A rare combination of beauty and grit, Yaga was someone who could soften even the hardest of hearts.

After a moment, Admir turned towards him.

"Yaga is really something, isn't she?" he said.

As the words floated through the air, Alexey continued staring into the void beyond the balcony, his eyes fixed on the dark forms enshrouded by the night.

"She's brilliant, actually. And beautiful," Admir continued. "I mean—she's not *my* type—but I can see why someone like yourself would be drawn to her."

Alexey flashed an understanding grin, for he knew Admir was not interested in Yaga—or in any woman at all. His smile was replaced by a look of consternation, however, for as Alexey stood in the cool night air, he felt a small upwelling of urgency spreading through his chest. Behind him, the warm light of the manor melded with the sounds of blithe merriment, and yet—he wanted only to leave. He wished to see Yaga right then.

Glancing over his shoulder, his eyes swept over the windows and glass doors, hoping she would be there. Of course, she wasn't. His shoulder slumping, Alexey gave a dejected sniff as he leaned his arms on the stone rail. For a few minutes, the two men stood in silence once again, Alexey pushing the food around on his plate.

As the stars slowly emerged overhead, Admir's eyes sparkled with something like nostalgia. He was envisioning Yaga—remembering her from their childhood. He saw her wild hair and mischievous grin, her hazel eyes flashing up from a book as she lay cocooned in a hammock at her family's estate. He saw her giggling, too—her hands braiding a crown of cornflowers and daisies for Admir, placing it atop his head.

Suddenly, his expression was replaced with something more pensive.

"Yaga is one of a kind, Alexey," Admir started, his gaze unchanging. "But you should know—the world hasn't always been kind to her."

Alexey stiffened upon hearing this—something almost protective arising within him.

"What do you mean, Admir?"

Admir gathered his thoughts, his breath hitching and he searched for the words.

"When Yaga was twelve, her mother died. It was an accident. And Yaga—well," he shook his head. "It changed her..."

Alexey fell silent. His thoughts circled back to his brief time with Yaga—the way she had seemed so capable and strong.

"Her heart is still the same—and she is wonderful, truly. But she carries the weight of her mother's death like a heavy stone," Admir said.

Alexey considered the way Yaga had tended to Misha with such care; how patient and kind she had been. How she hadn't asked for anything in return—not *once*.

"What happened to her mother?" Alexey asked quietly.

"She and her mother, Vesna, were making soap," Admir said, his voice softening with sadness. "There was a—a terrible accident. Oh god—poor Yaga." Admir's face crumpled as his eyes welled with tears. "She saw everything," he said, his voice trembling with emotion. He turned, his gaze catching Alexey's. "It wasn't her fault—but she's never forgiven herself."

The revelation about Yaga's past settled gravely upon Alexey's chest—his heart beating harder with urgency. Now, the skin behind his ears felt hot—as though he needed to move. He glanced once more towards the doors of the manor—momentarily catching sight of Nadia, who had been eyeing him from beyond a window.

Turning back to Admir, his thoughts swirled. Knowing that Yaga had experienced such a tragedy now filled him with a desire to go to her—to tell her he wanted to protect her—even though she clearly didn't need him. She seemed not to need anyone, really. And yet—he couldn't put down the feelings that had ignited within him.

Unexpectedly, Nadia's voice cut through his thoughts.

"Alexey, are you going to join us for a dance, or have you been stolen away by gossip?"

"Oh, *ha ha,*" Admir sneered, quickly wiping the tears from his eyes. He placed a hand on Alexey's forearm, eyeing him earnestly—knowing the magnitude of what he had told him.

Alexey blinked, pulling himself back to the present.

"I'm sorry, Nadia, but I... I need to go," he said firmly, excusing himself. With a hurried bow to Nadia, Alexey nodded at Admir before departing. Nadia watched as he slipped into the manor, disappearing into the crowd—a frown of disappointment forming on her face.

As Alexey walked briskly through the dining hall, he knew going to Yaga's cottage was out of the question. *You barely know her,* he thought. Yet, being at the gala any longer was torture; he had to leave. The only person he wanted to talk to that night was tucked away upon a stand of ancient oaks, and he would have to wait until the morning to see her. Until then, he needed to be alone with his thoughts. He felt it then as he weaved through the crowd—something far beyond sympathy and chivalry. Whatever it was, it tugged at him from beyond the veil itself—an undeniable thread twisting over his mortal skein from her own.

Soon, he stood before his mother, still mingling with the other attendees near the edge of the room.

"Mother, I'm going to turn in for the night. I'll take Misha back to the estate with me and send the carriage back for you and Father after."

Tatiana eyed her son, sensing something had disturbed him.

"Very well, then—why don't we all depart together," she said, her gaze shifting to Dmitri.

With a small, compliant nod, her husband set off towards Misha, now dancing with several other children. Taking his youngest son's hands,

Dmitri twirled Misha playfully for a moment, then walked him back across the room towards Tatiana and Alexey.

Soon, having bid goodbye to Casimir, they stood within the foyer, pulling their coats on. Then, the Grishaevs headed out into the brisk night, with Misha's laughter echoing over the landscape.

From a corner window in the dining hall, Branka and Nadia watched as the family moved down the path. Branka's gaze was sharp as she observed Alexey. Something felt... off. As though she could detect within his demeanor a complication. A threat.

She sighed—a wave of steadfast determination quickly replacing her disappointment. Turning her gaze back to Nadia, she smoothed the front of her dress.

"Be patient, darling. Let us show the other guests what a delight you can be. Your reputation *will* precede you," Branka told her daughter.

They were playing the long game now, and she dared not squander the opportunity to create a thirst—for where there was desire, there would be competition. With her mouth turned upward into a forced smile, Branka drew her daughter close, pulling her back into the night's festivities—determined to make an impression on the guests who remained.

With the outside world cloaked in darkness, the washroom of the cottage was quiet—its walls bathed in the amber light of a few candles. Perched at the head of a basin filled with hot water, Yaga readied herself for her bath, her fingers unlacing the front of her linen shirt. As she undressed, her long, chestnut-brown hair fell over her bare shoulders, cascading down the middle of her back. Slipping off the last of her clothing, she tossed it into a tall woven basket in the corner of the washroom. Turning to the basin, she stepped each of her feet into the hot water slowly, the scent of aromatic herbs wafting through the room.

Sinking down into the bath, steam pooled around her face, settling over her skin like dew. She let out a sigh of contentment—relieved that her day's work was complete. Now, as her skin glistened in the candle-light, she felt the water's warmth soaking into every muscle.

Softly, she began to hum, taking a bar of soap from a small table near the basin and working up a lather. Soon, the words of a gentle lullaby from her childhood drifted through the cottage.

"Sleep, sleep, my little sparrow—old oaks will sing to you,
Lullabies of forest dreams, shadows linger out of view.
Whispers carried on your wings—
Evening tears now morning dew,
Hmm, hmm, hmm, hmm..."

The song echoed through the kitchen and faintly up the stairs. Vasilisa, working at her loom, smiled as she listened. The Vila hummed along with her, her fingers gliding over the warp with a shuttle of crimson-colored yarn dyed with bloodroot the previous autumn.

Downstairs, steam from the bath wafted through the air like smoke, fogging up the single window of the washroom. Yaga closed her eyes, her arms resting on the edges of the basin, her fingers tapping at the placid surface of the bath water as she sang. In that moment, as she sank down into the water, the cares of the day vanished—the world beyond, distant.

But, there was something there—a shadowy figure lurking just past the window. Beyond the fogged glass, it moved silently—a creature peering in as Yaga bathed. Its gaze was unblinking and cold as it stared through the windowpane, watching her resting peacefully.

After a few minutes, the door to the washroom opened slowly, a faint creaking sound cutting through the warm air. Yaga stopped singing abruptly, craning her head behind her. There, in the doorway, stood Vasilisa.

"What is it, Vasa?"

But the Vila pressed her finger to her lips, instructing her to stay silent. Yaga's heart began to beat harder in her chest. Something was wrong.

Without a word between them, the two women remained motionless. Then—a small scraping sound just beyond the walls. The Vila tilted her head as though straining to hear.

Abruptly, Yaga turned—her eyes flicking to the small window. As she squinted at the glass, fear rose up within her. She stood up quickly, water sloshing over the side of the basin and across the wooden floorboards. She had the urge to run then—though she remained still, too afraid to make a sudden movement. Her breathing heavier now, only the water dripping faintly from her breasts and arms punctuated the quiet.

Just then, a blazing white light poured in through the window from outside.

Zhar had awakened.

The Firebird's eyes, scanning the yard below like twin suns, illuminated the cottage on all sides. The creature—lurking just outside—let out a guttural screeching sound before descending to all fours. Yaga and Vasilisa listened to the beating of its hooves over the duff as it loped away, deep into the forest undergrowth.

The steam continued to waft around Yaga as she and Vasilisa waited in silence—wondering if whatever had been watching her was truly gone. After a moment, however, the light flashed out. The cottage walls creaked softly as the Firebird shifted in her roost above them.

The danger had passed—but for how long?

Now in the quiet of the cottage, the two women stood with a palpable sense of unease lingering. From the doorway, Vasilisa pulled a towel off a nearby hook, tossing it to Yaga. She couldn't return to her bath—not now. Something had come—something large enough to have crept near the washroom window, set high above the ground.

"It's gone," Vasilisa said as Yaga stepped from the tub, wrapping herself in the towel. The Vila paused, shifting her head slightly, as though reading the energy beyond the cottage walls. "For now."

Seated at her loom just before, the Vila had sensed the intrusion. She had *felt* the creature—its presence vile and twisting with an old magic. Now, though there was some distance between the thing and their cottage, she felt wary. Whatever it was, it carried with it the same sour malevolence she had been sensing for weeks.

Back in their room, Vasilisa sat once again before the loom as Yaga dressed. The Vila sighed as she faced the tapestry. It had grown quickly in recent days. Pausing, she gathered up a tuft of her own hair, glistening like a raven's wing between her small hands. Then, with a forceful yank, she wrenched the hair from her head, a bit of blood clinging to the roots from the wound created in her scalp. Running her fingers through the clump of hair, she straightened it—before weaving the shining black strands into the tapestry before her.

Their carriage trundling along the uneven country road, Alexey leaned his head against the inside wall. The chatter between his mother and father about the gala and the other attendees had filled the journey home. Though, Alexey's own thoughts had been far away. He could not help but think of Yaga.

In his mind, he pictured her standing in her kitchen, herbs swaying overhead. He saw the profile of her face—her button nose turned up just slightly at the tip. As his head jostled along, he smiled—imagining the freckles splashed across her complexion. And her eyes—pulling him toward her in his mind—hidden behind dark lashes and filled with mystery.

Yaga had a graceful, self-assured demeanor as she moved about her world, and the thought of her filled him with something more than physical desire. He wanted to be near her—to be a part of her world. Indeed, Yaga was unlike anyone he had ever met. She seemed at once both ancient and wise—yet, she was surely the fairest maiden he had seen. Alexey's thoughts circled back to her over and over, as if she were some mystery he needed to unravel.

"Alexey," his father's voice broke into his thoughts. "You're awfully quiet, my son. Is something on your mind?"

Alexey blinked, sitting upright—offering his father a faint smile.

"I'm just tired from the gala, that's all."

His mother, sitting across from him, exchanged a glance with his father. As the carriage bumped over a small dip in the road, Alexey placed his arm around Misha, who had fallen asleep. Leaning back against the carriage window, Alexey peered outside. Across the countryside, the moonlight filtered through a growing mist—the land now cast in a pale glow. He sighed as his mind went back to Yaga, lulled by the rhythmic jostling of the carriage as it continued towards his family's estate.

Back at the gala, the revelry continued into the later hours of the night. Lively music filled the grand hall as the sounds of laughter and plucked strings melded seamlessly. Men and women continued to dance over the white marble floors beneath the warm, bright lights of the chandeliers above them.

Away from the merrymaking, a young couple had slipped through the doors, out into the cool night air, hoping for a bit of privacy. Outside, the air had thickened with a damp fog that swallowed up the edges of the garden, seeping around the outbuildings like a tide coming in.

Giggling quietly, the couple exchanged playful nudges as they wandered toward the stables. Soon, they had arrived—the air filled with the scent of hay and horses. They found a stable, quiet and empty—lit only by a few bars of moonlight streaming through a window. Freshly bedded with straw, it seemed the perfect place to escape the watchful eyes of the party's other guests.

Closing the door to the stall behind them, the couple flopped down onto the soft pile of hay. The man—tall and handsome with unruly blonde hair—leaned in close to his paramour. His hands brushed against her waist, caressing her low back as he kissed her neck tenderly. She flashed him a coy smile, their eyes locking with desire. With slender hands, she tousled his hair, drawing her finger down the front of his chest slowly.

Without warning, a sound—raspy and faint—drifted through the window, circling through the air inside the stables. It was a whisper, almost too soft to be noticed—though the man's head jerked up. He frowned, his eyes shifting around the dark space.

"Did you hear that?"

The young woman smiled sweetly as she tugged playfully at his shirt.

"You're imagining things," she teased, brushing a strand of her auburn hair away from her face. "It's just the wind," she told him, leaning in for another kiss, which he obliged.

But the horses in the adjoining stables began shifting uneasily, their hooves thudding against the wooden floors. They chuffed and snorted—disturbed by something unseen. Soon, the strange sound drifted once again through the stable window—a hushed pulse of air brushing past the young man like a whisper in his ear. It was louder this time—enough to startle him, the hair on his neck standing on end. Quickly, he stood, his body stiffening as his hand reached towards the woman.

"We should go back," he said firmly.

Her eyes rolled slightly as she sighed. Still, she offered her hand to him. Abruptly, he pulled her to her feet, leading her out of the stall.

As the stable door shut behind them, the two walked briskly back toward the estate. A sense of unease clung to them now, and with every step they took, the mist seemed to pool around their shoes. They hurried back into the manor, a wave of relief washing over them—now safely indoors and bathed in the bright, warm gaiety within.

Down the narrow streets of the village, Admir staggered over the cobblestones, his voice shrill and crooning. The crimson-colored scarf he wore around his neck fluttered behind him in the cool night breeze as he swayed—his dissonant singing echoing out into the empty night. With wine buzzing through his veins, he stumbled towards his home.

He chattered here and there to himself as he walked—barely noticing the fog that had begun pouring in around him. Oblivious, he gestured around wildly, shouting out to no one in particular as he meandered through the streets.

"Oh—early in the morning, while it's dark—all the world is still in bed!"

He slurred the words of a song, tripping over a loose stone. Stopping, he chuckled at his own clumsiness, followed by an amused sigh.

In his state, Admir barely noticed the shift in the breeze. It had taken on a strange sort of chill—pulling with it plumes of fog down the edges of the street. After a few minutes, it began to take on a faint, rasping whisper.

Turning, Admir wandered down an alleyway—where the sound grew loud enough for him to take notice. For a moment, it seemed to swirl around him—though it quickly faded out.

Admir stopped mid-step, his head swiveling as he squinted into the darkness.

"Who's there?" His body swayed and he laughed again. *"Radegast! Is that you? Oh Radegast!"* he called out into the black, his voice lilting and playful. Inebriated and oblivious, he wondered if perhaps a god himself might have come to pay him a visit. He hiccupped, gazing down at his feet for a time, his balance unsteady.

Suddenly, the sound had returned—this time louder. It was accompanied by a flash of movement in the corner of Admir's vision. Something had darted past him in the darkness, jolting him out of his stupor. Whipping around, he felt his heart pounding hard within his chest.

"Show yourself!" he demanded, his voice trembling.

The night grew into a kind of stillness that felt unnatural then. Admir, breathless now, stumbled backwards as he noticed the fog filling the space around him like flowing water. It swallowed the forms of the houses and buildings—leaving him completely alone, staring at a dark, gray haze. All at once, the whispers returned, this time growing louder and louder—becoming a cacophony of voices clawing into his ears. As the deafening noise pressed in all around him, Admir's chest tightened with panic.

Then, without warning, something moved. Impossibly fast, it was a blur—striking before he could react. In a flash, he was gone—dragged off into the night, the misty fog filling in the gap where he once stood.

And there, strewn limply over the cobblestones—a silken scarf, the only trace of Admir that remained.

Back at the Grishaev Estate, Alexey stood in the stables, gently petting Kolya. The wolf pressed his head into Alexey's leg. The night was calm here, though just beyond the grounds, a faint mist had begun to swirl. Abruptly, Kolya's ears twitched. With a low growl, his eyes flicked to the window, his gaze scanning the darkness beyond.

Alexey frowned. "What is it, boy?" he asked softly, looking toward the window. "What do you hear?" Alexey strained to listen, though he heard nothing except the quiet chirping of some frogs in a nearby pond.

"It's probably nothing," he said reassuringly. "I bet it's the wind."

He scratched Kolya behind the ears as he glanced in the direction of Yaga's cottage.

"Tomorrow, we are going on a walk, old friend. It will be an adventure. Misha and I are taking you to meet someone," Alexey said, smiling.

Kolya stared back at him, his amber-colored eyes gleaming brightly in the light of the lantern hanging from the rafters above. For a moment, Alexey got the impression that the wolf was reading him; that he sensed something beyond his words.

"She's been helping Misha. Yaga is... special." Alexey stood up, reaching for the lantern.

Kolya whimpered as he watched Alexey open the stable door.

"Don't worry, Kolya," he said, closing the door behind him as he left. He stared at Kolya through the small barred window in the door for a moment before turning.

"It's just the frogs," Alexey called over his shoulder as he walked back toward the manor.

As he moved, however, the fog seemed oddly thicker now, clinging to the ground as his boots squished down in the wet earth. As he walked up the stairs to the porch, he sensed something stirring in the night air beyond his view—something hidden out in the darkness. Perhaps it was not just frogs after all. His brow furrowed as he closed the manor door behind him, latching it—even as he pushed the feeling aside.

Beyond the village, deep in the forested hills, a creature lumbered through the heavy underbrush. Its massive form moved steadily, its hooves clomping down over the duff. It was dragging something; a person. Behind it, Admir's limp, unconscious body—pulled by the collar of his shirt—thudded over roots and stones.

The creature walked with purpose, its strong legs like those of a stag. Atop its head, too, sat a pair of heavy, branching antlers. The beast's face resembled something like a monstrous elk, with steam curling up in plumes from its wide nostrils as it huffed through the trees. Yet—its muscular frame was built more like a man's—moving upright with broad shoulders. With human-like hands blanketed in heavy, silvery fur, the beast gripped Admir's shirt tightly as it pushed forward, deeper into the woods.

Finally, it reached a clearing where a gauzy mist hung over the ground beneath several small trees. Dropping Admir against the base of a birch tree, the creature straightened. It towered over the unconscious man for only a moment before turning and loping off into the shadows.

Unexpectedly, out of the darkness, another figure emerged. He was tall and lean—his skin far too pale beneath the moonlight. He moved with an air of quiet elegance as he stepped into the clearing, each footstep seeming to glide over the matted grass. The man's sharp, handsome features seemed eerily bemused. He approached Admir, still unconscious.

"A Bes is really quite a useful creature," the tall man said, kneeling beside Admir. He shifted his gaze in the direction the beast had taken before disappearing into the undergrowth. "Such loyalty—even if they are a bit ungainly."

He reached out his palm, cradling Admir's chin atop his long, slender fingers.

"Well—look at *you*. What a shame it would be for such beauty to go to waste," he murmured, his voice smooth and low. He studied Admir's face for a moment, his gaze lingering.

With a soft sigh, the man leaned in close, pressing a gentle kiss to Admir's forehead. In an instant, Admir's eyes fluttered open, dilating in confusion as he found himself face-to-face with a stranger. But, before he could speak, he felt the man's finger pressed against his lips, silencing him.

"Shh," the man said. A strange tension formed between them—as if the man were savoring the anticipation of what came next.

Slowly, the man's lips parted—revealing two large fangs, their tips glinting in the moonlight. A sinister smile formed in the corners of his mouth, and—without warning—the man plunged his fangs deep into Admir's neck. The sharp pain of the bite gave way to a sudden flood of ecstasy, causing Admir to let out a faint groan. His eyes rolled back in his head as his body became limp once more.

High above them, the birch trees clattered against one another as the strange wind rasped over the canopy once more. Tonight, it seemed that a darkness had seeped into the lands surrounding Valen. Like drops of blood expanding out into water before disappearing from view, a creeping malevolence had settled in. Yet—the townspeople slept, blissfully unaware of what had intruded into their quiet part of the Thrice-Nine. Soon, however, everything would be clear; the peace within their small village was beginning to unravel.

Chapter Seven

BLOODROOT

Beside the shallow brook flowing through the woods behind the cottage, Yaga crouched, rinsing her hands in the chilly water. It was midmorning now as she watched the current rushing over her fingers, carrying with it the rust-colored remnants of the plant she was using to dye a bolt of cotton fabric. The cloth was destined to become clothing for Vasilisa—with any leftovers set aside for bundling up bars of soap and a few aprons for Yaga herself.

Presently, the fabric lay submerged in a large, outdoor cauldron—a massive iron basin tempered by the blacksmith in Valen years ago for Yaga's mother. The once-white cloth had been swallowed up in what looked to be blood—though the resulting dye would be a more subdued shade of rust.

Returning to the dye bath, Yaga gave the fabric a gentle stir with a wooden spoon. She watched as it bobbed up to the surface before sinking back down—a crimson whirlpool sucking it below. Afterwards, she gathered up a bit of kindling from the wood hutch, tossing it beneath the vat. Immediately, the fresh tinder ignited, sending flames up the sides of the pot's low, bulbous belly.

Yaga wiped her hands across her apron. She turned, crossing the yard and ascending the porch steps to the cottage. Inside, Vasilisa sat quietly at the worktable, her face cast in wide, alternating bands of shadow and light filtering through the shutters on one of the windows. In the air, the earthy aroma of tea leaves melded with the rising yeasts of fresh pastries prepared by the Vila that morning. Now, she was making eggs for breakfast as Yaga tended to chores—a typical morning at the cottage.

As Yaga entered, she moved to the kitchen, gathering up a few items for the dyeing process—a few oak galls and a bit of salt. After a moment, she paused—overcome with a sense she was being watched. She set down a few items on the table, turning toward Vasilisa, her face expectant.

Vasilisa sighed. This was a conversation she didn't want to have with Yaga—not now.

Not *ever*.

But—it had to be done. And she feared the consequences of leaving things unsaid more than how uncomfortable the truth made her. She turned to face Yaga, her expression serious.

Yaga's breath hitched, her thoughts flashing to the night before. The fear she had felt began to settle over her chest as she considered the details once more. A creature had lurked in the darkness beyond the walls of the cottage. The window was set high up off the ground; too high for any person—or animal—to reach. And...

"Something is coming for you, Yaga."

A grave expression creased the Vila's forehead beneath the pale green kerchief she wore. Yaga swallowed hard, her stomach already in knots. For a moment, there was silence as she gathered herself. Yet—she felt as though she couldn't comprehend the words—that they had no recognizable meaning.

What could an unknown creature with dark energy want with *her*?

Vividly, she conjured the moment once more within her mind. Though she hadn't seen what crept outside in the darkness, the feeling had been unmistakable; a prickling at the back of her neck—almost hot—and a restlessness that hadn't gone away until dawn.

Despite the upset, she and the Vila had tucked themselves away in the inner sanctum, each feeling a sense of safety beneath the roost of the Firebird. They had left a candle burning—though, despite their implicit trust that Zhar would protect them, sleep had been scarce.

Yaga pressed her fingers into her temples. There had never been such an intrusion into her small corner of the world. Yet, she knew that the Vila sensed magical energy in a way she could not, and now a mixture of apprehension and need for certainty overwhelmed her.

"What is? What is coming, Vasa?" Yaga's eyes narrowed, her trepidation mounting.

Vasilisa's fingers ran absently along the edge of the cloth tied over her eyes.

"Not 'what'...but... *who*. Somebody is coming for you, Yaga. I can feel it."

Yaga's mouth fell open slightly. With her brow rumpling into a vertical crease, she turned, staring out the window. Her eyes fixed on the pot of dye water boiling away outside as she stood in stunned silence. The deep red liquid had seeped into the wooden spoon resting in the cauldron, its rhythmic bobbing almost hypnotic.

Abruptly, a jar of eyeballs set upon the windowsill where she stood tipped over, scattering across the floor below her. The Kikimorra, perhaps—or was it? Sometimes, she couldn't tell anymore: was it the House Spirit, or the vibrations of the anima within the object creating movement?

Or was it Yaga herself?

Her mind churned like the amalgam of water and bloodroot outside as she watched the eyeballs rocking back and forth on the floor like metronomes, eventually coming to a stop. She stooped, picking one up. Its pupil was eerily distorted within a red, fractured iris—a bad batch set aside in the early days. Kneeling, she scooped the others back into the jar. Just then, Dobra began slinking over the tops of her feet, purring.

"They can sense it—the House Spirits," Vasilisa said. She tilted her head at an angle as though listening to something above them in the rafters.

"Honestly, I think I have, too. For weeks, maybe," Yaga murmured.

She now had an unshakable feeling that whatever—or whoever—was coming, it was somehow connected to the boy in the castle she had seen during her quietings. *But how?* She placed the jar back on the sill, the light scattering through the myriad hues of irises over her hands.

Yaga shook her head solemnly as she made her way to the worktable.

"Whatever it is, it's—"

"*Evil*," the Vila finished Yaga's sentence. "I sense darkness."

Yaga glanced up towards the ceiling, knowing that the Firebird sat perched in the oak branches beyond the rooftop. Zhar could be as small as a chicken if she wanted to—though there were times when she was as big as the cottage itself. Without question, the bird would defend them against any intruder, yet it was a prospect that only brought more discomfort to Yaga's heart. She could never ask for such a thing—at least she hoped never to have to.

"No more walking in the woods or working outside after dusk," Yaga said. A steely reserve settled over her face. "Or before dawn," she added. "I don't know what's coming, but I know we're safe in here."

Vasilisa nodded, her face becoming unreadable again. From across the worktable, however, Yaga could feel the Vila's worry, a detail which evoked a sense of alarm within her. The Vilé were a race of magical beings tied to the Old Gods in ways humans couldn't understand. Even a Witch like herself couldn't fathom the level of perception Vasilisa had. She only knew that the Vila was greatly impressioned by the energies around her; like a dowsing rod to water, she was a locator.

Now, internally, Yaga struggled with the reality of the ominous prediction; their world had been peaceful. Valen was a simple, remote village tucked within the forests of the Northern Thrice-Nine.

138

And yet, Vasilisa had been clear in her warning: someone was coming.

In the village, Alexey walked the streets with Misha high upon his shoulders. The brothers' chatter filled the morning air, with Misha excitedly recounting the spread of food from the gala the night before. Kolya walked beside them now, his nose to the ground as though he had caught a scent. The three were heading southward along a path, making their way towards the now-familiar farmlands bordering the thick wall of forest leading to Yaga's cottage.

That morning, the townspeople, already beginning their outdoor chores, eyed the trio with a mixture of curiosity and slight apprehension. Alexey knew it was the wolf that created a small spectacle—though by now most of the villagers were used to seeing him.

As Kolya's feet padded along next to the brothers, Misha let out a small squeal that pierced the air around them.

"Look!" he said, pointing down the street.

Lying a short distance ahead of them was a bit of fabric, discarded and out of place amongst the dirty cobblestones. Alexey knelt to pick it up, turning it over in his hands. The vibrant red fabric glinted softly in the morning light as he examined it. Immediately, he thought it looked familiar—though the memory of where he'd seen it now escaped him.

Kolya sniffed at the garment. Without warning, he let out a low growl, his hackles raising into a jagged ridge along his back. The wolf's eyes scanned a distant tree line bordering the farmlands near the village center. Seeing the tension rippling through him, Alexey, too, searched the countryside sprawling out from Valen, though he saw nothing. He studied the soft fabric in his hands once more, his brow furrowing.

"I've seen this scarf before," Alexey said.

He shrugged, stuffing it into his coat pocket. Still, as they continued their walk, Alexey moved his hand to the hilt of the dagger he kept at his waistline. His eyes flicked back to Kolya. The wolf's energy was off, his posture stiffened and alert. Alexey's gaze swept over the trees beyond the village one last time. Yet, there was nothing—at least nothing he could see.

"Ok, Mish. Let's go to Yaga's, shall we?" Alexey tilted his head, eyeing his younger brother.

Misha, oblivious to Kolya's strange demeanor, smiled back at him expectantly. Raising a small finger above his head, he gestured exuberantly towards the road leading south out of the village.

"Onward!" he called out, giving a little kick against Alexey's chest with his heel as though he were a horse. And so they went—the two brothers and Kolya, meandering towards the forest and Yaga's cottage beyond.

With a steamy mist rising from the rooftops, the sun drifted higher over Valen. The streets had just begun to bustle with energy as the shopkeepers lifted their shutters, sweeping out their entryways against a backdrop of muted conversations and hoof steps. The sky above was clear and blue, with no trace of the fog from the previous night. A light breeze coursed through the busy streets, the autumn air smelling of firewood and warm pastries.

At the booth of the fabric seller, Branka's servants stood haggling over rolls of silk jacquard. Chosen for a dress for Nadia, the material was rich and textured, its deep burgundy hue shimmering in the sunlight. Days before, when Branka herself had held it, she sensed it could capture an aesthetic she could work with—a fabric that conveyed something at once both austere and regal. Against Nadia's perfect porcelain skin, it would communicate both status *and* modest elegance—a simple, effective tool for signaling her daughter's virtuosity while making her shine.

On this particular morning, Branka had sent a messenger to the Grishaev estate, inviting Alexey's family for dinner the following week. With an acceptance now in hand, she had prompted two of her servant women to head to the market with haste.

The bolt of fabric was important. It was also much too heavy for the servants to carry along the road back to the estate on their own. The shopkeeper, a woman with graying auburn hair and a modest dress, had been eager to make the sale—agreeing to bring the fabric to Branka's estate by that evening, so that the seamstress might begin her work at once.

As the servant women shuffled away from her booth, the fabric seller slipped the heavy sack of coins into her apron pocket, patting it firmly. She glanced at her horse, her brow pressing into a line with frustration.

"Don't go lame on me today, Ruda," she said, her tone admonishing. This delivery was far too important for the horse to be obstinate. Branka was one of her best customers, after all. And, while the horse had been resistant of late—some strange nervousness having overtaken the animal—she would see that the fabric made it. It had to be done, even if she had to cart it out of the village herself.

Indeed, she told herself as she tended to the other reams of fabric—*she just had to keep her head about her.*

At the cottage, Yaga carefully worked a poultice of fresh nettle leaves, accompanied by the blue-tinged oil, over Misha's joints. She smiled kindly at him, pleased with the progress he had made in such a short time. He stood afterwards, stretching and testing his limbs before wandering over to a dish of eyeballs on a nearby shelf. Outside, Alexey and Kolya waited on the ground below the porch.

Soon, Yaga and Misha had made their way outdoors, Misha scampering down to the ground towards Alexey and Kolya. Yaga slowed her steps as she descended, studying the wolf thoughtfully. As she approached, she reached her hand out toward him, scratching him gently behind his ears. Kolya let out a pleased, heavy groan, pressing his head into Yaga's belly firmly.

"He likes you." Alexey smiled, bemused by the interaction.

Yaga paused, gazing for a moment into Kolya's eyes. Amber colored, with flecks of honey-brown, they seemed to stare straight into Yaga's spirit. She sensed something in the wolf—a subtle energy.

Just then, Vasilisa appeared at the threshold of the cottage. She stepped to the porch, a bit of sweet pastry in her mouth.

"He's got magic," she offered, still chewing—as though she had read Yaga's mind.

Alexey's eyebrow arched, his gaze shifting from the Vila to the wolf, and back again.

"He... what?" Alexey said.

Vasilisa paused, swallowing.

"I can't say exactly how—but I can feel it. He's not from... *here*." She gestured towards the forest and around the air, then plopped another piece of the pastry into her mouth.

"Where's he from then?" Misha asked, his expression curious. He leaned over Kolya, throwing his arms around him and hugging him roughly.

Vasilisa's feet seemed to glide as she moved to the ground below where she stood next to Kolya. Now, as she reached her small hand out to him, the wolf appeared gargantuan—as though he were the size of a draft horse next to the doll-like Vila. Immediately, Kolya sniffed at her fingertips, licking them.

Vasilisa seemed to be quietly reading him. She plucked off a piece of pastry, offering it. Kolya nibbled the morsel from her hand, then stared at her intently. Leaning over her, he pressed his nose to the side of her head, his snout nuzzling the handkerchief. He gave two long sniffs—as if to read the place where her eyes had once been—as Yaga and the others watched with curiosity.

"I'm not sure where he's from. He's just not from Yav," Vasilisa added, stuffing another bite of pastry into her mouth.

Alexey and Yaga exchanged an inquisitive glance. Yav—or Jawia—was the realm of mortals and magical beings, the material world in which their lives, and all of the Thrice-Nine Kingdoms, was located. If Kolya wasn't from Yav, they pondered silently, then it meant he was from somewhere else. The realm of the gods, Prav—or, perhaps, the underworld.

Alexey's face drew a blank, his expression contorting with confusion. This bit of information was certainly news to him—though, somehow, not *completely* unexpected. Something about Kolya had always been different—and not just his size or the circumstances of how he had entered Alexey's life. Now, Alexey stared at Kolya, his mind tumbling with questions.

"How...do you know?" Alexey asked.

Vasilisa turned towards him, her face impassive as though she were reading him, too.

"It's just a sense I have," Vasilisa replied.

Alexey's face twisted, his confusion growing.

"Vasilisa is a Vila, Alexey," Yaga said.

Vasilisa nodded, her expression unreadable as she continued chewing.

"What's a Vila? And where's Yav?" Misha asked, tugging on Alexey's sleeve.

Alexey shook his head, trying to push away his sense of bewilderment.

"Yav is here. It's where we all live," Yaga told him. She turned, her gaze scanning the forest and clear autumn sky above. "We live here in Yav. Some of us have magic—like Vasilisa. And some of us do not."

"Like me?" Misha frowned slightly.

"Oh, but you *do* have magic, Misha—it's just a different kind. You're very, *very* brave and full of life. Everyone's important in Yav—even if they don't have magical abilities." Noticing Misha's puzzlement, she paused, her gaze shifting to Alexey.

"Misha and I are Karelian," Alexey said. "We were raised with the Sclaveni stories, but he doesn't know them all," he added.

Yaga smiled, her eyes catching Misha's once more, before shifting her focus to the tree line behind the cottage. In the light of day, the outdoors seemed welcoming and warm. And, even though the night before had brought a dark intrusion to her home, she knew instinctively that whatever had come, it was gone—too far for either her or the Vila to sense. At least for now.

"Well, alright then," she said. "How about a small walk—to meet some of our neighbors here in Yav?" Yaga took a few steps, walking towards small path that lead to the brook behind the cottage.

Without a word, Vasilisa stuffed another bit of pastry into her mouth, tossing the last piece into the air behind her. Kolya snapped it up, swallowing it eagerly, then padded away after the two women.

Alexey and Misha looked at one another, a grin sparking across the boy's face before he scampered hastily after the others.

"Lead the way," Alexey called out, jogging to catch up. And, though his thoughts were still humming around the possibilities of Kolya's true nature, he forced himself to set the detail aside.

The path beside the brook was peaceful, the tranquil sounds of babbling water flowing over stones mixing with the light rustle of leaves in the autumn air. The group stepped over roots and gnarled branches, walking a single file in silence over the winding trail leading towards the nearby pond.

Soon, they had arrived, finding the water's surface cluttered with crimson-colored leaves along its edges. Woodland creatures took cover as the group neared the embankment, dodging into the thickets and reeds, watching them silently. As they reached the shoreline, Yaga and the others stared out over the placid waters, the pond's surface sparkling in the midmorning sun as though covered in tiny diamonds.

Abruptly, a look of disbelief spread across Misha's and Alexey's faces—their eyes widening at the sight of the nearly naked Rusalkas. Their appearance was almost like fair maidens, sensuous and wild as they danced and played in the water. Splashing at one another, the creatures' silvery grey skin glistened in the sunlight. Their laughter, strangely musical, sounded like lilting chimes in a breeze as it floated over the air toward them. Some of the Rusalkas paused, taking an immediate interest in Alexey. They giggled, whispering mischievously amongst themselves as they cast alluring stares in his direction.

"It's fine to watch the creatures play—but don't go near them, Misha," Yaga warned, her voice gentle, yet firm.

Misha had moved in silence with Kolya towards the water's edge, marveling at the playful beings from several yards away. Vasilisa followed close behind, standing quietly nearby, while Fairies—like delicate dragonflies—alighted on the scarf upon her head. Arranging themselves like a crown, their forms sparkled, seemingly flickering in and out of existence.

Alexey was speechless. Seeing how captivated he was, a sly smile formed at the edges of Yaga's lips.

"I take it you've never seen Rusalkas or Fairies?" she asked him, already knowing the answer.

The truth was, humans had grown distant from magical creatures, rarely encountering them at all anymore. For hundreds of years—perhaps longer—all across the Thrice-Nine, the old ways of seeing had been replaced. Much of the Kingdoms had embraced a new vision of the world, and within it, gods and magic were out of place.

And *feared*.

The Kingdoms had not abandoned gods and magic by accident. More and more, it seemed humans were afraid of those with magic because they were terrified of what had once been. Before Yaga's time, magic had come at a cost; some had used it for evil.

Now, the past was a place that felt far, far away. The magical inhabitants of Yav seemed to have disappeared from existence—or from view, in the very least. And, while there were many who still prayed to the Old Gods scattered over the Thrice-Nine, much of the magical world had mostly been forgotten or abandoned by human beings.

Yaga shifted her gaze to Alexey, who stared forward, unresponsive.

"Alexey."

Yaga's eyes flicked to the Rusalkas, who were pouring water from shells across their bodies, bathing one another provocatively.

"I guess... I... um..." Alexey stammered, his eyes strangely vacant. He shook his head. Blinking hard, he glanced toward Yaga as though abruptly regaining consciousness.

"I've—I've only ever read about them... in... storybooks..." His voice softened into a distant murmur as his eyes drifted back toward the water.

Alexey continued staring at the Rusalkas as they preened themselves. They had begun motioning at him seductively as their feminine laughter floated above the pond like an invitation. The spectacle formed a strange haze of desire in the air between him and the creatures, seemingly pulling him further and further down the embankment—if only in his mind.

Yaga noticed right away: Alexey was in a trance.

Without warning, his feet began moving him methodically towards the water's edge, each boot sinking a bit into the soft earth. Yaga reached her hand out quickly, touching his forearm. Immediately, Alexey's eyes flicked towards her. Her touch had felt electric to him, and as their gaze locked, the magnetism he felt for her caused him to catch his breath, blushing.

"Don't watch them for too long, Alexey. They're beautiful—but they *kill* men."

Her words startled him. He hadn't meant to stare—yet as soon as they had neared the pond, he hadn't been able to look away. He felt hypnotized. He remembered then, the Sclaveni stories he had learned in childhood; Rusalkas were playful forest nymphs who delighted in the fiendish pastime of luring men towards a watery death.

He swallowed, a lump forming in his throat. Looking down at his feet, he scratched at the back of his head, embarrassed.

"It's ok. They're part of the magic that exists here in Yav. That's part of their power," Yaga said, gently squeezing his arm, as though sensing his humiliation.

As she spoke, Alexey stared into her eyes. Hazel in color, they were filled with flecks the color of jade—captivating from beneath the frame of her thick brown lashes. Alexey sensed then that she held a deeper mystery then—as though he were being drawn in on some primal level. He felt a burning need to know her better. *To be with her.*

In that moment, he was struck with the realization that—unlike the enchanted allure of the Rusalkas—the attraction he felt for Yaga was real. He felt it deep within his bones: unequivocally, Yaga's heart was pure—and he cared for her more with every passing day.

As they stood next to one another, Alexey turned his focus to Misha, watching as his younger brother scampered after frogs on the embankment. Still, he felt a tugging in his chest that urged him to talk to Yaga, despite the embarrassment that lingered for what had happened just before. He cleared his throat.

"You weren't at the gala last night," he said.

Yaga wrinkled her nose, the sight of which caused him to let out a small chuckle.

"Did *you* enjoy it?" she asked, her tone one of mild curiosity as she watched the Fairies pulling at Misha's jacket collar.

"I could think of places I'd rather be," he replied with a shrug, glancing at her from the corner of his eyes. A small, unspoken tension grew between them.

"But you—it seems like you like it out here where there's..." Alexey searched for the words. "... not too many people."

Yaga's expression shifted, her posture shrinking just slightly. She stared past the others on the embankment, watching the Rusalkas silently as their glossy forms dove into the water and splashed about. Her eyes flicked in the direction of Valen.

"Well, after my father died, I had no reason to stay in the village." She paused, her lip stiffening. "I tried to live with my stepmother and stepsisters for a time, but..." Yaga's voice trailed off, leaving the rest unsaid.

Alexey, sensing the weight of her past now pressing down in the space between them, said nothing more. He knew that whatever had happened—whatever had brought her into the forest years ago—it was best to let her tell him in her own time.

Yaga sighed. She glanced at Alexey briefly, then back towards the water. As they stood watching Misha and Vasilisa, a tiny Fairy flitted by, landing on Yaga's shoulder like a butterfly. Alexey stared, marveling at the Fairy's luminous wings.

Smiling, he reached for it—only for the Fairy to dart away suddenly. Instead, his hand brushed softly against Yaga's cheek. He kept it there, slowly moving a tendril of chestnut hair out from in front of her eyes.

For a moment, they stood in stillness, as though cast in amber—a shared sense of heat rising between them.

They were interrupted by Misha's gleeful shouting as he splashed into the water. Immediately, Kolya leapt into the water behind him, grabbing him by the back of his trousers and pulling him to the shore. Turning abruptly, Misha splashed water playfully towards Vasilisa and Kolya, his laughter ringing through the forest around them.

"Misha—stay out of the water or you'll catch a cold," Alexey said. The bottom third of his younger brother's pants was wet now. And even though the day was unseasonably warm, he didn't want to risk anything—not with how well his brother had been feeling of late.

Misha stuck his tongue out at Alexey before scampering after a frog up the embankment.

Yaga chuckled softly as she watched the spectacle. Soon, however, she had the sense of being watched. Her eyes flicked to Alexey, who smiled at her, his half-grin framed by a strong, handsome jaw. Standing nearly a foot taller than her, she scanned his physique unconsciously—her gaze drawn upwards towards his muscular neck—then down to his broad shoulders and biceps, snug beneath a shirt decorated with red embroidery.

Her face flushing, she quickly glanced back towards the water. For several minutes, they stood together, silently watching the others—the palpable tension between them growing steadily. Still, neither of them felt ready to acknowledge it—least of all, Yaga. For her, the feelings of desire were tempered by an overwhelming sense of fear—as though letting Alexey into her world somehow posed a threat.

Abruptly, she sighed, pushing the tangle of emotions aside as she stepped forward a few feet. Stretching her arms overhead, she closed her eyes, feeling the warmth of the sun on her cheeks and inhaling the fresh air. She would shift her focus—moving it away from the tension she felt for the man standing a few feet behind her—placing it firmly on the world around her. She had to, for there was precious little energy she could give to romance; not with the unanswered questions she had about the creeping malevolence lurking in the world beyond, stalking her for reasons unknown.

For now, in this moment, Yaga wanted to put it all away. She wanted to enjoy the last few weeks of autumn, before the cold winds of winter settled over the land.

Soon, minutes had turned to hours, and with the early afternoon sky overhead, the time had come for Alexey and Misha to return to the village. At the cottage, Yaga and Vasilisa bid the two brothers and Kolya goodbye—though Yaga offered little more than a polite glance and a wave at their parting.

Alexey, sensing her distance, expressed his gratitude for her care and generosity as he hoisted a tired Misha upon his back for the trek home. After confirming his intention to return the following day, he departed, heading across the clearing with Kolya at his side.

As the brothers disappeared up the path towards Valen, Yaga and Vasilisa moved up the porch steps, entering the cottage. Making their way to the kitchen, Vasilisa studied Yaga quietly. To her, Yaga seemed deep in thought—her energy strange and conflicted.

"You're forming a bond with him," Vasilisa observed softly. "I felt it when he first arrived."

Yaga's nose crinkled, though she said nothing—even as a faint blush pooled in her cheeks. She wasn't ready to think about the feelings growing between her and Alexey. Getting close to someone was difficult for her—if not impossible—ever since her mother had passed.

Yet, despite this reticence, Yaga had been able to forge a deep bond of sisterhood with Vasilisa and the Firebird—seemingly from the very moment they had met. Now, the two women sat together in silence, tucked below Zhar as she roosted in the canopy above. With the afternoon sunlight warming the floorboards beneath their feet, Yaga and Vasilisa—each hoping to put their fears to rest—enjoyed a bit of stew and tea in the quiet.

In the forest, Alexey and Misha made their way back towards Valen. Beside them, with his nose trailing over roots and stones, Kolya focused intently—apparently caught on a scent. Abruptly, he raised his head, his ears pricking slightly. The wolf's snout wiggled as he sniffed heavily at the air; something was nearby.

High above, an owl watched them from the branch of an oak, the bird's head craning as he shadowed their movements. His gaze lingered as they continued up the path. After a moment, the owl leapt into the air, unseen by the trio as he swooped low, landing out of view behind a mass of leaves.

Just as quickly, a crow emerged from the same place, the creature's loud cackle reverberating through the understory and startling the brothers. Pausing briefly, they continued walking, unconcerned with the crow's presence. Kolya, however, began to whine; he sensed something unusual now, his eyes scanning the branches overhead expectantly.

He was searching for something—though it wasn't a bird.

The crow suddenly took flight, soaring downward from the tree and landing in the nearby undergrowth. Immediately, a fox darted out from behind a cluster of ferns, his pale-yellow eyes gleaming in the dimly lit forest. Kolya growled again, deep within his throat—the sound alerting Alexey to the creature's presence.

The fox, nimble and quick, slipped between some bushes, creating a ripple of movement through the vegetation. Alexey and Misha stopped abruptly. Turning their heads, Misha caught his breath, grabbing Alexey's arm tightly. The brothers watched as the fox scampered over a moss-covered boulder, disappearing behind a tree. Then—unexpectedly—a large stag slowly emerged, his antlers scraping on the low branches above him.

Alexey and Misha froze, their eyes widening with surprise as the animal stepped from the duff onto the path. Without warning, the beast moved towards them—transforming before their eyes into *a man*.

Alexey and Misha gasped.

The brothers stared in shock. Clearly, the older man who had transformed before them had magic. His features were unusual—his clothes seemingly woven from the woodland itself. Mice scurried in and out of his pockets as insects shimmered and writhed over his shoes. His body buzzed and hummed with a thousand forms of animals—each of the man's features shifting in subtle ways. His hands became hooves or paws—then his nose, a beak or snout—until, for a few fleeting seconds, he once again appeared human.

Previously guarded, Kolya let out a soft, pleading whine—moving towards the man and pressing his large head against the man's leg. Leaning forward, the stranger stroked the wolf's neck gently. Alexey watched with wide eyes, nearly speechless. He knew immediately who—or *what*, rather—stood before them.

"You're—you're a..." he struggled to find the words, mesmerized by the shimmering mirage of forest creatures flickering before him.

"A Leshy!" Misha squealed, squeezing Alexey's shoulders tightly with nervous excitement. Of all the Sclaveni tales read to him by his parents, the story of the Leshy had always stood out to Misha as something fascinating and strange.

The old man raised an eyebrow, genuinely surprised the young boy recognized him. It was rare that he stood before any human nowadays—and for those he did, they mostly ran away in fear.

"I am," the Leshy replied. He extended his hand graciously, its surface cloaked in a mass of wriggling millipedes.

Misha's eyes rounded as he watched the mice and a cascade of insects darting in and out of the Leshy's shirt sleeve. With his other hand, the man tipped his hat, the brothers watching as it turned into a robin's nest filled with greenish-blue eggs. Then, as it transformed into a clump of leaves, the Leshy placed the hat back upon his head gingerly.

Misha grimaced as he eyed the creatures crawling over the Leshy's outstretched hand. Still, he stuck his small finger toward it, reaching to touch one anyways. Alexey brushed his brother's hand down, a serious expression forming over his face. After the encounter with the Rusalkas earlier, Alexey was on guard for anything mischievous or malevolent from anyone—magic or otherwise.

The Leshy, sensing Alexey's reservation, took a single step backward, gently clasping his hands together behind his body.

"Ah, well. I don't blame you. It's not every day you meet someone with magic."

He paused, studying Alexey's face for a moment.

"Except that's not really true for *you* these days, is it?"

Alexey's brow furrowed. Had he been watching them?

"Ok, now—just a minute," Alexey began—though the Leshy interrupted him.

"What I mean is—you've been visiting our Yaga."

The Leshy smiled kindly, his eyes twinkling affectionately. He glanced at Misha, looking down at the boy's knees and ankles—his condition barely perceptible anymore.

Alexey felt himself growing more defensive. Taking a step forward, his strong form loomed over the man. Still, the Leshy seemed undisturbed—instead staring into Alexey's eyes, his gaze penetrating. Then, with an ominous tone, he offered something piercing.

"You came here for your brother, but it's you who needs healing—your *heart*."

He pointed up toward the center of Alexey's chest, his finger now coiled with a slithering snake. Alexey simply stared, his brow furrowing—too bewildered by the absurdity to react. He started to speak—but the Leshy interrupted once again, this time turning his attention toward Kolya. The wolf lay beside the man now, his massive head resting over the Leshy's foot.

"I see you have one of Devanna's wolves... or at least one of her pups," he said, his gaze narrowing as he observed Kolya. The wolf groaned contentedly as the Leshy stooped, scratching him behind his ears.

"Devanna's wolves? What exactly are you saying?" Alexey asked, confusion spreading over his face.

Misha, who had been watching the exchange with intense curiosity, tugged at Alexey's shirt sleeve.

"*Pup*?" Misha whispered, his face puzzled.

Kolya, plainly, was a giant—and the idea he could still be growing sounded preposterous, even to the ears of a six-year-old.

A sly smile spread over the Leshy's face.

"Ah, well..." he began, his face morphing into that of a gray wolf with striking amber eyes, "you know Devanna, the most powerful ancient goddess of our world. Surely your parents read the tales to you, my boy."

Alexey, still wary of the Leshy's intention—moved his hand to the hilt of his dagger as he considered the question. He searched his memory for stories of the Sclaveni people he had been told since he was a child.

Unlike most Karelian children, Alexey and Misha had grown up with the same fairy tales as Yaga, though for very different reasons. His parents had wanted them to know the folklore of the people in the nearby lands so as to be more cultured—and to fit in. His father was, after all, a businessman with ventures spanning the Sclaveni territories to the south of Severyn and beyond. His parents thought it best if he and his brother had a shared sense of their world—knowing that eventually, they would be a part of it. Still, his own people at the northernmost edge of the world were largely animistic—their beliefs differing vastly from the disorderly pantheon of wandering gods found in other corners of the Thrice-Nine.

Despite his exposure to much of the Sclaveni lore, as Alexey tumbled over the stories in his head, he really could not recall the Goddess Devanna, or the tales about her.

The Leshy eyed him curiously as he placed his hand between Kolya's shoulder blades, running his fingers over the wolf's back slowly. He continued, his tone shifting.

"Devanna is the Goddess of Yav. Or *was*. She once ruled over our world, though thousands of years ago, she waged a battle with Perun, God of Prav and the world of immortal beings... blah, blah, blah... challenging him for control and such over the three realms, Prav, Yav, and Nav..." the Leshy waved his free hand through the air with exaggeration.

"Anyways, in the ensuing fray, the veil between worlds thinned. Time and space bent, and the fabric keeping the dimensions apart was ripped open suddenly by the torrent of energy released in the battle. In Devanna's defeat, her wolves scattered across the forests—never to be seen again—or so it was said. Until this one found *you*."

For a moment, the Leshy settled his fingers on Kolya's back as though he had found something. An expression of recognition flashed briefly across his face. Quickly, he pulled his hand away, clasping it behind his back once more.

"You have one of her pups—but this one is... unusual," the Leshy said, his gaze meeting Kolya's amber-colored eyes.

Misha, now intensely curious, scrambled off of Alexey's back, rushing to Kolya's side. Alexey reached for him—though he just missed—watching as Misha wrapped his arms around Kolya's neck. The child's face beamed up at the Leshy.

"How do you know?" Misha asked.

The Leshy leaned forward.

"I can feel his magic," he whispered. "Just as I can feel that. You. Have. *None*." His hand morphing into a soft, sable rabbit's foot, the Leshy gently bopped the tip of Misha's nose. Though free of hostility, his words had landed with a finality between them. The Leshy glanced meaningfully at Alexey. Once again, before Alexey could gather his thoughts to respond, the Leshy shifted his focus, offering them a word of warning.

"I'm not the only one who can sense your lack of magic. Ordinarily, that wouldn't be much of a danger to you here—but something else has come into these woods of late. *Something dark*. It's drawn to her, you see. To her magic." The Leshy's eyes narrowed.

"Be careful now—especially at night. These creatures... they're not natural. They're fueled by a malevolence that grows with every passing day. I've not seen such darkness here in Yav for a long, long time—not in a millennia or more."

Alexey exchanged a glance with Misha. The Leshy was impossibly old—a fact stunning on its own. Yet, today, of all the revelations, a creeping darkness intruding into their small part of the world—and its connection to Yaga—was by far the most alarming.

Alexey's posture shifted, his mind more alert to the surrounding forest. He glanced back up the path towards Yaga's cottage, worried for her safety. *What do they want from her—these creatures?* Fear swelled at the edges of his mind. Narrowing his eyes, he squinted, scanning the canopy and the understory as far as he could until the woods disappeared into shadow.

The Leshy sighed, turning to leave, though he paused briefly.

"It's not just these creatures you should worry about. It's who made them," he said, shuddering.

Then, the Leshy turned to Misha, offering a gentle smile and a bow. Without another word, the brothers watched as the man abruptly transformed into a lynx, bounding away and disappearing into the thick woodland brush.

Alexey, shaken, stared once more up the path toward Yaga's cottage. Something was shifting in the forest, and his understanding of Yaga had become unexpectedly complicated. He sighed, not knowing what to do—despite being overcome with the sense that he needed to prepare somehow.

"Let's go," he said quietly, lifting Misha onto his back. Then, with his hand on the hilt of his dagger and Kolya at his side, they made their way out of the woods—the Leshy's words now heavy on Alexey's heart.

As the sun dipped beneath the horizon, Valen settled into the quiet hum of the evening. Shopkeepers, having packed up the last of their booths at the marketplace, bustled toward their homes, the smell of their waiting dinners wafting down the empty streets. Through the air, the soft clatter of hooves and creaking carts echoed faintly, forming a quiet din.

The fabric seller stood next to her horse now, the reins still hitched to a post beside her booth. In the fading daylight, the woman stared pensively at the large bolt of fabric destined to become a dress for Branka's daughter, Nadia. The burgundy silk, with its delicate jacquard pattern of florets, gleamed like a garnet in the low light. For a brief moment, she was struck by its beauty.

She sighed. One last stop, she thought wearily. Just one.

Her expression hardened as she eyed her horse. Lately, the beast had gone lame, refusing to pull the large cart she used to transport her heavy reams of material. With a sigh of frustration, the fabric seller resigned herself to hauling the silk to Branka's estate by hand. Her eyes flicked to the small wooden cart laying propped against the side of the booth.

Though she was tired, she had no other choice; Branka's patronage was much too valuable to her. Still, the journey through the countryside stretched before her like a test of endurance. As she loaded the pushcart and started off, her horse began to whinny and snort, stomping over the cobblestones fervently.

"Oh, hush. I'll be back for you soon enough," she grumbled, annoyed at her stubbornness.

The woman made quick work of the narrow streets leading out of the village. Soon, she came to a gravel road winding through the countryside to the east of Valen. As she trudged along, she strained beneath the weight of the handcart.

With the gloaming settling in around her now, no other travelers remained. She was alone, with only the sound of crickets to keep her company. Presently, a creeping fog had begun swirling around the edges of the wetlands and fields as she passed through. Swallowing the forests flanking the pasturelands, it seemed to be moving closer.

Not wishing to lose her visibility, the woman quickened her pace. After a time, however, she paused, catching her breath; the long day had taken a toll on her body. She leaned on the pushcart briefly from the exertion. As she did, it tipped to the side, startling her as the fabric almost spilled over the roadway.

"All this way, and for nearly nothing!" she said, admonishing herself.

The metal stand of the pushcart scraped on the gravel road as she steadied it, the sound cutting through the graying quiet that had settled over the area.

As she grasped the wooden handles, preparing to resume her walk, the woman heard a faint rustling coming from a stand of nearby reeds. At first, the sound caused her to stiffen—though soon, she relaxed her posture. *It had to be an animal,* she told herself sheepishly, despite the fear that had arisen in her chest. Pushing the cart forward, the woman struggled beneath its weight before settling into a steady pace once again.

Though she continued to tell herself otherwise, she felt a creeping *nervousness* gnawing at her now as she moved up the road. She was rarely on her own at this hour; her horse Ruda was usually her faithful companion, pulling her large cart home with her at the end of the day. She grimaced as she imagined the horse tethered beside her booth at this hour. *What would a passerby think?* She shook her head, muttering something to herself as she continued onward.

Soon, the woman started to hum—an attempt to chase away her sense of unease and isolation. Yet, as she walked along the path, she struggled to push down the worry growing within her.

Just a little bit further, she thought.

A few minutes passed, and—tired once more—she was about to pause for a small break. That was when the whispers began. They were soft at first—barely perceptible, like a faint clattering of birch leaves in the breeze, just at the edge of her hearing.

She tried to dismiss the sounds at first. *Certainly, it's just the reeds,* she thought. Yet, soon, the sounds grew louder—more distinct. Her heart pounded in her chest as she glanced around her, unsure of where the sounds had originated.

Then, without warning, the sounds became deafening. She dropped the handles of the pushcart as a torrent of noise swelled in her ears. Panic surged within her, and—abandoning the cart entirely—she broke into a desperate run towards a faint glow in the distance. It was a lantern, hanging just outside of Branka's carriage house.

I can make it, she thought.

But the fog, like a white muslin fabric, enveloped her on all sides, thickening into an opaque wall. It swallowed up the path until the dim light ahead had vanished from view entirely. The woman stopped, her chest heaving, her vision completely blinded by the fog. Suddenly, the chorus of sound stopped.

A heavy silence closed in around her.

She stood, panting—sweat beading on her temples.

Then she heard it—the unmistakable sound of a horse's hooves clopping up the road towards her. Her relief was immediate.

A rider!

The woman, straining her eyes to see through the fog, called out into the hazy void—her voice shaky but hopeful.

"Hello there? I—I can't see you just yet."

The thudding sound of hooves echoed into the stillness, drawing closer. Yet—no voice answered. She squinted in the direction of the sound, watching as a tall, dark shape slowly emerged through the blanket of fog.

"Oh, thank the heavens," the woman said.

As the rider came closer, she extended her hand towards him, sighing with relief.

The woman's breath caught in her throat. Something... something was wrong.

Her eyes went wide as her blood ran cold.

Looming over her was a hulking, monstrous figure—a horseman. What she saw was no man, however. Instead, what stood before her was something demented—an abomination of a man fused to his horse, the animal's eyes glowing red and deep within their sockets.

It was Todorats—a nightmare she had heard whispered about only in superstitions. A scary story told to frighten children. A rider of the dead—a being of pure malice.

Terror gripped her as she stumbled backward, her eyes bulging from their sockets.

"No... no... please!" Her voice trembled as she begged. The woman fell to her bottom and, scrambling backwards a few feet over the ground, she attempted to stand. To run away.

Todorats walked towards her then—each hoof step slow and deliberate. From the scabbard on his back, he drew out a massive sword, advancing. The horse's movement was unyielding now—the woman's last desperate steps faltering.

The countryside seemed to hold its breath for a moment as the misty fog climbed higher—like plumes of smoke rolling up everything beneath a gauzy burial shroud. Then, the air was split by a bloodcurdling scream—high, piercing, and filled with terror and finality.

The woman's death cry echoed far over the countryside, heard by every living thing in Valen and the forested lands beyond. Zhar, roosting above the cottage, was awakened by the sound, her feathers ruffling in alarm. In an instant, her blazing eyes scanned over the nearby woodlands.

Farther away, Kolya rested peacefully within the stables at the Grishaev Estate. The scream jolting him awake, his head lifted abruptly. His ears pricked at the unnatural sound as he stood, walking towards the stable door and nuzzling it open.

As the scream echoed through the twilight air, the entire region seemed to pause to hear it. Then, the village fell into a silence, tense and fearful. Fog clung to the fields and homes, wrapping the land in an eerie, opaque cloak. No one dared leave their homes to investigate—lest they meet the same fate of the unknown victim. But no one was mistaken about what they heard.

Someone had died tonight.

In the cottage, Yaga had sat up in her bed at once, her hand frozen over the pages of the large leather-bound grimoire. Vasilisa, who had been seated by the hearth, jerked her head toward the window, her face hidden beneath a lavender-colored kerchief. The cottage shook slightly as Zhar left her roost high above them in the oaks.

Yaga appeared at the top of the staircase, her feet carrying her down swiftly. There, she found Vasilisa, now standing near the front door of the cottage.

"Someone's been killed," Vasilisa whispered. "By something." She paused, moving to the window sill. "A demon."

To the magical creatures living near Valen, the sound of the woman's scream had carried a certain resonance. Within it, an ancient magic echoed. Something dark and twisted had arrived, revealing its presence to all within earshot.

Yaga joined the Vila, peering out the window at the unnatural fog hanging over the clearing. It floated like a white wall beneath the moonlight—cut through by the occasional bright band of light cast down by the Firebirds movements in the sky above.

"We should go look," Vasilisa said, moving towards the door. "It came from the direction of your father's estate."

Yaga's face fell. Could the scream have come from Branka or her stepsisters?

"You should stay here, Vasa," Yaga said. The last thing she wanted was to endanger Vasilisa.

Vasilisa's face stared back at her in silence.

"No," she told Yaga firmly, "we go together."

Yaga's breath hitched. She was worried for her friend, her frame delicate and small. Yet, she knew better than to argue with the Vila, and that ultimately, they were safer together. Cautiously, the two women opened the door of the cottage, walking down the steps into the hazy darkness.

Immediately, they were greeted by the descending, massive form of Zhar, who landed in the yard as though called by Yaga's intention alone.

Yaga and Vasilisa exchanged a glance at one another. Yaga had never climbed atop the Firebird before—and yet, she knew it was what the moment required. Moving towards the Firebird, she extended her hand to the Vila, hoisting her up the bird's back, then climbing up to join her. Together, they clung to Zhar's thick feathers, huddling against her body's warmth. With a few heavy flaps of her wings, the Firebird ascended, soaring into the night and racing over the countryside in the direction of the sound.

At the Grishaev Estate, Alexey had bolted upright in bed, his heart pounding in his chest. The scream had ripped through his dreams, wrenching him from the warmth of sleep into a cold, waking terror. He turned his head, seeing his younger brother beside him. Misha, who had fallen asleep after a bedtime story, stirred only slightly—somehow unawakened by the sound.

Alexey swung his legs over the side of the bed, moving quickly to the window. The night was unnaturally still now, with mist curling against the glass like spectral vines. He had heard stories growing up—old superstitions about creatures that roamed the Sclaveni wildlands. Yet, as a Karelian, he had never taken them in earnest; they were simply the folktales of another people. Now, fear swelled in his chest. His thoughts went to Yaga immediately. Yet—that wasn't the direction the sound had come from. It had come from the eastern farmlands of Valen, near Branka's estate.

As he dressed, Alexey's mind raced back to the Leshy's warning earlier that day. Something had moved into the forest... something drawn to

Yaga's magic. Could this be what he meant? A sharp pang of worry for Yaga and Vasilisa overtook him. They were all alone out there in the cottage.

Quickly, he dressed. Grabbing a lantern, he exited the bedroom quietly. As he entered the hall, he saw the household staff huddled together, speaking in hushed tones. As he crept down the stairs, he found his parents standing in the foyer with the stableman, worried expressions wrought over their faces. Seeing him, Tatiana opened her arms, her forehead etched with fear.

"Alexey—where is your brother?" she asked, her voice filled with anxiety.

"He's asleep in my room, Mother," Alexey said.

Tatiana and Dmitri sighed loudly in relief.

Then, Alexey caught something from the corner of his eye. Craning his neck to see out the glass of the door to the porch beyond, he saw him; there, with his back facing them as he stared out into the darkness, sat Kolya.

"The wolf came shortly after the scream," the stableman said. "He's been here waiting."

Alexey reached for the handle of the door, but his father moved abruptly, blocking him.

"Surely you can't mean to leave, son. It's not safe!"

Alexey looked back at his mother, her lips pressed down into a thin frown, her hands trembling. Beyond her, several women of the household staff huddled in the corner of the parlor. His eyes returned to his father, his hand flat against the front door.

Alexey took hold of the doorknob.

"I am going, Father. I don't know who—or *what*—we heard, but I am going to find out whatever I can."

His father's brow furrowed, his hand pressing more firmly to block his son. Gently, Alexey peeled his father's palm away from the door.

Turning towards Tatiana, Dmitri's face sank with resignation.

Despite his mother's protests, Alexey left her with a quick kiss on the forehead, slipping out into the darkness. Behind him, he could hear his mother begin to sob. He hated to cause her worry—yet, he had to leave. To find out what had happened—and to whom.

Outside, the foggy air clung to Alexey's skin like a strange, wet blanket. Beside him, Kolya kept his nose low to the ground, his movement punctuated with short pauses as he sniffed at the air. He was trailing a scent now—something pungent carried on the wind across the countryside from the east. The unmistakable odor of *blood*.

Alexey and the wolf cut through fields—the cold wet grass squishing underfoot as they moved. After some time, a shape formed ahead of them. There in the distance was Branka's estate, its dark silhouette barely visible through the swirling mist.

As they neared, the dim lights within the house came into view. Even from outside, the activity within was palpable; the manor was a hive of activity, with servants darting about, their hurried and frantic movements casting shadows over the curtains. Kolya sniffed the air again. The scent of blood growing stronger, he let out a low growl, causing Alexey's heart to quicken.

Finally, they had arrived at the base of the porch. Drawing in a deep breath, Alexey marched up toward the front door, unsure of what he would find inside. He knocked firmly, the sound thudding loudly into the night air. Suddenly, there was rustling and hushed tones. After a few seconds, the curtains in a nearby window shifted, a servant's terrified face peering through a small gap. Another moment passed before the door creaked open just a crack—enough for a sliver of a man's face to be visible.

"What do you need? What do you want?" the man asked, his voice tight with fear.

"I—I came because I heard the scream," Alexey said firmly.

Abruptly, the door flung open, the servant hurriedly tugging Alexey inside before slamming the door behind him and bolting it shut. The man's eyes flicked nervously to the figure of the wolf just beyond the window. Despite his trepidation, however, he knew—just as the rest of the house did—no wolf had caused the horror that had unfolded that evening.

With his voice trembling, the servant explained to Alexey that he had been pacing the grounds just before the scream—waiting for a merchant woman to arrive with a ream of fabric. He shuddered at the retelling, his face ashen and pale. His eyes shifted to the windows, then to the lock on the door, as though checking them again to be certain.

Just then, Branka descended the staircase, her face drawn and fearful. Seeing Alexey standing in the entry, she let out a small shriek of relief. Nadia, following closely behind her, peeked over her mother's shoulder.

"What is it, Mommy?" she said, clutching at her mother's arm and hiding behind her.

As soon as the two women reached the bottom of the stairs, Nadia noticed Alexey. Surging forward, she threw herself into his arms, burying her face into his chest, as her muffled sobs filled the foyer.

"Oh, thank the gods you're here!" Branka exclaimed. "We've just been beside ourselves with terror. Whatever do you think happened, Alexey? Are we in danger?"

Alexey, placing his hands gently on Nadia's shoulders, moved her back firmly, positioning her next to her mother.

"Everything's going to be ok," he said. He glanced around at the others—perhaps a dozen servants—seeing the terror in their eyes. Whatever had happened, it was close. The scream must have been deafening from within the manor.

"I'll head down the road to investigate further," Alexey said. "Stay inside. If I see any danger, I'll come back."

With that, he slipped back out the door—the servant shutting it behind him forcefully. As Alexey walked beside Kolya, their breath curled in plumes into the darkness. Nearing the road, Alexey turned, glancing back over his shoulder. Above them, in an upper window of the manor, he noticed a figure watching him. It was Marfa, Branka's youngest daughter. Her eyes peered at him with curious intensity. Catching his gaze, she shut the curtains abruptly.

Soon, he and Kolya were trudging up the road, making their way past the carriage house in the direction of the scream. And the blood. As they closed in, the fog seemed to grow thicker with every step, swallowing their forms whole while a damp chill beaded over their skin like sweat.

Soaring through the night, Yaga and the Vila's hands clung tightly to the Firebird's plumage. The air was brisk and biting as they flew—a howling cold rushing over their faces as they raced to the area where the killing had taken place.

Zhar, too, had been tracking the scent of blood. Now, she swooped lower to the ground. As she descended, her luminous eyes flared, casting bright beams over the misty fields. Passing over the roadway, the light illuminated two figures standing near an overturned cart. Landing a short distance up the road, Yaga and Vasilisa dismounted swiftly, their bootsteps clopping over the dirt and gravel as they approached.

Alexey, bewildered and shocked, lifted his hand in front of his face, shielding his eyes from the blazing white wall emanating from the Firebird's gaze. Suddenly, to his astonishment, Yaga and Vasilisa emerged onto the road before him. His stared in disbelief; he had never seen a creature like Zhar before—nor could he have imagined the two women descending on one from the sky.

Yaga, seeing his expression, took his hand gently. He blinked a few times. The day had been filled with too many extraordinary revelations. Now, his mind was struggling to adjust. *Nothing will ever surprise me again*, he thought.

Still, with Yaga's warm hand clasped over his own, his shoulders dropped in relief; she was safe.

"We came as soon as we could after the scream," Yaga told him. "Did you see what happened?"

Alexey shook his head, a grim expression overtaking his face. He squeezed Yaga's hand as he drew her towards a ditch a few feet away. There lay the lifeless body of the woman at the roadside—her red blood pooling at the base of several cattails, mingling with the brackish water swirling over their roots. Together, they stared down, each of their minds churning over the horror that had befallen the woman and their peaceful village that night.

"This is the work of Todorats," Vasilisa said, her voice breaking through the heavy quiet. "He's gone—for now. I can feel the magic fading, but he was here."

"Todorats?" Alexey asked, his brow furrowing.

"He's a demon—tortured and malevolent. He lived a long time ago when dark magic swallowed up parts of the Northern Thrice-Nine. Half horse, half rider—he has no mercy for those he encounters," the Vila explained.

"I've seen him in the pages of my grandmother's book," Yaga said. "But he hasn't been spotted anywhere for hundreds of years or more."

Alexey's gaze shifted between Yaga and Vasilisa, disbelief etched over his features. Kolya sniffed at the woman's body, wrinkling his nose and whimpering at the scent of her death.

There was a long pause then, with only the croaking sounds of unseen frogs in the wetland nearby. Yaga knew that a question now hung in the air like the mist itself.

Why had Todorats come?

Yaga wished she knew for sure. Yet—how could any of them understand the meaning of the creature's appearance? Nothing made sense to her anymore. Still, even if she didn't understand why Todorats had suddenly appeared, she felt with certainty that the intrusion into their world was *tied to her.*

And—somehow—to the boy in the castle.

"I don't know why this creature came here, but tonight, we need to be safe—and to rest," Alexey said, turning towards her. "Yaga—are the two of you going to be ok alone at the cottage? I'm... I'm worried." His eyes searched hers intently.

Yaga took Alexey's hand gently again—her touch sending a pulse of feeling through him. Even with the grim scene before them, sensing her skin upon his own sent a wave of desire and angst from beneath his belly into the top of his head. He never wanted to let go—especially now. He wanted to protect her.

"We're ok," she said, glancing beyond her shoulder at the Firebird. "Are you going to be alright?" She studied Kolya, her face pensive. "Zhar can bring you back to your family's estate."

Alexey paused—surprised by the question.

"That.. that won't be necessary," he assured her. "Kolya and I will be safe together on the ground."

Yaga chewed the inside of her cheek. Todorats was formidable—even for someone as strong as Alexey appeared. Yet, she knew Alexey was far safer with the wolf by his side than if he had been alone. She nodded hesitantly, releasing his hand as she and Vasilisa turned to walk back up the road towards Zhar.

"Tomorrow," Alexey called to her. "I want to see you tomorrow," he said, his voice firm.

Yaga paused, offering a soft smile before nodding solemnly. Climbing atop the back of the Firebird, she pulled Vasilisa up beside her. Soon, Zhar's wings expanded, and with several strong beats, she lifted them into the air—flying back through the darkness towards the cottage.

Alexey stood in the middle of the road next to Kolya, listening to the sound of the Firebird's wings fading into the distance. He glanced briefly towards the manor, knowing they would be safe—or at least, he hoped so. But, after seeing the horror that had befallen the poor fabric seller, he felt an urgency to return home, to protect his own family.

In case Todorats *did* return.

With his hand resting on the hilt of his dagger, he and Kolya walked back through the fields towards his family's estate. Together, they moved in the quiet—each more alert to the dangers lurking in the misty world beyond. Though—as they walked along, the fog began to slowly lift. A partition soon formed in the haze above their heads, the stars clearly visible against the midnight sky. Beneath the heavens, they pressed onward through the countryside—both man and wolf with a watchful ear to the wind.

The next morning, just as first light broke over Valen, Branka's groundskeeper crept passed the front door of the manor and onto the porch. He had tossed and turned throughout the night on a settee in the parlor—too scared to venture out of the house until after dawn.

A faint covering of mist still clung to the ground, swallowing his boots as he walked down the road. At first, he noticed the pushcart, abandoned and overturned—the fabric partially spilled across the path. Stepping closer, the hair on his neck stood on end, for, lying in the reeds nearby and half-covered by the foggy air, was the body of the fabric seller. Her dress had been soaked through with blood—the dark, crimson color still seeping into the damp earth by the roadside.

But it wasn't just the blood that turned his stomach; *the woman had no head.*

A surge of terror overtook him, and without a second thought, he spun around, running back towards the manor as fast as his legs would carry him. He barely stopped to breathe as he reached the stables, screaming for the stableman, his words tumbling over one another as he described what he had found—or rather, had not.

She had no head!

By midmorning, the news had spread like wildfire. In the town square, a large crowd had gathered—a low din of commotion flowing through like somber music played in a funeral procession. The shops were closed, the merchants standing idle—their faces tight with fear and suspicion.

Spotting the fabric seller's horse, Ruda, someone untied the poor creature, leading her away from the marketplace and into the warm stall of a nearby stable to rest. The horse, having heard the guttural scream of her master the night before, had spent the night standing upright on the cobblestones—her heart pounding with anguish for what had happened—and what might yet come.

Now in the daylight, the voices of the villagers had grown into a fearful cacophony—a sense of urgency rising into the air.

"Without a head! Could you imagine? The poor groundskeeper!" one villager shouted.

"Could it be wolves? Or—perhaps a bear?" another said.

The tension was palpable as they wondered aloud to one another.

171

The blacksmith, a large man with soot-streaked hands, lumbered into the center of the group.

"Yaga," he said, his voice low and ominous. "It could have been her. Everyone knows she has magic—who else could have done something like this?"

A few heads turned, nodding in quiet agreement, while others gasped with incredulity, shaking their heads as if to say *No! Certainly not Yaga.*

Then, another voice broke through.

"That's right! I saw what she did to Glúpyj's hands. Burned them clean off, she did! Magic like that—who knows what else she could be capable of!"

"And that massive bird with its blazing eyes she keeps—it could kill a man, I say! I saw it flying near the village just last night!" a woman shouted.

Anxious murmurs rippled through the crowd, the embers of suspicion stoked with every word. For some of them, a fearfulness twisted around Yaga's name, growing with each retelling of the rumors the villagers had heard.

Just then, Velimir stepped forward, raising a firm hand to quiet the crowd.

"Now, hold on," he said. "We've all known Yaga for a long, *long* time. She was born here, just like all of us. You've been going to her for help over the years—whenever you've had so much as a sniffle—and buying her soaps from me. She may have magic, yes—but it's not dark magic. And you..." he looked at the blacksmith directly, then back to the others, "You all know just as well as I that she's not capable of something so... *terrible.*"

The crowd quieted as they considered his words. It was true; Yaga was a bit odd, but they all knew her to be a kind and generous young woman. Someone to go to were they to fall ill—who rarely asked for much in return. In the silence that fell over the town square, the flames of accusation cooled. But it couldn't stop the rising tide of the villagers fears.

"What kind of evil is in these woods now?" Another woman called out as she clutched at her child next to her, pulling the young boy close.

"And why? *Why* is this happening?" yelled the potter, his booth boarded up behind him.

Just then, Mitza walked slowly into the center of the fray carrying a soap box in one hand. She tossed it to the ground with a thud, stepping onto it. She paused, her eyes scanning the villagers' faces.

"That's ENOUGH!" she shouted, her voice echoing across the cobblestones and down the adjoining streets.

"You all know quite well what's done this—you just don't want to admit it!"

A gasp rippled through the crowd, the villagers glancing round at one another.

"That's right! It's easier to point a finger at one of our own—because then we don't have to deal with the TRUTH!" Mitza said.

Now the crowd fell into a dead silence. Even the outspoken blacksmith said nothing. He feared, like the others, that to say the demon's name would summon it; that the creature might come for him, next.

"It was Todorats!" the boy exclaimed, his mother grabbing him and clasping her hand across his mouth to hush him.

It was true—no one wanted to admit that it had been Todorats. Yet they knew it at once when they heard the woman's head was nowhere to be found, her body carelessly discarded without so much as a scratch. Still, to think that the fabled creature of pure evil had stricken their small part of the world was utterly incomprehensible. Now, each of the villagers present was filled with a sense of rising dread—knowing that an unstoppable horror roamed freely through the countryside at night.

"How can we feel safe sending our children out with Todorats here?" a man shouted.

A wave of nods went through the crowd. Near the back, someone raised their voice.

"It might not have been Yaga, but maybe she still knows what's happening. She *must* know something!"

Just then, someone else remembered seeing Alexey the previous morning on his walk toward the cottage.

"That new boy, Alexey—he's been visiting her! Ask him to go speak with her. Then we can find out what's going on!"

The suggestion of Alexey sparked more commotion, with whispers of agreement all around.

"He's got a wolf," the potter said, his voice hushed. "Bigger than any wolf I've ever seen."

"Could a wolf do that—what happened to the woman?" somebody asked.

There was a pause as the crowd exchanged uneasy glances, as if trying to picture such a terrible thing.

"That wolf's no threat!" the town stableman declared, his muscular arms crossed over his chest. "But we should pay Alexey a visit—and send him to talk to Yaga!"

A chorus of agreement swept through the villagers as two other men, their faces resolute, flanked the stableman. They set off at once, marching together down the streets towards the Grishaev Estate, leaving those who remained to worry and whisper in the square.

The people of Valen were afraid now, and desperate for answers. They felt like children—huddled scared in the darkness as they clutched at the covers. Only—they hadn't awakened from a nightmare. Instead, the chilling, terrible dream had swallowed up the countryside and all of their homes and livelihoods with it. Now they hoped that someone—Yaga perhaps—could tell them there was nothing to be scared of, tucking them back down with soothing words into the safety and warmth of their beds.

Despite this vain hope, each of the villagers knew deep down that Todorats was a hellish, merciless fiend—and none of them would be safe so long as the monstrous demon could return.

Beyond Valen, deep in the shadowed woods where Yaga's cottage stood, things had settled into a state of worry and unease. Dobra had been pacing for hours; paranoid, he had begun lunging at the flickering shadows. The Kikimorra, too—normally a subtle presence haunting the corners of the house—had been unusually active since the killing. Now she scurried about, flashing in and out of sight, taking the forms of inanimate objects and the faces of strange, disembodied creatures. Since the scream, both House Spirits had been restless, disturbed by the dark energy now wrapping itself over the lands.

So, too, was the house itself—and all the things within it. Stones shook, vibrating in place, occasionally dropping off the shelves and landing with a thud upon the floor. The embers in the hearth crackled and popped, as though driven by unseen, angry bellows. Bottles clanked against one another on the worktable while pages of nearby books fluttered open before the covers slammed shut abruptly. There was a kind of madness that had been aroused in the anima of the things—as though the world around Yaga was effusing its discontent.

Sitting before the hearth—half ignoring the commotion of the restless house around her, Yaga's impassive face was illuminated by the orange glow of the fire. Within her mind, however, a torrent of concerns roiled, threatening to burst out from her entirely. She sensed it was her fault. That whatever was happening, she had caused it somehow. It was a crushing feeling—to think she could be at the center of someone else's demise.

For a brief moment, Yaga's eyes flicked to the cauldron—a vision of her mother's last moment cracking into her thoughts and sucking the wind from her lungs. She buried her head into her hands, her heart sinking down into her stomach.

You bring pain, she thought.

Upstairs, Vasilisa knelt before her loom, her hands whipping and pulling with a maddening intensity. Upon their arrival home the previous night, the Vila had whispered something to the Firebird beyond Yaga's hearing. Hugging Zhar's large neck, she had grasped a single feather, plucking it gently from the bird's breast. Now, she weaved it into the warp, the feather's shimmering blackness somehow refracting the light within the room like a prism.

At present, neither of the women sensed any immediate danger. The Firebird, alert and nestled above, was a formidable shield with her sharp, merciless claws. Yet, the specter of Todorats lurked inside the cottage with them still. Someone had died, and worse—the woman's death was tainted with an ancient, malevolent magic.

Both women knew the truth—that the signs had been there for weeks, creeping closer like shadows at the edges of their vision. First the creature lurking beyond the washroom window, and now, Todorats. Sinister things had been drawn to their part of the Thrice-Nine Kingdoms.

And now, more than ever, there was a question: what could they want with Yaga?

As Yaga sat before the fire, a chair materialized out of thin air beside her. It was the Kikimorra, no doubt. Remorseful for her irredeemable past, perhaps now she wanted to be seen as a comfort or a help. Yaga, however, ignored the House Spirit, her attention focused intently on her own thoughts. She stared at her hands resting upon her lap, noting the bits of bloodroot from the previous morning staining the flesh beneath her fingernails. Her breath hitched.

Just then, Vasilisa appeared at the top of the stairs, as though summoned by Yaga's worry. Yaga glanced up at her, then back at her hands, her face solemn. After a moment, she felt the small, doll-like hand of the Vila on her shoulder. Yaga lifted her head, staring into the fire, watching the flames lick up the iron belly of the cauldron.

"My quietings, Vasa. They have been pulling me to places filled with an energy that feels... *dark*."

Her gaze flicked towards the Vila as she sat on the chair beside her, then returned to the fire before them.

"It's as though something is pulling me in deeper, each time I leave my body," Yaga said. "There is a castle. And a boy. He has magic—I think." Yaga's brow furrowed as she tried to picture the boy in her mind. "The castle he's in—its musty and old. It feels soaked in—"

"Evil," Vasilisa said. She had felt the energy, too—a strange signature in the air that had accompanied Yaga as she came back into her body during each of the recent quietings.

Yaga glanced at Vasilisa. This was the first time Yaga had talked about the boy in the castle. She felt a strange solace that the Vila somehow had a shared knowledge of things—as though the burden was no longer Yaga's own to carry. In truth, she worried she was powerless, knowing nothing about where the boy was—or *who* he was.

Or, why she had returned to the castle—again and again.

"I just wish I knew the reason," Yaga said. She felt overwhelmed by responsibility now. And yet, she had no answers. Not yet.

Vasilisa tilted her head as though she were listening for something. For a moment, it was quiet—save the hissing and popping from beneath the cauldron.

"You need to go back, Yaga," Vasilisa said.

The Vila stood, placing her delicate hand on Yaga's shoulder once more. Yaga glanced up at her, her eyes searching her face for something—an answer, perhaps. Instead, Vasilisa turned, moving across the cottage towards the stairs. She was returning to the loom.

Alone again in front of the fire, Yaga's mind churned over the possibilities. She needed to know who the boy was—and who the castle belonged to. And she needed to know how it was connected to her—and to the creatures intruding into their peaceful world.

"It's the only way," Yaga said aloud, her voice hardening with resolve.

Suddenly, the Kikimora's form flashed, changing from the chair into a soft brown moth, flitting through the cottage towards the lantern by the staircase. In the warm amber light emanating from the hearth, Dobra soon appeared next to Yaga, his dark eyes staring up at her as though he wished to speak. Yaga patted her lap, inviting him up.

Nestling onto her legs, Dobra purred—though more for her comfort than his own. He knew, just like the other House Spirit, that Yaga's energy was changing—that *she* was changing.

And before long, nothing would ever be the same.

As the midafternoon sun filtered through the windows in the cottage, Yaga prepared for the quieting. She gathered up her kettle and a bundle of dried, freshly bound herbs. Gently, she slid a small wooden doll—given to her by her mother—from a shelf. It was a charm to keep her anchored to the physical world, and as she tucked it down into her apron pocket, she let out a sigh. She wanted to be prepared in every way possible.

With a lit beeswax candle in her hand, she climbed the twisting stairwell, making her way through each set of tapestries towards the inner sanctum. Inside, the space was quiet—wrapped in a heavy stillness and a lingering scent of smoke and tea. Beyond the smoke hole, a breeze rustled through the forest canopy, the leafy branches of the oaks scraping lightly over the wooden shingles of the roof.

Back in the bedroom, the Vila's fingers moved with focused intention over the loom. She had been working for hours—barely stopping to eat. From here, Vasilisa could keep a close read on Yaga—her senses attuned to the slightest shifts in magic. As her hands pushed and pulled the bits of fabric and yarn through the warp, the house fell into a quiet lull. Beyond the walls, the faint groaning of the trees cradling the cottage seemed to announce what came next.

Yaga sat down upon the sheepskin rug, steadying her breath. She knew that soon, the room around her would fade, leaving her spirit body in the liminal space beyond their world. She would cross it, hoping she could find answers.

For the boy, and for the villagers.

For the fabric seller.

And for herself.

Chapter Eight

THE BELL

For a single moment, the stillness of the inner sanctum merged with Yaga's consciousness. As her body lay on the sheepskin rug cradling her like a cocoon, her awareness spread out beyond the confines of her physical form, diffusing throughout the space. Then, her spirit drifted—slipping through the partition in the gossamer-like veil between worlds.

Yaga felt herself pulled through the ether—a sudden whooshing and popping sound ushering her beyond the bounds of her flesh. She felt herself whirring through the vastness of the space beyond the material, its hazy darkness passing over her like an endless, dense mist. Soon, she had the familiar sensation of her spirit body condensing within something.

She was back in the castle.

This time, it was a simple earthenware pitcher of warm milk that held her. Surrounded by the rough clay interior, the liquid contents gently sloshing back and forth within, Yaga felt herself carried along the corridors of the castle.

The hands holding the vessel belonged to a servant woman dressed in a dreary, slightly tattered frock—the threads worn bare in places and patched over in others. The garments were impossibly old—far older than the woman herself. Yet, the servant woman hardly took notice anymore, resigned to her gloomy, meager existence within the castle walls.

She moved quietly, though now she quickened her pace with every step. Her face was filled with a strange tension as she walked, her footsteps barely a whisper against the cold stone floors. By her side was another servant, herself carrying a neat stack of folded clothes. Yaga noticed the clothing items were small—most certainly for the child. The two women spoke in hushed tones, their voices edged with fear as they continued facing forward.

"Did you see him today?" one of the servants whispered.

The other servant's face tightened at the mention of the Sorcerer, shaking her head. "No, and I hope I don't—Master Koschei is more upset than usual."

Without a word, each of the women increased their pace, their eyes flicking up the hall and towards the blackened corridor behind them nervously.

For Yaga, the mention of the name Koschei landed with a heavy thud—a flash of recognition rippling through her consciousness. She had heard the name before; Sorcerer Koschei was an infamous monster from stories told to scare young children in her part of the Thrice-Nine. He appeared in tales about the before-times, passed down for hundreds—perhaps thousands—of years. Accounts of things that had happened in an era when magic had been abundant and the Old Gods walked amongst humans.

And yet—could it actually be him?

Was this really the castle of the immortal Sorcerer, Koschei the Deathless?

The servants had fallen back into silence, only the subtle sound of milk within the pitcher sloshing in time with the soft, rhythmic clacking of their heels over the stone floors. Soon, they stopped, reaching a simple wooden door. Yaga recognized it immediately by the heavy bolt securing it from opening—and the tremendous iron lock fashioned into the door itself. This was the boy's room.

From a small loop at her waistline, one of the servants inserted a key into the lock, turning it. Then, passing the pitcher to the other, she raised both of her arms, wrapping her hands over the heavy bolt above it and drawing it to the side with all her might. A loud clanging reverberated in the space around them. The second servant gave a soft knock, the door creaking open as the women let themselves inside.

They moved in silence, setting the pitcher down on a small wooden table and placing the folded clothing in a cupboard in the corner. Just as quickly as they had arrived, they exited, the door thudding shut behind them. Yaga, still inside the pitcher, heard the lock clicking closed, followed by the bang of the bolt sliding into place. Then, the muffled sound of the women's footsteps fading down the corridor.

As Yaga expanded her consciousness just beyond the vessel, she saw the boy sitting at a desk at the window, his small hands folded over his lap. She observed him, sensing a profound sadness—beneath which she could feel a quiet, steady magic humming from his slumped frame.

Abruptly—as though the boy sensed he was being watched, he lifted his head. Turning, he stared down at the floor, his face drawn and pale.

"I know you're here," he said.

Yaga's awareness sharpened, her consciousness lifting towards the ceiling. Taking in the chamber more fully, she could see the boy was completely alone.

Does he mean me?

Yaga was puzzled. She wished she could speak to him, a strange feeling of resonance arising within her; there was a connection between them; a thread pulling tighter.

The boy turned, his eyes fixing directly on the pitcher.

"You came through the smoke," he said quietly. "You look like her—my mother."

The words sent a jolt through Yaga's spirit.

His mother?

A vague, fragmented memory stirred within her—the face of a woman she hadn't thought of in years flashing before her mind's eye. *Aunt Mira.* Yaga's memories of her aunt were faint—her fair-skinned face framed by tawny waves of hair, out from which gleamed wide, amber-colored eyes in the shape of half-moons.

Mira had vanished from her life so long ago—almost as though she had never been there at all. Since then, she was a ghost haunting the edge of Yaga's memory. She had never learned why her Aunt had left—nor why she had come in the first place—or *from where*. Now, Mira was little more than a pale, beautiful shadow at the periphery of her early life.

The boy's words had pierced something between them. The need to speak to him burned within her, yet she remained utterly powerless. Still, she wanted desperately to ask him questions about where he was—and *why* he was there.

As though he could read her thoughts, the boy abruptly stood, walking toward the table and picking up the pitcher. He cupped it between his small hands, squinting down into the milky shadows within.

"You're not really in here, are you?" he asked, his eyes scanning back over the room despondently, as though he didn't expect an answer.

"Where are you really, Yaga?"

She was stunned. He knew her *name.*

A torrent of questions flooded her mind, the urge to speak growing with furious intensity. Perhaps the child sensed her frustration, for she heard his small voice piercing through her thoughts once more.

"I'm Ivan," he said.

Just as he had spoken the words, however, he fell silent.

Wait—what's happening, Ivan?

Yaga watched as the boy's expression changed, his body beginning to shake. And then, the sound of bootsteps—a methodical, slow walking up the corridor that abruptly stopped just outside the door. She glanced at Ivan, his faze frozen in fear.

Then, a heavy clanging sound as the iron bolt unlatched, followed by the click of the metal as the lock within the door turned. Ivan startled, the pitcher dropping from his hands. As it crashed to the floor, the pottery burst into shards, splattering the milk everywhere.

Without warning, Yaga's consciousness moved involuntarily to another object—this time into a brass bell mounted on the wall by the door. Slowly, the door swung open. In the darkness of the hallway, a shadowy figure loomed in silence. A cold, suffocating presence poured into the room like rolling fog, sending a chill through Yaga's spirit body. Across the room, Ivan stiffened, his eyes widening.

"What a mess," a voice hissed, still cloaked in shadow beyond the threshold.

Ivan's heart raced. The boy feared Koschei would find out about Yaga—that somehow he would know she was there. And if he did—if the Sorcerer knew about her—Ivan worried that he would hide him away again. Perhaps never to be found.

"Don't be slovenly, boy," the figure said, his voice carrying an edge of irritation. "I'm sure you'll have this cleaned up before your supper—won't you," the Sorcerer said, his tone threatening.

With a final disapproving sigh, the door to the room slammed closed abruptly—followed by a clanging sound of the iron locks once more. Soon, heavy footsteps echoed over the stone floor of the corridor beyond the door.

Grief and sorrow welled up within Yaga as she watched Ivan bend forward, collecting the broken pottery shards. She knew it had been the Sorcerer there in the darkness, his vile energy permeating the space. There could be no doubt that the child was terrified of Koschei. More than ever, Yaga knew with intensity that she needed Ivan to be *free* of this awful place.

And yet—knowing exactly where Ivan was being held would be a challenge. Despite how well-known Koschei was—his fabled tales of terror and domination passing amongst the Sclaveni across untold generations—there would be a certain difficulty in finding the Sorcerer. According to legend, he held dominion over the Dark Lands—a vast, mysterious region tucked far away in the Northwestern Thrice-Nine. It was filled with the ruins of eons past—ancient fortresses toppled and abandoned during the Sorcerer's supreme reign as a veritable god amongst men. No one ventured into those places anymore and returned to tell. So, while yellowed maps of the desolate terrain certainly existed, Yaga had no way of knowing where to begin.

Collecting the shards, Ivan's small fingers glistened with a dingy mixture of dirt and milk. With his face turned away from her, she heard him sigh—a soft sound of hopelessness and defeat over the wet scraping over the floor.

"Will you come for me?" Ivan asked. His voice was barely a trembling whisper now. "You are coming for me, aren't you, Yaga?"

She wanted to assure him that she would—that he would be free of this desolate place one day soon. Yet, the unanswered question of how to find him still swirled within her mind. Before she could gather her thoughts, however, a familiar voice cut through the haze, rippling through the liminal space itself.

"*Yaga... wake... up.*"

It was Vasilisa, and although the sound of her speaking wasn't loud, it was *everywhere*. The sound of the Vila's words reverberated over the walls, filling the air of the bedroom chamber.

"*Yaga. Yaga, wake up.*"

Her name, spoken across the folded fabric of the material plane, faded in and out—at times distant and inaudible. Yaga's grip on the bell began to weaken, and, though she tried to hold on, the Vila's voice pulled at her, tugging her back toward her body. Back to the cottage.

"Who is that?" Ivan asked, his small face twisting in confusion as his head craned around the room.

In an instant, Yaga sensed an impending shift; she was being pulled away again. The veil between the realms grew thinner by the second, the room blurring from view, the world of the castle fading away. Soon, the coldness of the stone walls was replaced once more by the warm glow of the cottage.

Yaga gasped as she felt the texture of the sheepskin rug upon her skin, her eyes jolting open. Above her, Vasilisa's expectant face greeted her from beneath a rose-colored kerchief.

"Yaga," she said quietly. "It's time."

The Sorcerer's boots clopped ominously as he slowly made his way down a long corridor. Even the sparse torches along the walls gave way, each bowing to Koschei's shadow as it loomed, winding its way toward a distant reach within the castle.

Soon, he had arrived in a large, cylindrical chamber. At the far end, an arched threshold led to a narrow spiral staircase. Koschei descended, and with every step, the air seemed to grow impossibly cold until his breath rose in plumes before his face. Unaffected beneath his fur robes, the Sorcerer continued downward into the castle's depths.

Now in the dungeon, the air was thick with the scent of mildew. Several torches cast an eerie glow over the space through which Koschei moved briskly, walking with purpose towards a heavy iron door off to one side.

With a simple flick of his wrist, a metallic clanging echoed around him. The door opened—untouched by his hands—revealing a rounded chamber. Within the room, dozens of pillar candles were arranged in a perfect circle. At the center, a massive, ancient sigil was etched over the stone façade of the floor. Koschei walked into the room, the pillar candles igniting at once as he stepped across the threshold.

This was Koschei's inner sanctum. As he stood in the center, the door closed with a heavy bang, the bolt sliding over and locking from within.

The Sorcerer flung his robes to the side. He struggled for a moment as he lowered his aging body down upon a single crimson cushion, the surface worn threadbare from years of use. Folding his legs in front of him, Koschei rested his long, bony fingers over his knees. Then, he closed his eyes, the deep silence of the space overtaking his awareness.

Yet, something gnawed at the edge of his mind. A restlessness now grew within him, threatening to take over his thoughts. The Sorcerer had felt a *disturbance* earlier. Something strange; a slight tear in the magic of the castle. Now, his mind would not still, the cause of the intrusion eluding him. He knew better than to ignore it, feeling exposed in some small way that he hadn't before. Not in a millennia or more.

It was as though he was being *watched.*

But—how?

His mind combed over the possibilities. For reasons he did not understand, pieces of his carefully laid plans were shifting. Something—someone—was interfering.

His eyes snapped open then, cold and calculating. There was work to be done—and though the strange new energy caused him pause, he had other important matters to attend to. At that very moment, far from the walls of the castle, past the arboreal borders of the Northwest Thrice-Nine, powerful forces were in motion. The Sorcerer could no longer ignore the shifts happening in the world outside his dominion. It seemed that life had continued beyond the borders of the darkened lands he reigned over, and soon, he would be forced to act.

Koschei took a deep breath. Exhaling sharply, he closed his eyes once more.

On the other side of a wall adjoining the inner sanctum sat an older man—a scribe with gray hairs flanking a balding scalp. He was accompanied by a messenger boy of no more than sixteen years. The two were positioned before a desk within a small, dimly lit room. The scribe, his breathing quick, worked diligently as the boy observed him tensely. The older man's hands labored nervously over a piece of parchment, each of his strokes crafted with meticulousness as sweat beaded on his brow. Even with the Sorcerer out of sight, Koschei seemed to loom in the shadows—the sinister promise of a threat were the man to err.

The scribe, his fingers stained black with ink, reread the message on the thin strip of parchment paper one last time. With a final scratch of words and a flourish of the quill, he rolled the paper up, handing it to the boy, their eyes meeting in the bated quiet.

"Be quick," the scribe instructed, his voice hushed. He cast a wary glance toward the stone wall separating them from Koschei's sanctum. "He does *not* tolerate delay."

His hands trembling slightly, the boy nodded. Swallowing hard, he held the message up before the light of a candle, eyeing it as he slipped it down within a metallic tube engraved with laurels and the rays of a sun. Soon, he had exited the room, his feet carrying him up the stone steps and beyond, out from the bowels of the castle.

He broke into a small run, his heart pounding in his chest. The boy felt a sense of desperation welling up; he did not want to disappoint the master. *Not ever.*

He climbed what seemed like hundreds of spiraling steps and crossed over long lengths of empty corridors, finally arriving at a small room with a single window. Along the far wall, there was a cage—within it, a sleek black bird. She was a carrier bird—a raven, bred for speed and endurance.

The boy squinted in the low light as he opened the wire door. Without prodding, the bird stepped out to a wooden perch affixed on the front of the cage, her black eyes gleaming as she stretched her neck and wings in anticipation. The messenger boy stooped over the creature, securing the metal tube containing the message to her leg as she waited patiently. After, he picked the raven up, moving her towards the window.

The raven's feathers glistened in the afternoon sunlight as the boy pushed open the pane of glass, placing her gently upon the sill. As soon as she could, the bird instinctively darted out into the open expanse of sky—the messenger boy's face becoming smaller and smaller as she ascended.

Now, the raven's wings sliced through the air, her body rising swiftly. The wind lifted her far beyond the castle, out over the countryside. Beneath her, forests stretched out like dark green seas, and beyond them, a blur of rolling hills sat cloaked beneath a thick blanket of fog. She moved quickly; the bird was driven by pure instinct, heading toward the distant land from whence she had come.

But the raven was not alone.

Unbeknownst to the bird, nestled within the metal tube strapped to her leg, Sorcerer Koschei's consciousness lay coiled like a waiting serpent. Long ago, he had mastered the art of forcing his consciousness into objects, inhabiting them and using them to spy. Now, after leaping from his body through the stone walls of the inner sanctum, the Sorcerer had passed into the metal tube just as the scribe was finishing.

He had a week—perhaps two—before he would need to return to his physical form. Everything would depend on a *reply*—lest the Sorcerer spend the rest of his existence bound to objects in a distant land.

It was a risk he was willing to take.

As the raven soared onward, the Sorcerer's awareness expanded outward. He seeped into the surrounding air, the rush of wind flowing through him as the motion of the bird's wings formed a steady rhythm. With the raven as his guide, Koschei was heading towards a place far beyond the edges of his dominion.

In truth, he understood little of the land to which he travelled—only that he was to go beyond the western wilds of the Northern Kingdoms. He would move past the vast expanse of the dominions he had conquered—heading out to a part of the Thrice-Nine he had never cared to know. Moving towards a sender who had somehow taken note of him at the far edge of the world.

As they moved, Koschei's thoughts continued to spin. He sensed with certainty that whoever waited for the bird at the other end of this journey was of great importance. Not merely a king or a lord—but *something else*. He recalled the message that the raven had brought to him; it bore a red waxen seal with the imprint of a dove. It's wings upturned, the bird's head sat beneath a crown of rays—like the sun. A halo. *A show of strength*, Koschei thought.

The Sorcerer's mind toiled over the identity of the sender. Though he himself was aging physically, he remained driven by an unquenchable thirst for *power*. So it seemed for another. Now, the world he had created was set to grow smaller. Yet, he had no intention of obeisance.

Not ever.

Instead, he needed answers; to know what lay beyond the Dark Lands and his ancient conquests of castles and forests, now overgrown and forgotten by the rest of the Kingdoms—until now. The Sorcerer wanted to see who would have the audacity—who would dare ask him for fealty.

Unaware of her cargo, the raven flew onward. Beneath her small body, the world of Koschei's dominion spread out like a bleak, tattered tapestry. It had been a long, long time since there had been movement on the skein of the Sorcerer's life. And now, as the warp shifted, so did his own sense of what could be possible.

What could be his.

Yaga blinked, still disoriented. She took in a deep breath, steadying herself. Her heart ached; the image of Ivan—his eyes pleading—emblazoned over her mind. She had no answers for him yet, but the weight of his suffering pressed down heavily upon her chest. Beside her, Vasilisa rested her hand with surprising firmness on Yaga's shoulder, as though to anchor her to the material world itself.

"Alexey is here," the Vila said softly. "He's waiting for you."

Slowly, Yaga sat upright, her body protesting what had been by far the most abrupt transition across the veil she had ever endured. She steadied herself on the small table before her, pushing up to her feet with trembling hands. Then, with Vasilisa slipping under her arm to shoulder some of her weight, she moved through the upper rooms and down the staircase.

Alexey, with Kolya at his side, stood in the doorway. His face was etched with concern as his eyes tracked Yaga moving slowly towards the lower level of the cottage. She glanced at him, immediately noticing the tightness of his expression. It was clear that whatever had brought him to her, it was urgent.

"Yaga," Alexey began as she neared the bottom. "It's the villagers. They're—they're scared. After what happened to the fabric seller, a few of them came to see me at my family's estate."

Yaga nodded. Already sensing the weight of what he was about to say, she gestured for him to sit in a nearby chair. Instead, Alexey lifted the chair with haste, placing it nearer to her as Vasilisa guided Yaga to sit down. Finding her way to its cushioned surface, she slumped forward, more exhausted than she realized.

Alexey knelt at the base of the chair, placing a hand lightly on her knee. She gazed at him wearily, taken by his gentleness despite the heaviness of his expression. It was as though he knew she didn't want or need this burden—whatever it was he was coming to tell her. And yet, things was different now in Valen, the townspeople justifiably afraid.

"What is it?" Yaga asked, her eyes searching his.

Alexey glanced at Vasilisa, then back to Yaga.

"The villagers ... they need answers. They're desperate to know what's happening... and how to stop it. No one feels safe."

Yaga's eyes flicked to Kolya, noticing his gaze trained upon her. He watched her intently, as though reading the impact of the sudden transition of her spirit slamming back into her body. He whined softly, resting his large head upon his paws on the floor, a worried groan escaping his muzzle.

"The villagers think that because you have magic, you can tell them what's been happening. They're worried, Yaga." Alexey paused, his gaze shifting in the direction of the village. He shook his head solemnly. "The townspeople are terrified."

Yaga closed her eyes, letting the weight of his words settle over her. She didn't want to be the one the townspeople turned to for answers. Not like this. She wanted her world to go back to the shape it had taken for so long—a peaceful, quiet existence. She wanted to heal people when needed and *stay out of the way*. She had worked hard to build a life where she answered to no one but herself. Her skills as a healer were precise and controlled; as long as she made no mistakes, she wouldn't have to hurt or disappoint anyone.

And yet—she had no real answers for the villagers.

Whatever was happening lay far outside her understanding of the world—each fragment of information murkily connected to one another within her psyche. Still, she knew the villagers were right to be afraid. The malevolent forces creeping into their small part of the Thrice-Nine were real. And dangerous. And, without question, Yaga knew these intrusions were connected to something far darker than any of them could understand—she and Vasilisa included.

What was even more daunting was her certainty that what had happened to the fabric seller was linked to her. And to Ivan, too

She inhaled deeply, her mind still churning. She didn't have all the answers—not yet. But the growing danger and the all-consuming fear of the people in Valen urged her to act. She would need to face the villagers—to hear them, no matter how much discomfort it brought her.

"I'll speak with them," Yaga said. She felt a twinge in her chest—a sense of trepidation for was to come. She closed her eyes, wishing in that instant that none of this were real. Yet—she couldn't shake the feeling that she already knew the truth.

That the killing was somehow her fault.

"I'll try to ease their minds... I'll..." Her voice trailed off as her gaze became distant.

Sensing her depletion, Vasilisa cradled Yaga's face within her small hands.

"First, you rest," she told her. The Vila turned towards Alexey. "Tomorrow—Yaga will sleep tonight and depart for Valen in the morning to meet with the villagers at the market square."

Yaga's eyes lifted towards Alexey one last time, her pupils carrying a strange haze that unsettled him. He bit the inside of his cheek, rising to his feet. With a nod, he moved towards the door of the cottage. Turning towards her once more, he gazed at Yaga with a mixture of gratitude and concern knit into his forehead.

"Yaga, please—get all the rest you need. I'll tell them you'll meet with them tomorrow." Without another word, he stooped below the threshold, departing into the autumn air with Kolya at his side.

Yaga turned her head towards Vasilisa. The Vila's face seemed to stare back at her silently—a certain kind of sturdiness contained in her expression.

"Thank you, friend," Yaga whispered, leaning her head to the side and resting it against the Vila's shoulder. She knew that sleep was the remedy she needed now to recover from the quieting—and to face the villagers the next morning.

After a few minutes, Vasilisa moved towards the hearth, collecting the kettle and a mug from a shelf in the kitchen. She placed a few sprigs of nettle into the cup, pouring hot water over them, their green juices steeping into the liquid. Yaga would need her strength. The nettles, along with food to nourish her and an early end to their day, was the most important thing right now.

As the Vila moved about the kitchen preparing a small meal for the two of them, Yaga centered her thoughts back on Ivan. Whatever lay ahead, she knew she would have to face it. Still—she wasn't at all certain *what exactly* she needed to do. And now, she would have to speak to the villagers—putting herself firmly in the center of their confusion and terror. She didn't want this responsibility—not any of it. And yet, here it was before her.

Yaga would have to act—to take a leap of faith in a direction where the path was unclear—her own peril uncertain. It seemed the fate of Ivan and Valen, indeed, of Yaga's entire world, now hung in the balance.

Chapter Nine

A GOLDEN APPLE

L ong before dawn had broken over the cottage, preparations for the day ahead had already begun. Yaga had been exhausted on all levels the previous afternoon, her consciousness seemingly lagging behind her body. Not long after Alexey had departed back to Valen, she had fallen into a deep, dreamless sleep. Hours later, she awoke to the rhythmic purring of Dobra, his furry body planted firmly upon her chest, his face expectant. And, though the urge to stay within the safety and comfort of her bed had been strong, eventually, the pressure of what awaited her finally won out.

It was just after first light when Alexey arrived with Kolya. His soft knock at the door surprised her, and as she opened it, he could see the expression of concern wrought over her face. Alexey knew the time of his arrival revealed he and the wolf had made the journey to the cottage in total darkness.

"We were fine," Alexey said, stooping to enter the cottage with Kolya following behind. The wolf turned in a circle before settling down over the wooden floorboards.

"I swear he's getting bigger by the day—even Todorats might think twice," Alexey added, flashing a toothy grin.

His smile vanished quickly as the grim reality of things settled back over them. Though Todorats was gone, it wasn't likely to be the last time that he, or another monstrous creature, came to terrorize the people of Valen. The Leshy's warning crept back into Alexey's mind: dark things were being drawn to Yaga—pulled to her. And, though Alexey knew little of Yaga's own understanding of things, he felt with certainty she hadn't caused it herself.

"I'll be ready to leave in just a moment," Yaga told him, interrupting his thoughts.

She glanced up the staircase. Vasilisa was asleep, having collapsed from exhaustion still seated before her loom, a shuttle of turquoise yarn held limply within her hand. Yaga had covered the Vila with a quilt shortly after waking, taking care not to disturb her. Now, she gave a half-smile as she considered her friend's diligent toiling over the loom. She paused briefly, considering it with quiet curiosity, before moving to the worktable to finish her preparations. It was nearly time to leave.

As Yaga readied for the trip to the village, Alexey stood by the door—he and Kolya each absorbed in watching her. Their eyes followed Yaga as she retrieved a leather satchel from a hook near the stairs. Returning to the worktable, she drew the flap back from the top of the bag.

And that's when something strange happened.

The book beside her—the grimoire—lifted right off the surface of the worktable, slipping down into her satchel all on its own.

Alexey's eyes flicked to Yaga, bewildered. He wondered if he had imagined it; after all, the last few days had been stressful and fraught. *Perhaps it had finally taken a toll on his mind.* Beneath him on the floor, Kolya tilted his head to the side—as though he too found the occurrence confounding.

Yaga, however, seemed oblivious. Instead, she simply twisted the brass clasp on the satchel closed as she made her way towards the front door.

Noticing Alexey's eyes fixed on the bag—his mouth slightly agape—she paused. She glanced at the satchel, then back to Alexey.

"Oh—it's not what it looks like," she told him, patting the book gently through the cloth.

Alexey scratched the back of his head.

"I mean—what it *looks* like... what was that, exactly?"

"I didn't make it move—or any of the other things. At least I don't think," she said, hesitantly.

"Other things?" Alexey asked curiously.

In truth, so much had been changing in Yaga's world, she wasn't at all certain what she really understood anymore. About *anything*.

She moved past him and out the door of the cottage, giving a soft smile.

"Come on," she said.

As Yaga and Alexey made their way through the forest, Kolya padding alongside them, a crisp autumn breeze drifted through the undergrowth. A few of the remaining leaves floated from the branches, each spiraling slowly towards the heavy blanket accumulated over the path.

As they crunched along in silence, Yaga—though filled with worry lately and little more—felt a strange sense of peace unfolding between them. It was as though, for just that moment, she had permission to leave her problems far, far away.

She glanced up at Alexey, her mind flashing to the time they shared beside the pond days before. She imagined his hand brushing over her cheek—the charge of energy she had felt coursing through her body at his touch.

Alexey paused, pulling a few low-hanging branches out of the way as they moved through a narrow section of the path. As Yaga passed beneath, he smiled down at her sweetly. She watched him duck below the branches, feeling her attraction for him returning. Her eyes swept over his strong physique. At his waist, she noticed his hand resting on the hilt of his dagger again. Catching her gaze, he grinned, hoping to keep the mood light for as long as possible.

"So…" he said, clearing his throat. "Books that move on their own?"

Yaga sighed, her eyes returning to the path ahead. As she moved, the dappled light filtered through the patchy canopy, her chestnut braid glinting as though woven with strands of gold. Alexey's heart leapt as he watched the parting of her curved, full lips while she considered her words.

"Well," she said, pulling her satchel tighter to her body, "ever since I was little, things around me just seemed to… move. On their own."

She glanced back up at Alexey, searching his expression—wondering if he thought her to be strange. Though, he only nodded silently, his face pensive.

"It's not me," she added. "At least, I don't think so."

Her brow furrowed slightly as she considered the best way to explain the phenomena. Stopping abruptly, her hand grasped at the twiggy branch of a shrub growing beside the path.

"What I mean is," she started. "Things have their own energy. I think they're responding to me. Or perhaps not? Honestly, I don't know anymore."

Yaga studied the twig as she chewed the inside of her lip. Alexey nodded, the two of them resuming their walk. For several minutes, the only sounds were the percussion of their bootsteps moving through the leafy duff, accompanied by the melody of a gentle breeze moving through the understory.

"I get it, actually," Alexey said.

He studied the crimson foliage of a cluster of shrubs as they continued down the path.

"My family—we're Karelian," he said. "Our people in the far Northern Thrice-Nine are animists."

Yaga paused, turning toward him. Alexey reached up, plucking a leaf from the air as it spiraled towards the ground between their bodies.

"It's just as you say, Yaga. Everything—this leaf, those stones," he said, gesturing towards the path. "Everything has their own energy. Their own anima. *A spirit.*"

"Exactly!" Yaga said, feeling for the first time that someone beyond the Vila and the Firebird understood.

"Though, I haven't actually ever seen..." Alexey looked back in the direction of the cottage.

"You haven't seen something move like that—like what happens with me," she finished, her expression changing.

Alexey shook his head.

"No—I haven't. Not that there's anything wrong with it," he said. "It's just, only certain people—certain kinds of people—talk to the spirit of things in that way."

Yaga's lips pressed together, her brow rumpling as her feet carried her forward along the path. Suddenly, she felt Alexey's warm hand clasp around her arm firmly. She turned to face him abruptly, her face twisting slightly; she felt she would never be truly understood by anyone but the Vila and Zhar.

"What I mean is that where I'm from, the people who speak to the anima of things are *special.*"

Alexey's gaze swept over Yaga, settling on her hazel eyes—the flecks of green within them catching in the sunlight. Beside them, Kolya stood silently, his gaze penetrating the understory beyond. Yaga glanced down at Alexey's hand gripped over her forearm. Suddenly, her heart began to beat harder within her chest. Gazing up into his eyes that appeared like sapphire oceans, she swallowed, her face flushing.

"Yaga, *you*... are special," Alexey said. He pulled her towards him then, each of them feeling the heat rise between their bodies. He wanted to hold her—to tell her everything would be ok. To tell her she was good. And *brave*.

He wanted to tell her what he felt for her.

Abruptly, Kolya let out a loud boof, his posture stiffening. Somewhere in the distance, something had moved. An animal—or perhaps the Leshy. Alexey's hand released Yaga's arm as it moved instinctively to the hilt of his dagger once more, pulling it up just slightly from the sheath. Yet, whatever it had been, it was silent now.

Alexey's eyes glanced back at Yaga, though the moment had passed—each of them rattled back to the reality before them. The villagers were afraid because they weren't safe. No one was.

"We should keep going," Yaga said.

Alexey nodded, scanning the shadowed woodland. As they walked ahead, his stomach twinged. He would have to tell her his feelings. *He had too.* Yet, this intense sense of connection he felt for her—which he hoped she shared—would have to wait.

Their pace quickened, and before long, they had stepped out into the meadow—now patched with frost-bitten browns over the green. In the distance, the village was visible beneath a bright, gray-toned sky. Forging ahead, they reached the road, winding their way towards Valen—each unable to escape the thoughts of what was to come.

The time to find the answers to this hardship was closing in around Yaga now. As she moved through the countryside, fear pressed down on her. With every step, she imagined some horror—the fabric seller, Ivan, and now the terrified villagers. Soon, her mind began to spin, pulling her thoughts in a dark direction. Images of her mother flashed before her, and of the cauldron.

Abruptly, Yaga felt Alexey's warm hand take hold of her own. Though, instead of stopping, he continued walking beside her—his hand firmly clasped around hers.

Casting her eyes up to him, he nodded, as if to say: you've got this.

Yet, despite the surprising sturdiness she felt in his presence, for the first time since her mother had passed, Yaga worried that she *wouldn't* be able to handle something. Or even if anything could be done at all about the mysterious chaos that had enveloped their lives.

Sensing her worry, Alexey squeezed her hand gently. As they continued the walk together, they remained connected this way, a pulse of energy moving between them. It was as though their hands fit together—their feet moving in sync up the road towards what lay ahead.

For Yaga, while she knew without question that Alexey could not share her burden, he seemed to care for her deeply. That alone, she felt, would be enough to face the villagers. She sighed. For now, she would consider what she understood with any certainty about recent events—and what she didn't. Perhaps the answers to the questions she turned over in her mind would lay somewhere in between.

At the market square, the villagers had already gathered in droves by the time Alexey and Yaga arrived. Their faces were pale with worry and unease, their postures stiff and defeated. As Yaga and Alexey made their way towards the center of the crowd, a wave of commotion and movement sparked. Whispers soon thrummed in the cold air like a hive of buzzing, disturbed bees. Soon the crowd pressed in around them, their voices taking on a desperate quality. They began shouting over one another, each plea more fearful than the last.

"Yaga, you must help us!"

"What's happening to our land, Yaga?"

"Tell us what more there is to come!"

Yaga stood still, letting the torrent of questions wash over her. She felt the villagers' panic. Her own instincts screamed at her to retreat—to run and leave this burden far behind. Yet, she knew she had a responsibility to talk to them. And to act, for without a doubt, the threads of her own existence were woven deeply within the changing fabric of their small part of the world.

She closed her eyes, her head throbbing from the mob's fever pitch. In her mind, she pictured Ivan's mortal skein, each strand interlocking with her own. Somehow, she and this boy—a nephew she hadn't known existed until now—were connected to the darkness seeping into Valen.

And so was Koschei.

Abruptly, Mitza appeared, tossing a soap box down onto the cobblestones next to Yaga. Yaga's eyes opened, shifting to Alexey, unsure of whether to take the next step. His gaze searched her own—as though to ask her if she were ready. She nodded, feeling him pull her up onto the wooden box's sturdy boards.

It was time.

Looking out over the group of villagers, she saw the fear in their faces—the terror that lingered in their eyes. She cleared her throat.

"I—I don't know what's happening," she said.

A wave of moans swept through the crowd—only for Mitza's voice to blare loudly above them.

"Let her speak!" Mitza commanded.

The crowd fell silent, all eyes turning toward Yaga.

"I... I'm as confused as all of you are—and I don't have all the answers. But I know someone who might," she said.

There was a bated silence as Yaga scanned the crowd. She paused, closing her eyes for a single moment as her hand gently pressed through the cloth of her satchel, feeling the shape of the grimoire beneath its fibers. The book had a certain sturdiness to it—a heft that felt just like the first time she had held it. She opened her eyes, the vision of the villagers spreading out before her like a painting—a still life of expectant, frightened faces.

"*Baba Roga,*" Yaga said.

An audible gasp ripped through the square, followed by an eerie hush. The villagers exchanged fearful, incredulous glances at one another, their mouths falling open in disbelief.

Alexey, too, stared at Yaga—his brow knit together with fear and alarm.

Not Baba Roga, he thought.

Yaga continued, her voice becoming steadier with every word.

"She knows things," Yaga said. She opened her satchel, pulling out the leather-bound book, its pages yellowed with age. Holding it above her head, she raised her voice beyond the growing chorus of concern starting to reverberate all around her.

"It's in here—she's in this book. This was my grandmother's, and it's filled with the stories of the before times—ancient tales about those with magical ability..." Yaga paused, her throat tightening.

"People like *me.*"

A gasp surged all around her, the villagers shaking their heads in disbelief. They had always known that Yaga was different—that she possessed magic, even. A floating vial here, a strange encounter there. By now, the villagers were used to her eccentricity.

But she was *nothing* like Baba Roga. The Cave Witch of the Sclaveni legends seemed *incomprehensibly dangerous.* In the minds of the villagers, now even uttering her name could invite misery and death.

"And for that reason," Yaga continued, "I must go to see her—to ask her for answers."

"Yaga! You can't!" Alexey blurted out, stepping towards her as the villagers' horrified gasps washed over the square once more.

He looked at Yaga pleadingly. He and every person there—indeed, everyone in the northern lands of the Thrice-Nine—knew well of the dangers she would face seeking Baba Roga. There had to be another way to find the answers they needed. The malodorous Cave Witch, with her beady eyes and bloodthirst—her gnashing *iron teeth*. She was more than a folktale. Hers was not a simple story like so many fabled others of the ancient world; Baba Roga was a *real* monster—just like Todorats.

But it wasn't just Alexey and the Sclaveni who knew the stories well: Roga's infamy was widespread amongst the many tribes of the Northern Thrice-Nine. From the reindeer-herding Karelians nestled next to the Ebon Tors at the northernmost edge of the world, to the eastern alpine tundra, their tribespeople banging out their love for the life-breath Selün Spirit upon drums while keeping time by the moon—*there were many who knew the demon Witch's name.*

Velimir stepped towards Yaga, his expression fearful.

"Surely, you can't mean to go alone, dear. She could hurt you," he said, hoping to change her mind.

Yaga glanced around at the villagers. Once more, she closed her eyes, centering herself, inhaling the crisp morning air down deep into her lungs. In that instant, she felt the tension of the moment slipping away, the autumn breeze brushing gently over her skin. She exhaled, opening her eyes once more—the green flecks within them glittering in the sun like jewels.

"I have to," Yaga said. Her voice resounded through the square, firm and decisive. "But I must go *alone*," she said, her eyes shifting to Alexey. "Baba Roga will eat anyone but another Witch."

Alexey's jaw tightened, his eyes flashing with frustration.

"Yaga, please—let me come with you. I'll stay hidden—I will," he said. "But you can't—"

Yaga shook her head.

"No. She'll sense you—and that would put us both in danger. I must do this alone."

A wave of defeat crashed over Alexey. He couldn't force her to stay—or to bring him. His heart sank into the pit growing within his stomach.

The crowd shifted uncomfortably now, each villager concerned for Yaga. That anyone could venture alone into Baba Roga's lair seemed preposterous. Yet—how much did they really understand of what Yaga was capable of—after all, *she too* was a Witch. She had a better chance than any of them to reach Baba Roga and live to tell.

Alexey's eyes scanned over the crowd. Yaga had made up her mind to go; she would not be swayed. Still, he wasn't ready to let her leave unprotected, and in an instant, an idea sparked.

"Take Kolya with you, then," Alexey said, his voice insistent. "Please—he'll stay back, outside of the cave. He won't interfere, I promise. But just *take* him—so he can be there if you need help."

Yaga hesitated, her gaze shifting towards the massive wolf. Kolya lifted his head, staring up at her. Apprehension filled her then; she didn't want to endanger anyone else. Yet, in that moment, she felt the grounding energy of the wolf's spirit. His presence was calm and steady—and something within told her he would be ok. Perhaps she didn't have to be completely alone in this fool's journey.

"Alright," she said, her forehead creasing. "Kolya comes, too. But the rest of you must stay here."

With her hand down at her side, she gave a tender squeeze to Alexey's arm. He swallowed hard as he helped her down from the wooden crate. This was not going to be easy for any of them—not for Yaga and Kolya, or those they would leave behind.

Reluctantly, the villagers accepted her decision. They began to disperse slowly, speaking in low tones amongst themselves, their eyes downcast. Stepping to the cobblestones, Yaga prepared to leave the square.

Suddenly, a small voice rang out over the din. It was a young girl, no more than twelve. She had been watching from her mother's close embrace.

"We believe in you, Yaga!" the girl said.

The market fell silent. Yaga turned, unsure of where the girl stood—touched by the certainty in the child's voice.

"That—that's right!" her mother echoed. "You can do this, Yaga!"

Now the tenor of the crowd began to change—a sense of growing reverence replacing the gravity of the moment. Their own Yaga. A healer of unmatched skill... *a Witch*.

"Yaga, thank you!" a man said, his wife nodding beside him.

"Show her what you're made of!" the blacksmith bellowed.

What followed was an uproar of cheering—the villagers shouting and whistling encouragement to Yaga as she made her way with Alexey and Kolya out of the market square.

The villagers' eyes followed her as she moved, each one of them now certain of her bravery.

For everyone, despite the fears that lingered for their own lives, a new-found sense of hope burgeoned—seemingly forged by Yaga's courage alone. Perhaps it really was true: Yaga could help them, saving Valen from this unknown and growing terror.

The villagers, more than ever, needed her— and now they were counting on her.

The walk back through the forest had been silent—the air between Yaga and Alexey heavy with tension. There was so much Alexey wanted to say—to protest—and yet, he knew she was right. Though he wanted to protect her, throwing his body before her to stop whatever lay waiting at

Roga's lair, he knew the truth deep down: Yaga could take care of herself. Still, his heart ached with fear—a burning spear plunged into its center.

Back at the cottage, with Kolya and Alexey waiting on the porch, Yaga began gathering what she needed for the journey. As she packed up food and a few supplies, her hands moved swiftly, though they trembled beneath the weight of the fear she carried. With her mind turned toward the confrontation ahead, her thoughts became a torrent of questions and concerns for the future.

Sitting by the hearth in silence, Vasilisa watched her.

"I know you have to do this alone, Yaga—so I won't try to stop you," the Vila said.

Yaga seemed not to hear her. Instead, she continued moving around the cottage, her mind and body locked into a frenzied holding pattern of preparation.

Bottles and stones started rattling upon the shelves then—books opening and closing with increasing agitation. All at once, a tremendous vibration moved through the walls around them, the floorboards creaking as the walls groaned. On the porch, Alexey and Kolya squinted through the windows, unsure of what was happening within the cottage. Yaga's pace quickened, her mind a blur of thoughts—of Ivan and the villagers. Of Baba Roga and Koschei.

"Yaga!" the Vila said, her voice dropping like a hammer upon the anvil of Yaga's consciousness.

Yaga stopped suddenly before the kitchen sink, her chest heaving. She leaned back, sinking to the floor.

"Breathe," Vasilisa said, her feet gliding toward the crumpled heap that had become Yaga's form.

She stooped over her, cradling her face within her hands. Yaga stared back at her through matted strands of chestnut hair that clung to her brow with sweat. The Vila's delicate hand brushed the hair away from

Yaga's sweat-covered brow— her lips quivering with fear in the dim light of the cottage.

"I... I don't think I can do this," Yaga said. "They're all counting on me. All of them! Vasa, I'm nobody—I'm—"

Vasilisa pulled Yaga's face against her small belly, cradling her hands around the back of her head. Yaga began to sob—the sound of her weeping muffled within the Vila's linen dress.

"It's ok, Yaga, *shh*..." Vasilisa said. She held onto her friend, patting the back of her neck.

The movements of the cottage and restless objects within began to slow—returning the space back to quiet. Soon, Yaga pulled her head away from the Vila, her face swollen and wet with tears. Vasilisa pulled the kerchief from her own face—her dark, empty eye sockets staring back at Yaga. Slowly, she dabbed Yaga's skin, drying her cheeks.

"Yaga—you are the strongest person I know," Vasilisa said. "It's ok to be afraid. Fear is good—it means you're alive. It means you have something to care for—to *fight* for."

Yaga blinked, soaking up her friend's words.

She was right. Yaga felt afraid *because* she cared. Because she was brave. And, though she was beyond tired—overwhelmed by the magnitude of what lay before her—she knew without question that she would continue. For the sake of everything she loved, she had to do the one thing she could: get answers from the only person who might have them.

Yaga lifted her gaze to Vasilisa. Taking a deep breath, she wiped away the last of her tears.

"Thank you, Vasa," she said, wrapping her arms around Vasilisa and hugging her tightly.

As she did so, worry suddenly flashed over Yaga's face.

Vasilisa peeled herself away, moving towards the hearth where she lifted a small log from a nearby stack of wood. Tossing it into the embers below, she turned back to face Yaga.

"I'll be fine," she said firmly. "Please don't worry about me. Now, how about a few of these rolls I made?" She moved to the worktable and began packing a small bag with butter, bread, and venison. Finishing, she placed it next to Yaga's satchel.

Yaga sighed as she watched the Vila. Vasilisa was by far the most capable person she knew. She couldn't let her worry for her friend overtake her now. There was too much at stake for her to lose sight of the plan. With a forceful inhale, she set an intention; from now on, she would focus only on the goal: find Baba Roga and get the answers they needed, before something worse happened in their world.

With the grimoire, along with its map of Baba Roga's bastion far to the northwest tucked safely inside her pack, Yaga stepped outside, followed by the Vila. It was late afternoon now as she approached Alexey and Kolya waiting at the bottom of the steps.

As she neared Alexey, he smiled up at her—though his eyes betrayed a deeper emotion. Her heart leapt; she wished they could be frozen in time together, as though encased in amber. Still, she resisted the thought. There would be time for their connection—whatever it was becoming—after she returned. *If* she returned.

As she stood next to him in the yard, the oak trees upon which the cottage rested began to creak and shift as the Firebird descended from her perch. They were connected—Zhar and Yaga—by some unseen thread, as though their minds worked in synchrony, like a mother and her child. Zhar landed in the yard nearby, stretching out her wings for the long flight ahead.

Together, Yaga, Vasilisa, Alexey, and Kolya walked towards the Firebird. Yaga could feel Alexey's trepidation as he walked beside her—the type of concern that can only come from one place: love. For a single moment, she was taken aback as she considered the weight of how he might feel in this position—powerless to change the course of something for someone he might care for. She pushed the thought aside, however—her mind shifting to the immediacy of her departure, and what lay ahead.

Soon, Yaga and Kolya climbed atop the back of the Firebird, settling down into the thick plumes of her feathers. As they nestled in, Yaga noticed once more how grounding the wolf's presence was. He would have to remain hidden somehow, yet there was something about his energy that gave her a sense of safety. A traveler from afar, he was not of their world. Now, they would journey together into a land from where few returned. She smiled at him, her heart sparking with gratitude for his presence—and for Alexey having pushed her to accept the help of another.

From atop the Firebird's back, Yaga looked to where her friends remained on the ground. She was struck in that moment by the differences between Alexey and Vasilisa. Alexey towered above the small Vila, his face perfect—his body muscular and broad. Yet, there was something rugged and unruly about him; something feral and unbridled. Vasilisa, on the other hand, seemed scarred and frail—yet she exuded an unmatched poise and quiet, almost regal confidence. Yaga smiled, thinking how fortunate she was to have such loyal, unique companions—one like a sister to her, the other quickly becoming something altogether new and unfamiliar. She nodded at them—her strength growing in her realization that she could count on them. For anything.

Pausing, Yaga grounded herself once more, turning her attention to Zhar. To get to Baba Roga's cave—located high in a range of cavernous mountains—the Firebird would have to fly for at least two days. There would be little—if any—time for her to stop and rest. Yaga closed her eyes, placing her palm between the tufts of the Firebird's feathers, onto her warm skin below. Their connection, made of magic and loyalty—of love, and trust—pulsed between Yaga's hand and the bird's flesh.

Thank you, Zhar.

Without a sound, the Firebird spread her massive wings, lifting Yaga and Kolya up into the gray sky. Alexey and Vasilisa looked on as the Firebird ascended far above the countryside.

Soon, she soared over the forest, leaving the cottage within the clearing as a faint, distant speck. Beneath Zhar and her riders, rolling fields cut by streams stretched out in all directions—a patchwork quilt of tree-covered hills and meadowlands. With everything cloaked in long shadows, Yaga, Kolya, and the Firebird barreled onward in the direction of the setting sun.

Throughout the afternoon and deep into the night, Zhar flew. Her massive body, floating over vast forests and rivers, moved like a whale through the sea. Occasionally, the signs of a quiet village would appear, a small cluster of lights settled amongst rolling hills. Yaga watched as the world passed by below them, wondering about the people in those places—curious about their lives.

By sunrise, they had stopped to rest in a small grove of birch trees. It was a chance to stretch their bodies and drink from a spring—yet there was no time to linger. Baba Roga's cave lay far beyond the reach of normal travelers, and Yaga knew that they were fighting against time to help the villagers of Valen.

And Ivan.

For much of the journey, Yaga had snuggled against Kolya's heavy frame, the two of them tucked down beneath the feathers on Zhar's back. Yaga combed over her thoughts, again and again, for everything she knew about the boy in the castle—and what she didn't. And the creatures she feared were drawn to her—where had they come from? *And why?*

These thoughts and more filled her mind—only ceasing when she drifted into a dreamless sleep. But by the time the following day stretched towards dusk, Yaga's previous feelings of dread and worry had been all but replaced by a newfound sense of resolve. Her belly burned with a fire now—a determination to find answers. She would find the *truth*.

As the evening sun descended, the landscape was cast in hues of pink and orange—seemingly in defiance of the oppressive cold swallowing the world around them. They were soaring over the jagged, western mountains now—craggy cliffs and limestone spires sparsely dotted with twisting, gnarled trees. Snow dusted the ground below them—the last villages having long disappeared from view. A palpable shift permeated the air—an old, dark magic growing all around them.

They were nearing Baba Roga's lair.

With every passing second, Zhar moved closer to the ground. In the fading daylight, a barren no-man's land was revealed—the hair on Yaga's neck standing on end as Kolya stiffened. Soon, the trees had disappeared, save for a few deformed and tangled masses whose frames seemed to claw towards the darkness itself.

And in the distance beyond, the soft glow of two fires.

Yaga squinted as they drew nearer to the flames. She had an eerie sense that somehow, Baba Roga *knew* they were coming. Descending, they passed through a rolling blanket of fog, Yaga's cheeks burning in the frigid, damp mountain air. Soon, the mouth of a cave came into view, its gaping blackness flanked by two large torches.

And then, she saw the bones.

Yaga glanced at Kolya, who sniffed intently. The breeze was filled with the smell of death—a musty stench of decay and rot that hovered over the landscape. This was a bad place, Baba Roga's dominion. It was a place one did not come back from.

Yaga scanned the ground, the bones of untold numbers of men and beasts piled up into heaps and elsewhere scattered across the craggy mountainside beyond the mouth of the cave. A chill ran down Yaga's spine just as Zhar let out thin whimper. The sound startled her, for the majestic bird rarely made noise at all, save the beating of her massive wings. Yaga knew the Firebird sensed evil here. And, although she wanted to turn and take her passengers far, far away—she pressed on.

In the darkness, Yaga dismounted—her boots crunching down on the gravel beneath. As Kolya stepped to the ground, he emitted a growl, low and fierce—as if to tell her he sensed immediate danger. She nodded at the wolf, her eyes passing over the shadowed terrain as her feet carried her towards the entrance of the cave. They moved in silence as Zhar ascended toward the top of a lone, towering tree upon a nearby cliff where she would wait in restless anticipation until she was needed.

Drawing in a breath, Yaga steeled herself for what was to come; she knew Baba Roga would not give answers easily. There would be a trick—or a trade. And she would have to face the formidable Witch alone.

Standing at the entrance of the cave, Yaga peered down into the dark chasm with trepidation. Her eyes flicking to the periphery, she watched as Kolya walked intently to a nearby pile of bones. As the wolf rummaged around, Yaga studied him, her nose wrinkling. He began tugging at a large bone, its end slicked with something oiled and fleshy. Padding towards her, he dropped it at her feet, looking up at her expectantly.

Yaga knelt to pick it up, shuddering at the greasy film dripping off one end. Her gaze searched Kolya's eyes, the flames of the torches reflecting over their amber spheres. Instantly, she understood him; this was to be her torchlight.

At once, Yaga moved to one of the large, eternal flames at the front of the cave. She plunged the end of the bone into the fire. A terrible scent of burning gristle billowed into the air, filling her lungs. She coughed, gagging—trying hard not to vomit. *This will have to do*, she thought. With a final nod at Kolya, she stepped into the cave—its mouth swallowing up her form into darkness.

Descending deeper, Yaga's footsteps echoed off the damp, jagged walls. As she moved, the small ember on the end of her stick revealed the gruesome details of Baba Roga's lair—piles of human bones, broken and scattered over the entirety of the passage.

The air within—thick with the smell of must and decay—had grown considerably warmer with each passing minute, forcing her to undo the front of her heavy coat. Yaga's stomach churned, for in the moist air, rotting flesh of years past flowed into greasy pools scattered across the path.

All around her, Yaga saw signs she might come to regret this journey. She really hadn't been able to fathom what the Cave Witch was capable of. Now, she moved past collections of skulls set atop ledges and hanging off boney limbs like fence posts, each one staring back at her with empty, hollow eyes. Every so often, with their jaws agape, one seemed to warn, *"Go back! Go back while you still can!"*

The twisted skeletons of fallen beasts, too, lay strewn across the floor as she passed, forcing Yaga to climb over them like fallen logs. And then there were the stains on the walls—though she dared not examine them too closely, the remnants of dark rituals she shuddered to imagine.

More than once, Yaga caught her breath as she passed by piles of gold and silver coins—and jewels. Thousands of sparkling gem-encrusted rings and necklaces mixed in with the bullion, stacked and heaped in ambivalent disarray. There was even a crown—its rubies and emeralds embedded in gold and gleaming in the low light of the torch. All the riches of the world, it seemed. All abandoned, for Baba Roga had no use for the shallow desires of men.

No—she wanted misery and death more than anything. It was rare that someone escaped alive from her lair, or so the stories told. Her captives would have to offer her far more than fame and fortune if they were to bargain for their freedom. Roga, possessed of an ancient magic that hungered endlessly, was much more interested in destruction. She wanted *chaos*.

Pressing on, Yaga feared she would have nothing worthwhile to trade to the demon Witch. Nonetheless, she kept her resolve as she moved through the bone-laden passage. Perhaps she would want a favor—or something that held meaning beyond the value of glittering stones. Yaga knew she had little to barter that would be of use to Roga. She considered the grimoire in her satchel, wincing. It was her most prized possession.

As she rounded a corner, she passed a headless skeleton, the bones seemingly chewed upon. She cringed, knowing full well the terrifying stories of Baba Roga's iron teeth—how they tore through bones and more with ease. She thought of the image in the grimoire that rendered Baba Roga with a gaping mouth and a single, massive horn protruding from her forehead—a dark symbol of the ancient power she wielded.

Yaga closed her eyes, centering herself. She focused on her breath for a moment—every inhale and exhale a chance to become more grounded. Peering down the dark passage once more, she felt her fear pushed off to the edges of her mind just enough. She would need to stay strong, knowing only one thing with any certainty: if there was anyone who could help Yaga get the answers she needed, it would be the ghoulish being dwelling in the depths of this cave.

Soon, after stooping to pass through a narrow part of the passage, Yaga saw the light of a large fire. Shadows spanned upward along the walls of the cave, the pathway widening into a vaulted chamber. She continued on, her eyes focusing toward the center of the room. There, standing with her back to Yaga, stood Baba Roga. She was hunched over a cauldron, humming a dissonant melody. As Yaga took another step forward, an abrupt silence fell over the space.

Yaga froze, her heart pounding.

Baba Roga remained standing there, her hands busily dropping items into the bubbling amalgam before her.

"Well, well, well. What have we here?" She opened a jar, tossing a screeching creature into the roiling liquid.

Plop.

Yaga stood silently, the small ember on her stick wafting a tiny plume of smoke around her.

"Ah, well, it's disappointing, really. I had been hoping for a *different* kind of company," Baba Roga continued, licking her lips.

Abruptly, she turned in Yaga's direction, her face illuminated by several torches in the room. In the orange glow, Yaga could see the Cave Witch's wild, menacing eyes, and a massive, smiling mouth lined with rows of giant, iron teeth. Yaga let out a small gasp, though she quickly straightened, attempting to regain her composure.

In the low light, Baba Roga squinted, studying Yaga.

"Ugh, such a pity. I mean—you *really do* look delicious," Roga told her. "But that book in your bag is correct—I won't kill you," she continued, though she paused.

"Probably."

Yaga swallowed hard. She knew she had to ask for the Witch's help. And, while she might very well die in this forsaken place, it was a risk she was willing to take. *It's now or never*, she thought. Yet, before the words could leave her mouth, she heard Baba Roga's voice.

"You've come," Baba Roga croaked, gliding eerily across the chamber towards Yaga and circling around her, "for the boy."

Yaga inhaled sharply, setting aside her fear.

"I need answers," Yaga said. "There is a darkness that's been drawn to the village where I live. And to me. I've—I've come to try to understand *why*."

Baba Roga stopped her pacing, positioning herself squarely in front of her. Yaga was struck by how slight the Cave Witch actually was; such power in so frail a form. Roga tilted her head, her gaze penetrating as she studied the young woman before her. After a moment, she shrugged, walking back towards a stone table across the room, calling out behind her as she did.

"Yes, well. The boy, the Sorcerer, the beasts... It's all the same really."

Yaga raised her eyebrow. Baba Roga *did know* about the connection. She took a step forward again, her persistence growing.

"Yes, and I—I need to understand why these things are happening. That's the reason I'm here," she finished.

Back at her table, Baba Roga began fiddling with an assortment of items, shifting them around with purposeful movements—bones, stones, and other objects. She was aligning them into a circle, creating a sort of sigil and muttering to herself.

"Mmm... yes. Answers. You. Seek."

She paused, jerking her head in Yaga's direction and staring at her from across the room—her eyes strange, black beads reflecting light from the nearby torches. Her gaze was unsettling, though soon she had turned once more to her preparations at the table.

"Then we shall have a trade. Your wolf—I am so, *so hungry*," Baba Roga said, her smile widening as she began to hum—this time a low, gravelly sound emanating from deep in her throat. She gave a small chuckle, glancing over at the pot of liquid bubbling away.

"No," Yaga said firmly. "He's not for trade."

219

Baba Roga stopped her movements, cocking her head slightly. She was amused by Yaga's defiance. *How remarkably brave*, the Cave Witch thought. Seemingly, the bone yard—with all its fetid horrors—had been no deterrent to this girl's courage. A smile crept at the corners of her giant mouth, her iron teeth glinting faintly in the firelight. Her eyebrows raised, she turned back to the items on her table, continuing to arrange them.

"I see," she murmured. "Very well, then. I'll take a feather from the Zhar-Ptitsa." Roga smirked, though she did not look up. To refuse again would be a very defiant action, indeed. She licked her lips.

Yaga blinked, swallowing hard. She knew Zhar would be uneasy with the act of giving such a malodorous creature as Baba Roga one of her feathers. Each one was laced with an ancient magic—a wish for whoso-ever received one. To be given one was a singular opportunity, with the potential to confer great power once the wish was granted.

Yaga squirmed inside at the idea of giving the Cave Witch such potent magic. Yet—for Baba Roga to eat Kolya was out of the question. So was leaving without answers. Yaga stiffened, knowing she had no other choice. The information she sought might well determine the fate of her people—and of Ivan.

"Ok," Yaga said, her face solemn.

The quiet of the cave shattered suddenly as a loud, raucous cackle burst out of Baba Roga. It was a throaty, primal sound that rattled the bones scattered over the floor, echoing throughout the cave.

"Good," Baba Roga hissed. *"Then we shall begin."*

Without warning, the Cave Witch moved with unsettling speed, her body barreling towards Yaga. She grabbed Yaga by the shoulders with ancient, gnarled hands, dragging her hastily towards a large dripstone glinting at the edge of the chamber, its tip sharpened into a point. Baba Roga yanked Yaga's hand beneath it, plunging it upward, the tip of the stone piercing into her flesh. Yaga screeched in pain as blood pooled within her palm. Yet, before she could react, Baba Roga had whisked her over to a small woven mat beside the wall of the cave. Holding a shallow bowl below her hand, Roga balled Yaga's hand into a fist.

She squeezed *hard*, blood pouring down into the bowl.

"*Oww!*" Yaga cried, wincing in pain as Baba Roga pushed her backwards.

"*Sit,*" Baba Roga commanded.

Yaga landed with a thud upon the mat. She steadied herself, her eyes widening with confusion. *What's happening?* She gripped her hand, pressing into her palm to stop the blood from seeping out.

Then she watched as Baba Roga returned to the table, snatching fistfuls of dried herbs, strange fats, and substances Yaga could scarcely identify at a distance. The Cave Witch's body whirled about, a dissonant hum emanating from within that reverberated through the depths of the caverns connected to the chamber.

Roga was working diligently on... *something*.

Occasionally, a small, ghoulish chuckle punctuated her humming—a strange detail that only increased Yaga's alarm. Yet, she continued watching as Baba Roga mixed the strange assortment of items together in a rough stone bowl—a foul smell wafting through the air.

Yaga grimaced, and, for a moment, she contemplated running.

"*I. Wouldn't. Do. That,*" the Cave Witch warned, her voice lilting as though she were singing a song. Her eyes gleamed menacingly in the light as she continued her intensive focus on the items before her.

Soon, she had transferred the mixture into the bowl of Yaga's blood. In the low light, Yaga could see it was a dish carved from the bone of some unknown creature. Roga lit the contents aflame, then walked swiftly towards Yaga at the wall of the cave. The smoke billowing out from the bowl was thick and acrid—the smell causing Yaga's stomach to churn. By the time the Cave Witch stood in front of her, the smoke had died out; within the bowl, only ashes remained. There was a short pause as Roga stared down at Yaga, her eyes seeming especially deranged. Her mouth widened into a gaping grin.

Without warning, Baba Roga bent forward, blowing the ashes within the dish straight into Yaga's face. Yaga gasped as the putrid substance filled her lungs. Her chest tightened as she coughed, a sputtering panic seizing her. She gasped, clutching desperately at her throat.

I'm choking! I'm dying!

Then her eyesight blurred, a torrent of energy slamming into her body. Yaga slumped backwards, her last vision only Baba Roga looming over her, a fiendish cackle echoing throughout the chamber.

Yaga felt her consciousness shattering immediately—as though she was disintegrating, reforming, and breaking apart, again and again. Voices screamed within her mind as a flood of images flashed before her eyes. She felt her body hurtling across time and space as strange shapes, colors she had no names for, and symbols from worlds long forgotten moved like a river over her mind's eye. She was being pulled through a maelstrom of magic—her spirit slingshot across an endless void. Until, in an instant, she was somewhere else.

Yaga focused her awareness as the sound of a howling breeze filled her senses. Above her, wispy white clouds dotted over an abyss of blue sky. As she looked around, she noticed she was in a nest of some kind. She expanded her vision—hoping to see things more clearly.

Her consciousness had been projected into a single large egg. It was tucked snugly within a giant nest, perched upon a twisting, massive tree. The tree grew perilously out from the side of a cliff, against which a moaning wind whipped in gusts. Beyond the tree—a vast, sparkling blue sea. It was a tremendous sight—yet seemed strangely desolate.

How will I find answers here? She wondered.

No sooner had the thought arisen, Yaga heard the heavy flapping of massive wings. A giant bird—its head that of a beautiful woman—landed upon the edge of the nest. The Birdwoman's hair flowed like black coils of rope over her shoulders, her plumage a kaleidoscope of shimmering color. Yaga recognized the towering creature from Sclaveni lore; this was an ancient, all-knowing being of magic—the *Gamyun.*

The Birdwoman's eyes sparkled like amethysts as she peered down at the egg. She spoke to Yaga through her thoughts, her lips unmoving.

"You... are familiar," she said, her head tilting to one side.

The Gamyun's voice sounded like a soft, gossamer echo within Yaga's mind. The Birdwoman studied the egg as though she could see Yaga within it.

"Why have you come?"

Yaga summoned a response within her own consciousness.

"I'm here to find answers," she said.

The wind began to pick up, blowing across the body of the Gamyun, her feathers whipping violently in all directions.

"There are dark beasts that have come to my village. And there is a boy, Ivan. He's kept in a castle by a Sorcerer—Koschei," Yaga said.

At the mention of the Sorcerer's name, the Birdwoman seemed startled, her eyes growing wide. A crack of lightning, followed by a colossal clap of thunder filled the air around them as the clear sky suddenly flashed to gray.

"Koschei!" The Gamyun boomed, her voice reverberating through Yaga's consciousness. *"And who are YOU?"*

The Gamyun clutched at the egg with her massive, clawed foot, as though she might break it. The air above her swirled—arcs of lightning snaking beyond her head. Terrified, Yaga continued.

"My name is Yaga, and I'm... I'm here to help my people. I'm here to..."

Suddenly, the Birdwoman released the egg back into the nest, the expression on her face shifting. The sky above her flashed to pale blue once more, the only sounds now the howling coastal winds against the bluffs.

"Yaga," she said, her voice softer.

The Gamyun closed her eyes. She turned her face towards the breeze, her feathers moving in waves like a wind-swept grassland. Yaga watched the Birdwoman intently—unsure of what would come next. The Gamyun seemed deep in thought—as though she were considering something she hadn't thought of for a long time. Opening her eyes, the Birdwoman gazed off into the distance as though witnessing something in the abyss beyond.

Suddenly, she turned back to face the egg that held Yaga's consciousness. What she said next would change Yaga's life forever.

"The world has been waiting for you, Yaga Luchanova."

The Gamyun's words penetrated deep into her psyche as though it were a key unlocking an ancient chest of secrets—a torrent of sensations flooding through Yaga's spirit. There was silence as Yaga searched the Birdwoman's eyes.

"How—how do you know my name?"

The sound of the moaning wind permeated the air between them, the surface of the sea glittering like diamonds behind the Birdwoman. In bated silence, Yaga waited for the Gamyun to answer.

"I can show you the answers you seek."

Without warning, a multitude of images appeared before Yaga's eyes. A blurry, dream-like vision replaced the nest and the world beyond. Now, Yaga saw a field—and within it, a young man wearing a long black cape.

"This is a story of immortality and curses," began the Gamyun, her voice an ethereal, distant whisper resounding through Yaga's consciousness.

The Gamyun told Yaga a story then—of a young Sorcerer's ambition to kill one of the Birdwoman's sisters, the *Sirin*.

Throughout time, men who listened to the song of the Sirin had been forever cursed to search for her. Cruelly, they were invariably unable to find her—their minds plunging into *madness*. Poor spirits, forever lost to the world, their lives were laid to waste and ruin. In the time of the ancients, this was how things were: magic could give, and magic could *take*.

One afternoon, Koschei—then young and strong—made his way through a field of wheat. The midday sun beat down over the rolling, tawny grasses, warming his dark cloak as he walked. He was heading straight towards an apple tree at the center of the field—the nesting place of the Sirin bird. He wasted no time, ambushing the unsuspecting Birdwoman who rested in the boughs of the tree.

He wanted her *dead*.

Wrapping his hands around the bird's neck, a torch emanated from his palm. The young Sorcerer was ready to end her life. Yet, just as he was about to kill her, her other sister—the *Alkonost*—appeared. Alighting on the branch beside them, the Alkonost wept desperately, begging Koschei to spare her beloved sister.

The Alkonost was a creature of pure peace—a symbol of happiness and mirth. As she sobbed, her tears fell over the tree below, dripping like rain upon the branches and the apples they held. As she pleaded for mercy, the Alkonost's agony rippled over the field like a shiver, where it reached the Goddess Noonwraith who stood threshing wheat nearby, a sickle in her hand.

Taking pity on the Alkonost and her sister, the Noonwraith walked towards the tree, her blonde braid dragging through the wheat behind her. Her voice moved like a soft song through the air, calling out to intervene.

Seeing the Sirin's death was imminent, the Noonwraith offered to grant the Sorcerer a form of immortality—twisted as it was. It was exactly midday when she proclaimed that Koschei could live forever, his own spirit transferred into the physical form of his male descendants upon their twelfth birthday. One year of life, they would be given—for every hour that had passed that day before he had captured the Sirin.

For as long as his spirit remained within a male descendant's form, the Noonwraith promised, the Sorcerer would be *immortal*. Within each vessel, Koschei would retain his own magical gifts—along with the original power of the descendant, so long as their body walked upon the earth.

The Sorcerer paused, his hands still gripping the neck of the Sirin as he considered the offer before him. The curse was cruel, for Koschei would never know the everlasting joy of loving his own child. The cycle would only repeat—a constant reminder to him of his unnatural need for power. Yet—Koschei's heart had long been dark, and this grim prospect had no bearing. Driven by a dark contempt, the young Sorcerer agreed, releasing the Sirin in disgust.

Yet, before he could descend from the tree, another goddess, Devanna, appeared. She was the most ancient goddess of their world, ruling over all of Yav. A fierce protector of balance in the realm, she had been watching from a nearby grove of oaks. Her blood boiled at the Sorcerer's defiance of the natural law; he was a merciless killer—obeying no god and loving no other.

In an instant, her words rang out across the field like a thunderclap. Each and every drop of the Alkonost's tears, she proclaimed, would one day be the source of Koschei's demise. Having fallen upon the apples of the tree, they would one day bear the fruit which would destroy him. And so would the Sorcerer.

Devanna commanded then that on a full moon, each and every tree within its line would produce *a golden apple*. When consumed by a female descendant of the Sorcerer, this apple would grant her the power to end his life *forever.*

As Devanna said these final words, every apple upon the tree dropped from its branch, hovering but for a single moment in the air. Then, in a flash, the apples hurtled away at an unfathomable speed, moving outward in every direction. Disappearing far into the distance, the apples, fueled by Devanna's magic, had been sent to the farthest reaches of the Thrice-Nine Kingdoms.

Koschei's face twisted into an arrogant smile as he descended, his black boots stomping over the wheat below him.

"No matter," he told Devanna, his eyes narrowing as a sinister expression formed over his face.

As the goddesses looked on, Koschei turned, departing through the field. With a wave of his hands, he set the field ablaze, a roaring fire rendering the dry grasses to ash. Behind him, the apple tree, too, erupted into a towering pyre—the Birdwomen flying off in escape towards the horizon line. Then, Sorcerer Koschei slipped from view, disappearing behind a thick black wall of smoke.

As the story wove itself through Yaga's consciousness, the Gamyun addressed her once more.

"For three millennia, the dark Sorcerer has taken the life of every female heir. No daughters had ever been spared—until Vesna and Mira."

Finding herself back within the nest, Yaga steadied her consciousness, still disoriented by the shift.

"Yaga—you are the female descendant who will end his reign, born of a secret line hidden away by your real grandmother. The manchild Ivan was born to the only daughter the Sorcerer has ever known. He spared Mira in

his desperation to live, lest he perish without a vessel. The boy's spirit is pure, though he is the most powerful male descendant to ever be born. Koschei cannot be allowed to take control of Ivan's body."

A gust of wind sent the plumage of the Birdwoman whipping and swirling, a moaning breeze sounding all around them. The sky darkened as lightning and thunder returned over the skyline. Yaga sensed the energy between them changing, burdened with the weight of the grim duty the Gamyun had proclaimed for her.

"What about my Aunt Mira?" Yaga asked as the winds grew louder. *"Why should it be me and not her?"*

The Gamyun stared out at the vast expanse of sparkling blue ocean, her feathers blowing in disarray over her impassive face. Abruptly, she turned, her expression flashing with ferocity as her deafening words boomed across the coal-black sky.

"Yaga, Mira's magic is a pale, flickering flame compared to the blazing sun that is your birthright. The world has been waiting for YOU, Yaga! It is your *destiny and can be no other's. If Koschei takes Ivan as a vessel, his power will grow to a level the world has never seen. He will be unstoppable, filling the world with a darkness never known! Be quick girl—now! The deathless Sorcerer MUST DIE!"*

The Birdwoman's voice rattled and echoed through Yaga's mind like a thousand silver plates crashing onto stone. In an instant, Yaga's thoughts flooded with a torrent of images—first of Ivan, then Alexey. She saw places she had never been—people she didn't know the names of. A young girl crying—an old woman dying within her bed.

Then there was a flash of someone else—her face caked in clay and paint, standing before a large outdoor fire. Within her hands, a leather pouch dangled, and in that moment—Yaga sensed the figure saw her, too. Quickly, the vision disappeared, replaced by a large black serpent writhing in the air before her. Then another—smaller and red—growing quickly, uncontrollably. Without warning, the large black snake coiled, striking at the red—before they both disappeared into thin air.

Suddenly, Yaga found herself standing on a darkened plain—a vast, empty expanse. In the distance, she saw a figure walking towards her. She recognized her as they drew closer; it was her mother. Vesna moved in a white linen dress with red embroidery down the front and sleeves. She smiled at Yaga, making her way towards her until she had almost reached the place where Yaga stood. Abruptly, Vesna's expression changed to horror—her flesh melting off her skull and bones. Screaming in agony, her mother dropped to the ground. Yaga called out to her, reaching for her desperately as the vision faded.

"No! No! It cannot be me!" Yaga screamed, her mind returning to the Gamyun's nest once more. *"I cannot be the one. I'm a monster! A monster!"* she wailed.

The Gamyun stared down at her, her expression unchanged. A long silence followed—only the wind gusting off the cliffs sounding in the air around them.

"Yaga, you are the one the world has been waiting for. Now go and claim your birthright—GO!" the Gamyun's consciousness bellowed, her massive wings spreading out from her body.

In an instant, the Gamyun's nest faded away—only to be replaced by the dark, damp interior of Baba Roga's cave. Yaga gasped as her consciousness snapped back into her body, jolting her upright. She opened her eyes to find the Cave Witch looming above, her gleaming eyes staring down at Yaga expectantly.

"Well. You have what you came for," Baba Roga rasped, grasping Yaga's arm and yanking her up to her feet. "And now, *my feather*."

Yaga's heart pounded, her chest heaving as the revelations settled over her. Ivan was in grave danger; she had to free him from the Sorcerer before it was too late. But then, she remembered—the people of Valen. They were terrified—yet, she still had no answer.

"Wait!" Yaga called out, struggling to keep her balance. The room seemed to slosh back and forth within her vision, the effects of the concoction Roga gave her lingering.

The Cave Witch, now standing at the edge of the dark passage leading towards the entrance, paused. Yaga moved towards her, steadying herself on a nearby boulder, her hands slipping over its slimy surface.

"The beasts—the ones that have come to my village. Why have they come? How—how can I stop them?" Yaga called out to Baba Roga breathlessly.

Baba Roga sighed, rolling her eyes slightly as though annoyed by the question.

"It's you, dear. You must feel it—can't you? You're becoming quite popular these days. You're the reason they come—*and the reason they'll leave*," she said flatly. "Koschei's not the only one with a growing power, you know."

Baba Roga stood silently before adding something unexpected—as though she could read Yaga's mind.

"A word of caution: you won't be able to *wish* your way out of this. A Firebird's feather cannot undo the curse of a god. Shift it, perhaps. But it can only do so much. You're better off finding the boy yourself, though you must be warned: the Deathless Sorcerer will stop at nothing—*nothing*—to have the power contained within that child."

She paused, gesturing impatiently towards the dark tunnel.

It was time to leave.

With Baba Roga trailing behind her, Yaga stumbled over bones and splashed through fetid pools as she moved towards the mouth of the cave. It was nearly dawn now, and when they arrived, the Firebird stood waiting near the entrance. Already, Zhar had plucked out a single feather, placing it on the ground nearby. It shimmered in the torchlight, an iridescent sparkle hinting of its latent magic.

Baba Roga snatched it up hastily. With a final glance at Yaga, she turned back. Soon, the Witch had shuffled once more down into the darkness, disappearing into the depths of the cave.

Yaga, still disoriented, squinted in the low light of the morning. Her head pounded as her stomach gurgled unpleasantly. She glanced back at the cave, half expecting the malodorous Baba Roga to reappear.

Suddenly, Kolya slipped out from behind a large pile of bones. He moved to Yaga's side, his eyes watchful as he studied the entrance of the cave. She steadied herself against him, feeling a wave of relief wash over her.

Still, Yaga felt a newfound urgency upwelling within her. The real journey had yet to begin. She would have to find Ivan. In that moment, she realized with anguish that—in her disorientation from the transition across the veil—she had not thought to ask *where he was*. Her eyes flicked back to the cave entrance. She dared not go back inside and tempt the Cave Witch's patience. Not when it was her duty to save the boy—preventing Koschei from taking his form and claiming another innocent life.

And, if the prophecy were true, one day, she would have to face Koschei himself—to stop him once and for all. Despite Yaga's overwhelm with everything at stake, the Gamayun had been clear: eons before her time, there had been a cosmic injustice—and it was her destiny alone to balance the scales. For now, however, her only mission was to save Ivan—and she worried time would run out.

In the days following the fabric seller's killing, Yaga's stepmother Branka had settled her focus on the meticulous planning of the dinner she had arranged with the Grishaevs. She was determined to use this gathering—despite the recent morbid event—to strengthen her daughter's prospects with Alexey. For her, securing a marriage between the two was of utmost importance; nothing would deter her. And, the atmosphere in Valen fraught with uncertainty, Branka knew that the warmth and comfort of a shared meal had the potential to restore a sense of normalcy and stability.

It was one of the servants at the estate who broke the news of Yaga's departure, having just returned from the market square after being sent to purchase a slab of salt pork from the butcher. The woman had been the first to go into the village since the body of the woman had been collected the day after the killing—her headless remains carted away beneath a crisp white sheet. She would be buried far from the village—lest Todorats come back to claim the rest of her from their midst.

Upon the servant's return to the manor, she sparked an immediate commotion with a revelation of the most unthinkable development: Yaga Luchanova had travelled to find the infamous Cave Witch Baba Roga in a search of answers. Immediately, the revelation spread like a fire throughout the household.

Most of the servants had known Yaga since she was a child—each of them coming to live in the manor shortly after Yaga's father had married Branka. They had sensed Yaga to be peculiar, yes—though most thought kindly of her. Especially when she called at their bedside after they had fallen ill.

Branka, upon hearing of Yaga's travels from the hive now buzzing within the manor, felt at first a sense of *shock*. Yet, this was quickly replaced by a competing emotion which she dared not express aloud: Branka hoped, for reasons she and few others knew, that her stepdaughter might never return. She secretly wished for Yaga to be lost somewhere—marooned in a faraway place. *Or worse.*

Still, on the outside, Branka expressed her disturbance loudly as though devastated by the development.

"Oh, my dearest daughter," she said, gazing out the window into the gray haze of the midday sky. "I do pray to the gods for her return."

The servants merely stared at their shoes, their heads turned solemnly downward. In closed quarters, however, they grimaced and shook their heads—mistrustful of Branka's sentiments entirely. They knew the mistress of the manor to be guiling and hateful, never once having a kind word to say of Yaga before. Still, they kept this to themselves—none deigning to utter it aloud, save within their private spaces.

Despite this turn of events, Branka of course thought it best to proceed with the dinner as planned. In truth, the spreading word of her stepdaughter's bravery only fueled her ambition: she could use this terrible turn of things to garner sympathy amongst the villagers. And perhaps favor.

Preparations for the gathering began immediately, despite the servants' secret misgivings in planning such a happy occasion, all things considered. In the days that followed, several of the women were sent with lists, instructed to fetch what they could from remained of the market. Though, most of its booths and stalls still lay shuttered—neither patron nor shopkeeper ready to forget.

Grimly, the path Branka's servants travelled to the village sent them directly past the scene of the killing. A brown stain still lingered on the road there, and as the women neared it, they averted their eyes. Each was terrified they could be next—their feet carrying them swiftly to and from the market when the sun was high overhead. As soon as the carriage house came back into view, they practically sprinted, desperate to be back behind locked doors long before dusk.

Then, a few days after Yaga's departure, the countryside had been soaked with rain—all physical traces of the grisly killing washed away. Inside the manor, the preparation for the upcoming dinner was in full swing. And, though it was days away, Branka now moved about the space, levying a battery of instructions.

It was much to the chagrin of the servants that Branka found it necessary to personally oversee every agonizing detail of the preparations, right down to the individual selection of fresh vegetables and the spices to be used for the roasted meats. She instructed the staff on how to set the table, too—insisting an intensive polish be applied to the silverware. And the wine, she told them, was to be purchased from a neighboring village nearly half a day's ride from Valen—the finest vintage available to her.

Nadia, who had been in her bedroom chamber admiring herself in her mirror all morning, now preened and hummed aloud as a servant looked on from her position on the floor beside the bed. Branka's oldest daughter was dressed in a lace-trimmed chemise, perched near the footboard, seemingly oblivious to the servant woman filing her toenails.

Truly, Nadia was lost in thought: within a few short days, she hoped she would be seated across from her future husband. She beamed, playing with one of her curls, before leaning backward upon the fluffy covers of the bed, besotted. She sighed loudly, her mind filling with visions of Alexey's handsome face.

The servant's stomach turned, for hanging in the corner of the room was a perfect, delicate gown made of the very fabric that had been the cause of so much horror—the bolt of burgundy silk. The day after the tragedy, Branka had quietly instructed the seamstress to cut off the section caked in a crust of dark residue—something she had insisted was *just a bit of mud.*

From the remaining material, a stunning dress had been fashioned—the seamstress working feverishly on it over an entire day and night without stopping, just to be done. Afterward, the woman had soaked herself in two hot baths in succession—scrubbing her hands raw and downing a flask of birchshine in the hopes it would help her to *forget*.

Branka, however, had no misgivings whatsoever about the choice to proceed with the fabric and the upcoming dinner. Nadia would look exquisite, despite the backdrop of inauspicious events just days before. Her eldest daughter's future with Alexey was within her sights now. In Branka's eyes, he held the key to bigger, better things for her daughter. And for her, for although the money left after Zoren's death had been ample, Branka's eyes sparkled with the ambition of what could be.

Across Valen, Tatiana Grishaev was also thinking about the upcoming dinner. The light sound of rain created a soft din in the background of the manor as she moved through the dimly lit halls, contemplating Alexey's future. Meeting Nadia had ignited a small ember of hope within her that she might have *finally* found a match for her son. The girl was especially beautiful, with poise and feminine talents; an apparently kind-hearted, nurturing young woman. Surely, Alexey would be satisfied with her for a wife.

Tatiana hummed gently as she moved, visions of a future filled with children laughing and running through the hallways warming her heart. After a moment, a member of the household staff passed her.

"Oh, pardon me—have you seen Alexey?" Tatiana asked.

"In the parlor, my lady," he responded.

Tatiana returned a warm smile, thanking him. He nodded, departing to resume his duties elsewhere in the house. Tatiana turned, heading towards the parlor, her blithe humming continuing as she walked.

Upon her arrival, she found Alexey seated on a large, upholstered chair. He was hunched forward, his body facing the window with his arms resting against his knees. His gaze was fixed on the rainy ground beyond the window, the green grass of summer now patched with beige and strewn with a mess of wet brown autumn leaves. As Tatiana entered, she noticed immediately the faraway look on his face.

"Alexey, my dear. Have you seen Misha?" Tatiana asked.

She studied him quietly, her mind combing over the potentials of what could be ailing him. He remained quiet for a moment, his stare unbroken at the rain.

"Mother, Misha is in his room, I believe," he said, sighing.

Tatiana looked over her son's appearance, struck by the pain she could see etched across his face.

"My son, you seem unhappy. Is this about the... the... incident?"

A sense of apprehension arose within her; she had taken great pains—almost out of superstition—to avoid referencing the killing of the merchant woman.

Alexey stood, turning. Walking towards her, he placed his hands gently on his mother's shoulders.

"Mother, I'm fine."

Yet—she could see in his eyes plainly that he was not. That he was hiding something from her.

"Well, alright," she said, watching as Alexey moved to a shelf, his finger absently tracing over the spines of several books.

"In a few days, we are heading to Branka's for the evening—for a dinner she so graciously invited us to attend. Nadia will be there..."

A faint, discontented groan escaped Alexey's mouth. Ever since Yaga had departed on her journey to seek Baba Roga, he had been drowning beneath the weight of his emotions. He worried about Yaga every moment that passed, unable to think of much else.

"I'm sorry, Mother, but I can't focus on that right now," he told her, his feet carrying him to the door of the parlor to leave.

As she observed him depart, Tatiana's expression tightened with worry. She knew that his thoughts were elsewhere—far from the festive warmth of the upcoming dinner party. Unaware of the growing connection between Alexey and Yaga, she felt her focus shifting towards overcoming the rising distance she felt between her and her eldest son. She feared that, whatever was paining him, it would only steer him further from the life she hoped he would lead. She knew better than to push, however, letting him leave without saying another word.

"I'll think about it," he said absently, moving down the hall.

Now alone in the parlor, Tatiana listened to the sounds of his footsteps fading. After a moment, she turned, walking to the window. Through the panes of glass, fogged around the edges with humidity, she noticed the rain had momentarily stopped.

Within the yard, a single robin had alighted to the ground. Feverishly, the bird tugged at a worm—though it wriggled desperately from the bird's grasp, slipping back beneath the soil. The rains abruptly returned, Tatiana watching as the robin took refuge in a nearby tree. The creature, it seemed, was waiting for things to subside again; for a break in the clouds.

For another chance to capture the worm.

Over the next three days, the sun returned to Valen, baking the countryside in warm, golden rays that harkened to the summer. Alexey and Misha spent much of their time then away from the Grishaev Estate—instead preferring the company of Vasilisa and the House Spirits at the cottage. And, while Alexey and the Vila shared an unspoken worry, they kept themselves busy rather than speak their fears aloud.

The cottage, though incomplete without Yaga's presence, still held a sense of her magic—a fact on its own which provided a quiet comfort to all within its walls. And so, nestled upon the gnarled, ancient oaks, her friends took refuge, passing the time away in anticipation of her return.

Vasilisa, when not working at her loom or doing small chores, had begun to assist Alexey in tending to Misha's bandages each day. Alexey—hoping to be a help—worked outdoors with Misha at times—feeding and caring for the chickens and chopping wood. Occasionally, he helped Vasilisa with small tasks inside—the Vila finding his presence useful in her efforts to declutter and organize the many objects upon high shelves laying just beyond her reach.

With each passing day, the cottage became tidier, the brothers growing closer with Vasilisa and the House Spirits. Misha, having an especial fondness for the creatures, could often be found seated by the hearth with a suspicious mouse in his shirt pocket, and a cat on his lap.

Settling into a routine, the brothers departed each day in the midafternoon, only to return the following morning with fresh bread and other sundries. Vasilisa and Alexey had grown accustomed to one another—even finding the presence of the other soothing. And so, Yaga's friends sought to pass their time in productive, meaningful ways as best they could in her absence.

Mostly, however, they waited.

On the day of the dinner at Branka's estate, all preparations had accounted for the gathering to end long before darkness could descend over the land. As the Grishaev's carriage trundled through the countryside, the region was baked in the soft glow of early afternoon sun. Still, the birch trees appeared like towering skeletons that loomed oppressively over the landscape—the white bark of their denuded branches transformed into ominous, spindly bones by the recent rain.

The door to the manor opened as Tatiana and Dmitri ascended the porch steps, an awaiting cluster of servants ushering them inside. As they entered the foyer, Misha emerged from behind his mother, his eyes marveling at the glittering chandelier overhead. The awaiting servants slipped off the guests' jackets, wordlessly walking them to a nearby closet as a houseman greeted them at the threshold of the living room.

"Welcome," he said, guiding them into the space where Branka stood waiting.

As the Grishaevs entered, Branka smiled, though her eyes flicked beyond them and out the door. Seeing no sign of Alexey—her smile faltered only briefly. She cleared her throat, focusing her attention on Tatiana.

"Welcome, welcome—oh, what a lovely dress you're wearing, dear," Branka said, her eyes scanning over Tatiana's simple gray dress with embroidered florals.

Branka winced inside, wondering if she had miscalculated Nadia's attire. The gears within her mind began to turn while she exchanged pleasantries with Tatiana and Dmitri, her thoughts vacillating as to how to rectify what she perceived to be a near-fatal error to her scheming. Nadia's burgundy dress was too formal; it would be almost gaudy next to Tatiana's. She couldn't risk losing the ground she had gained, and so she acted quickly.

"Oh, why don't you have a seat right here," she said, gesturing to a few chairs and a settee in the living room.

The servants and the houseman exchanged confused glances—knowing full well the highly curated dinner was to begin at the dining table with a fresh loaf of bread and compote being plated in the kitchen at that very moment.

As Misha flopped down on a chair, followed by Tatiana and Dmitri, Branka's eyes cut across the room towards the servants. She cocked her head briskly, directing the two women to follow her to another room.

"If you'll excuse me, I'll be right back," Branka said—though her heart was beating hard.

Time was limited; Nadia could appear at any moment. Branka, along with the summoned servants, slipped into the dining room and around a corner.

"You must find Nadia at once and remove the burgundy dress," she rasped. She paused, looking over her shoulder to ensure she was not being observed by the Grishaevs.

"Put her in the yellow dress—the one with the delicate pelerine of lace."

The servants knew better than to ask any questions, instead moving quietly and nimbly through an adjoining hall and up the staircase, unseen.

Branka smoothed the front of her dress down, her breathing slowing. As she saw it, she had narrowly avoided a disaster—what could have been a complete undoing of her work thus far. Now Nadia would be dressed in something pretty but spare. Yet—even this could be of use, for the sunny yellow color of the gown might come across as earnest and unpretentious. Branka felt a small pang when she considered her own elegant dress, though she put the thought aside. She had put out one fire, and now there were guests that needed tending to.

As Branka reemerged into the living room, she found Tatiana, seated on one of the two upholstered wingback chairs and tickling a wriggling, giggling Misha upon her lap. Branka smiled, seating herself across from her. Just as she did, a pair of servants entered the room carrying a loaf of warm bread upon a cutting board and a dish of butter and raspberry compote, along with a few porcelain saucers.

Misha's eyes widened as he squirmed away from his mother, seating himself next to his father near the bread.

"*Mmm,*" Misha said as he sniffed the air.

He was just about to stick a finger into the compote when his father pulled him back. Misha pouted, though he resigned himself to sitting upon the cushion next to Dmitri.

Soon, a servant had cut the bread, plating up slices and offering them to Branka and her guests. A polite exchange followed—mostly involving Dmitri and Misha remarking to the servants about how tasty the raspberries were with the butter.

Branka and Tatiana, however, were each consumed by their own thoughts as they slowly chewed each morsel. For her part, Tatiana wished terribly that her oldest son were in attendance. She suffered the absence like a wound—knowing that he was both stricken in some way, and that the opportunity to further her own ambitions for his future would have to be placed *on hold*—at least the part where he was concerned. She could do well on her own, despite his absence, feeling without question she knew what was best for Alexey. She was, after all, his mother, and could rightly gauge the suitability of a prospective partner in marriage.

Branka, too, now ruminated about Alexey and Nadia from her chair—even as each bite she swallowed fought to move past the tension in her throat. She wanted desperately to ask where on earth the boy was—though she said nothing. It would be too forward. Too obvious.

Just as the two women set their empty plates back on the low table at the center of the seating area, Nadia appeared in the doorway. She looked simple yet radiant in her yellow gown, her blonde curls shining in the light of the chandelier. Only—she knew at once that Alexey was not in attendance, her shoulders slumping just slightly.

Her gaze immediately flicked to her mother, searching for reassurance. Alexey's absence was not auspicious—yet Branka would not let it deter them. She gave a small, nearly imperceptible nod to Nadia. Immediately, her daughter turned, smiling at Tatiana and Dmitri sweetly.

"Hello," she said pleasantly, giving a small bow and curtsy.

Still, despite Nadia's best efforts, her anticipation had been dashed terribly by Alexey's absence. Now, a faint disappointment clouded her features. Just then Marfa slipped into the living room quietly—almost unnoticed. Nadia's breath hitched as she caught her sister's shared look of surprise. She couldn't let this turn of events dampen the mood; Nadia was determined to make a good impression—if not on Alexey himself, then on his mother. If she could not captivate Alexey Grishaev, then she would focus her efforts on his parents.

They would want her.

Soon, having moved to the dining room, the afternoon was in full swing around the dinner table. The conversations meandered around the village's history and the niceties expected for a shared meal. The food was impeccable, the wine flowing and elevating the atmosphere—nudging everyone to forget the recent events, if only for a short while.

Conspicuously absent was any talk of Yaga's departure. For Tatiana, the heroic journey of the woman in the woods was a casualty of the fabric seller's killing—a topic she wanted to avoid, unsettling as it was. But for Branka, the calculated choice not to discuss her stepdaughter's bravery at this juncture was twofold: she wanted the mood of the dinner light, with Nadia shining above all else. And, she wanted her own inevitable display of grief should Yaga not return—especially having been so brave for her dinner guests—to engineer future efforts at consolation from Tatiana.

For a bit of entertainment in the middle of dinner, Nadia moved toward the mantle where she played a small harp for the guests. Her hair framed her rosy cheeks as her fingers moved gracefully over the strings. She was lovely—her charming demeanor making her sparkle like a star in the eyes of everyone present.

Everyone except for Misha and Marfa—and the servants who rolled their eyes from behind closed doors. Watching Nadia's and Branka's displays, they groaned silently, revolted by the overtures dripping in a saccharine mirth they knew to be utterly false. Still, Marfa and the servants alike were impressed by the sheer skill involved at pretending with such conviction.

Marfa, for one, knew her sister to be vain and callous. She was a cruel and vacant sibling—always hoping to best Marfa, even when Marfa herself preferred to blend into the paper adorning the walls. In Marfa's eyes, Nadia was undeserving of someone like Alexey and his family—her older sister a dull piece of coal amongst people who seemed good and kind. Yet, here Nadia was, polished like a diamond.

Still, Marfa wanted to make the best of the evening—itself a reprieve from staring out the window of her bedroom. As such, she soon discovered that by silently pantomiming her older sister's giddy laugh, she could amuse Misha to no end.

The two sat next to one another at the table, Marfa, too, finding the boy's mischievous antics absolutely delightful. To her, Misha seemed like the only person remotely relatable at the table—the two of them captives in a foreign land.

At one point, Nadia had begun to wax on about her love for small animals. Misha had caught Marfa rolling her eyes at the fraudulent details, knowing full well that Nadia hated all creatures, finding them wretched. Her older sister would no sooner help a kitten than she would lay in a puddle of mud.

As Nadia continued, Misha's eyes flicked to Marfa, his eyebrows furrowing as an impish expression flashed across his face. Silently, he stabbed at the small bits of meat on his plate—as if he were performing a sacrifice of some poor beast. Marfa snickered aloud at the amusing display—something which only the servants seemed to notice, themselves exchanging knowing smirks from across the room.

By the end of the dinner, Misha and Marfa had found an unusual alliance in one another. Still, it was nothing at all like the scheming Nadia and Branka had done for weeks. What's more, it seemed that Branka's plan was *working*; Tatiana seemed at ease—even impressed. Several times, Branka had caught Tatiana glancing at Dmitri, an enthused, hopeful smile forming on her lips. This pleased Branka and Nadia to no end, of course—fueling their ambitions to new heights by the time the Grishaevs departed.

As she rode back to their estate in the carriage, Tatiana's eyes passed over the countryside—the stands of oaks like hands grasping upward towards the open sky.

This could be the girl, she thought.

A small part of her twinged, however—her heart beyond remiss that Alexey had not been there that evening. Throughout the dinner, her mind had consistently wandered back to him and his crumpled demeanor over the past several days, the image of her son staring despondently out the parlor window seared into her mind.

As the carriage bumped along, she watched the sun beginning its descent towards the darkened ranges in the distance. Pondering her son's strange misery, she felt unsure of how she might break through to him; she wanted to be there for him. Soon, too, she would see to it that he came around in other ways—if not on his own, then by her loving direction as she steered him towards new horizons.

Back at the cottage, Alexey sat by the fire across the room from Vasilisa. Gazing into the hearth, he watched as the orange flames devoured a fresh log, a stark contrast with the sky-blue hue of his eyes. He was deep in thought, his stomach now growling to be fed as darkness descended over the forest beyond the cottage walls.

Yet, he couldn't eat. He feared Yaga was lost at sea in the wide world beyond Valen. Adrift in his emotions, his fear and worry grew with every passing second of her absence. Tonight, he would sleep by the hearth, his mind returning endlessly to his burning need to see Yaga returned home safely. His longing to be in her presence was a gap within his heart—an injury for which the balm was Yaga herself.

Staring into the flames, he waited.

Chapter Ten

THE RAVEN

I n the southern lands of the Thrice-Nine Kingdoms, a palatial building stood atop a craggy coastal outcropping. At the far end of the
rooftop nearest the open sea, encircled by a parapet on all sides, was a
terrace whereupon an aviary stood—its high walls and ceiling made of
glass. Inside, a cage constructed of fragrant rosewood sat nestled amongst
a veritable forest of potted greenery.

It was quiet inside—save the chirping of the hatchlings emanating
from the roosting boxes. With a few of the windows open, a fresh cross
breeze from the ocean gently pulled at the plumage on the mother ravens'
faces. They hopped between branches, each ducking in and out of the
cage to check on their brood.

Within one of the boxes, tucked amongst his brothers and sisters the
color of obsidian, lay a fuzzy raven chick, pale and gleaming as a sliver of
moonlight. Like the others, he was a bird born to return home—belong-
ing to a breed of ravens known as the Kedra' Hasran. They were messenger birds, bred for centuries or more. Swift and unerring, once grown,
each of the hatchlings would be sent elsewhere to live the Thrice-Nine
over—all destined to make the return trip to the palace should a message
need conveyance.

Except for him.

Every so often, when the moon was full and the night was still, a single hatchling could be born silvery-white amongst the others. This bird was known as the Argynfeather—though by their first molt, their pale color would darken. Still, the light remained hidden beneath their feathers, the priests said—etched into the birds' bones and within a hidden quill. This faint trace of moon-color, so it was believed, granted the Argynfeather their rare gift: *the power to seek the bearer of a Name.*

Once spoken, the word would become a beacon; the Argynfeather could find them, travelling to places near and far. And so, they spent their lives in the palace—only departing to locate those *who needed to be found.* The bird's gift was called providence by the priests—a sanctioned miracle of the One True God. Still, the oldest handlers of the Kedra' Hasran whispered the truth: the magic in the blood of the Argynfeather was older than any prayer uttered within the hallowed halls of the empire.

After hours of relentless movement, the raven's muscles burned. The ache she felt was dull and unending, pulsing in time with the beating of her wings. This was a journey far beyond anything she had undertaken before; the flight to the castle in the remote wilds of the Northwestern Thrice-Nine had been arduous. Now, doubling back without more than a few days rest was a test of endurance unlike any other.

Day and night, she carried forth, each gust of wind scraping against the feathers of her face. Her plumage was in tatters now—each feather snagged by stray breezes, dragged slightly out of alignment. Still, she continued onward, flapping her wings with an unyielding persistence, as though each of her tendons were synchronized by the mechanical pull of an invisible cord. She was born for this; seeing the world pass by underneath was how the bird had spent most of her life. Nevertheless, the repeated contraction and extension of her wings had driven an unabating fatigue deep into her joints.

Far below, the raven passed over long stretches of forested mountain valleys—each filled with perches beckoning to her like an oasis—a brief reprieve from this now-hellish task. Her sharp eyes, too, felt strained—the pale abyss of sky blurring at the edges of her vision. She closed them at times, barreling forward like a meteor, her destination wrought down into her very core. A small speck against an endless blue haze, the raven soldiered on.

Yet, something more than a physical burden weighed upon the bird. Ever since she had departed the moldering, damp castle tucked into the overgrown forests in the far northwest, she had *sensed something*. She couldn't contemplate what it was, though it chilled her far more than the winds ripping across the skies. A dark energy clung to her now; she could feel it.

Nearly a week had passed since the raven had left the castle with the Sorcerer's consciousness coiled within the metal tube affixed to her leg. Though she remained unaware, the urgency with which she had been shuttled back into the sky was a testament to Koschei's insatiable thirst for power; nothing else mattered to him—not anything. And so, the raven flew—unaware of her cargo.

For the Sorcerer, too, the flight had begun to feel like an eternity. Days had bled into one another, marked only by the rising and setting of the sun. The landscape below was an ever-changing tapestry—a feast for the eyes of majestic, breathtaking scenery. Yet, Koschei's mind no longer marveled at the world's beauty. He was indifferent, his heart pulled down into the depths of his own depravity, held there by the dark currents of a hunger never faded.

Still, within him, a newfound curiosity had been awakened; he was tantalized by the prospect that the world beyond had risen up from its ancient past of magic and chaos. With the Old Gods gone and nearly forgotten, the world outside of his dominion seemed to lay waiting for him. And so, there was but a singular purpose for this journey: learn everything he could about the sender of the message—the one brought to him by the enchanted bird who ferried him at present. He could sense the magic contained within the creature, and now, he needed to see who had sent it and from where. He wanted to know who dared address him with such authority.

He wanted to see what could be *his*.

Attached to the raven, Koschei had soared for days over dense forests, the stands of tree-covered hills and valleys stretching out in undulating waves of green. As the days passed, the world beneath began to shift. Far in the distance, mountain ranges had sprung up from the earth like jagged teeth. The forests grew more sparse, the air warm and rolling over the distant grasslands in waves. A balmy breeze replaced the sharp winds of the Northern Thrice-Nine, carrying with it the scent of salt and fragrant vegetation. Below him, the waters of vast rivers now snaked lazily through fertile plains towards the horizon—each an endless, languid mirror in the midday sun.

Soon, the raven flew over bustling villages and small towns, the rooftops tiled in a fashion unfamiliar to the Sorcerer. Much of what he saw before him of mankind was a surprise to Koschei. After all, he had lived for thousands of years, rarely venturing past the borders of the Dark Lands, save for when necessity required it.

Back then—in the before times—the veil between worlds had been more permeable. It was an era when Gods and magic creatures had walked amongst humans the world over, meddling in their affairs.

Koschei had conquered the first kings of the early Northern King-doms. Over time, the lands he subsumed had become twisting and fal-low—devoid of nearly anyone or anything. And, while there were people still living within the borders of the Dark Lands, the sorcerer had never felt the need to expand his reach. All he had ever wanted, he had already taken—the ancient kings falling to his immense power.

Now, it was clear that humans had risen up from the ashes of their past. Perhaps the Old Gods had truly abandoned the world of men, for all around him, he saw signs of development and growth.

What was more, as he soared over dense cities and bustling market squares, it occurred to him he had become *obscure*. Just a morbid legend—a fearsome conqueror, now nothing but a fabled shut-in to the Sclaveni. The Dark Lands surrounding his castle seemed more a relic of the past than a bastion of his immortal magic. He recoiled at the thought.

Yet—he knew it to be *true*. Without a challenge, Koschei had grown bored—complacent, even. And so, a renewed desire began to take shape as he watched the world below him grow more vast and strange than he had ever cared to dream.

By the time the raven had reached the coastline, the lands beneath had transformed entirely. Below, a channel of deep blue stretched towards a boundless expanse of open sea. The ocean waters glistened like a jewel, and for a moment, Koschei was mesmerized.

How could it be—that I had thought the world so small?

At the far edge of the horizon line, masts of ships dotted against the pale blue skies—each one a tiny speck and spire, sailing off to points unknown. As the raven drew nearer, the shoreline itself bristled with activity, too—crowded with vessels from distant lands and teeming with merchants and citizens going about their lives.

As the bird continued on her course, Koschei's thoughts turned inwards. These new lands—with their spiced, warm air, their sprawling cities and monuments of stone—germinated a dormant seed deep within him. He had been content to live in his forgotten, remote part of the world for so long—unaware—no, *ambivalent* to the rest of the Kingdoms. Yet here—far from the Sorcerer's spoils from eons past—the scale of wealth and ambition was *staggering*. Massive statues now lined the roads leading into the cities, their stone faces gazing impassively over throngs of people who barely took note of them. Enormous buildings of marble and stone gleamed in the sun, while towers pierced the sky. Each edifice of importance was adorned with grand columns. Everywhere he looked, he saw signs of a vast pulsating organism of trade and progress.

Then, Koschei saw them—the expansive military battalions spread across endless swaths of open terrain. Some of the men marched in unison while others sparred, their bodies glistening in the sun with sweat and grit. A pulse of power ran through him as he watched the young soldiers grappling, while others moved in a synchronized march beneath shining armor. He could practically taste it; the throbbing rhythm of wealth and conquest made him drip with desire. Envy filled him in a way it hadn't in thousands of years.

It made him feel *alive*.

As the raven descended, she circled slowly around a sprawling palace set high upon a hill. Koschei's mind burned with curiosity now.

What ruler commands this place? What sorcery—what power—could have built such wealth?

Soon, the bird landed upon a stone balcony overlooking the water. The warm air was thick with the scent of the sea, its waves lapping at the rocky base upon which the fortress stood. Within a glass structure atop the terrace, a figure moved—a man clad in long, flowing robes. He turned when he saw the bird, a gentle smile forming on his face. After a moment, however, the man's brow furrowed.

With haste, he fetched a small cage, then emerged onto the terrace with a pensive expression. Koschei's consciousness, still connected to the tube, watched as the man moved toward the raven with slow, deliberate steps. Grimacing, he seemed to be studying her as he approached. He sighed, adjusting the spectacles he wore.

"Now, why would someone be so cruel, Diamonda?"

The man shook his head as he placed a gentle hand at the back of the bird's head, softly patting her plumage.

"You poor dear—here," he said, unclasping the metal tube from her leg. "You'll not be heading out again for some time. It's rest for you, my darling," he told her. The raven stepped wearily into the open cage. She was exhausted—and now she was home.

After placing the cage upon a stand within the glass room—an aviary of some kind—the man set a small dish of water within it. Then, he draped a silken cloth over the metal frame—an invitation for the raven to rest. He stepped back, retrieving the metal tube containing the message from a nearby table. Then, with a sweet farewell whispered to the bird, he slipped out of a set of doors leading further into the palace.

Perched within the shaded respite of the cage, the raven finally took in a deep, contented breath. She felt warmth returning inside of her—a stark contrast to the chill she had been unable to shake since she had set out on her return. As the man in robes moved down a far corridor, the distance grew between her and the feeling of dread and darkness that had remained with her day and night, with every beat of her wings. Shuddering, she drifted off into a deep sleep.

With the metal tube clutched in his hand, the man—a servant of the emperor—moved dutifully through a series of hallways within the palace. His breath was measured—his pace steady and unbothered. Walking upright, he showed not a hint of fear in his body, clearly confident of his place in the world.

How strange, the Sorcerer thought. This man serves—yet he remains ruled by himself somehow, his heart seemingly unbent beneath the will of another.

Soon, they had ascended a set of wide stone steps. It expanded into a circular room that truncated outward in different directions. They were navigating the inner labyrinthian halls of a palace steeped in majesty and grandeur. Now Koschei marveled at the vision before him, tantalized by the opulence. Every surface gleamed—every wall adorned with shining silver plaques. Each archway and window had been draped in tapestries of fine silk, while beneath him, the sandal-clad feet of the man carrying the tube glided over massive, intricately tiled mosaics.

As the corridor widened, the Sorcerer noticed portraits of noblemen stretching down its length, all set within ornate, gilded frames. The figures wore regal robes, their olive skin surrounded by dark, curly hair. As Koschei whisked by, their honey-colored eyes seemed to stare back at him, following his movement as he passed through the palace undetected.

For the Sorcerer, every turn seemed to reveal something more splendid than the last. Statues bearing imperious expressions flanked doorways, while floral arrangements burst into vibrant plumes of color, spilling out of towering, finely decorated porcelain vases. Exotic plants loomed from every corner, the sunlight streaming across their giant, shining leaves. This place, he told himself, seemed befitting of someone with far more power than a king. It was as though a god himself lived here. Koschei could barely contain his envy—outmatched only by his growing contempt for whoever had sent the message.

For what he saw before him, he thought, should be his.

Abruptly, the man stopped, having arrived at a set of large, intricately carved doors made of heavy black wood. Before it sentries stood guard, each wearing leather armor and dome-shaped copper helmets with a metallic mesh sash draped over their faces—beneath which only their eyes were visible.

With a small nod, the guards opened the doors, holding them for the man as he moved to the interior of the room. A heavy thud echoed over the basalt floor within as the doors closed behind him. They had entered a vast chamber, the center of which was dominated by a large wooden table.

Seated at its head was a man unlike any Koschei had ever encountered. His face was framed with dark ringlets, over which he wore a golden crown of laurels. Jewels adorned his fingers and his ears—each one sparkling in the sunlight streaming through the windows. His strong physique was draped in a blazing red tunic. The man's face was steely and impassive, his posture exuding imminent power.

This place—this land in which Koschei found himself to be a mere passerby—was an empire.

And this man, *the emperor*.

Moving towards a wall, the man carrying the tube silently took his place beside several others—each of whom seemed to be awaiting the opportunity to speak to the emperor.

The Sorcerer observed the emperor now. His brow was furrowed as he contemplated something. He seemed to be scrutinizing a set of parchments laid out before him as a man robed in blue spoke inaudibly next to him. Soon, the emperor nodded, and—without a word—the man in blue gathered the papers up. With a deferential bow, he turned sharply, exiting the room.

The emperor's eyes fell briefly upon the tube which held Koschei's message. Quickly, as though summoned, the man holding it approached the side of the table, placing it in front of the emperor silently, followed by a slight bow. The emperor's gaze narrowed, an eyebrow raising as he squared his attention on the man who had delivered it.

"It's from the Northern Thrice-Nine, Caesar," the man said. "From King Koschei in the far Western Kingdoms."

The Sorcerer listened now with great intrigue. Indeed, he had been referred to as *King* Koschei in the original correspondence—something which had seemed outrageously offensive to him. He was an *immortal*

Sorcerer—one who had walked the earth since the times of gods and men. To be called a mere king was *insolence*. It also belied the sender had no recognition of Koschei's formidable dominion—or at least that he was unbelieving.

I am a destroyer of kings, Koschei thought.

His consciousness fumed from within the tube. Now, a mixture of fascination and animus overtook the Sorcerer's mind as he continued observing the scene before him.

Upon hearing the correspondence had come from Koschei, the emperor's gaze flicked towards another man at the far end of the room. He wore robes of white, his aging body seated upon a simple wooden chair. The man's eyes were a silvery gray color—a hue which matched the halo of hair surrounding the bald crown of his head.

Beside him stood yet another man in similar garb. He leaned forward, whispering to the first. After a moment, Koschei watched the seated man give a faint, nearly imperceptible nod across the room to the emperor. The emperor cleared his throat.

"Let's have it then," he said, his eyes watchful as the man beside him slid the rolled parchment out from the tube.

Soon, Koschei heard the very words his scribe had penned just days before falling into the air around him. As he watched the emperor, he noticed his expression was unchanging—save for a slight narrowing of his eyes. Koschei had expected this; his reply had been filled with false humility and pledges of fealty. It was all a lie, of course—a ruse he had crafted to stall, though just enough pressure to ensure a hasty reply.

He *needed* the emperor to respond. Indeed, this trip could well be the Sorcerer's last—a gamble he had been willing to take to see what lay beyond his dominion. Still, he knew the hearts of men; he would return by hitting just the right chord. He had beseeched the sender for *help*. His dominion was falling upon desperate times, he had said.

Yet, the emperor had experience with men of power, and so, behind Koschei's careful words, he sensed the truth: Koschei had no intention of being a subject. It was a thought which unnerved the emperor—though not for the contempt and insubordination he heard between each word. Koschei, he knew, was unlike the others.

The emperor's eyes moved towards a large copper repousse of a dove with upturned wings upon the wall. The bird was depicted as centered within the rays of a sun. He sighed, for he knew there would be no diplomacy. The emperor, unbeknownst to the Sorcerer, knew that Koschei was no mere man. He was a magician—a heretic in his eyes. And he would *need to be stopped.*

Yet, the emperor too would play the game.

After all, he had one hundred thousand soldiers at the ready in the capitol alone, all but ensuring the outcome. He studied the bird upon the wall, his eyes fixed on a band of sunlight streaming through the open window and falling over the metal plaque.

Koschei watched the emperor intently—studying the man's expression. He knew more than he was saying. Koschei admitted to himself then that perhaps he had underestimated the sender, for this man could be no fool—not with the riches and conquests he had beneath his seat of power.

Abruptly, the emperor turned—his eyes meeting with the awaiting gaze of a tall, slender scribe. The emperor nodded, causing him to move towards the table—a quill and fresh sheet of parchment already held within his hand. Appearing at the side of the emperor, the scribe stood ready to compose his reply. At that moment, Koschei took his opportunity: it was time *to move.*

The Sorcerer's consciousness slipped from the tube, darting between objects through the room and out the door. He moved through vases and candlesticks, oil lamps and goblets, surging through the halls as quickly as possible. He had little time to waste now, for he wanted to know more about this place, and had not a moment to spare.

Everywhere he looked, Koschei saw wealth beyond imagination. His mind overflowed with desire and envy. And greed.

And, something *darker.*

As he hurled his consciousness from one object to another, he passed by a door so quickly he almost missed it. Emanating from an adjoining room was the sweet smell of jasmine, pulling him back and beckoning him through the keyhole. Slipping into the space, from a tall vase standing near the door, he saw her then—a woman, seated on a balcony.

Koschei leapt from the vase into a glass just as she lowered it from her lips. Laying on a settee, her tan shoulders dripped in a soft white tunic, her black hair falling like vines over her chest. The Sorcerer was awestruck; to him, the woman and her sun-drenched skin radiated beauty unlike any he had ever seen.

He watched as she placed the glass of water on a small table. With an attractive, slender hand, she moved a small bit of hair out from in front of her face. Koschei studied her, taken by her calm eyes—each a glistening sphere the color of raw umber. And her lips—soft and supple with a bow—smiling faintly toward her handservants positioned nearby.

The Sorcerer felt the stir of something primal then.

This was the empress.

His gaze took in the fullness of her bosom, and the blush within her cheeks. In that moment he wished that she would place the glass again to her lips...*just* once more. His thirst for power shifted now—*to lust.*

Unexpectedly, Koschei heard the screeching of a gull beyond the balcony, soaring above the waters below the palace promontory. Instantly, the sound brought him back to the urgency of things: he had seen enough of this place and needed to get back to the silver tube in time—lest he never be able to leave. With a final gaze at the empress, he passed through the keyhole of the doorway once more and out into the corridor.

Like a gust of wind, Koschei's consciousness surged back through the halls, returning him to the grand room where the emperor sat. As he arrived, the scribe was penning the last of the emperor's words. The Sorcerer watched as the quill scratched across the parchment, his final flourishes making a sound like a metronome—sturdy and deliberate. Standing upright, the scribe turned, passing the parchment to the man with glasses solemnly, before returning to his position against a nearby wall.

The emperor left his seat, his fingers snapping in command as he walked towards one of the windows within the room. His eyes were fixed upon the waters then as though he were daring the universe itself to oppose him. Gazing out over the sparkling sea, he spoke with his back turned, his voice shifting in a way that made the Sorcerer uncomfortable.

"Read it back to me," he said.

The man cleared his throat as he adjusted the pair of spectacles perched on his nose, his eyes scanning over the parchment.

"To King Koschei, and no other," the man began, his voice steady.

Koschei's mind focused intently now, taking on an undulating rhythm as though it were a snake's tongue flicking in the air, sensing.

"Your message has been received," the man continued. "Your blessed allegiance will pay dividends for years to come for you and yours."

The Sorcerer's thoughts simmered. *Dividends?*

The very word tasted bitter to him. To be offered dividends as if he were some minor lord—some vassal to this emperor! Koschei's pride flared—the boiling lava flow of his contempt threatening to melt the metal tube within which he lay coiled. Yet, he forced himself to listen.

"We sense the urgency of your situation," the man continued reading, "And thusly, have decided to accelerate the timeline. The Imperial Forces should be expeditious in their march towards the lands of the

Northwestern Thrice-Nine—with envoys to arrive in no longer than six months' time."

Six months.

Koschei's thoughts quickened.

Six months until the emperor's army marches upon his dominion.

The Sorcerer winced; his false humility had been overdone. It had seemed too pathetic—too eager. Or perhaps not—perhaps this was all just a game. All along, the emperor truly *had* seen through him.

An image of the Sorcerer's own scribe being incinerated beneath a raging torrent of fire flashed before him as his anger and newfound fear collided.

He would have but a few short months to prepare; to scheme. Yet Koschei knew he needed far more time before Ivan would be ready; nearly *two years*. He sensed the boy to be the strongest by far of all his descendants—and with Ivan's form, Koschei would become *unstoppable*. He would seize the entirety of this empire to the south, then—perhaps the whole of the Thrice-Nine Kingdoms.

Yet—six months. This was a prospect that posed a significant problem indeed.

The man's voice broke through the Sorcerer's thoughts as he finished reading the message aloud.

"We wish you peace and prosperity pending our arrival."

Peace and prosperity, Koschei mused darkly. *What a hollow promise.*

He tasted the lie woven within those words; the emperor's forces would not bring peace. Instead, they would bring war, subjugation, and the iron grip of conquest over the path the battalions traversed. And, while Koschei himself had never desired peace, the idea that this so-called emperor would seek to bend an immortal such as he beneath his will—pacifying and subjugating him—brought a grim pleasure to his dark heart. He would kill the emperor, and all who served him.

"With Regards," the man concluded, his voice almost reverent as he spoke, "Caesar Justinian."

The title hung in the air, weighty and commanding. Koschei lingered on the sound, burning with rage at the audacity of the man who claimed it. *Caesar Justinian.* It rang through the metal tube, echoing over his consciousness as the man stuffed the rolled message inside, replacing the cap.

The man glanced in the direction of the emperor, who offered him a slight, approving nod. With a deferential bow, the man turned abruptly, exiting the way he had come. Beyond the heavy door and travelling down the hallway, Koschei watched as the guards peered out through the slits within the chainmail overhanging their faces. One day, he thought, it would be *he* these men would give their lives to protect.

As the man walked through the palace, retracing his steps, the tube bobbed up and down with his stride. Koschei, besieged by the weight of what was to come, retreated into the deepest part of his psyche. The journey home would be days, and he would use every moment to focus on preparing for the emperor's arrival.

A vision of Ivan flashed over the Sorcerer's mind then—along with the proclamation uttered by the Noonwraith so many countless years before. Like all the others, Ivan would have to turn twelve before Koschei could take him as a vessel.

Yet, the Sorcerer would have to do something—he had no choice.

Now, against the hushed din of the man's footsteps against the floor, the Sorcerer heard his own name whispered within his mind's eye, as though destiny itself had uttered it: *Tsar Koschei.*

And to his vain, dark heart, those words sounded irresistibly delicious—like golden honey dripping off the skin of a ripe, juicy apple.

By the time the Firebird's feet touched down on the cold, damp ground just beyond the cottage, the forests of Valen were blanketed in darkness. It had been a week since she had left for Baba Roga's lair, and now, with Kolya nestled against her, the motion of their landing jostled Yaga to consciousness.

Opening her eyes, she took in the twinkling stars embedded in the black velvet sky above. Ever since leaving the boneyards of the demented Cave Witch, she had been in a deep, dreamless sleep. Inhaling the chilly air laced with the familiar comfort of woodsmoke and dried herbs, Yaga was wide awake. Her mind sharpened as she stared up into the abyss of night—her thoughts focusing in on the journey ahead. She would free Ivan before the Sorcerer could hurt him any more than he already had.

Before it was too late.

As she dismounted, a fierce determination arose within her like a fire hungering for fresh kindling. An image of Ivan flashed through her mind—his face etched with pain and fear. Reaching the earth below, she paused, her gaze catching Zhar's giant eyes, shining like glass in the glow from the cottage. Yaga paused, sending her thoughts across the space between them.

You will need to rest, my love. The travels ahead will be long and full of unknown danger.

The Firebird gave a soft cooing sound before turning, flapping her massive wings and alighting into the night air. She was heading to her roost to sleep; she would need to renew her energy before their journey could begin.

And then, there would be no resting. No safe harbor until Ivan had been brought to safety—away from Koschei's clutches.

The revelations now weighed heavily upon her—solidifying her desire to act more than ever. In some ways, Yaga felt she was no longer the same person as when she had left. She had a special purpose now; destiny had given her a mission. The Gamyun had been clear: Yaga's fate was to one day face the Sorcerer. Yet—she could not allow the darkness that had consumed her ancestors for generations to claim another innocent life. Ivan was to be protected at all costs. And though some small part of her wanted to turn away from it all, she knew without question *she would not.*

Yaga's thoughts were interrupted suddenly as Alexey and Vasilisa burst out of the cottage door. Alexey leapt over the porch steps, running towards her through the yard. He paused only briefly before throwing his arms around her, hugging her tightly to his chest and lifting her from the ground. He held her firmly as the Vila made her way down the steps—as though he were afraid of letting her go.

Vasilisa, having sensed Yaga's return home for several hours, moved slowly and quietly across the yard to where they stood. Yaga, still held above the ground within Alexey's embrace, reached her hand out to her. Vasilisa let out a small laugh as she grasped Yaga's pinky.

Alexey cleared his throat, gently setting Yaga down on her feet—though he remained close. Bending forward, Yaga wrapped her arms around the Vila gently—squeezing her affectionately as each woman gave a heavy sigh. Seeing Kolya, Alexey bent forward, hugging the wolf firmly against his chest and scratching him behind the ears.

"Hi, friend," Alexey said as he nuzzled Kolya.

With the return of Yaga and Kolya, Alexey felt his heart beginning to beat in a steady rhythm for the first time in a week. Vasilisa, too, moved her hand over Kolya's silvery fur, welcoming him back as a sense of relief began to settle over her. Suddenly, however, the Vila's head tilted towards Yaga. Catching the shift, Alexey—having come to know Vasilisa's sensitivity—felt a wave of alarm washing over him.

Yaga's eyes flicked to the ground as she felt the penetrating stare of the Vila burrow into her psyche. Alexey studied her expectantly. Yaga's lips tugged to one side, her expression growing solemn.

"What—no. No. *Yaga—no,*" Alexey said, fear spreading across his face.

Alexey searched her eyes, hopeful he was mistaken. But no—he saw it then: a bright, sparkling resolve tucked between the flecks of jade strewn over the hazel of her irises.

She was leaving—again.

"Yaga, you can't!" he said, throwing his arms up in frustration.

He emitted a pained, frustrated groan—his feet carrying him into the yard several feet as a burning fear threatened to consume him once again. *This cannot be happening.* He had just gotten her back; she was safe now. Abruptly, he turned to face her.

"I'm going with you."

Alexey's voice was deep and firm, carrying an assertiveness she hadn't yet heard. It was a command—landing in the air like a shovel slamming down into the duff. Yaga began to object, though he stopped her.

"Yaga—I'm going with you. I don't care where you are going—or what you are doing. *I'm coming with you.*"

Yaga's eyes shifted to Vasilisa, the Vila's face impassive as ever.

"Same, Yaga. We go where you go."

From her periphery, Yaga felt Kolya's stare following her now. He—just as the others—seemed to be studying her, as though awaiting her next words.

Yaga closed her eyes, focusing on her breath. She knew she needed them—all of them. Yet, she had spent much of her life being self-sufficient—not wanting anything from anyone. Since her mother's passing, she had believed that if she were to *truly* need someone, she would be hurt. Or she would hurt them. Now, however, she recognized that her friendships—and the love they felt for one another—made her *stronger.* And she knew, deep down—no matter what the prophecy said—she could not face the Sorcerer on her own. Not yet.

She exhaled, her eyes opening to the expectant faces of her friends.

"We leave in three days," she said. "I'll explain everything later, but we have to go while there's still time."

Alexey nodded firmly, stepping towards her and extending his hand to her.

"Whatever you need, Yaga. Anything at all," he said.

Looking up into his eyes, Yaga was taken with how much sturdier the ground felt in his presence. She placed her hand within his, Alexey closing his strong fingers around them. Smiling faintly, Yaga leaned forward, pressing her head into his chest. She let out a deep sigh as he wrapped his arms around her firmly once more.

Vasilisa glanced back at the cottage. There would be many things to do before they could depart. She turned to make her way back—but before she could leave, she felt Yaga's hand upon her forearm, pulling her into the embrace.

For a moment, the three friends lingered, Kolya resting on the ground beside them.

This was it. They only had each other now. Together, with Zhar, they were all that stood between Ivan and the Sorcerer's terrible plan. And soon, they would find out just how much they would have to depend on one another.

Before long, Vasilisa had ascended the steps to the cottage. Yaga and Alexey stood for a time in the darkness beyond the cottage walls—the two of them finding a quiet, unexpected strength in one another.

"Thank you," Yaga whispered as she softened, allowing herself to be supported by his broad frame.

Alexey stared down at her intently, his blue eyes shining like sapphires in the low light.

"I can't lose you, Yaga," he told her, his hand wrapping around her waist, pulling her body closer.

They remained this way for several minutes before turning to head inside, both of them aware of the pressure they now faced. There was much to do.

They needed to free Ivan.

But first, they had to *find* him.

Yaga still didn't know exactly where the Sorcerer's castle was located. Unlike Baba Roga, Koschei's lair wasn't in the pages of the grimoire—not anymore, at least. Long ago, it seemed, several pages had been torn from the ancient book. Now, what remained of the maps of those areas were dotted with dozens—perhaps hundreds—of abandoned castles from eons past. Ivan could be anywhere.

In the stillness of the following evening, Yaga prepared for one last quieting—one final projection of her spirit form into the liminal space beyond her body.

She and the others had spent the day readying for the journey ahead. Wanting to leave as soon as they were able, Yaga, Vasilisa, and Alexey had gone to the market to procure food and other items. Stopping off at the town clerk, they had borrowed a map of the northern Kingdoms—including the Dark Lands far to the west—promising to bring it back once they returned.

Importantly, Yaga and the others had met with some of the villagers in the market square—the blacksmith, Velimir, and Mitza amongst the small crowd in attendance. With Alexey and the Vila at her side, Yaga informed them that Todorats—and other terrors like him—were fueled by a malevolent energy emanating from the distant Dark Lands. She told them she and the others would journey to confront Koschei the

Deathless—a revelation that brought gasps and concerned looks to their faces.

Despite this admission, Yaga concealed that the true aim of this mission was to save Ivan. Unlike her friends, the villagers needed as little detail as possible; she didn't want them to worry any more than they had to. She wanted them to be able to resume their lives in peace and safety.

Still—even Vasilisa and Alexey remained unaware of the magnitude of the fate woven within Yaga's mortal skein. She would tell them, one day—about the revelations the Gamyun had proclaimed for her. Until then, she felt it best to focus on their efforts to free Ivan.

Following the announcement, the market had erupted into a wave of unsettled whispers. Like Todorats, the Deathless Sorcerer had been little more than a superstition for as long as anyone could remember. That he was behind the intrusions into Valen somehow was truly a horrifying detail to comprehend.

Yet ultimately, the villagers had offered Yaga words of support and affirmation, expressing a resounding gratitude. Still, Yaga could see the desperation in their eyes; they were afraid. The villagers needed them now. They needed *Yaga*.

With twilight settling over the landscape, cloaking the world in darkness, Yaga sat upon the sheepskin rug within the inner sanctum of the cottage. She took a few centering breaths, her senses sharpening. Tonight, Yaga would attempt something for the first time: projecting her consciousness outward from her body without a vessel to receive her.

Cross-legged with her back straight and her eyes closed, she focused on the ebb and flow of her breath. The house was quiet, the scent of incense still lingering in the air around her. The space felt particularly thick with magic now, each candle's flickering flame casting a long shadow up the walls. Pooling her awareness, she listened to the faint rustling of the last leaves clinging to the ancient oaks high above.

Let my spirit ride the wind tonight.

Yaga's eyes fluttered as her consciousness shifted, her mind's eye pulling her deeper into the quieting. She felt her breathing fall into a quickened rhythm. Her hands, resting upon her knees, began to lift into the air without effort.

Something different was happening—though she knew to remain focused. She had learned in those first quietings with her mother so many years before that if she questioned the process, or if she tried to control it too much—she could lose the thread. So she waited, allowing the moment to take the shape it intended.

She soon felt her hands moving in a strange pattern—each alternating in unison, tapping her fingers over points along the center of her body. Suddenly, something—like a current—pulsed up her spine, moving into the top of her head. Yaga felt her spirit form beginning to peel away from her physical body.

And then, it was though her eyes were open. She could see the inner sanctum clearly. Standing, she turned, looking back at her physical form still seated behind her. For a single moment, Yaga was taken by how peaceful her expression was.

Then—unbound from her physical body—Yaga leapt into the air, floating up toward the ceiling and passing effortlessly through the small hole in the roof. Beyond the cottage, the cool winds of autumn greeted her. As she continued to drift upward through the canopy, Zhar stirred—as though sensing Yaga in some way. Shifting slightly on her perch, the Firebird's dark, iridescent feathers rustled and shimmered like a raven's wing in the moonlight.

As she continued higher, up above the forest, Yaga hovered in the air. She was listening to the breeze whispering all around her. In this state, every gust seemed to carry a unique melody—like voices, soft and faint. At first, they melded together—each one distant and elusive. Yet, as she focused her mind intently, she began to hear distinct rivers of sound. A current of air sweeping past, Yaga felt instinctively it would guide her to where she needed to go.

Soon, she found herself pulled along slowly, noticing the warmth and magic that seemed to ferry her through the night sky. It was accompanied by a lilting song, a melody sang by voices, soft and gentle. The current of sound was a beacon from the spirit world, and before she knew it, Yaga's consciousness had alighted upon it—soaring over the forested hills beyond her cottage.

Abruptly, the wind began pulling her forward at tremendous speed, vaulting her spirit body far from the sleepy countryside of Valen. Hurtling over the vast darkness, she sensed the fabric of time and space itself folding. Impossibly fast, Yaga passed over valleys and mountains—the rivers and forests a blur below her.

For hours, her consciousness flashed like a meteor past the tiny plumes of smoke arising from the villages scattered in tight clusters beneath. She moved southward at first—and then, far to the west. As time continued to pass, the landscape below, illuminated by the pale light of the moon, grew increasingly desolate. She began to slow, no longer seeing the warm glow of lamplight scattered beneath her—only ragged wisps of woodsmoke coiling upward from darkened hovels.

Then an eerie feeling crept upon her, as though the very air through which she moved had become saturated with *malevolence.*

She was getting closer.

The landscape suddenly changed to a perilous, overgrown carpet of gnarled, ancient trees. There was a faint chattering, too—like whispers of the damned rasping at the edges of the psyche as she continued onward. And then she saw it—faint at first but growing brighter with each moment. In the shrinking distance, a single candle flame flickered in a high window.

This could be Ivan's room, she thought, a pang of urgency swelling within her heart.

Her spirit slowed as the shape of a castle appeared, the wind guiding her gently towards the castle's outer wall. There inside, she saw him; Ivan, sitting quietly at his desk, his small hands clasped together. His eyes seemed sunken—his gaze distant as he stared out the window. It was as though the boy's thoughts were somewhere else entirely—somewhere far from this desolate prison.

But then, Ivan felt something—a soft, inexplicable tug in his chest. He looked up as his heart skipped a beat. He couldn't see her, but *he knew*: Yaga was there, somewhere beyond the veil of the physical world. She had *finally* found him.

In an instant, he knew she would come for him.

Hope sparking within his heart—his eyes twinkled in the flame of the candle before him. Yaga studied his expression from just beyond the panes of wavy, ancient glass. She wanted to warn him—to tell him he was in grave danger. Tell him she would find him again soon. Yet, it was all she could do to make the solemn promise within her heart: she *would* return to this place, and one day, he would be safe and free.

Or she would die trying.

She pulled back from the castle, rising upwards into the night sky. It was just as she had imagined—its walls towering and impenetrable. Yet, there were signs of aging and disrepair, too, with crumbling stone façades and vines threatening to overtake the embattlements.

Very strange indeed, she thought. Koschei's castle was a place outside of time—a fortress forgotten and degraded by the eons.

Yaga glanced down at the window for a final, fleeting moment. Ivan's small, somber face stared winsomely into the darkness. She steeled herself; she would waste no time. Up into the sky she barreled at great speed until the whole of the dark, forested lands surrounding the castle came into view. Taking in one last image of the landscape below—its farthest edges now cloaked in the early light of dawn—Yaga emblazoned it within her memory.

And then—in an instant—she willed herself back into her body.

A heaviness returned as her spirit snapped abruptly through the veil, back into her physical form. Still seated on the lambskin rug, her eyes fluttered open. Light streamed downward through the smoke hole now. As she settled into the quiet rhythm of her breath, she watched the movement of sunlight dappling over the floor—each candle before her having burned down into a pool of wax.

Except for one.

A single flame remained, protruding upward from its melted base.

Shifting her gaze, Yaga stared at the tiny plume of fire. For a time, she focused on it, centering her thoughts. She knew exactly where to go to find the isolated castle littered amongst the ruins of so many others within the bounds of the Dark Lands. If it was drawn upon the map, she would recognize it.

She understood, however, that her spirit body traveling over the veil had been warped in some way. The castle—and Ivan—would be many days' journey from Valen, even on the back of the Firebird. Travelling through the material world of Jav, things would be slower—and more dangerous.

Yaga sighed deeply. Leaning forward, she blew out the remaining candle—a thread-like wisp of smoke coiling and snaking through the air before her.

It was time.

Yaga's thoughts were focused—each movement deliberate as she and Vasilisa moved about the cottage. Throughout the morning and afternoon, they had worked tirelessly, making their final preparations. Dobra seemed to follow Yaga across the house, disappearing in a poof, then reappearing wherever her feet took her. He was worried. The Kikimorra, too, stirred—though she skittered as a mouse atop the cupboards, knocking over stones and vials as she moved, her restlessness evidence of Yaga's own suppressed fears. Yet, Yaga ignored the rising tension of the House Spirits—and the rest of the objects around her as they kicked up their own kinetic frenzy of angst. She had work to do.

Early on, Alexey had stopped by to see the women. Together, they planned to meet in a clearing near his family's estate just after dusk. Gathering remedies for Misha, he headed back to Valen to make preparations of his own—and break the news to his family, a moment he tensed at the thought of.

Now, as the late afternoon sun slipped beyond the trees, Yaga paused amidst the quiet bustle of her movements, surveying the interior of the cottage. The familiar scents of lavender and rose permeated the air—though she felt a growing distance from their comfort. She traced her fingers along a finished bar of soap upon the worktable—one of several she planned to pack for the journey.

Lavender calms the senses—and the heart.

She heard her mother's voice within her mind—like a song playing in another room. Lifting the bar of soap to her nose briefly, she inhaled it sweet scent. She placed it within her satchel alongside the others before gathering her remaining items.

Vasilisa, too, was readying for the departure. Earlier, she led a troupe of squawking chickens into a large enclosure stocked with enough food and water to last for weeks should they need it. After, in the silence of the bedroom, the Vila's nimble fingers had worked to finish the last touches on the tapestry she had been weaving for weeks. Pulling it from the warp, she ran a thick wooden needle through, sewing a few of its edges together.

Stepping back, she admired her work. Before her was a cloak—a small pewter clasp affixed to the front. The garment sparkled in the low light streaming in through the window. It seemed *alive*—each tuft of Kolya's fur she had added the night before a shimmering, silvery contrast to the black feather of the Firebird and her own dark hair.

Quietly, Vasilisa pulled the cloak towards her face. She pressed her forehead into it, whispering in the tongue of the Vilé.

"Fira ptica, vestra vei... Firebird's feather, cloak thy wearer."

Vasilisa could feel the latent magic she held within her hands. The cloak was an enchanted shield now, concealing the form of whoever wore it. And, though she couldn't see the finished cloth, she knew the power it contained intimately—a reflection of the fierce magic within her own heart.

For a moment, she recalled dark energy that had been seeping into Valen. The unknown beast that had lurked beyond the cottage windows. The merciless horror of Todorats. Whatever else was out there—whoever—she knew the cloak would offer protection. *Perhaps sooner than later.*

With dusk descending over the whole of the Northern Thrice-Nine, Alexey stood within the foyer of his family's estate. His face was pensive as he considered the ramifications of his decision to go on the journey with the others. Misha had always been so fragile; leaving him behind sent a pang of worry through Alexey's heart. But there would be no turning back.

The tension during dinner with his parents had nearly suffocated him. Now, standing near the front door, the walls of the manor vibrated with his mother's anguish. Her eyes were filled with fear and sorrow as she clutched at her oldest son's arm. Tatiana was terrified—desperately pleading with him to change his mind. She had looked to her husband for comfort—begging him to stop their son from leaving. Yet, Dmitri had not protested.

The truth was he admired his son's bravery—even if his heart screamed at him to barricade the door to keep him from departing. Yet, he knew son's actions were courageous, and in this very moment, he was somehow more certain of his son's character ever before. Alexey had *chosen* something—called to do something honorable with his life. As he stood before him in the foyer now, Dmitri stared at his son knowing the full circle Alexey had come. More than ever, he knew he was standing before a *man*.

Indeed, this very moment felt a lifetime in the making. For many years, Dmitri had taken his oldest son to the city of Volhynia in the south—a bustling place of commerce and trade nestled against an expansive, land-locked sea. At the southernmost edge of the Northern Thrice-Nine Kingdoms, it was a place filled with ported ships and bustling city streets.

Dmitri had brought Alexey there while he attended to business affairs, staying for weeks and sometimes months at a time, before returning back to Severyn. The fact of the matter was, Alexey had been taken by his father on these trips because the boy *couldn't* be left behind. Growing into his adolescence, his eldest son had become something of a miscreant—having developed an insatiable penchant for *fighting*. Yet, despite the change of scenery, Alexey had been rather incorrigible—his mood brooding and braced for conflict. Even under the watchful eye of a governess, he would slip out through the staff quarters beyond the kitchen—only to be found hours later by officials as he tussled with local boys within the streets.

On one occasion in particular, a local nobleman had witnessed Alexey—just fourteen at the time—scrapping with some older boys in Volhynia who had taunted him for the fine clothing he wore. Upon Dmitri's arrival, the nobleman pulled Alexey's father aside. Impressed, he suggested Dmitri enroll his son in a nearby training center for young merchant marines.

"It will build character—and give him a place to let out all that anger," the man had said.

At the time, Dmitri had winced at the thought of his young son training alongside paid soldiers. But then—he was truly at his wit's end; both he and Tatiana worried desperately over their son's future. So, for years after, Alexey had trained amongst the ranks of aspiring marines. And though he had started out as a disgruntled and uncoordinated child, over time the boy—now outsizing nearly any man—had become a formidable opponent, besting even the most seasoned fighter.

Perhaps, Dmitri thought, his son's capabilities would save his life—or the life of another—as he ventured forth to protect the vulnerable people of Valen now. At that moment, pride swelled within Dmitri's heart. All he had ever wanted was for his son to feel *called by something*. To have purpose and direction. Now, with tears forming in his eyes, he cleared his throat.

"Do come back to us, my son."

Alexey took hold of his father's forearm, squeezing it firmly. Then he turned, leaning forward to hug his mother before pulling on his heavy fur coat. Slinging his knapsack over his broad shoulders, he faced them both once more. Despite his mother's protests, he was going to leave.

Defeated, Tatiana crumpled onto a chair along the wall.

Alexey turned towards Misha, who was flanked by two household staff. He extended a velvet satchel towards one of the women, depositing it into her hand solemnly.

"Just as we discussed—please follow the instructions word for word," he said.

The small bag contained vials, a pair of leather gloves for handling the nettle, along with instructions for changing Misha's bandages and applying the medicine to his joints. He knew that soon, the supply of fresh nettles would be lost to the winds of winter. Until then, Alexey wanted to ensure the focused effort on his brother's healing continued uninterrupted. The woman nodded dutifully, clutching the bag to her chest.

Finally, Alexey knelt, taking Misha into his gaze. The brothers stared at one another—each wishing they could stay that way; this absence would be difficult for both of them. Abruptly, however, Misha cracked a smile, leaning into Alexey's giant frame and squeezing him tightly. Alexey hugged him firmly—his heart soaking up his brother's sweetness one last time. Smiling, Alexey tousled Misha's hair before standing upright.

A serious expression overtook Alexey's face. His mind had turned towards the journey. With a kiss to Misha's forehead, he straightened, his hand pulling his satchel tightly across his shoulder. With a final nod to all who had gathered in the foyer, he gazed towards Tatiana.

"Mother—I love you," he said.

Tears began pouring from her eyes. While it pained him to see her this way, he had no choice. This could be the *only way*. Without another word, he exited out into the evening air where Kolya lay waiting.

As the door closed behind him, he heard his mother shriek out, a guttural cry akin to the animal sounds of childbirth. For a moment, he stood motionless in the darkness, his breath pooling around his face in plumes. Soon, however, he found himself descending the steps—Kolya at his side—their feet crunching over the gravel towards the road. As the stars glittered above them, he and Kolya walked briskly along the path leading away from the estate.

As they gathered in the clearing, each of the travelers felt a sense of finality overtake them. Zhar, with her brilliant, dark feathers shimmering in the twilight, stretched her massive wings in preparation for the long flight ahead.

Kolya stood watch, his amber eyes scanning the distant darkness beyond the tree line. The wolf had been restless since returning from Roga's lair, pacing and growling softly—his ears and nose to the wind. Now, he appeared alert and ready for danger—as though he could sense the peril that lay waiting for them all.

The first to climb atop the back of the Firebird, Vasilisa's delicate hands grazed the feathers as she ascended with Yaga's help. Neatly folded, the cloak she had woven sat tucked down within her knapsack. Kolya followed behind, the two of them nestling down into the warmth.

Without hesitation, Yaga climbed atop Zhar's back. Glancing back at Alexey, she extended her hand, steadying his gait with a strength that surprised him. Together, they settled beneath the blanket of the Firebird's plumage, the heat of the bird's body seeping through their jackets. In silence, the travelers glanced at one another one last time. Then, Vasilisa's voice broke through the still air.

"I can feel something," she whispered. "Dark magic is growing. With every minute that passes, it..." her voice trailed off. She shifted her head to the side as though she were reading something on the night itself.

"There are monsters with no master—no allegiance to anyone but their own dark hearts," she said. The Vila placed her hands on the knapsack she carried, now set upon her lap.

"Inside is a cloak that conceals its wearer."

Alexey's gaze flicked to Yaga. This was becoming more real—the threat of unknown dangers increasing without ever leaving the ground.

"Thank you, Vasa," Alexey said, his large hand reaching out and squeezing her shoulder softly.

Vasilisa smiled warmly, comforted by the energy she sensed within him. He was fearless—something she had felt from the moment she and Yaga had walked past him at the market weeks before. She knew he would protect them if he had the chance. And what's more, she knew his heart; the only thing stronger than the man himself was the energy of goodness she felt emanating from deep within.

And now, as they readied to sail into waters uncharted, Vasilisa sensed with certainty that they would protect *each other*—all of them. She leaned back against the warmth of Kolya's belly, who let out a soft groan.

With a small nod towards Alexey, Yaga closed her eyes. Her long, chestnut hair—tied back into a braid—fell across the fur of her jacket collar, framing her face in the moonlight. Even now—even with the unknown terror of what lay ahead, Alexey was taken by her beauty. And by her fierce, brave abandon—for Yaga, he knew, was a warrior unlike any other.

Breathing deeply, Yaga moved her hand down through Zhar's plumage, gently pressing her hand against the Firebird's warm skin. She closed her eyes, focusing her awareness on the connection between them. She could feel Zhar's heartbeat, and in that moment, a transcendent bond pulsed between them in time with its rhythm.

It is time, friend.

Zhar shifted her weight, readying for flight. Spreading her wings outward, a shadowed curve like a crescent moon spanned over the ground beneath them. With a mighty beat, she lifted into the air, rising swiftly above the dampened cold that overhung the clearing. The world below them blurred as they ascended, the crisp night breeze whipping past their faces as they picked up speed.

Below, the lights of Valen receded, becoming smaller and smaller, until they had disappeared from view like candles burning out. Yaga stared up through the plumes of Zhar's feathers, her gaze sweeping over the vast tapestry of stars overhead. Her thoughts turned to the castle. The evil that awaited them there was unlike anything she or the others had ever faced before. Yet, Ivan's face—sad and broken—haunted her now.

She could not fail him.

She considered her friends, then—each sheltered within the feathers on Zhar's back. She felt her heart swell—her hand unconsciously moving down toward Alexey's, slipping beneath it. For the first time in her life, Yaga felt she truly understood the meaning of friendship: it was a profound loyalty and warmth, fueled by a sacred connection between kindred spirits. Her friends believed in her—perhaps more than she ever had. And she believed in them, too—needing them in ways she could never have imagined.

Now, as they rode upon the back of the Firebird towards an uncertain future, she was struck by the wild courage binding them all together. It filled her, soothing the ache that had long inhabited her heart—knowing that whatever might come, they would face it *together*. Yet, in the depths of Yaga's bones, she knew without question: once this journey began, a fire would be lit—and none of them would ever be the same again.

ACKNOWLEDGMENTS

I am deeply grateful to my family, who believed in this story as it took shape. To my mother, who nurtured her child of the wild wolves with fortitude and love. To my son, Robyn, for being the brightest star: may you always follow the guidance of your own true north. To Carrie, my stalwart editor; I am blessed by your extraordinary talent. And to Andrew—thank you for your endless faith in me (*and Yaga*) on this journey.

ABOUT THE AUTHOR

With her lifelong love of folklore, Shea Michaels weaves themes of resilience, transformation, and the power of the unseen into her writing. She grew up captivated by stories that celebrated courage, imagination, and the untamed spirit. From the worlds of *Pippi Longstocking* and *The Boxcar Children* to the adventurous charm of *Swiss Family Robinson*, she found early blueprints for the wonder she now brings to her own fiction. Her work is also deeply influenced by Clarissa Pinkola Estés' writings on feminine archetypes and myth, as well as the grounding teachings of Buddhism.

When not dreaming up fantasy, she can be found collecting antique oddities, wandering the forests of Maine, or taking a walk with her son, Robyn. This is her debut novel.

Learn more about her books at Yagabooks.com

ALSO BY

Shea Michaels

Young Yaga and the Thrice-Nine Kingdoms, *Tears of the Alkonost*
Book One of the Maiden Trilogy
Young Yaga and the Thrice-Nine Kingdoms, *The Bonefire Gaze*
Book Two of the Maiden Trilogy (coming soon)